PRAISE FOR ED McBAIN
AND DOL

"Ed McBain is ba [illegible] lence. . . . The w [illegible] suspense runs h [illegible] pretty solution-gimmick [illegible] in the title."

—**Anthony Boucher,**
New York Times Book Review

"Suspense is all the better. . . . A spell of gory and sexy scenes delivered at first hand."

—San Francisco Chronicle

"The best . . . crammed with excitement, violence, and sex."

—Kansas City Star

"Engrossing. . . . Another excellent crime detection story."

—Newsday

"Familiarity with the cops of the 87th Precinct builds something like devotion: the more we know about them the more we want to know."

—Newsweek

more . . .

"Ed McBain is, by far, the best at what he does. Case closed."

—*People*

"Nobody writes better detective fiction than Ed McBain. Nobody."

—*West Coast Review of Books*

"Amazing. . . . McBain's telegraphic style gives his story a hard, reportorial surface. Characters are caught in a few memorable strokes; things happen economically. What is surprising in such terse circumstances is how much you have felt, or have been led to understand that the characters were feeling."

—*Los Angeles Times*

"No one writes dialogue among cops as convincingly as McBain."

—*Chicago Sun-Times*

"The best writer of police procedurals working today."

—*Houston Chronicle*

"A master storyteller."

—*Washington Times*

"I never read Ed McBain without the awful thought that I still have a lot to learn. And when you think you're catching up, he gets better."

—Tony Hillerman

"McBain has a great approach, great attitude, terrific style, strong plots, excellent dialogue, sense of place, and sense of reality."

—Elmore Leonard

"McBain has stood the test of time. He remains one of the very best."

—San Antonio Express-News

"McBain is the unquestioned king. . . . Light-years ahead of anyone else in the field."

—San Diego Union

"The hot wire style has kept McBain ahead of the competition for three decades."

—Philadelphia Inquirer

"No living mystery writer creates more suspenseful scenes or builds plots better than McBain."

—Greensboro News & Record

more . . .

"McBain is a top pro, at the top of his game."

—*Los Angeles Daily News*

"McBain's characters age, change, and stay interesting."

—*Arizona Daily Star*

"You'll be engrossed by McBain's fast, lean prose."

—*Chicago Tribune*

"Ed McBain is a national treasure."

—*Mystery News*

"McBain redefines the American police novel. . . . He can stop you dead in your tracks with a line of dialogue."

—*Cleveland Plain Dealer*

"He keeps getting better. . . . His plots have become more complicated, and he juggles his subplots, his sidebar stories, with practiced—and improved—skill and surety. . . . McBain remains a literary boss on his chosen turf."

—*Tulsa World*

"McBain has . . . an unfailing ability to create tricky, engaging plots."

—*Roanoke Times & World-News*

"The best crime writer in the business."

—*Houston Post*

"It is hard to think of anyone better at what he does. In fact, it's impossible."

—**Robert B. Parker**

"The McBain stamp: sharp dialogue and crisp plotting."

—*Miami Herald*

Ed McBain is one of the most illustrious names in crime fiction. Famous for his 87th Precinct series of police procedurals—a genre he pioneered and perfected—he is also, as Evan Hunter, the author of books ranging from the classic *The Blackboard Jungle* to the bestselling *Privileged Conversation*. McBain's 87th Precinct novel *Ice* was named by *Newsweek* as one of the ten best crime novels of all time.

Also by Ed McBain

The 87th Precinct Novels

Cop Hater • The Mugger • The Pusher (1956) The Con Man • Killer's Choice (1957) Killer's Payoff • Killer's Wedge • Lady Killer (1958) 'Til Death • King's Ransom (1959) Give the Boys a Great Big Hand • The Heckler • See Them Die (1960) Lady, Lady, I Did It! (1961) The Empty Hours • Like Love (1962) Ten Plus One (1963) Ax (1964) He Who Hesitates • Doll (1965) Eighty Million Eyes (1966) Fuzz (1968) Shotgun (1969) Jigsaw (1970) Hail, Hail the Gang's All Here (1971) Sadie When She Died • Let's Hear It for the Deaf Man (1972) Hail to the Chief (1973) Bread (1974) Blood Relatives (1975) So Long As You Both Shall Live (1976) Long Time No See (1977) Calypso (1979) Ghosts (1980) Heat (1981) Ice (1983) Lightning (1984) Eight Black Horses (1985) Poison • Tricks (1987) Lullaby (1989) Vespers (1990) Widows (1991) Kiss (1992) Mischief (1993) And All Through the House (1994) Romance (1995) Nocturne (1997)

The Matthew Hope Novels

Goldilocks (1978) Rumpelstiltskin (1981) Beauty and the Beast (1982) Jack and the Beanstalk (1984) Snow White and Rose Red (1985) Cinderella (1986) Puss in Boots (1987) The House That Jack Built (1988) Three Blind Mice (1990) Mary, Mary (1993) There Was a Little Girl (1994) Gladly the Cross-Eyed Bear (1996)

Other Novels

The Sentries (1965) Where There's Smoke • Doors (1975) Guns (1976) Another Part of the City (1986) Downtown (1991)

And as Evan Hunter

Novels

The Blackboard Jungle (1954) Second Ending (1956) Strangers When We Meet (1958) A Matter of Conviction (1959) Mothers and Daughters (1961) Buddwing (1964) The Paper Dragon (1966) A Horse's Head (1967) Last Summer (1968) Sons (1969) Nobody Knew They Were There (1971) Every Little Crook and Nanny (1972) Come Winter (1973) Streets of Gold (1974) The Chisholms (1976) Love, Dad (1981) Far From the Sea (1983) Lizzie (1984) Criminal Conversation (1994) Privileged Conversation (1996)

Short Story Collections

Happy New Year, Herbie (1963) The Easter Man (1972)

Children's Books

Find the Feathered Serpent (1952) The Remarkable Harry (1959) The Wonderful Button (1961) Me and Mr. Stenner (1976)

Screenplays

Strangers When We Meet (1959) The Birds (1962) Fuzz (1972) Walk Proud (1979)

Teleplays

The Chisholms (1979) The Legend of Walks Far Woman (1980) Dream West (1986)

ED McBAIN

DOLL

WARNER BOOKS

A Time Warner Company

WARNER BOOKS EDITION

Cover design by Diane Luger
Cover photo by Herman Estevez
Hand lettering by Carl Dellacroce

This Warner Books Edition is published by arrangement with the author.

Warner Books, Inc.
1271 Avenue of the Americas
New York, NY 10020

A Time Warner Company

Visit our Web site at
http://pathfinder.com/twep

Printed in the United States of America
First Warner Books Printing: January, 1997
10 9 8 7 6 5 4 3 2 1

This, too, is for Dodie and Ray Crane

The city in these pages is imaginary.
The people, the places are all fictitious.
Only the police routine is based on established investigatory technique.

DOLL

One

The child Anna sat on the floor close to the wall and played with her doll, talking to it, listening. She could hear the voices raised in anger coming from her mother's bedroom through the thin separating wall, but she busied herself with the doll and tried not to be frightened. The man in her mother's bedroom was shouting now. She tried not to hear what he was saying. She brought the doll close to her face and kissed its plastic cheek, and then talked to it again, and listened.

In the bedroom next door, her mother was being murdered.

Her mother was called Tinka, a chic and lacquered label concocted by blending her given name, Tina, with her middle name, Karin. Tinka was normally a beautiful woman, no question about it. She'd have been a beautiful woman even if her name was Beulah. Or Bertha. Or perhaps even Brunhilde. The Tinka tag only enhanced her natural good looks, adding an essential gloss, a necessary polish, an air of mystery and adventure.

Tinka Sachs was a fashion model.

She was, no question about it, a very beautiful woman.

She possessed a finely sculptured face that was perfectly suited to the demands of her profession, a wide forehead, high pronounced cheekbones, a generous mouth, a patrician nose, slanted green eyes flecked with chips of amber; oh, she was normally a beauty, no question about it. Her body was a model's body, lithe and loose and gently angled, with long slender legs, narrow hips, and a tiny bosom. She walked with a model's insinuating glide, pelvis tilted, crotch cleaving the air, head erect. She laughed with a model's merry shower of musical syllables, painted lips drawing back over capped teeth, amber eyes glowing. She sat with a model's carelessly draped ease, posing even in her own living room, invariably choosing the wall or sofa that best offset her clothes, or her long blonde hair, or her mysterious green eyes flecked with chips of amber; oh, she was normally a beauty.

She was not so beautiful at the moment.

She was not so beautiful because the man who followed her around the room shouting obscenities at her, the man who stalked her from wall to wall and boxed her into the narrow passage circumscribed by the king-sized bed and the marble-topped dresser opposite, the man who closed in on her oblivious to her murmuring, her pleading, her sobbing, the man was grasping a kitchen knife with which he had been slashing her repeatedly for the past three minutes.

The obscenities spilled from the man's mouth in a steady unbroken torrent, the anger having reached a pitch that was unvaried now, neither rising nor falling in volume or intensity. The knife blade swung in a short, tight arc, back and forth, its rhythm as unvaried as that of the words that poured from the man's mouth. Obscenities and blade, like partners in an evil copulation, moved together in perfect rhythm and pitch, enveloping Tinka in alternating splashes of blood and spittle. She kept murmuring the man's name pleadingly, again and again, as the blade ripped into her flesh. But the glittering arc was relentless. The razor-sharp blade, the monotonous flow of obscenities, inexorably forced her bleeding and torn into the far corner of the room, where the back of her head collided with an original Chagall, tilting it slightly askew, the knife moving in again in its brief terrifying arc, the blade slicing parallel bleeding ditches across her small breasts and moving lower across the flat abdomen, her peignoir tearing again with a clinging silky blood-sotted sound as the knife blade plunged deeper with each step closer he took. She said his name once more, she shouted his name, and then she murmured the word 'Please', and then she fell back against the wall again, knocking the Chagall from its hook so that a riot of framed color dropped heavily over her shoulder, falling in a lopsided angle past the long blonde hair, and the open red gashes across her throat and naked chest, the tattered blue peignoir, the natural brown of her exposed pubic hair, the blue satin slippers. She fell gasping for breath, spitting blood, headlong over the painting, her forehead colliding with the wide oaken frame, her blonde hair covering the Chagall reds and yellows and violets with a fine misty golden haze, the knife slash across her throat pouring blood onto the canvas, setting her hair afloat in a pool of red that finally overspilled the oaken frame and ran onto the carpet.

Next door, the child Anna clung fiercely to her doll.

She said a reassuring word to it, and then listened in terror as she heard footfalls in the hall outside her closed bedroom door. She kept listening breathlessly until she heard the front door to the apartment open and then close again.

She was still sitting in the bedroom, clutching her doll,

when the superintendent came up the next morning to change a faucet washer Mrs. Sachs had complained about the day before.

April is the fourth month of the year.

It is important to know that—if you are a cop, you can sometimes get a little confused.

More often than not, your confusion will be compounded of one part exhaustion, one part tedium, and one part disgust. The exhaustion is an ever-present condition and one to which you have become slowly accustomed over the years. You know that the department does not recognize Saturdays, Sundays, or legal holidays, and so you are even prepared to work on Christmas morning if you have to, especially if someone intent on committing mischief is inconsiderate enough to plan it for that day—witness General George Washington and the unsuspecting Hessians, those drunks. You know that a detective's work schedule does not revolve around a fixed day, and so you have learned to adjust to your odd waking hours and your shorter sleeping time, but you have never been able to adjust to the nagging feeling of exhaustion that is the result of too much crime and too few hours, too few men to pit against it. You are sometimes a drag at home with your wife and children, but that is only because you are tired, boy what a life, all work and no play, wow.

The tedium is another thing again, but it also helps to generate confusion. Crime is the most exciting sport in the world, right? Sure, ask anybody. Then how come it can be so boring when you're a working cop who is typing reports in triplicate and legging it all over the city talking to old ladies in flowered house dresses in apartments smelling of death? How can the routine of detection become something as prescribed as the ritual of a bullfight, never changing, so that even a gun duel in a nighttime alley can assume familiar dimensions and be regarded with the same feeling of ennui that accompanies a routine request to the B.C.I.? The boredom is confusing as hell. It clasps hands with the exhaustion and makes you wonder whether this is January or Friday.

The disgust comes into it only if you are a human being. Some cops aren't. But if you are a human being, you are sometimes appalled by what your fellow human beings are capable of doing. You can understand lying because you practice it in a watered-down form as a daily method of smoothing the way, helping the machinery of mankind to function more easily without getting fouled by too much truth-stuff. You can understand stealing because when you were a kid you sometimes swiped pencils from the public school supply closet, and once a toy airplane from the five and ten. You can even understand murder because there is a dark and secret place in your own heart where you have hated deeply enough to kill. You can understand all these things, but you are nonetheless disgusted when they are piled upon you in profusion, when you are constantly confronted with liars, thieves and slaughterers, when all human decency seems in a state of suspension for the eight or twelve or thirty-six hours you are in the squadroom or out answering a squeal. Perhaps you could accept an occasional corpse—death is only a part of life, isn't it? It is corpse heaped upon corpse that leads to disgust and further leads to confusion. If you can no longer tell one corpse from another, if you can no longer distinguish one open bleeding head from the next, then how is April any different from October?

It was April.

The torn and lovely woman lay in profile across the

bloody face of the Chagall painting. The lab technicians were dusting for latent prints, vacuuming for hairs and traces of fiber, carefully wrapping for transportation the knife found in the corridor just outside the bedroom door, the dead girl's pocket book, which seemed to contain everything but money.

Detective Steve Carella made his note and then walked out of the room and down the hall to where the little girl sat in a very big chair, her feet not touching the floor, her doll sleeping across her lap. The little girl's name was Anna Sachs—one of the patrolmen had told him that the moment Carella arrived. The doll seemed almost as big as she did.

"Hello," he said to her, and felt the old confusion once again, the exhaustion because he had not been home since Thursday morning, the tedium because he was embarking on another round of routine questioning, and the disgust because the person he was about to question was only a little girl and her mother was dead and mutilated in the room next door. He tried to smile. He was not very good at it. The little girl said nothing. She looked up at him out of very big eyes. Her lashes were long and brown, her mouth drawn in stoic silence beneath a nose she had inherited from her mother. Unblinkingly, she watched him. Unblinkingly, she said nothing.

"Your name is Anna, isn't it?" Carella said.

The child nodded.

"Do you know what my name is?"

"No."

"Steve."

The child nodded again.

"I have a little girl about your age," Carella said. "She's a twin. How old *are* you, Anna?"

"Five."

"That's just how old my daughter is."

"Mmm," Anna said. She paused a moment, and then asked, "Is Mommy killed?"

"Yes," Carella said. "Yes, honey, she is."

"I was afraid to go in and look."

"It's better you didn't."

"She got killed last night, didn't she?" Anna asked.

"Yes."

There was a silence in the room. Outside, Carella could hear the muted sounds of a conversation between the police photographer and the m.e. An April fly buzzed against the bedroom window. He looked into the child's upturned face.

"Were you here last night?" he asked.

"Um-huh."

"Where?"

"Here. Right here in my room." She stroked the doll's cheek, and then looked up at Carella and asked, "What's a twin?"

"When two babies are born at the same time."

"Oh."

She continued looking up at him, her eyes tearless, wide, and certain in the small white face. At last she said, "The man did it."

"What man?" Carella asked.

"The one who was with her."

"Who?"

"Mommy. The man who was with her in her room."

"Who was the man?"

"I don't know."

"Did you see him?"

"No. I was here playing with Chatterbox when he came in."

"Is Chatterbox a friend of yours?"

"Chatterbox is my *dolly,*" the child said, and she held up the doll and giggled, and Carella wanted to scoop her into his arms, hold her close, tell her there was no such thing as sharpened steel and sudden death.

"When was this, honey?" he asked. "Do you know what time it was?"

"I don't know," she said, and shrugged. "I only know how to tell twelve o'clock and seven o'clock, that's all."

"Well . . . was it dark?"

"Yes, it was after supper."

"This man came in after supper, is that right?"

"Yes."

"Did your mother know this man?"

"Oh, yes," Anna said. "She was laughing and everything when he first came in."

"Then what happened?"

"I don't know," Anna shrugged again. "I was here playing."

There was another silence.

The first tears welled into her eyes suddenly, leaving the rest of the face untouched; there was no trembling of lip, no crumbling of features, the tears simply overspilled her eyes and ran down her cheeks. She sat as still as a stone, crying soundlessly while Carella stood before her helplessly, a hulking man who suddenly felt weak and ineffective before this silent torrent of grief.

He gave her his handkerchief.

She took it wordlessly and blew her nose, but she did not dry her eyes. Then she handed it back to him and said, "Thank you," with the tears still running down her face endlessly, sitting stunned with her small hands folded over the doll's chest.

"He was hitting her," she said. "I could hear her crying, but I was afraid to go in. So I . . . I made believe I didn't hear. And then . . . then I *really* didn't hear. I just kept talking with Chatterbox, that was all. That way I couldn't hear what he was doing to her in the other room."

"All right, honey," Carella said. He motioned to the patrolman standing in the doorway. When the patrolman joined him, he whispered, "Is her father around? Has he been notified?"

"Gee, I don't know," the patrolman said. He turned and shouted, "Anybody know if the husband's been contacted?"

A Homicide cop standing with one of the lab technicians looked up from his notebook and said, "He's in Arizona. They been divorced for three years now."

Lieutenant Peter Byrnes was normally a patient and understanding man, but there were times lately when Bert Kling gave him a severe pain in the ass. And whereas Byrnes, being patient and understanding, could appreciate the reasons for Kling's behavior, this in no way made Kling any nicer to have around the office. The way Byrnes figured it, psychology was certainly an important factor in police work because it helped you to recognize that there were no longer any villains in the world, there were only disturbed people. Psychology substituted understanding for condemnation. It was a very nice tool to possess, psychology was, until a cheap thief kicked you in the groin one night. It then became somewhat difficult to imagine the thief as a put-upon soul who'd had a shabby childhood. In much the same way, though Byrnes completely understood the trauma that was responsible for Kling's current behavior, he was finding it more and more difficult to accept Kling as anything but a cop who was going to hell with himself.

"I want to transfer him out," he told Carella that morning.

"Why?"

"Because he's disrupting the whole damn squadroom, that's why," Byrnes said. He did not enjoy discussing this, nor would he normally have asked for consultation on any firm decision he had made. His decision, however, was anything but final, that was the damn thing about it. He liked Kling, and yet he no longer liked him. He thought he could be a good cop, but he was turning into a bad one. "I've got enough bad cops around here," he said aloud.

"Bert isn't a bad cop," Carella said. He stood before Byrnes's cluttered desk in the corner office and listened to the sounds of early spring on the street outside the building, and he thought of the five-year-old girl named Anna Sachs who had taken his handkerchief while the tears streamed down her face.

"He's a surly shit," Byrnes said. "Okay, I know what happened to him, but people have died before, Steve, people have been killed before. And if you're a man you grow up to it, you don't act as if everybody's responsible for it. We didn't have anything to do with his girl friend's death, that's the plain and simple truth, and I personally am sick and tired of being blamed for it."

"He's not blaming you for it, Pete. He's not blaming any of us."

"He's blaming the *world,* and that's worse. This morning, he had a big argument with Meyer just because Meyer picked up the phone on his desk. I mean, the goddamn phone was ringing, so instead of crossing the room to his own desk,

Meyer picked up the closest phone, which was on Kling's desk, so Kling starts a row. Now you can't have that kind of attitude in a squadroom where men are working together, you can't have it, Steve. I'm going to ask for his transfer."

"That'd be the worst thing that could happen to him."

"It'd be the best thing for the squad."

"I don't think so."

"Nobody's asking your advice," Byrnes said flatly.

"Then why the hell did you call me in here?"

"You see what I mean?" Byrnes said. He rose from his desk abruptly and began pacing the floor near the meshed-grill windows. He was a compact man and he moved with an economy that belied the enormous energy in his powerful body. Short for a detective, muscular, with a bullet-shaped head and small blue eyes set in a face seamed with wrinkles, he paced briskly behind his desk and shouted, "You see the trouble he's causing? Even you and I can't sit down and have a sensible discussion about him without starting to yell. That's *just* what I mean, that's *just* why I want him out of here."

"You don't throw away a good watch because it's running a little slow," Carella said.

"Don't give me any goddamn similes," Byrnes said. "I'm running a squadroom here, not a clock shop."

"Metaphors," Carella corrected.

"What*ever,*" Byrnes said. "I'm going to call the Chief tomorrow and ask him to transfer Kling out. That's it."

"Where?"

"What do you mean *where*? What do I care where? Out of here, that's all."

"But *where?* To another squadroom with a bunch of

strange guys, so he can get on *their* nerves even more than he does ours? So he can—"

"Oh, so you admit it."

"That Bert gets on my nerves? Sure, he does."

"And the situation isn't improving, Steve, you know that too. It gets worse every day. Look, what the hell am I wasting my breath for? He goes, and that's it." Byrnes gave a brief emphatic nod, and then sat heavily in his chair again, glaring up at Carella with an almost childish challenge on his face.

Carella sighed. He had been on duty for close to fifty hours now, and he was tired. He had checked in at eight-forty-five Thursday morning, and been out all that day gathering information for the backlog of cases that had been piling up all through the month of March. He had caught six hours' sleep on a cot in the locker room that night, and then been called out at seven on Friday morning by the fire department, who suspected arson in a three-alarm blaze they'd answered on the South Side. He had come back to the squadroom at noon to find four telephone messages on his desk. By the time he had returned all the calls—one was from an assistant m.e. who took a full hour to explain the toxicological analysis of a poison they had found in the stomach contents of a beagle, the seventh such dog similarly poisoned in the past week—the clock on the wall read one-thirty. Carella sent down for a pastrami on rye, a container of milk, and a side of French fries. Before the order arrived, he had to leave the squadroom to answer a burglary squeal on North Eleventh. He did not come back until five-thirty, at which time he turned the phone over to a complaining Kling and went down to the locker room to try to sleep again. At eleven o'clock Friday night, the entire squad, working in flying wedges of three detectives to a team, culminated a two-month period of surveillance by raiding twenty-six known numbers banks in the area, a sanitation project that was not finished until five on Saturday morning. At eight-thirty a.m., Carella answered the Sachs squeal and questioned a crying little girl. It was now ten-thirty a.m., and he was tired, and he wanted to go home, and he didn't want to argue in favor of a man who had become everything the lieutenant said he was, he was just too damn weary. But earlier this morning he had looked down at the body of a woman he had not known at all, had seen her ripped and lacerated flesh, and had felt a pain bordering on nausea. Now—weary, bedraggled, unwilling to argue—he could remember the mutilated beauty of Tinka Sachs, and he felt something of what Bert Kling must have known in that Culver Avenue bookshop not four years ago when he'd held the bullet-torn body of Claire Townsend in his arms.

"Let him work with me," he said.

"What do you mean?"

"On the Sachs case. I've been teaming with Meyer lately. Give me Bert instead."

"What's the matter, don't you like Meyer?"

"I *love* Meyer, I'm tired, I want to go home to bed, will you please let me have Bert on this case?"

"What'll that accomplish?"

"I don't know."

"I don't approve of shock therapy," Byrnes said. "This Sachs woman was brutally murdered. All you'll do is remind Bert—"

"Therapy, my ass," Carella said. "I want to be with him, I want to talk to him, I want to let him know he's still got some people on this goddamn squad who think he's a decent human being worth saving. Now, Pete, I *really* am very tired and I don't want to argue this any further, I mean it. If you want to send Bert to another squad, that's your business, you're the boss here, I'm not going to argue with you, that's all. I mean it. Now just make up your mind, okay?"

"Take him," Byrnes said.

"Thank you," Carella answered. He went to the door. "Good night," he said, and walked out.

Two

Sometimes a case starts like sevens coming out.

The Sachs case started just that way on Monday morning when Steve Carella and Bert Kling arrived at the apartment building on Stafford Place to question the elevator operator.

The elevator operator was close to seventy years old, but he was still in remarkable good health, standing straight and tall, almost as tall as Carella and of the same general build. He had only one eye, however—he was called Cyclops by the superintendent of the building and by just about everyone else he knew—and it was this single fact that seemed to make him a somewhat less than reliable witness. He had lost his eye, he explained, in World War I. It had been bayoneted out of his head by an advancing German in the Ardennes Forest. Cyclops—who up to that time had been called Ernest—had backed away from the blade before it had a chance to pass completely through his eye and into his brain, and then had carefully and passionlessly shot the German three times in the chest, killing him. He did not realize his eye was gone until he got back to the aid station. Until then, he though the bayonet had only gashed his brow and caused a flow of blood that made it difficult to see. He was proud of his missing eye, and proud of the nickname Cyclops. Cyclops had been a giant, and although Ernest Messner was only six feet tall, he had lost his eye for democracy, which is as good a cause as any for which to lose an eye. He was also very proud of his remaining eye, which he claimed was capable of twenty/twenty vision. His remaining eye was a clear penetrating blue, as sharp as the mind lurking somewhere behind it. He listened intelligently to everything the two detectives asked him, and then he said, 'Sure, I took him up myself.'

"You took a man up to Mrs. Sachs's apartment Friday night?" Carella asked.

"That's right."

"What time was this?"

Cyclops thought for a moment. He wore a black patch over his empty socket, and he might have looked a little like an aging Hathaway Shirt man in an elevator uniform, except that he was bald. 'Must have been nine or nine-thirty, around then.'

"Did you take the man *down,* too?"

"Nope."

"What time did you go off?"

"I didn't leave the building until eight o'clock in the morning."

"You work from when to when, Mr. Messner?"

"We've got three shifts in the building," Cyclops explained. "The morning shift is eight a.m. to four p.m. The afternoon shift is four p.m. to midnight. And the graveyard shift is midnight to eight a.m."

"Which shift is yours?" Kling asked.

"The graveyard shift. You just caught me, in fact. I'll be relieved here in ten minutes."

"If you start work at midnight, what were you doing here at nine p.m. Monday?"

"Fellow who has the shift before mine went home sick. The super called me about eight o'clock, asked if I could come in early. I did him the favor. That was a long night, believe me."

"It was an even longer night for Tinka Sachs," Kling said.

"Yeah. Well, anyway, I took that fellow up at nine, nine-thirty, and he still hadn't come down by the time I was relieved."

"At eight in the morning," Carella said.

"That's right."

"Is that usual?" Kling asked.

"What do you mean?"

"Did Tinka Sachs usually have men coming here who went up to her apartment at nine, nine-thirty and weren't down by eight the next morning?"

Cyclops blinked with his single eye. "I don't like to talk about the dead," he said.

"We're here precisely so you can talk about the dead," Kling answered. "And about the living who visited the dead. I asked a simple question, and I'd appreciate a simple answer. Was Tinka Sachs in the habit of entertaining men all night long?"

Cyclops blinked again. "Take it easy, young fellow," he said. "You'll scare me right back into my elevator."

Carella chose to laugh at this point, breaking the tension. Cyclops smiled in appreciation.'

"You understand, don't you?" he said to Carella. "What Mrs. Sachs did up there in her apartment was *her* business, not anyone else's."

"Of course," Carella said. "I guess my partner was just

wondering why you weren't suspicious. About taking a man up who didn't come down again. That's all."

"Oh," Cyclops thought for a moment. Then he said, "Well, I didn't give it a second thought."

"Then it *was* usual, is that right?" Kling asked.

"I'm not saying it was usual, and I'm not saying it wasn't. I'm saying if a woman over twenty-one wants to have a man in her apartment, it's not for me to say how long he should stay, all day or all night, it doesn't matter to me, sonny. You got that?"

"I've got it," Kling said flatly.

"And I don't give a damn what they do up there, either, all day or all night, that's their business if they're old enough to vote. You got that, too?"

"I've got it," Kling said.

"Fine," Cyclops answered, and he nodded.

"Actually," Carella said, "the man didn't *have* to take the elevator down, did he? He could have gone up to the roof, and crossed over to the next building."

"Sure," Cyclops said. "I'm only saying that neither me nor anybody else working in this building has the right to wonder about what anybody's doing up there or how long they're taking to do it, or whether they choose to leave the building by the front door or the roof or the steps leading to the basement or even by jumping out the window, it's none of our business. You close that door, you're private. That's my notion."

"That's a good notion," Carella said.

"Thank you."

"You're welcome."

"What'd the man look like?" Kling asked. "Do you remember?"

"Yes, I remember," Cyclops said. He glanced at Kling coldly, and then turned to Carella. "Have you got a pencil and some paper?"

"Yes," Carella said. He took a notebook and a slender gold pen from his inside jacket pocket. "Go ahead."

"He was a tall man, maybe six-two or six-three. He was blond. His hair was very straight, the kind of hair Sonny Tufts has, do you know him?"

"Sonny *Tufts*?" Carella said.

"That's right, the movie star, him. This fellow didn't look at all like him, but his hair was the same sort of straight blond hair."

"What color were his eyes?" Kling asked.

"Didn't see them. He was wearing sunglasses."

"At night?"

"Lots of people wear sunglasses at night nowadays," Cyclops said.

"That's true," Carella said.

"Like masks," Cyclops added.

"Yes."

"He was wearing sunglasses, and also he had a very deep tan, as if he'd just come back from down south someplace. He had on a light grey raincoat; it was drizzling a little Friday night, do you recall?"

"Yes, that's right," Carella said. "Was he carrying an umbrella?"

"No umbrella."

"Did you notice any of his clothing under the raincoat?"

"His suit was a dark grey, charcoal grey, I could tell that by his trousers. He was wearing a white shirt—it showed up here, in the opening of the coat—and a black tie."

"What color were his shoes?"

"Black."

"Did you notice any scars or other marks on his face or hands?"

"No."

"Was he wearing any rings?"

"A gold ring with a green stone on the pinky of his right hand—no, wait a minute, it was his left hand."

"Any other jewelry you might have noticed? Cuff links, tie clasp?"

"No, I didn't see any."

"Was he wearing a hat?"

"No hat."

"Was he clean-shaven?"

"What do you mean?"

"Did he have a beard or a mustache?" Kling said.

"No. He was clean-shaven."

"How old would you say he was?"

"Late thirties, early forties."

"What about his build? Heavy, medium, or slight?"

"He was a big man. He wasn't fat, but he was a big man, muscular. I guess I'd have to say he was heavy. He had very big hands. I noticed the ring on his pinky looked very small for his hand. He was heavy, I'd say, yes, very definitely."

"Was he carrying anything? Briefcase, suitcase, attaché—"

"Nothing."

"Did he speak to you?"

"He just gave me the floor number, that's all. Nine, he said. That was all."

"What sort of voice did he have? Deep, medium, high?"

"Deep."

"Did you notice any accent or regional dialect?"

"He only said one word. He sounded like anybody else in the city."

"I'm going to say that word several ways," Carella said. "Would you tell me which way sounded most like him?"

"Sure, go ahead."

"Ny-un," Carella said.

"Nope."

"Noin."

"Nope."

"Nahn."

"Nope."

"Nan."

"Nope."

"Nine."

"That's it. Straight out. No decorations."

"Okay, good," Carella said. "You got anything else, Bert?"

"Nothing else," Kling said.

"You're a very observant man," Carella said to Cyclops.

"All I do every day is look at the people I take up and down," Cyclops answered. He shrugged. "It makes the job a little more interesting."

"We appreciate everything you've told us," Carella said. "Thank you."

"Don't mention it."

Outside the building, Kling said, "The snotty old bastard."

"He gave us a lot," Carella said mildly.

"Yeah."

"We've really got a good description now."

"*Too* good, if you ask me."

"What do you mean?"

"The guy has one eye in his head, and one foot in the grave. So he reels off details even a trained observer would have missed. He might have been making up the whole thing, just to prove he's not a worthless old man."

"Nobody's worthless," Carella said mildly. "Old or otherwise."

"The humanitarian school of criminal detection," Kling said.

"What's wrong with humanity?"

"Nothing. It was a human being who slashed Tinka Sachs to ribbons, wasn't it?" Kling asked.

And to this, Carella had no answer.

A good modeling agency serves as a great deal more than a booking office for the girls it represents. It provides an answering service for the busy young girl about town, a baby-sitting service for the working mother, a guidance-and-counseling service for the man-beleaguered model, a *pied-à-terre* for the harried and hurried between-sittings beauty.

Art and Leslie Cutler ran a good modeling agency. They ran it with the precision of a computer and the understanding of an analyst. Their offices were smart and walnut-paneled, a suite of three rooms on Carrington Avenue, near the bridge leading to Calm's Point. The address of the agency was announced over a doorway leading to a flight of carpeted steps. The address plate resembled a Parisian street sign, white enameled on a blue field, 21 Carrington, with the blue-carpeted steps beyond leading to the second story of the building. At the top of the stairs there was a second blue-and-white enameled sign, Paris again, except that this one was lettered in lowercase and it read the cutlers.

Carella and Kling climbed the steps to the second floor, observed the chic nameplate without any noticeable show of appreciation, and walked into a small carpeted entrance foyer in which stood a white desk starkly fashionable against the walnut walls, nothing else. A girl sat behind the desk. She was astonishingly beautiful, exactly the sort of receptionist one would expect in a modeling agency; if she was only the receptionist, my God, what did the *models* look like?

"Yes, gentlemen, may I help you?" she asked. Her voice was Vassar out of finishing school out of country day. She wore eyeglasses with exaggerated black frames that did nothing whatever to hide the dazzling brilliance of her big blue eyes. Her makeup was subdued and wickedly innocent, a touch of pale pink on her lips, a blush of rose at her cheeks, the frames of her spectacles serving as liner for her eyes. Her hair was black and her smile was sunshine. Carella answered with a sunshine smile of his own, the one he usually reserved for movie queens he met at the governor's mansion.

"We're from the police," he said. "I'm Detective Carella; this is my partner, Detective Kling."

"Yes?" the girl said. She seemed completely surprised to have policemen in her reception room.

"We'd like to talk to either Mr. or Mrs. Cutler," Kling said. "Are they in?"

"Yes, but what is this in reference to?" the girl asked.

"It's in reference to the murder of Tinka Sachs," Kling said.

"Oh," the girl said. "Oh, yes." She reached for a button on the executive phone panel, hesitated, shrugged, looked up at them with radiant blue-eyed innocence, and said, "I suppose you have identification and all that."

Carella showed her his shield. The girl looked expectantly at Kling. Kling sighed, reached into his pocket, and opened his wallet to where his shield was pinned to the leather.

"We never get detectives up here," the girl said in explanation, and pressed the button on the panel.

"Yes?" a voice said.

"Mr. Cutler, there are two detectives to see you, a Mr. King and a Mr. Coppola."

"Kling and Carella," Carella corrected.

"Kling and Capella," the girl said.

Carella let it go.

"Ask them to come right in," Cutler said.

"Yes, sir." The girl clicked off and looked up at the detectives. "Won't you go in, please? Through the bull pen and straight back."

"Through the what?"

"The bull pen. Oh, that's the main office, you'll see it. It's right inside the door there." The telephone rang. The girl gestured vaguely toward what looked like a solid walnut wall, and then picked up the receiver. "The Cutlers," she said. "One moment, please." She pressed a button and then said, "Mrs. Cutler, it's Alex Jamison on five-seven, do you want to take it?" She nodded, listened for a moment, and then replaced the receiver. Carella and Kling had just located the walnut knob on the walnut door hidden in the walnut wall. Carella smiled sheepishly at the girl (blue eyes blinked back radiantly) and opened the door.

The bull pen, as the girl had promised, was just behind the reception room. It was a large open area with the same basic walnut-and-white decor, broken by the color of the drapes and the upholstery fabric on two huge couches against the left-hand window wall. The windows were draped in diaphanous saffron nylon, and the couches were done in a complementary brown, the fabric nubby and coarse in contrast to the nylon. Three girls sat on the couches, their long legs crossed. All of them were reading *Vogue.* One of them had her head inside a portable hair dryer. None of them looked up as the men came into the room. On the right-hand side of the room, a fourth woman sat behind a long white Formica counter, a phone to her ear, busily scribbling on a pad as she listened. The woman was in her early forties, with the unmistakable bones of an ex-model. She glanced up briefly as Carella and Kling hesitated inside the doorway, and then went back to her jottings, ignoring them.

There were three huge charts affixed to the wall behind her. Each chart was divided into two-by-two-inch squares, somewhat like a colorless checkerboard. Running down the extreme left-hand side of each chart was a column of small photographs. Running across the top of each chart was a listing for every working hour of the day. The charts were covered with plexiglass panels, and a black crayon pencil hung on a cord to the right of each one. Alongside the photographs, crayoned onto the charts in the appropriate time slots, was a record and a reminder of any model's sittings for the week, readable at a glance. To the right of the charts, and accessible through an opening in the counter, there was a cubbyhole arrangement of mailboxes, each separate slot marked with similar small photographs.

The wall bearing the door through which Carella and Kling had entered was covered with eight-by-ten black-and-white photos of every model the agency represented, some seventy-five in all. The photos bore no identifying names. A waist-high runner carried black crayon pencils spaced at intervals along the length of the wall. A wide white band under each photograph, plexiglass-covered, served as the writing area for telephone messages. A model entering the room could, in turn, check her eight-by-ten photo for any calls, her photo-marked mailbox for any letters, and her photo-marked slot on one of the three charts for her next assignment. Looking into the room, you somehow got the vague impression that photography played a major part in the business of this agency. You also had the disquieting feeling that you had seen all of these faces a hundred times before, staring down at you from billboards and up at you from magazine covers. Putting an identifying name under any single one of them would have been akin to labeling the Taj Mahal or the Empire State Building. The only naked wall was the one facing them as they entered, and it—like the reception-room wall—seemed to be made of solid walnut, with nary a door in sight.

"I think I see a knob," Carella whispered, and they started across the room toward the far wall. The woman behind the counter glanced up as they passed, and then pulled the phone abruptly from her ear with a "Just a second, Alex," and said to the two detectives, "Yes, may I help you?"

"We're looking for Mr. Cutler's office," Carella said.

"Yes?" she said.

"Yes, we're detectives. We're investigating the murder of Tinka Sachs."

"Oh. Straight ahead," the woman said. "I'm Leslie Cutler. I'll join you as soon as I'm off the phone."

"Thank you," Carella said. He walked to the walnut wall, Kling following close behind him, and knocked on what he supposed was the door.

"Come in," a man's voice said.

Art Cutler was a man in his forties with straight blond hair like Sunny Tufts, and with at least six feet four inches of muscle and bone that stood revealed in a dark blue suit as he rose behind his desk, smiling, and extended his hand.

"Come in, gentlemen," he said. His voice was deep. He kept his hand extended while Carella and Kling crossed to the desk, and then he shook hands with each in turn, his grip firm and strong. "Sit down, won't you?" he said, and indicated a pair of Saarinen chairs, one at each corner of his desk. "You're here about Tinka," he said dolefully.

"Yes," Carella said.

"Terrible thing. A maniac must have done it, don't you think?"

"I don't know," Carella said.

"Well, it *must* have been, don't you think?" he said to Kling.

"I don't know," Kling said.

"That's why we're here, Mr. Cutler," Carella explained. "To find out what we can about the girl. We're assuming that an agent would know a great deal about the people he repre—"

"Yes, that's true," Cutler interrupted, "and especially in Tinka's case."

"Why especially in her case?"

"Well, we'd handled her career almost from the very beginning."

"How long would that be, Mr. Cutler?"

"Oh, at least ten years. She was only nineteen when we took her on, and she was . . . well, let me see, she was thirty in February, no, it'd be almost *eleven* years, that's right."

"February what?" Kling asked.

"February third," Cutler replied. "She'd done a little modeling on the coast before she signed with us, but nothing very impressive. We got her into all the important magazines, *Vogue, Harper's, Mademoiselle,* well, you name them. Do you know what Tinka Sachs was earning?"

"No, what?" Kling said.

"Sixty dollars an hour. Multiply that by an eight- or ten-hour day, an average of six days a week, and you've got somewhere in the vicinity of a hundred and fifty thousand dollars a year." Cutler paused. "That's a lot of money. That's more than the president of the United States earns."

"With none of the headaches," Kling said.

"Mr. Cutler," Carella said, "when did you last see Tinka Sachs alive?"

"Late Friday afternoon," Cutler said.

"Can you give us the circumstances?"

"Well, she had a sitting at five, and she stopped in around seven to pick up her mail and to see if there had been any calls. That's all."

"Had there?" Kling asked.

"Had there what?"

"Been any calls?"

"I'm sure I don't remember. The receptionist usually posts all calls shortly after they're received. You may have seen our photo wall—"

"Yes," Kling said.

"Well, our receptionist takes care of that. If you want me to check with her, she may have a record, though I doubt it. Once a call is crayoned onto the wall—"

"What about mail?"

"I don't know if she had any or . . . wait a minute, yes, I think she did pick some up. I remember she was leafing through some envelopes when I came out of my office to chat with her."

"What time did she leave here?" Carella asked.

"About seven-fifteen."

"For another sitting?"

"No, she was heading home. She has a daughter, you know. A five-year-old."

"Yes, I know," Carella said.

"Well, she was going home," Cutler said.

"Do you know where she lives?" Kling asked.

"Yes."

"Where?"

"Stafford Place."

"Have you ever been there?"

"Yes, of course."

"How long do you suppose it would take to get from this office to her apartment?"

"No more than fifteen minutes."

"Then Tinka would have been home by seven-thirty . . . *if* she went directly home."

"Yes, I suppose so."

"Did she say she was going directly home?"

"Yes. No, she said she wanted to pick up some cake, and *then* she was going home."

"Cake?"

"Yes. There's a shop on the street that's exceptionally good. Many of our mannequins buy cakes and pastry there."

"Did she say she was expecting someone later on in the evening?" Kling asked.

"No, she didn't say what her plans were."

"Would your receptionist know if any of those telephone messages related to her plans for the evening?"

"I don't know, we can ask her."

"Yes, we'd like to," Carella said.

"What were *your* plans for last Friday night, Mr. Cutler?" Kling asked.

"*My* plans?"

"Yes."

"What do you mean?"

"What time did *you* leave the office?"

"Why would you possibly want to know *that*?" Cutler asked.

"You were the last person to see her alive," Kling said.

"No, her *murderer* was the last person to see her alive," Cutler corrected. "And if I can believe what I read in the newspapers, her *daughter* was the *next*-to-last person to see her alive. So I really can't understand how Tinka's visit to the agency or *my* plans for the evening are in any way germane, or even related, to her death."

"Perhaps they're not, Mr. Cutler," Carella said, "but I'm sure you realize we're obliged to investigate every possibility."

Cutler frowned, including Carella in whatever hostility he had originally reserved for Kling. He hesitated a moment and then grudgingly said, "My wife and I joined some friends for dinner at *Les Trois Chats.*" He paused and added caustically, "That's a French restaurant."

"What time was that?" Kling asked.

"Eight o'clock."

"Where were you at nine?"

"Still having dinner."

"And at nine-thirty?"

Cutler sighed and said, "We didn't leave the restaurant until a little after ten."

"And then what did you do?"

"Really, is this necessary?" Cutler said, and scowled at

the detectives. Neither of them answered. He sighed again and said, "We walked along Hall Avenue for a while, and then my wife and I left our friends and took a cab home."

The door opened.

Leslie Cutler breezed into the office, saw the expression on her husband's face, weighed the silence that greeted her entrance, and immediately said, "What is it?"

"Tell them where we went when we left here Friday night," Cutler said. "The gentlemen are intent on playing cops and robbers."

"You're joking," Leslie said, and realized at once that they were not. "We went to dinner with some friends," she said quickly. "Marge and Daniel Ronet—she's one of our mannequins. Why?"

"What time did you leave the restaurant, Mrs. Cutler?"

"At ten."

"Was your husband with you all that time?"

"Yes, of course he was." She turned to Cutler and said, "Are they allowed to do this? Shouldn't we call Eddie?"

"Who's Eddie?" Kling said.

"Our lawyer."

"You won't need a lawyer."

"Are you a new detective?" Cutler asked Kling suddenly.

"What's that supposed to mean?"

"It's supposed to mean your interviewing technique leaves something to be desired."

"Oh? In what respect? What do you find lacking in my approach, Mr. Cutler?"

"Subtlety, to coin a word."

"That's very funny," Kling said.

"I'm glad it amuses you."

"Would it amuse you to know that the elevator operator

at 791 Stafford Place gave us an excellent description of the man he took up to Tinka's apartment on the night she was killed? And would it amuse you further to know that the description fits you to a tee? How does *that* hit your funny bone, Mr. Cutler?"

"I was nowhere near Tinka's apartment last Friday night."

"Apparently not. I know you won't mind our contacting the friends you had dinner with, though—just to check."

"The receptionist will give you their number," Cutler said coldly.

"Thank you."

Cutler looked at his watch. "I have a lunch date," he said. "If you gentlemen are finished with your—"

"I wanted to ask your receptionist about those telephone messages," Carella said. "And I'd also appreciate any information you can give me about Tinka's friends and acquaintances."

"My wife will have to help you with that." Cutler glanced sourly at Kling and said, "I'm not planning to leave town. Isn't that what you always warn a suspect not to do?"

"Yes, don't leave town," Kling said.

"Bert," Carella said casually, "I think you'd better get back to the squad. Grossman promised to call with a lab report sometime this afternoon. One of us ought to be there to take it."

"Sure," Kling said. He went to the door and opened it. "My partner's a little more subtle than I am," he said, and left.

Carella, with his work cut out for him, gave a brief sigh, and said, "Could we talk to your receptionist now, Mrs. Cutler?"

Three

When Carella left the agency at two o'clock that Monday afternoon, he was in possession of little more than he'd had when he first climbed those blue-carpeted steps. The receptionist, radiating wide-eyed helpfulness, could not remember any of the phone messages that had been left for Tinka Sachs on the day of her death. She knew they were all personal calls, and she remembered that some of them were from men, but she could not recall any of the men's names. Neither could she remember the names of the women callers—yes, some of them were women, she said, but she didn't know exactly how many—nor could she remember why *any* of the callers were trying to contact Tinka.

Carella thanked her for her help, and then sat down with Leslie Cutler—who was still fuming over Kling's treatment of her husband—and tried to compile a list of men Tinka knew. He drew another blank here because Leslie informed him at once that Tinka, unlike most of the agency's mannequins (the word "mannequin" was beginning to rankle a little) kept her private affairs to herself, never allowing a date to pick her up at the agency, and never discussing the men in her life, not even with any of the other mannequins (in fact, the word was beginning to rankle a lot) Carella thought at first that Leslie was suppressing information because of the jackass manner in which Kling had conducted the earlier interview. But as he questioned her more completely, he came to believe that she really knew nothing at all about Tinka's personal matters. Even on the few occasions when she and her husband had been invited to Tinka's home, it had been for a simple dinner for three, with no one else in attendance, and with the child Anna asleep in her own room. Comparatively charmed to pieces by Carella's patience after Kling's earlier display, Leslie offered him the agency flyer on Tinka, the composite that went to all photographers, advertising agency art directors, and prospective clients. He took it, thanked her, and left.

Sitting over a cup of coffee and a hamburger now, in a luncheonette two blocks from the squadroom, Carella took the composite out of its manila envelope and remembered again the way Tinka Sachs had looked the last time he'd seen her. The composite was an eight-by-ten black-and-white presentation consisting of a larger sheet folded in half to form two pages, each printed front and back with photographs of Tinka in various poses.

Carella studied the composite from first page to last.

The only thing the composite told him was that Tinka posed fully clothed, modeling neither lingerie nor swimwear, a fact he considered interesting, but hardly pertinent. He put the composite into the manila envelope, finished his coffee, and went back to the squadroom.

Kling was waiting and angry.

"What was the idea, Steve?" he asked immediately.

"Here's a composite on Tinka Sachs," Carella said. "We might as well add it to our file."

"Never mind the composite. How about answering my question?"

"I'd rather not. Did Grossman call?"

"Yes. The only prints they've found in the room so far are the dead girl's. They haven't yet examined the knife, or her pocketbook. Don't try to get me off this, Steve. I'm goddamn good and sore."

"Bert, I don't want to get into an argument with you. Let's drop it, okay?"

"No."

"We're going to be working on this case together for what may turn out to be a long time. I don't want to start by—"

"Yes, that's right, and I don't like being ordered back to the squadroom just because someone doesn't like my line of questioning."

"Nobody ordered you back to the squadroom."

"Steve, you outrank me, and you told me to come back, and that was *ordering* me back. I want to know why."

"Because you were behaving like a jerk, okay?"

"I don't think so."

"Then maybe you ought to step back and take an objective look at yourself."

"Damnit, it was *you* who said the old man's identification seemed reliable! Okay, so we walk into that office and we're face to face with the man who'd just been *described* to us! What'd you expect me to do? Serve him a cup of tea?"

"No, I expected you to accuse him—"

"Nobody accused him of anything!"

"—of murder and take him right up here to book him," Carella said sarcastically. "*That's* what I expected."

"I asked perfectly reasonable questions!"

You asked questions that were snotty and surly and hostile and amateurish. You treated him like a criminal from go, when you had no reason to. You immediately put him on the defensive instead of disarming him. If I were in his place, I'd have lied to you just out of spite. You made an enemy instead of a friend out of someone who might have been able to help us. That means if I need any further information about Tinka's professional life, I'll have to beg it from a man who now has good reason to hate the police."

"He fit our description! Anyone would have asked—"

"Why the hell couldn't you ask in a civil manner? And *then* check on those friends he said he was with, and *then* get tough if you had something to work with? What did you accomplish your way? Not a goddamn thing. Okay, you asked me, so I'm telling you. I had work to do up there, and I couldn't afford to waste more time while you threw mud at the walls. *That's* why I sent you back here. Okay? Good. Did you check Cutler's alibi?"

"Yes."

"*Was* he with those people?"

"Yes."

"And *did* they leave the restaurant at ten and walk around for a while?"

"Yes."

"Then Cutler couldn't have been the man Cyclops took up in his elevator."

"Unless Cyclops got the time wrong."

"That's a possibility, and I suggest we check it. But the checking should have been done *before* you started hurling accusations around."

"I didn't accuse anybody of anything!"

"Your entire approach did! Who the hell do you think

you are, a Gestapo agent? You can't go marching into a man's office with nothing but an idea and start—"

"I was doing my best!" Kling said. "If that's not good enough, you can go to hell."

"It's not good enough," Carella said, "and I don't plan to go to hell, either."

"I'm asking Pete to take me off this," Kling said.

"He won't."

"Why not?"

"Because I outrank you, like you said, and *I* want you on it."

"Then don't ever try that again. I'm warning you. You embarrass me in front of a civilian again and—"

"If you had any sense, you'd have been embarrassed long before I asked you to go."

"Listen, Carella—"

"Oh, it's *Carella* now, huh?"

"I don't have to take any crap from you, just remember that. I don't care what your badge says. Just remember I don't have to take any crap from you."

"Or from anybody."

"Or from anybody, right."

"I'll remember."

"See that you do," Kling said, and he walked through the gate in the slatted railing and out of the squadroom.

Carella clenched his fists, unclenched them again, and then slapped one open hand against the top of his desk.

Detective Meyer Meyer came out of the men's room in the corridor, zipping up his fly. He glanced to his left toward the iron-runged steps and cocked his head, listening to the angry clatter of Kling's descending footfalls. When he came into the squadroom, Carella was leaning over, straight-armed, on his desk. A dead, cold expression was on his face.

"What was all the noise about?" Meyer asked.

"Nothing," Carella said. He was seething with anger, and the word came out as thin as a razor blade.

"Kling again?" Meyer asked.

"Kling again."

"Boy," Meyer said, and shook his head, and said nothing more.

On his way home late that afternoon, Carella stopped at the Sachs apartment, showed his shield to the patrolman still stationed outside her door, and then went into the apartment to search for anything that might give him a line on the men Tinka Sachs had known—correspondence, a memo pad, an address book, anything. The apartment was empty and still. The child Anna Sachs had been taken to the Children's Shelter on Saturday and then released into the custody of Harvey Sadler—who was Tinka's lawyer—to await the arrival of the little girl's father from Arizona. Carella walked through the corridor past Anna's room, the same route the murderer must have taken, glanced in through the open door at the rows of dolls lined up in the bookcase, and then went past the room and into Tinka's spacious bedroom. The bed had been stripped, the blood-stained sheets and blanket sent to the police laboratory. There had been blood stains on the drapes as well, and these too had been taken down and shipped off to Grossman. The windows were bare now, overlooking the rooftops below, the boats moving slowly on the River Dix. Dusk was coming fast, a reminder that it was still only April. Carella flicked on the lights and walked around the chalked outline of Tinka's body on the thick green carpet, the blood soaked into it and dried to an ugly brown. He went to an oval table serving as a desk on the wall opposite the bed, sat in the pedestal chair before it, and began rummaging through the papers scattered over its top. The disorder told him that detectives from Homicide had already been through all this and had found nothing they felt worthy of calling to his attention. He sighed and picked up an envelope with an airmail border, turned it over to look at the flap, and saw that it had come from Dennis Sachs—Tinka's ex-husband—in Rainfield, Arizona. Carella took the letter from the envelope, unfolded it, and began reading:

Tuesday, April 6

My darling Tinka—

Here I am in the middle of the desert, writing by the light of a flickering kerosene lamp, and listening to the howl of the wind outside my tent. The others are all asleep already. I have never felt farther away from the city—or from you.

I become more impatient with Oliver's project every day of the week, but perhaps that's because I know what you are trying to do, and everything seems insignificant beside your monumental struggle. Who cares whether or not the Hohokam traversed this desert on their way from Old Mexico? Who cares whether we uncover any of their lodges here? All I know is that I miss you enormously, and respect you, and pray for you. My only hope is that your ordeal will soon be ended, and we can go back to the way it was in the beginning, before the nightmare began, before our love was shattered.

I will call East again on Saturday. All my love to Anna . . .

. . . and to you.

Dennis

• • •

Carella refolded the letter and put it back into the envelope. He had just learned that Dennis Sachs was out in the desert on some sort of project involving the Hohokam, whoever the hell they were, and that apparently he was still carrying the torch for his ex-wife. But beyond that Carella also learned that Tinka had been going through what Dennis called a "monumental struggle" and "ordeal." What ordeal? Carella wondered. What struggle? And what exactly was the "nightmare" Dennis mentioned later in his letter? Or was the nightmare the struggle itself, the ordeal, and not something that predated it? Dennis Sachs had been phoned in Arizona this morning by the authorities at the Children's Shelter, and was presumably already on his way East. Whether he yet realized it or not, he would have a great many questions to answer when he arrived.

Carella put the letter in his jacket pocket and began leafing through the other correspondence on the desk. There were bills from the electric company, the telephone company, most of the city's department stores, the Diners' Club, and many of the local merchants. There was a letter from a woman who had done house cleaning for Tinka and who was writing to say she could no longer work for her because she and her family were moving back to Jamaica, B.W.I. There was a letter from the editor of one of the fashion magazines, outlining her plans for shooting the new Paris line with Tinka and several other mannequins that summer, and asking whether she would be available or not. Carella read these cursorily, putting them into a small neat pile at one edge of the oval table, and then found Tinka's address book.

There were a great many names, addresses, and telephone numbers in the small red leather book. Some of the people listed were men. Carella studied each name carefully, going through the book several times. Most of the names were run-of-the-mill Georges and Franks and Charlies, while others were a bit more rare like Clyde and Adrian, and still others were pretty exotic like Rion and Dink and Fritz. None of them rang a bell. Carella closed the book, put it into his jacket pocket and went through the remainder of the papers on the desk. The only other item of interest was a partially completed poem in Tinka's handwriting:

When I think of what I am
And of what I might have been,
I tremble.
I fear the night.
Throughout the day,
I push from dragons conjured in the dark
Why will they not

He folded the poem carefully and put it into his jacket pocket together with the address book. Then he rose, walked to the door, took a last look into the room, and snapped out the light. He went down the corridor toward the front door. The last pale light of day glanced through Anna's windows into her room, glowing feebly on the faces of her dolls lined up in rows on the bookcase shelves. He went into the room and gently lifted one of the dolls from the top shelf, replaced it, and then recognized another doll as the one Anna had been holding in her lap on Saturday when he'd talked to her. He lifted the doll from the shelf.

The patrolman outside the apartment was startled to see a grown detective rushing by him with a doll under his arm. Carella got into the elevator, hurriedly found what he wanted in Tinka's address book, and debated whether he should call the squad to tell where he was headed, possibly get Kling to assist him with the arrest. He suddenly remembered that Kling had left the squadroom early. His anger boiled to the surface again. The *hell* with him, he thought, and came out into the street at a trot, running for his car. His thoughts came in a disorderly jumble, one following the next, the brutality of it, the goddamn stalking animal brutality of it, should I try making the collar alone, God that poor kid listening to her mother's murder, maybe I ought to go back to the office first, get Meyer to assist, but suppose my man is getting ready to cut out, why doesn't Kling shape up. Oh God, slashed again and again. He started the car. The child's doll was on the seat beside him. He looked again at the name and address in Tinka's book. Well? he thought. Which? Get help or go it alone?

He stepped on the accelerator.

There was an excitement pounding inside him now, coupled with the anger, a high anticipatory clamor that drowned out whatever note of caution whispered automatically in his mind. It did not usually happen this way, there were usually weeks or months of drudgery. The surprise of his windfall, the idea of a sudden culmination to a chase barely begun, unleashed a wild energy inside him, forced his foot onto the gas pedal more firmly. His hands were tight on the wheel. He drove with a recklessness that would have brought a summons to a civilian, weaving in and out of traffic, hitting the horn and the brake, his hands and his feet a part of the machine that hurtled steadily downtown toward the address listed in Tinka's book.

He parked the car, and came out onto the sidewalk, leaving the doll on the front seat. He studied the name plates in the entrance hallway—yes, this was it. He pushed a bell button at random, turned the knob on the locked inside door when the answering buzz sounded. Swiftly he began climbing the steps to the third floor. On the second-floor landing, he drew his service revolver, a .38 Smith & Wesson Police Model 10. The gun had a two-inch barrel that made it virtually impossible to snag on clothing when drawn. It weighed only two ounces and was six and seven-eighths of an inch long, with a blue finish and a checked walnut Magna stock with the familiar S&W monogram. It was capable of firing six shots without reloading.

He reached the third floor and started down the hallway. The mailbox had told him the apartment number was 34. He found it at the end of the hall, and put his ear to the door, listening. He could hear the muted voices of a man and a woman inside the apartment. Kick it in, he thought. You've got enough for an arrest. Kick in the door, and go in shooting if necessary—he's your man. He backed away from the door. He braced himself against the corridor wall opposite the door, lifted his right leg high, pulling back the knee, and then stepped forward and simultaneously unleashed a piston kick, aiming for the lock high on the door.

The wood splintered, the lock ripped from the jamb, the door shot inward. He followed the opening door into the room, the gun leveled in his right hand. He saw only a big beautiful dark-haired woman sitting on a couch facing the door, her legs crossed, a look of startled surprise on her face. But he had heard a man from outside. Where—?

He turned suddenly. He had abruptly realized that the apartment fanned out on both sides of the entrance door, and that the man could easily be to his right or his left, beyond his field of vision. He turned naturally to the right because he was right-handed, because the gun was in his right hand, and made the mistake that could have cost him his life.

The man was on his left.

Carella heard the sound of his approach too late, reversed his direction, caught a single glimpse of straight blond hair like Sonny Tufts, and then felt something hard and heavy smashing into his face.

Four

There was no furniture in the small room, save for a wooden chair to the right of the door. There were two windows on the wall facing the door, and these were covered with drawn green shades. The room was perhaps twelve feet wide by fifteen long, with a radiator in the center of one of the fifteen-foot walls.

Carella blinked his eyes and stared into the semidarkness.

There were nighttime noises outside the windows, and he could see the intermittent flash of neon around the edges of the drawn shades. He wondered what time it was. He started to raise his left hand for a look at his watch, and discovered that it was handcuffed to the radiator. The handcuffs were his own. Whoever had closed the cuff onto his wrist had done so quickly and viciously; the metal was biting sharply into his flesh. The other cuff was clasped shut around the radiator leg. His watch was gone, and he seemed to have been stripped as well of his service revolver, his billet, his cartridges, his wallet and loose change, and even his shoes and socks. The side of his face hurt like hell. He lifted his right hand in exploration and found that his cheek and temple were crusted with dried blood. He looked down again at the radiator leg around which the second cuff was looped. Then he moved to the right of the radiator and looked behind it to see how it was fastened to the wall. If the fittings were loose—

He heard a key being inserted into the door lock. It suddenly occurred to him that he was still alive, and the knowledge filled him with a sense of impending dread rather than elation. *Why* was he still alive? And was someone opening the door right this minute in order to remedy that oversight?

The key turned.

The overhead light snapped on.

A big brunette girl came into the room. She was the same girl who had been sitting on the couch when he'd bravely kicked in the front door. She was carrying a tray in her hands, and he caught the aroma of coffee the moment she entered the room, that and the overriding scent of the heavy perfume the girl was wearing.

"Hello," she said.

"Hello," he answered.

"Have a nice sleep?"

"Lovely."

She was very big, much bigger than she had seemed seated on the couch. She had the bones and body of a showgirl, five feet eight or nine inches tall, with firm full breasts threatening a low cut peasant blouse, solid thighs sheathed in a tight black skirt that ended just above her knees. Her legs were long and very white, shaped like a dancer's with full calves and slender ankles. She was wearing black slippers, and she closed the door behind her and came into the room silently, the slippers whispering across the floor.

She moved slowly, almost as though she were sleepwalking. There was a current of sensuality about her, emphasized by her dreamlike motion. She seemed to possess an acute awareness of her lush body, and this in turn seemed coupled with the knowledge that whatever she might be—housewife or whore, slattern or saint—men would try to do things to that body, and succeed, repeatedly and without mercy. She was a victim, and she moved with the cautious tread of someone who had been beaten before and now expects attack from any quarter. Her caution, her awareness, the ripeness of her body, the certain knowledge that it was available, the curious look of inevitability the girl wore, all invited further abuses, encouraged fantasies, drew dark imaginings from hidden corners of the mind. Rinsed raven-black hair framed the girl's white face. It was a face hard with knowledge. Smoky Cleopatra makeup shaded her eyes and lashes, hiding the deeper-toned flesh there. Her nose had been fixed once, a long time ago, but it was beginning to fall out of shape so that it looked now as if someone had broken it, and this too added to the victim's look she wore. Her mouth was brightly painted, a whore's mouth, a doll's mouth. It had said every word ever invented. It had done everything a mouth was ever forced to do.

"I brought you some coffee," she said.

Her voice was almost a whisper. He watched her as she came closer. He had the feeling that she could kill a man as readily as kiss him, and he wondered again why he was still alive.

He noticed for the first time that there was a gun on the tray, alongside the coffee pot. The girl lifted the gun now, and pointed it at his belly, still holding the tray with one hand. "Back," she said.

"Why?"

"Don't fuck around with me," she said. "Do what I tell you to do when I tell you to do it."

Carella moved back as far as his cuffed wrist would allow him. The girl crouched, the tight skirt riding up over her thighs, and pushed the tray toward the radiator. Her face was dead serious. The gun was a super .38-caliber Llama automatic. The girl held it steady in her right hand. The thumb safety on the left side of the gun had been thrown. The automatic was ready for firing.

The girl rose and backed away toward the chair near the entrance door, the gun still trained on him. She sat, lowered the gun, and said, "Go ahead."

Carella poured coffee from the pot into the single mug on the tray. He took a swallow. The coffee was hot and strong.

"How is it?" the girl asked.

"Fine."

"I made it myself."

"Thank you."

"I'll bring you a wet towel later," she said. "So you can wipe off that blood. It looks terrible."

"It doesn't feel so hot, either," Carella said.

"Well, who invited you?" the girl asked. She seemed about to smile, and then changed her mind.

"No one, that's true." He took another sip of coffee. The girl watched him steadily.

"Steve Carella," she said. "Is that it?"

"That's right. What's *your* name?"

He asked the question quickly and naturally, but the girl did not step into the trap.

"Detective second/grade," she said. "87th Squad." She paused. "Where's that?"

"Across from the park."

"What park?"

"Grover Park."

"Oh, yeah," she said. "That's a nice park. That's the nicest park in this whole damn city."

"Yes," Carella said.

"I saved your life, you know," the girl said conversationally.

"Did you?"

"Yeah. *He* wanted to kill you."

"I'm surprised he didn't."

"Cheer up, maybe he will."

"When?"

"You in a hurry?"

"Not particularly."

The room went silent. Carella took another swallow of coffee. The girl kept staring at him. Outside, he could hear the sounds of traffic.

"What time is it?" he asked.

"About nine. Why? You got a date?"

"I'm wondering how long it'll be before I'm missed, that's all," Carella said, and watched the girl.

"Don't try to scare me," she said. "Nothing scares me."

"I wasn't trying to scare you."

The girl scratched her leg idly, and then said, "There's some questions I have to ask you."

"I'm not sure I'll answer them."

"You will," she said. There was something cold and deadly in her voice. "I can guarantee that. Sooner or later, you will."

"Then it'll have to be later."

"You're not being smart, mister."

"I'm being very smart."

"How?"

"I figure I'm alive only because you don't know the answers."

"Maybe you're alive because I *want* you to be alive," the girl said.

"Why?"

"I've never had anything like you before," she said, and for the first time since she'd come into the room, she smiled. The smile was frightening. He could feel the flesh at the back of his neck beginning to crawl. He wet his lips and looked at her, and she returned his gaze steadily, the tiny evil smile lingering on her lips. "I'm life or death to you," she said. "If I tell him to kill you, he will."

"Not until you know all the answers," Carella said.

"Oh, we'll get the answers. We'll have plenty of time to get the answers." The smile dropped from her face. She put one hand inside her blouse and idly scratched her breast, and then looked at him again, and said, "How'd you get here?"

"I took the subway."

"That's a lie," the girl said. There was no rancor in her voice. She accused him matter-of-factly, and then said, "Your car was downstairs. The registration was in the glove compartment. There was also a sign on the sun visor, something about a law officer on a duty call."

"All right, I drove here," Carella said.

"Are you married?"

"Yes."

"Do you have any children?"

"Two."

"Girls?"

"A girl and a boy."

"Then that's who the doll is for," the girl said.

"What doll?"

"The one that was in the car. On the front seat of the car."

"Yes," Carella lied. "It's for my daughter. Tomorrow's her birthday."

"He brought it upstairs. It's outside in the living room." The girl paused. "Would you like to give your daughter that doll?"

"Yes."

"Would you like to see her ever again?"

"Yes."

"Then answer whatever I ask you, without any more lies about the subway or anything."

"What's my guarantee?"

"Of what?"

"That I'll stay alive."

"*I'm* your guarantee."

"Why should I trust you?"

"You have to trust me," the girl said. "You're mine." And again she smiled, and again he could feel the hairs stiffening at the back of his neck.

She got out of the chair. She scratched her belly, and then moved toward him, that same slow and cautious movement, as though she expected someone to strike her and was bracing herself for the blow.

"I haven't got much time," she said. "He'll be back soon."

"Then what?"

The girl shrugged. "Who knows you're here?" she asked suddenly.

Carella did not answer.

"How'd you get to us?"

Again, he did not answer.

"Did somebody see him leaving Tinka's apartment?"

Carella did not answer.

"How did you know where to come?"

Carella shook his head.

"Did someone identify him? How did you trace him?"

Carella kept watching her. She was standing three feet away from him now, too far to reach, the Llama dangling loosely in her right hand. She raised the gun.

"Do you want me to shoot you?" she answered conversationally.

"No."

"I'll aim for your balls, would you like that?"

"No."

"Then answer my questions."

"You're not going to kill me," Carella said. He did not take his eyes from the girl's face. The gun was pointed at his groin now, but he did not look at her finger curled inside the trigger guard.

The girl took a step closer. Carella crouched near the radiator, unable to get to his feet, his left hand manacled close to the floor. "I'll enjoy this," the girl promised, and struck him suddenly with the butt of the heavy gun, turning the butt up swiftly as her hand lashed out. He felt the numbing shock of metal against bone as the automatic caught him on the jaw and his head jerked back.

"You like?" the girl asked.

He said nothing.

"You *no* like, huh, baby?" She paused. "How'd you find us?"

Again, he did not answer. She moved past him swiftly, so that he could not turn in time to stop the blow that came from behind him, could not kick out at her as he had planned to do the next time she approached. The butt caught him on the ear, and he felt the cartilage tearing as the metal rasped downward. He whirled toward her angrily, grasping at her with his right arm as he turned, but she danced out of his reach and around to the front of him again, and again hit him with the automatic, cutting him over the left eye this time. He felt the blood start down his face from the open gash.

"What do you say?" she asked.

"I say go to hell," Carella said, and the girl swung the gun again. He thought he was ready for her this time. But she was only feinting, and he grabbed out at empty air as she moved swiftly to his right out of reach. The manacled hand threw him off balance. He fell forward, reaching for support with his free hand, the handcuff biting sharply into his other wrist. The gun butt caught him again just as his hand touched the floor. He felt it colliding with the base of his skull, a two-pound-six-and-a-half-ounce weapon swung with all the force of the girl's substantial body behind it. The pain shot clear to the top of his head. He blinked his eyes against the sudden dizziness. Hold on, he told himself, hold on, and was suddenly nauseous. The vomit came up into his throat, and he brought his right hand to his mouth just as the girl hit him again. He fell back dizzily against the radiator. He blinked up at the girl. Her lips were pulled back taut over her teeth, she was breathing harshly, the gun hand went back again, he was too weak to turn his head aside. He tried to raise his right arm, but it fell limply into his lap.

"Who saw him?" the girl asked.

"No," he mumbled.

"I'm going to break your nose," she said. Her voice sounded very far away. He tried to hold the floor for support, but he wasn't sure where the floor was anymore. The room was spinning. He looked up at the girl and saw her spinning face and breasts, smelled the heavy cloying perfume and saw the gun in her hand. "I'm going to break your nose, mister."

"No."

"Yes," she said.

"No."

He did not see the gun this time. He felt only the excruciating pain of bones splintering. His head rocked back with the blow, colliding with the cast-iron ribs of the radiator. The pain brought him back to raging consciousness. He lifted his right hand to his nose, and the girl hit him again, at the base of the skull again, and again he felt sensibility slipping away from him. He smiled stupidly. She would not let him die, and she would not let him live. She would not allow him to become unconscious, and she would not allow him to regain enough strength to defend himself.

"I'm going to knock out all of your teeth," the girl said.

He shook his head.

"Who told you where to find us? Was it the elevator operator? Was it that one-eyed bastard?"

He did not answer.

"Do you want to lose all your teeth?"

"No."

"Then tell me."

"No."

"You have to tell me," she said. "You *belong* to me."

"No," he said.

There was a silence. He knew the gun was coming again. He tried to raise his hand to his mouth, to protect his teeth, but there was no strength in his arm. He sat with his left wrist caught in the fierce biting grip of the handcuff, swollen, throbbing, with blood pouring down his face and from his nose, his nose a throbbing mass of splintered bone, and waited for the girl to knock out his teeth as she had promised, helpless to stop her.

He felt her lips upon him.

She kissed him fiercely and with her mouth open, her tongue searching his lips and his teeth. Then she pulled away from him, and he heard her whisper, "In the morning, they'll find you dead."

He lost consciousness again.

On Tuesday morning, they found the automobile at the bottom of a steep cliff some fifty miles across the River Harb, in a sparsely populated area of the adjoining state. Most of the paint had been burned away by what must have been an intensely hot fire, but it was still possible to tell that the car was a green 1961 Pontiac sedan bearing the license plate RI 7-3461.

The body on the front seat of the car had been incinerated. They knew by what remained of the lower portions that the body had once been a man, but the face and torso had been cooked beyond recognition, the hair and clothing gone, the skin black and charred, the arms drawn up into the typical pugilistic attitude caused by post-mortem contracture of burned muscles, the fingers hooked like claws. A gold wedding band was on the third finger of the skeletal left hand. The fire had eaten away the skin and charred the remaining bones and turned the gold of the ring to a dull black. A .38 Smith & Wesson was caught in the exposed springs of the front seat, together with the metal parts that remained of what once had been a holster.

All of the man's teeth were missing from his mouth.

In the cinders of what they supposed had been his wallet,

they found a detective's shield with the identifying number 714-5632.

A call to the headquarters across the river informed the investigating police that the shield belonged to a detective second/grade named Stephen Louis Carella.

Five

Teddy Carella sat in the silence of her living room and watched the lips of Detective Lieutenant Peter Byrnes as he told her that her husband was dead. The scream welled up into her throat, she could feel the muscles there contracting until she thought she would strangle. She brought her hand to her mouth, her eyes closed tight so that she would no longer have to watch the words that formed on the lieutenant's lips, no longer have to see the words that confirmed what she had known was true since the night before when her husband had failed to come home for dinner.

She would not scream, but a thousand screams echoed inside her head. She felt faint. She almost swayed out of the chair, and then she looked up into the lieutenant's face as she felt his supporting arm around her shoulders. She nodded. She tried to smile up at him sympathetically, tried to let him know she realized this was an unpleasant task for him. But the tears were streaming down her face and she wished only that her husband were there to comfort her, and then abruptly she realized that her husband would never be there to comfort her again, the realization circling back upon itself, the silent screams ricocheting inside her.

The lieutenant was talking again.

She watched his lips. She sat stiff and silent in the chair, her hands clasped tightly in her lap, and wondered where the children were, how would she tell the children, and saw the lieutenant's lips as he said his men would do everything possible to uncover the facts of her husband's death. In the meantime, Teddy, if there's anything I can do, anything I can do personally, I mean, I think you know how much Steve meant to me, to all of us, if there's anything Harriet or I can do to help in any way, Teddy, I don't have to tell you we'll do anything we can, anything.

She nodded.

There's a possibility this was just an accident, Teddy, though we doubt it, we think he was, we don't think it was an accident, why would he be across the river in the next state, fifty miles from here?

She nodded again. Her vision was blurred by the tears. She could barely see his lips as he spoke.

Teddy, I loved that boy. I would rather have a bullet in my heart than be here in this room today with this, with this information. I'm sorry. Teddy I am sorry.

She sat in the chair as still as a stone.

Detective Meyer Meyer left the squadroom at two p.m. and walked across the street and past the low stone wall leading into the park. It was a fine April day, the sky a clear blue, the sun shining overhead, the birds chirping in the newly leaved trees.

He walked deep into the park, and found an empty bench and sat upon it, crossing his legs, one arm stretched out across the top of the bench, the other hanging loose in his lap. There were young boys and girls holding hands and whispering nonsense, there were children chasing each other and laughing, there were nannies wheeling baby carriages, there were old men reading books as they walked, there was the sound of a city hovering on the air.

There was life.

Meyer Meyer sat on the bench and quietly wept for his friend.

Detective Cotton Hawes went to a movie.

The movie was a western. There was a cattle drive in it, thousands of animals thundering across the screen, men sweating and shouting, horses rearing, bullwhips cracking. There was also an attack on a wagon train, Indians circling, arrows and spears whistling through the air, guns answering, men screaming. There was a fight in a saloon, too, chairs and bottles flying, tables collapsing, women running for cover with their skirts pulled high, fists connecting. Altogether, there was noise and color and loud music and plenty of action.

When the end titles flashed onto the screen, Hawes rose and walked up the aisle and out into the street.

Dusk was coming.

The city was hushed.

He had not been able to forget that Steve Carella was dead.

Andy Parker, who had hated Steve Carella's guts when he was alive, went to bed with a girl that night. The girl was a prostitute, and he got into her bed and her body by threatening to arrest her if she didn't come across. The girl had been hooking in the neighborhood for little more than a week. The other working hustlers had taken her aside and pointed out all the Vice Squad bulls and also all the local plainclothes fuzz so that she wouldn't make the mistake of propositioning one of them. But Parker had been on sick leave for two weeks with pharyngitis and had not been included in the girl's original briefing by her colleagues. She had approached what looked like a sloppy drunk in a bar on Ainsley, and before the bartender could catch her eye to warn her, she had given him the familiar "Wanna have some fun, baby?" line and then had compounded the error by telling Parker it would cost him a fin for a single roll in the hay or twenty-five bucks for all night. Parker had accepted the girl's proposition, and had left the bar with her while the owner of the place frantically signaled his warning. The girl didn't know why the hell he was waving his arms at her. She knew only that she had a John who said he wanted to spend the night with her. She didn't know the John's last name was Law.

She took Parker to a rented room on Culver. Parker was very drunk—he had begun drinking at twelve noon when word of Carella's death reached the squadroom—but he was not drunk enough to forget that he could not arrest this girl until she exposed her "privates." He waited until she took off her clothes, and then he showed her his shield and said she could take her choice, a possible three years in the jug, or a pleasant hour or two with a very nice fellow. The girl, who had met very nice fellows like Parker before, all of whom had been Vice Squad cops looking for fleshy handouts, figured this was only a part of her normal overhead, nodded briefly, and spread out on the bed for him.

Parker was very very drunk.

To the girl's great surprise, he seemed more interested in talking than in making love, as the euphemism goes.

"What's the sense of it all, would you tell me?" he said, but he did not wait for an answer. "Son of a bitch like Carella gets cooked in a car by some son of a bitch, what's the sense of it? You know what I see every day of the week, you know what we *all* of us see every day of the week, how do you expect us to stay human, would you tell me? Son of a bitch gets cooked like that, doing his job is all, how do you expect us to stay human? What am I doing here with you, a two-bit whore, is that something for me to be doing? I'm a nice fellow. Don't you know I'm a nice fellow?"

"Sure, you're a nice fellow," the girl said, bored.

"Garbage every day," Parker said. "Filth and garbage, I have the stink in my nose when I go home at night. You know where I live? I live in a garden apartment in Majesta. I've got three and a half rooms, a nice little kitchen, you know, a nice apartment. I've got a hi-fi set and also I belong to the Classics Club. I've got all those books by the big writers, the important writers. I haven't got much time to read them, but I got them all there on a shelf, you should see the books I've got. There are nice people living in that apartment building, not like here, not like what you find in this crumby precinct, how old are you anyway, what are you nineteen, twenty?"

"I'm twenty-one," the girl said.

"Sure, look at you, the shit of the city."

"Listen, mister—"

"Shut up, shut up, who the hell's asking you? I'm *paid* to deal with it, all the shit that gets washed into the sewers, that's my job. My neighbors in the building know I'm a detective, they respect me, they look up to me. They don't know that all I do is handle shit all day long until I can't stand the stink of it anymore. The kids riding their bikes in the courtyard, they all say, "Good morning, Detective Parker." That's me, a detective. They watch television, you see. I'm one of the good guys. I carry a gun. I'm brave. So look what happens to that son of a bitch Carella. What's the sense?"

"I don't know what you're talking about," the girl said.

"What's the sense, what's the sense?" Parker said. "People, boy, I could tell you about people. You wouldn't believe what I could tell you about people."

"I've been around a little myself," the girl said drily.

"You can't blame me," he said suddenly.

"What?"

"You can't blame me. It's not my fault."

"Sure. Look, mister, I'm a working girl. You want some of this, or not? Because if you—"

"Shut up, you goddamn whore, don't tell me what to do."

"Nobody's—"

"I can pull you in and make your life miserable, you little slut. I've got the power of life and death over you, don't forget it."

"Not quite," the girl said with dignity.

"Not quite, not quite, don't give me any of that crap."

"You're drunk," the girl said. "I don't even think you can—"

"Never mind what I am, I'm not drunk." He shook his head. "All right, I'm drunk, what the hell do you care what I am? You think I care what *you* are? You're *nothing* to me, you're *less* than nothing to me."

"Then what are you doing here?"

"Shut up," he said. He paused. "The kids all yell good morning at me," he said.

He was silent for a long time. His eyes were closed. The

girl thought he had fallen asleep. She started to get off the bed, and he caught her arm and pulled her down roughly beside him.

"Stay where you are."

"Okay," she said. "But look, you think we could get this over with? I mean it, mister, I've got a long night ahead of me. I got expenses to meet."

"Filth," Parker said. "Filth and garbage."

"Okay, already, filth and garbage, do you want it or not?"

"He was a good cop," Parker said suddenly.

"What?"

"He was a good cop," he said again, and rolled over quickly and put his head into the pillow.

Six

At seven-thirty Wednesday morning, the day after the burned wreckage was found in the adjoining state, Bert Kling went back to the apartment building on Stafford Place, hoping to talk again to Ernest Cyclops Messner. The lobby was deserted when he entered the building.

If he had felt alone the day that Claire Townsend was murdered, if he had felt alone the day he held her in his arms in a bookshop demolished by gunfire, suddenly bereft in a world gone cold and senselessly cruel, he now felt something curiously similar and yet enormously different.

Steve Carella was dead.

The last words he had said to the man who had been his friend were angry words. He could not take them back now, he could not call upon a dead man, he could not offer apologies to a corpse. On Monday, he had left the squadroom earlier than he should have, in anger, and sometime that night Carella had met his death. And now there was a new grief within him, a new feeling of helplessness, but it was coupled with an overriding desire to set things right again—for Carella, for Claire, he did not really know. He knew he could not reasonably blame himself for what had happened, but neither could he stop blaming himself. He had to talk to Cyclops again. Perhaps there was something further the man could tell him. Perhaps Carella had contacted him again that Monday night, and uncovered new information that had sent him rushing out to investigate alone.

The elevator doors opened. The operator was not Cyclops.

"I'm looking for Mr. Messner," Kling told the man. "I'm from the police."

"He's not here," the man said.

"He told us he has the graveyard shift."

"Yeah, well, he's not here."

"It's only seven-thirty," Kling said.

"I know what time it is."

"Well, where is he, can you tell me that?"

"He lives someplace here in the city," the man said, "but I don't know where."

"Thank you," Kling said, and left the building.

It was still too early in the morning for the rush of white-collar workers to subways and buses. The only people in the streets were factory workers hurrying to punch an eight-a.m. timeclock; the only vehicles were delivery trucks and an occasional passenger car. Kling walked swiftly, looking for a telephone booth. It was going to be another beautiful day; the city had been blessed with lovely weather for the past week now. He saw an open drugstore on the next corner, a telephone plaque fastened to the brick wall outside. He went into the store and headed for the directories at the rear.

Ernest Cyclops Messner lived at 1117 Gainesborough Avenue in Riverhead, not far from the County Court Building. The shadow of the elevated-train structure fell over the building, and the frequent rumble of trains pulling in and out of the station shattered the silence of the street. But it was a good low-to-middle-income residential area, and Messner's building was the newest on the block. Kling climbed the low flat entrance steps, went into the lobby, and found a listing for E. Messner. He rang the bell under the mailbox, but there was no answering buzz. He tried another bell. A buzz sounded, releasing the lock mechanism on the inner lobby door. He pushed open the door, and began climbing to the seventh floor. It was a little after eight a.m., and the building still seemed asleep.

He was somewhat winded by the time he reached the seventh floor. He paused on the landing for a moment, and then walked into the corridor, looking for apartment 7A. He found it just off the stairwell, and rang the bell.

There was no answer.

He rang the bell again.

He was about to ring it a third time when the door to the apartment alongside opened and a young girl rushed out, looking at her wrist watch and almost colliding with Kling.

"Oh, hi," she said, surprised. "Excuse me."

"That's all right." He reached for the bell again. The girl had gone past him and was starting down the steps. She turned suddenly.

"Are you looking for Mr. Messner?" she asked.

"Yes, I am."

"He isn't home."

"How do you know?"

"Well, he doesn't get home until about nine," she said. "He works nights, you know."

"Does he live here alone?"

"Yes, he does. His wife died a few years back. He's lived here a long time, I know him from when I was a little girl."

She looked at her watch again. "Listen, I'm going to be late. Who *are* you, anyway?"

"I'm from the police," Kling said.

"Oh, hi." The girl smiled. "I'm Marjorie Gorman."

"Would you know where I can reach him, Marjorie?"

"Did you try his building? He works in a fancy apartment house on—"

"Yes, I just came from there."

"Wasn't he there?"

"No."

"That's funny," Marjorie said. "Although, come to think of it, we didn't hear him last night, either."

"What do you mean?"

"The television. The walls are very thin, you know. When he's home, we can hear the television going."

"Yes, but he works nights."

"I mean before he leaves. He doesn't go to work until eleven o'clock. He starts at midnight, you know."

"Yes, I know."

"Well, that's what I meant. Listen, I really do have to hurry. If you want to talk, you'll have to walk me to the station."

"Okay," Kling said, and they started down the steps. "Are you sure you didn't hear the television going last night?"

"I'm positive."

"Does he usually have it on?"

"Oh, *con*stantly," Marjorie said. "He lives alone, you know, the poor old man. He's got to do *some*thing with his time."

"Yes, I suppose so."

"Why did you want to see him?"

She spoke with a pronounced Riverhead accent that

somehow marred her clean good looks. She was a tall girl, perhaps nineteen years old, wearing a dark-grey suit and a white blouse, her auburn hair brushed back behind her ears, the lobes decorated with tiny pearl earrings.

"There are some things I want to ask him," Kling said.

"About the Tinka Sachs murder?"

"Yes."

"He was telling me about that just recently."

"When was that?"

"Oh, I don't know. Let me think." They walked out of the lobby and into the street. Marjorie had long legs, and she walked very swiftly. Kling, in fact, was having trouble keeping up with her. "What's today, anyway?"

"Wednesday," Kling said.

"Wednesday, mmm, boy where does the week go? It must have been Monday. That's right. When I got home from the movies Monday night, he was downstairs putting out his garbage. So we talked awhile. He said he was expecting a detective."

"A detective? Who?"

"What do you mean?"

"Did he say *which* detective he was expecting? Did he mention a name?"

"No, I don't think so. He said he'd talked to some detectives just that morning—that was Monday, right?—and that he'd got a call a few minutes ago saying another detective was coming up to see him."

"Did he say that exactly? That *another* detective was coming up to see him? A *different* detective?"

"Oh. I don't know if he said just that. I mean, it could have been one of the detectives he'd talked to that morning. I really don't know for sure."

"Does the name Carella mean anything to you?"

"No." Marjorie paused. "Should it?"

"Did Mr. Messner use that name when he was talking about the detective who was coming to see him?"

"No, I don't think so. He only said he'd had a call from a detective, that was all. He seemed very proud. He told me they probably wanted him to describe the man again, the one he saw going up to her apartment. The dead girl's. Brrr, it gives you the creeps, doesn't it?"

"Yes," Kling said. "It does."

They were approaching the elevated station now. They paused at the bottom of the steps.

"This was Monday afternoon, you say?"

"No. Monday night. Monday *night,* I said."

"What time Monday night?"

"About ten-thirty, I guess. I told you, I was coming home from the movies."

"Let me get this straight," Kling said. "At ten-thirty Monday night, Mr. Messner was putting out his garbage, and he told you he had just received a call from a detective who was on his way over? Is that it?"

"That's it." Marjorie frowned. "It *was* kind of late, wasn't it? I mean, to be making a business visit. Or do you people work that late?"

"Well, yes, but . . ." Kling shook his head.

"Listen, I really have to go," Marjorie said. "I'd like to talk to you, but—"

"I'd appreciate a few more minutes of your time, if you can—"

"Yes, but my boss—"

"I'll call him later and explain."

"Yeah, you don't *know* him," Marjorie said, and rolled her eyes.

"Can you just tell me whether Mr. Messner mentioned anything about this detective the next time you saw him. I mean, *after* the detective was there."

"Well, I haven't seen him since Monday night."

"You didn't see him at *all* yesterday?"

"Nope. Well, I usually miss him in the morning, you know, because I'm gone before he gets home. But sometimes I drop in at night, just to say hello, or he'll come in for something, you know, like that. And I told you about the television. We just didn't hear it. My mother commented about it, as a matter of fact. She said Cyclops was probably—that's what we call him, Cyclops, everybody does, he doesn't mind—she said Cyclops was probably out on the town."

"Does he often go out on the town?"

"Well, I don't think so—but who knows? Maybe he felt like having himself a good time, you know? Listen, I really have to—"

"All right, I won't keep you. Thank you very much, Marjorie. If you'll tell me where you work, I'll be happy to—"

"Oh, the hell with him. I'll tell him what happened, and he can take it or leave it. I'm thinking of quitting, anyway."

"Well, thank you again."

"Don't mention it," Marjorie said, and went up the steps to the platform.

Kling thought for a moment, and then searched in his pocket for a dime. He went into the cafeteria on the corner, found a phone booth, and identified himself to the operator, telling her he wanted the listing for the lobby phone in

Tinka's building on Stafford Place. She gave him the number, and he dialed it. A man answered the phone. Kling said, "I'd like to talk to the superintendent, please."

"This is the super."

"This is Detective Kling of the 87th Squad," Kling said. "I'm investigating—"

"Who?" the superintendent said.

"Detective Kling. Who's this I'm speaking to?"

"I'm the super of the building. Emmanuel Farber. Manny. Did you say this was a detective?"

"That's right."

"Boy, when are you guys going to give us some rest here?"

"What do you mean?"

"Don't you have nothing to do but call up here?"

"I haven't called you before, Mr. Farber."

"No, not you, never mind. This phone's been going like sixty."

"Who called you?"

"Detectives, never mind."

"Who? Which detectives?"

"The other night."

"When?"

"Monday. Monday night."

"A detective called you Monday night?"

"Yeah, wanted to know where he could reach Cyclops. That's one of our elevator operators."

"Did you tell him?"

"Sure, I did."

"Who was he? Did he give you his name?"

"Yeah, some Italian fellow."

Kling was silent for a moment.

"Would the name have been Carella?" he asked.

"That's right."

"Carella?"

"Yep, that's the one."

"What time did he call?"

"Oh, I don't know. Sometime in the evening."

"And he said his name was Carella?"

"That's right, Detective Carella, that's what he said. Why? You know him?"

"Yes," Kling said. "I know him."

"Well, you ask him. He'll tell you."

"What time in the evening did he call? Was it early or late?"

"What do you mean by early or late?" Farber asked.

"Was it before dinner?"

"No. Oh no, it was after dinner. About ten o'clock, I suppose. Maybe a little later."

"And what did he say to you?"

"He wanted Cyclops' address, said he had some questions to ask him."

"About what?"

"About the murder."

"He said that specifically? He said, 'I have some questions to ask Cyclops about the murder'?"

"About the Tinka Sachs murder, is what he actually said."

"He said, 'This is Detective Carella, I want to know—' "

"That's right, this is Detective Carella—"

" '—I want to know Cyclops Messner's address because I have some questions to ask him about the Tinka Sachs murder.' "

"No, that's not it exactly."

"What's wrong with it?" Kling asked.

"He didn't say the name."

"You just said he *did* say the name. The Tinka Sachs murder. You said—"

"Yes, that's right. That's not what I mean."

"Look, what—?"

"He didn't say Cyclops' name."

"I don't understand you."

"All he said was he wanted the address of the one-eyed elevator operator because he had some questions to ask him about the Tinka Sachs murder. That's what he said."

"He referred to him as the one-eyed elevator operator?"

"That's right."

"You mean he didn't know the name?"

"Well, I don't know about that. He didn't know how to *spell* it, though, that's for sure."

"Excuse me," the telephone operator said. "Five cents for the next five minutes, please."

"Hold on," Kling said. He reached into his pocket, and found only two quarters. He put one into the coin slot.

"Was that twenty-five cents you deposited, sir?" the operator asked.

"That's right."

"If you'll let me have your name and address, sir, we'll—"

"No, forget it."

"—send you a refund in stamps."

"No, that's all right, operator, thank you. Just give me as much time as the quarter'll buy, okay?"

"Very well, sir."

"Hello?" Kling said. "Mr. Farber?"

"I'm still here," Farber said.

"What makes you think this detective couldn't spell Cyclops' name?"

"Well, I gave him the address, you see, and I was about to hang up when he asked me about the spelling. He wanted to know the correct spelling of the name."

"And what did you say?"

"I said it was Messner, M-E-S-S-N-E-R, Ernest Messner, and I repeated the address for him again, 1117 Gainesborough Avenue in Riverhead."

"And then what?"

"He said thank you very much and hung up."

"Sir, was it your impression that he did not know Cyclops' name until you gave it to him?"

"Well, I couldn't say that for sure. All he wanted was the correct spelling."

"Yes, but he asked for the address of the one-eyed elevator operator, isn't that what you said?"

"That's right."

"If he knew the name, why didn't he use it?"

"You got me. What's *your* name?" the superintendent asked.

"Kling. Detective Bert Kling."

"Mine's Farber, Emmanuel Farber, Manny."

"Yes, I know. You told me."

"Oh. Okay."

There was a long silence on the line.

"Was that all, Detective Kling?" Farber said at last. "I've got to get these lobby floors waxed and I'm—"

"Just a few more questions," Kling said.

"Well, okay, but could we—?"

"Cyclops had his usual midnight-to-eight-a.m. shift Monday night, is that right?"

"That's right, but—"

"When he came to work, did he mention anything about having seen a detective?"

"He *didn't*," Farber said.

"He didn't mention a detective at all? He didn't say—"

"No, he didn't come to work."

"What?"

"He didn't come to work Monday nor yesterday, either," Farber said. "I had to get another man to take his place."

"Did you try to reach him?"

"I waited until twelve-thirty, with the man he was supposed to relieve taking a fit, and finally I called his apartment, three times in fact, and there was no answer. So I phoned one of the other men. Had to run the elevator myself until the man got here. That must've been about two in the morning."

"Did Cyclops contact you at all any time yesterday?"

"Nope. You think he'd call, wouldn't you?"

"Did he contact you today?"

"Nope."

"But you're expecting him to report to work tonight, aren't you?"

"Well, he's due at midnight, but I don't know. I hope he shows up."

"Yes, I hope so, too," Kling said. "Thank you very much, Mr. Farber. You've been very helpful."

"Sure thing," Farber said, and hung up.

Kling sat in the phone booth for several moments, trying to piece together what he had just learned. Someone had called Farber on Monday night at about ten, identifying himself as Detective Carella, and asking for the address of the one-eyed elevator operator. Carella knew the man was named Ernest Messner and nicknamed Cyclops. He would not have referred to him as the one-eyed elevator operator. But more important than that, he would never have called the superintendent at all. Knowing the man's name, allegedly desiring his address, he would have done exactly what Kling had done this morning. He would have consulted the telephone directories and found a listing for Ernest Messner in the Riverhead book, as simple as that, as routine as that. No, the man who had called Farber was not Carella. But he had known Carella's name, and had made good use of it.

At ten-thirty Monday night, Marjorie German had met Cyclops in front of the building and he had told her he was expecting a visit from a detective. That could only mean that "Detective Carella" had already called Cyclops and told him he would stop by. And now, Cyclops was missing, had indeed been missing since Monday night.

Kling came out of the phone booth, and began walking back toward the building on Gainesborough Avenue.

The landlady of the building did not have a key to Mr. Messner's apartment. Mr. Messner has his own lock on the door, she said, the same as any of the other tenants in the building, and she certainly did not have a key to Mr. Messner's lock, nor to the locks of any of the other tenants. Moreover, she would *not* grant Kling permission to try his skeleton key on the door, and she warned him that if he forced entry into Mr. Messner's apartment, she would sue the city. Kling informed her that if she cooperated, she would save him the trouble of going all the way downtown for a search warrant, and she said she didn't *care* about his going all the way downtown, suppose Mr. Messner came back and learned she had let the police in there while he was away, *who'd* get the lawsuit then, would he mind telling her?

Kling said he would go downtown for the warrant.

Go ahead then, the landlady told him.

It took an hour to get downtown, twenty minutes to obtain the warrant, and another hour to get back to Riverhead again. His skeleton key would not open Cyclops' door, so he kicked it in.

The apartment was empty.

Seven

Dennis Sachs seemed to be about forty years old. He was tall and deeply tanned, with massive shoulders and an athlete's easy stance. He opened the door of his room at the Hotel Capistan, and said, "Detective Kling? Come in, won't you?"

"Thank you," Kling said. He studied Sachs's face. The eyes were blue, with deep ridges radiating from the edges, starkly white against the bronzed skin. He had a large nose, an almost feminine mouth, a cleft chin. He needed a shave. His hair was brown.

The little girl, Anna, was sitting on a couch at the far end of the large living room. She had a doll across her lap, and she was watching television when Kling came in. She glanced up at him briefly, and then turned her attention back to the screen. A give-away program was in progress, the m.c. unveiling a huge motor launch to the delighted shrieks of the studio audience. The couch was upholstered in a lush green fabric against which the child's blond hair shone lustrously. The place was oppressively over-furnished, undoubtedly part of a suite, with two doors leading from the living room to the adjoining bedrooms. A small cooking alcove was tucked discreetly into a corner near the entrance door, a screen drawn across it. The dominant colors of the suite were pale yellows and deep greens, the rugs were thick, the furniture was exquisitely carved. Kling suddenly wondered how much all this was costing Sachs per day, and then tried to remember where he'd picked up the notion that archaeologists were poverty-stricken.

"Sit down," Sachs said. "Can I get you a drink?"

"I'm on duty," Kling said.

"Oh, sorry. Something soft then? A Coke? Seven-Up? I think we've got some in the refrigerator."

"Thank you, no," Kling said.

The men sat. From his wing chair, Kling could see through the large windows and out over the park to where the skyscrapers lined the city. The sky behind the buildings was a vibrant blue. Sachs sat facing him, limned with the light flowing through the windows.

"The people at the Children's Shelter told me you got to the city late Monday, Mr. Sachs. May I ask where in Arizona you were?"

"Well, part of the time I was in the desert, and the rest of the time I was staying in a little town called Rainfield, have you ever heard of it?"

"No."

"Yes. Well, I'm not surprised," Sachs said. "It's on the edge of the desert. Just a single hotel, a depot, a general store, and that's it."

"What were you doing in the desert?"

"We're on a dig, I thought you knew that. I'm part of an archaeological team headed by Dr. Oliver Tarsmith. We're trying to trace the route of the Hohokam in Arizona."

"The Hohokam?"

"Yes, that's a Pima Indian word meaning "those who

have vanished." The Hohokam were a tribe once living in Arizona, haven't you ever heard of them?"

"No, I'm afraid I haven't."

"Yes, well. In any case, they seem to have had their origins in Old Mexico. In fact, archaeologists like myself have found copper bells and other objects that definitely link the Hohokam to the Old Mexican civilization. And, of course, we've excavated ball courts—an especially large one at Snaketown—that are definitely Mexican or Mayan in origin. At one site, we found a rubber ball buried in a jar, and it's our belief that it must have been traded through tribes all the way from southern Mexico. That's where the wild rubber grows, you know."

"No, I didn't know that."

"Yes, well. The point is that we archaeologists don't know what route the Hohokam traveled from Mexico to Arizona and then to Snaketown. Dr. Tarsmith's theory is that their point of entry was the desert just outside Rainfield. We are now excavating for archaeological evidence to support this theory."

"I see. That sounds like interesting work."

Sachs shrugged.

"Isn't it?"

"I suppose so."

"You don't sound very enthusiastic."

"Well, we haven't had too much luck so far. We've been out there for close to a year, and we've uncovered only the flimsiest sort of evidence, and . . . well, frankly, it's getting a bit tedious. We spend four days a week out on the desert, you see, and then come back into Rainfield late Thursday night. There's nothing much in Rainfield, and the nearest big town is a hundred miles from there. It can get pretty monotonous."

"Why only *four* days in the desert?"

"Instead of five, do you mean? We usually spend Fridays making out our reports. There's a lot of paperwork involved, and it's easier to do at the hotel."

"When did you learn of your wife's death, Mr. Sachs?"

"Monday morning."

"You had not been informed up to that time?"

"Well, as it turned out, a telegram was waiting for me in Rainfield. I guess it was delivered to the hotel on Saturday, but I wasn't there to take it."

"Where were you?"

"In Phoenix."

"What were you doing there?"

"Drinking, seeing some shows. You can get very sick of Rainfield, you know."

"Did anyone go with you?"

"No."

"How did you get to Phoenix?"

"By train."

"Where did you stay in Phoenix?"

"At the Royal Sands."

"From when to when?"

"Well, I left Rainfield late Thursday night. I asked Oliver—Dr. Tarsmith—if he thought he'd need me on Friday, and he said he wouldn't. I guess he realized I was stretched a little thin. He's a very perceptive man that way."

"I see. In effect, then, he gave you Friday off."

"That's right."

"No reports to write?"

"I took those with me to Phoenix. It's only a matter of organizing one's notes, typing them up, and so on."

"Did you manage to get them done in Phoenix?"

"Yes, I did."

"Now, let me understand this, Mr. Sachs . . ."

"Yes?"

"You left Rainfield sometime late Thursday night . . ."

"Yes, I caught the last train out."

"What time did you arrive in Phoenix?"

"Sometime after midnight. I had called ahead to the Sands for a reservation."

"I see. When did you leave Phoenix?"

"Mr. Kling," Sachs said suddenly, "are you just making small talk, or is there some reason for your wanting to know all this?"

"I was simply curious, Mr. Sachs. I know Homicide had sent a wire off to you, and I was wondering why you didn't receive it until Monday morning."

"Oh. Well, I just explained that. I didn't get back to Rainfield until then."

"You left Phoenix Monday morning?"

"Yes. I caught a train at about six a.m. I didn't want to miss the jeep." Sachs paused. "The expedition's jeep. We usually head out to the desert pretty early, to get some heavy work in before the sun gets too hot."

"I see. But when you got back to the hotel, you found the telegram."

"That's right."

"What did you do then?"

"I immediately called the airport in Phoenix to find out what flights I could get back here."

"And what did they tell you?"

"There was a TWA flight leaving at eight in the morning, which would get here at four-twenty in the afternoon—there's a two-hour time difference, you know."

"Yes, I know that. Is that the flight you took?"

"No, I didn't. It was close to six-thirty when I called the airport. I might have been able to make it to Phoenix in time, but it would have been a very tight squeeze, and I'd have had to borrow a car. The trains out of Rainfield aren't that frequent, you see."

"So what *did* you do?"

"Well, I caught American's eight-thirty flight, instead. Not a through flight; we made a stop at Chicago. I didn't get here until almost five o'clock that night."

"That was Monday night?"

'Yes, that's right."

"When did you pick up your daughter?"

"Yesterday morning. Today is Wednesday, isn't it?"

"Yes."

"You lose track of time when you fly cross-country," Sachs said.

"I suppose you do."

The television m.c. was giving away a fourteen-cubic-foot refrigerator with a big, big one-hundred-and-sixty-pound freezer. The studio audience was applauding. Anna sat with her eyes fastened to the screen.

"Mr. Sachs, I wonder if we could talk about your wife."

"Yes, please."

"The child . . ."

"I think she's absorbed in the program." He glanced at her, and then said, "Would you prefer we discussed it in one of the other rooms?"

"I thought that might be better, yes," Kling said.

"Yes, you're right. Of course," Sachs said. He rose and led Kling toward the larger bedroom. His valise, partially unpacked, was open on the stand alongside the bed. "I'm afraid everything's a mess," he said. "It's been hurry up, hurry up from the moment I arrived."

"I can imagine," Kling said. He sat in an easy chair near the bed. Sachs sat on the edge of the bed and leaned over intently, waiting for him to begin. "Mr. Sachs, how long had you and your wife been divorced?"

"Three years. And we separated a year before that."

"The child is how old?"

"Anna? She's five."

"Is there another child?"

"No."

"The way you said 'Anna,' I thought—"

"No, there's only the one child. Anna. That's all."

"As I understand it, then, you and your wife separated the year after she was born."

"That's right, yes. Actually, it was fourteen months. She was fourteen months old when we separated."

"Why was that, Mr. Sachs?"

"Why was what?"

"Why did you separate?"

"Well, you know." Sachs shrugged.

"No, I don't."

"Well, that's personal. I'm afraid."

The room was very silent. Kling could hear the m.c. in the living room leading the audience in a round of applause for one of the contestants.

"I can understand that divorce is a personal matter, Mr. Sachs, but—"

"Yes, it is."

"Yes, I understand that."

"I'd rather not discuss it, Mr. Kling. Really, I'd rather not. I don't see how it would help you in solving . . . in solving my wife's murder. Really."

"I'm afraid *I'll* have to decide what would help us, Mr. Sachs."

"We had a personal problem, let's leave it at that."

"What sort of a personal problem?"

"I'd rather not say. We simply couldn't live together any longer, that's all."

"Was there another man involved?"

"Certainly not!"

"Forgive me, but I think you can see how another man might be important in a murder case."

"I'm sorry. Yes. Of course. Yes, it would be important. But it wasn't anything like that. There was no one else involved. There was simply a . . . a personal problem between the two of us and we . . . we couldn't find a way to resolve it, so . . . so we thought it best to split up. That's all there was to it."

"What was the personal problem?"

"Nothing that would interest you."

"Try me."

"My wife is dead," Sachs said.

"I know that."

"Any problem she might have had is certainly—"

"Oh, it was *her* problem then, is that right? Not yours?"

"It was *our* problem," Sachs said. "Mr. Kling, I'm not going to answer any other questions along these lines. If you insist that I do, you'll have to arrest me, and I'll get a lawyer, and we'll see about it. In the meantime, I'll just have to refuse to co-operate if that's the tack you're going to follow. I'm sorry."

"All right, Mr. Sachs, perhaps you can tell me whether or not you mutually agreed to the divorce."

"Yes, we did."

"Whose idea was it? Yours or hers?"

"Mine."

"Why?"

"I can't answer that."

"You know, of course, that adultery is the only grounds for divorce in this state."

"Yes, I know that. There was no adultery involved. Tinka went to Nevada for the divorce."

"Did you go with her?"

"No. She knew people in Nevada. She's from the West Coast originally. She was born in Los Angeles."

"Did she take the child with her?"

"No. Anna stayed here with me while she was gone."

"Have you kept in touch since the divorce, Mr. Sachs?"

"Yes."

"How?"

"Well, I see Anna, you know. We share the child. We agreed to that before the divorce. Stuck out in Arizona there, I didn't have much chance to see her this past year. But usually, I see quite a bit of her. And I talked to Tinka on the phone, I *used* to talk to her on the phone, and I also wrote to her. We kept in touch, yes."

"Would you have described your relationship as a friendly one?"

"I loved her," Sachs said flatly.

"I see."

Again, the room was silent. Sachs turned his head away.

“Do you have any idea who might have killed her?” Kling asked.

“No.”

“None whatever?”

“None whatever.”

“When did you communicate with her last?”

“We wrote to each other almost every week.”

“Did she mention anything that was troubling her?”

“No.”

“Did she mention any of her friends who might have reason to . . . ?”

“No.”

“When did you write to her last?”

“Last week sometime.”

“Would you remember exactly when?”

“I think it was . . . the fifth or the sixth, I’m not sure.”

“Did you send the letter by air?”

“Yes.”

“Then it should have arrived here before her death.”

“Yes, I imagine it would have.”

“Did she usually save your letters?”

“I don’t know. Why?”

“We couldn’t find any of them in the apartment.”

“Then I guess she didn’t save them.”

“Did *you* save *her* letters?”

“Yes.”

“Mr. Sachs, would you know one of your wife’s friends who answers this description: Six feet two or three inches tall, heavily built, in his late thirties or early forties, with straight blond hair and—”

“I don’t know who Tinka saw after we were divorced. We led separate lives.”

"But you still loved her."

"Yes."

"Then why did you divorce her?" Kling asked again, and Sachs did not answer. "Mr. Sachs, this may be very important to us . . ."

"It isn't."

"Was your wife a dyke?"

"No."

"Are you a homosexual?"

"No."

"Mr. Sachs, *whatever* it was, believe me, it won't be something new to us. Believe me, Mr. Sachs, and please trust me."

"I'm sorry. It's none of your business. It has nothing to do with anything but Tinka and me."

"Okay," Kling said.

"I'm sorry."

"Think about it. I know you're upset at the moment, but—"

"There's nothing to think about. There are some things I will never discuss with anyone, Mr. Kling. I'm sorry, but I owe at least that much to Tinka's memory."

"I understand," Kling said, and rose. "Thank you for your time. I'll leave my card, in case you remember anything that might be helpful to us."

"All right," Sachs said.

"When will you be going back to Arizona?"

"I'm not sure. There's so much to be arranged. Tinka's lawyer advised me to stay for a while, at least to the end of the month, until the estate can be settled, and plans made for Anna . . . there's so much to do."

"*Is* there an estate?" Kling asked.

"Yes."

"A sizable one?"

"I wouldn't imagine so."

"I see." Kling paused, seemed about to say something, and then abruptly extended his hand. "Thank you again, Mr. Sachs," he said. "I'll be in touch with you."

Sachs saw him to the door. Anna, her doll in her lap, was still watching television when he went out.

At the squadroom, Kling sat down with a pencil and pad, and then made a call to the airport, requesting a list of all scheduled flights to and from Phoenix, Arizona. It took him twenty minutes to get all the information, and another ten minutes to type it up in chronological order. He pulled the single sheet from his machine and studied it:

AIRLINE SCHEDULES FROM PHOENIX AND RETURN

EASTBOUND:

Frequency	Airline & Flt.	Departing Phoenix	Arriving Here	Stops
Exc. Sat.	American #946	12:25AM	10:45 AM	(Tucson 12:57 AM— 1:35 AM
				(Chicago 6:35 AM—8:00 AM
Daily	American #98	7:25 AM	5:28 PM	(Tucson 7:57 AM— 8:25 AM
				(El Paso 9:10 AM— 9:40 AM
				(Dallas 12:00 PM—12:30 PM
Daily	TWA #146	8:00 AM	4:20 PM	Chicago 12:58PM—1:30 PM
Daily	American #68	8:30 PM	4:53 PM	Chicago 1:27 PM— 2:00 PM
Daily	American #66	2:00 PM	10:23 PM	Chicago 6:57 PM— 7:30 PM

WESTBOUND:

Frequency	Airline & Flt.	Departing H ere	Arriving Phoenix	Stops
Exc. Sun.	American #965	8:00 AM	11:05 AM	Chicago 9:12 AM—9:55 AM
Daily	TWA #147	8:30 AM	11:25 AM	Chicago 9:31 AM—10:15 AM
Daily	American #981	4:00 PM	6:55 PM	Chicago 5:12 PM—5:45 PM
Daily	TWA #143	4:30 PM	7:40 PM	Chicago 5:41 PM—6:30 PM
Daily	American # 67	6:00PM	10:10PM	(Chicago 7:12 PM—7:45 PM
				(Tuscon 9:08 PM—9:40 PM

* * *

It seemed entirely possible to him that Dennis Sachs could have taken either the twelve twenty-five flight from Phoenix late Thursday night, or any one of three flights early Friday morning, and still have been here in the city in time to arrive at Tinka's apartment by nine or nine-thirty p.m. He could certainly have killed his wife and caught an early flight back the next morning. Or any one of four flights on Sunday, all of which—because of the time difference—would have put him back in Phoenix that same night and in Rainfield by Monday to pick up the telegram waiting there for him. It was a possibility—remote, but a possibility nonetheless. The brown hair, of course, was a problem. Cyclops had said the man's hair was blond. But a commercial dye or bleach—

One thing at a time, Kling thought. Wearily, he pulled the telephone directory to him and began a methodical check of the two airlines flying to Phoenix. He told them he wanted to know if a man named Dennis Sachs, or any man with the initials D.S., had flown here from Phoenix last Thursday night or Friday morning, and whether or not he had made the return flight any time during the weekend. The airlines were helpful and patient. They checked their flight lists. Something we don't ordinarily do, sir, is this a case involving a missing person? No, Kling said, this is a case involving a murder. Oh, well in that case, sir, but we don't ordinarily do this, sir, even for the police, our flight lists you see . . . Yes, well I appreciate your help, Kling said.

Neither of the airlines had any record of either a Dennis Sachs or a D.S. taking a trip from or to Phoenix at any time before Monday, April 12th. American Airlines had him listed as a passenger on Flight 68, which had left Phoenix at eight-thirty a.m. Monday morning, and had arrived here at four-fifty-three p.m. that afternoon. American reported that Mr. Sachs had not as yet booked return passage.

Kling thanked American and hung up. There was still the possibility that Sachs had flown here and back before Monday, using an assumed name. But there was no way of checking that—and the only man who could make any sort of a positive identification had been missing since Monday night.

The meeting took place in Lieutenant Byrnes's office at five o'clock that afternoon. There were five detectives present in addition to Byrnes himself. Miscolo had brought in coffee for most of the men, but they sipped at it only distractedly, listening intently to Byrnes as he conducted the most unorthodox interrogation any of them had ever attended.

"We're here to talk about Monday afternoon," Byrnes said. His tone was matter-of-fact, his face expressed no emotion. "I have the duty chart for Monday, April twelfth, and it shows Kling, Meyer and Carella on from eight to four, with Meyer catching. The relieving team is listed as Hawes, Willis and Brown, with Brown catching. Is that the way it was?"

The men nodded.

"What time did you get here, Cotton?"

Hawes, leaning against the lieutenant's filing cabinet, the only one of the detectives drinking tea, looked up and said, "It must've been about five."

"Was Steve still here?"

"No."

"What about you, Hal?"

"I got here a little early, Pete," Willis said. "I had some calls to make."

"What time?"

"Four-thirty."

"Was Steve still here?"

"Yes."

"Did you talk to him?"

"Yes."

"What about?"

"He said he was going to a movie with Teddy that night."

"Anything else?"

"That was about it."

"I talked to him, too, Pete," Brown said. He was the only Negro cop in the room. He was sitting in the wooden chair to the right of Byrnes's desk, a coffee container clasped in his huge hands.

"What'd he say to you, Art?"

"He told me he had to make a stop on the way home."

"Did he say where?"

"No."

"All right, now let's get this straight. Of the relieving team, only two of you saw him, and he said nothing about where he might have been headed. Is that right?"

"That's right," Willis said.

"Were you in the office when he left, Meyer?"

"Yes. I was making out a report."

"Did he say anything to you?"

"He said good night, and he made some joke about bucking for a promotion, you know, because I was hanging around after I'd been relieved."

"What else?"

"Nothing."

"Did he say anything to you at any time during the afternoon? About where he might be going later on?"

"Nothing."

"How about you, Kling?"

"No, he didn't say anything to me, either."

"Were you here when he left?"

"No."

"Where were you?"

"I was on my way home."

"What time did you leave?"

"About three o'clock."

"Why so early?"

There was a silence in the room.

"Why so early?" Byrnes said again.

"We had a fight."

"What about?"

"A personal matter."

"The man is dead," Byrnes said flatly. "There are no personal matters anymore."

"He sent me back to the office because he didn't like the way I was behaving during an interview. I got sore." Kling paused. "That's what we argued about."

"So you left here at three o'clock?"

"Yes."

"Even though you were supposed to be working with Carella on the Tinka Sachs case, is that right?"

"Yes."

"Did you know where he was going when he left here?"

"No, sir."

"Did he mention anything about wanting to question anyone, or about wanting to see anyone again?"

"Only the elevator operator. He thought it would be a good idea to check him again."

"What for?"

"To verify a time he'd given us."

"Do you think that's where he went?"

"I don't know, sir."

"Have you talked to this elevator operator?"

"No, sir, I can't locate him."

"He's been missing since Monday night," Meyer said. "According to Bert's report, he was expecting a visit from a man who said he was Carella."

"Is that right?" Byrnes asked.

"Yes," Kling said. "But I don't think it *was* Carella."

"Why not?"

"It's all in my report, sir."

"You've read this, Meyer?"

"Yes."

"What's your impression?"

"I agree with Bert."

Byrnes moved away from his desk. He walked to the window and stood with his hands clasped behind his back, looking at the street below. "He found something, that's for sure," he said, almost to himself. "He found *something* or *somebody,* and he was killed for it." He turned abruptly. "And not a single goddamn one of you knows where he was going. Not even the man who was allegedly working this case with him." He walked back to his desk. "Kling, you stay. The rest of you can leave."

The men shuffled out of the room. Kling stood uncomfortably before the lieutenant's desk. The lieutenant sat in his swivel chair, and turned it so that he was not looking directly at Kling. Kling did not know where he was looking. His eyes seemed unfocused.

"I guess you know that Steve Carella was a good friend of mine," Byrnes said.

"Yes, sir."

"A good friend," Byrnes repeated. He paused for a moment, still looking off somewhere past Kling, his eyes unfocused, and then said, "Why'd you let him go out alone, Kling?"

"I told you, sir. We had an argument."

"So you left here at three o'clock, when you knew goddamn well you weren't going to be relieved until four-forty-five. Now what the hell do you call that, Kling?"

Kling did not answer.

"I'm kicking you off this goddamn squad," Byrnes said. "I should have done it long ago. I'm asking for your transfer, now get the hell out of here."

Kling turned and started for the door.

"No, wait a minute," Byrnes said. He turned directly to Kling now, and there was a terrible look on his face, as though as he wanted to cry, but the tears were being checked by intense anger.

"I guess you know, Kling, that I don't have the power to suspend you, I guess you know that. The power rests with the commissioner and his deputies, and they're civilians. But a man can be suspended if he's violated the rules and regulations or if he's committed a crime. The way I look at it, Kling, you've done *both* those things. You violated the rules and regulations by leaving this squadroom and heading home when you were supposed to be on duty, and you committed a crime by allowing Carella to go out there alone and get killed."

"Lieutenant, I—"

"If I could personally take away your gun and your shield, I'd do it, Kling, believe me. Unfortunately, I can't. But I'm going to call the Chief of Detectives the minute you leave this office. I'm going to tell him I'd like you suspended pending a complete investigation, and I'm going to ask that he recommend that to the commissioner. I'm going to *get* that suspension, Kling, if I have to go to the mayor for it. I'll get departmental charges filed, and a departmental trial, and I'll get you dismissed from the force. I'm *promising* you. Now get the hell out of my sight."

Kling walked to the door silently, opened it, and stepped into the squadroom. He sat at his desk silently for several moments, staring into space. He heard the buzzer sound on Meyer's phone, heard Meyer lifting the instrument to his ear. "Yeah?" Meyer said. "Yeah, Pete. Right. Right. Okay, I'll tell him." He heard Meyer putting the phone back onto its cradle. Meyer rose and came to his desk. "That was the lieutenant," he said. "He wants me to take over the Tinka Sachs case."

Eight

The message went out on the teletype at a little before ten Thursday morning:

MISSING PERSON WANTED FOR QUESTIONING CONNECTION HOMICIDE XXX ERNEST MESSNER ALIAS CYCLOPS MESSNER XXX WHITE MALE AGE 68 XXX HEIGHT 6 FEET XXX WEIGHT 170 LBS XXX COMPLETELY BALD XXX EYES BLUE LEFT EYE MISSING AND COVERED BY PATCH XXXXX LAST SEEN VICINITY 1117 GAINESBOROUGH AVENUE RIVERHEAD MONDAY APRIL 12 TEN THIRTY PM EST XXX CONTACT MISPERBUR OR DET/2G MEYER MEYER EIGHT SEVEN SQUAD XXXXXXXXX

A copy of the teletype was pulled off the squadroom machine by Detective Meyer Meyer who wondered why it had been necessary for the detective at the Missing Persons Bureau to insert the word "completely" before the word "bald." Meyer, who was bald himself, suspected that the description was redundant, over-emphatic, and undoubtedly derogatory. It was his understanding that a bald person had no hair. None. Count them. None. Why, then, had the composer of this bulletin (Meyer visualized him as a bushy-headed man with thick black eyebrows, a black mustache and a full beard) insisted on inserting the word "completely," if not to point a deriding finger at all hairless men everywhere? Indignantly, Meyer went to the squadroom dictionary, searched through balas, balata, Balaton, Balboa, balbriggan, and came to:

bald (bôld) adj. **1.** lacking hair on some part of the scalp: *a bald head or person.* **2.** destitute of some natural growth or covering: *a bald mountain.* **3.** bare; plain; unadorned: *a bald prose style.* **4.** open; undisguised: *a bald lie.* **5.** *Zool.* having white on the head: *bald eagle.*

Meyer closed the book, reluctantly admitting that whereas it was impossible to be a little pregnant, it was not equally impossible to be a little bald. The composer of the bulletin, bushy-haired bastard that he was, had been right in describing Cyclops as "completely bald." If ever Meyer turned up missing one day, they would describe him in exactly the same way. In the meantime, his trip to the dictionary had not been a total loss. He would hereafter look upon himself as a person who lacked hair on his scalp, a person destitute of some natural growth, bare, plain and unadorned, open and undisguised, having white on the head. Hereafter, he would be known zoologically as The Bald Eagle—Nemesis of All Evil, Protector of the Innocent, Scourge of the Underworld!

"Beware The Bald Eagle!" he said aloud, and Arthur Brown looked up from his desk in puzzlement. Happily, the telephone rang at that moment. Meyer picked it up and said, "87th Squad."

"This is Sam Grossman at the lab. Who'm I talking to?"

"You're talking to The Bald Eagle," Meyer said.

"Yeah?"

"Yeah."

"Well, this is The Hairy Ape," Grossman said. "What's with you? Spring fever?"

"Sure, it's a beautiful day out," Meyer said, looking through the window at the rain.

"Is Kling there? I've got something for him on this Tinka Sachs case."

"I'm handling that one now," Meyer said.

"Oh? Okay. You feel like doing a little work, or were you planning to fly up to your aerie?"

"Up *your* aerie, Mac," Meyer said, and burst out laughing.

"Oh boy, I see I picked the wrong time to call," Grossman said. "Okay. Okay. When you've got a minute later, give me a ring, Okay? I'll—"

"The Bald Eagle *never* has a minute later," Meyer said. "What've you got for me?"

"This kitchen knife. The murder weapon. According to the tag, it was found just outside her bedroom door, guy probably dropped it on his way out."

"Okay, what about it?"

"Not much. Only it matches a few other knives in the girl's kitchen, so it's reasonable to assume it belonged to her. What I'm saying is the killer didn't go up there with his own knife, if that's of any use to you."

"He took the knife from a bunch of other knives in the kitchen, is that it?"

"No, I don't think so. I think the knife was in the bedroom."

"What would a knife be doing in the bedroom?"

"I think the girl used it to slice some lemons."

"Yeah?"

"Yeah. There was a pitcher of tea on the dresser. Two lemons, sliced in half, were floating in it. We found lemon-juice stains on the tray, as well as faint scratches left by the knife. We figure she carried the tea, the lemons, and the knife into the bedroom on that tray. Then she sliced the lemons and squeezed them into the tea."

"Well, that seems like guesswork to me," Meyer said.

"Not at all. Paul Blaney is doing the medical examination. He says he's found citric-acid stains on the girl's left hand, the hand she'd have held the lemons with while slicing with the right. We've checked, Meyer. She was right-handed."

"Okay, so she was drinking tea before she got killed," Meyer said.

"That's right. The glass was on the night table near her bed, covered with her prints."

"Whose prints were covering the knife?"

"Nobody's," Grossman said. "Or I should say *everybody's.* A whole mess of them, all smeared."

"What about her pocketbook? Kling's report said—"

"Same thing, not a good print on it anywhere. There was no money in it, you know. My guess is that the person who killed her also robbed her."

"Mmm, yeah," Meyer said. "Is that all?"

"That's all. Disappointing, huh?"

"I hoped you might come up with something more."

"I'm sorry."

"Sure."

Grossman was silent for a moment. Then he said, "Meyer?"

"Yeah?"

"You think Carella's death is linked to this one?"

"I don't know," Meyer said.

"I liked that fellow," Grossman said, and hung up.

Harvey Sadler was Tinka Sachs's lawyer and the senior partner in the firm of Sadler, McIntyre and Brooks, with offices uptown on Fisher Street. Meyer arrived there at ten minutes to noon, and discovered that Sadler was just about to leave for the Y.M.C.A. Meyer told him he was there to find out whether or not Tinka Sachs had left a will, and Sadler said she had indeed. In fact, they could talk about it on the way to the Y, if Meyer wanted to join him. Meyer said he wanted to, and the two men went downstairs to catch a cab.

Sadler was forty-five years old, with a powerful build and craggy features. He told Meyer he had played offensive back for Dartmouth in 1940, just before he was drafted into the army. He kept in shape nowadays, he said, by playing handball at the Y two afternoons a week, Mondays and Thursdays. At least, he *tried* to keep in shape. Even handball twice a week could not completely compensate for the fact that he sat behind a desk eight hours a day.

Meyer immediately suspected a deliberate barb. He had become oversensitive about his weight several weeks back when he discovered what his fourteen-year-old son Alan meant by the nickname "Old Crisco." A bit of off-duty detective work uncovered the information that "Old Crisco" was merely high school jargon for "Old Fat-in-the-Can," a disrespectful term of affection if ever he'd heard one. He would have clobbered the boy, naturally, just to show who was boss, had not his wife Sarah agreed with the little vontz. You *are* getting fat, she told Meyer; you should begin exercising at the police gym. Meyer, whose boyhood had consisted of a series of taunts and jibes from Gentiles in his neighborhood, never expected to be put down by vipers in his own bosom. He looked narrowly at Sadler now, a soldier in the enemy camp, and suddenly wondered if he was becoming a paranoid Jew. Worse yet, an *obese* paranoid Jew.

His reservations about Sadler and also about himself vanished the moment they entered the locker room of the Y.M.C.A., which smelled exactly like the locker room of the Y.M.H.A. Convinced that nothing in the world could eliminate suspicion and prejudice as effectively as the aroma of a men's locker room, swept by a joyous wave of camaraderie, Meyer leaned against the lockers while Sadler changed into his handball shorts, and listened to the details of Tinka's will.

"She leaves everything to her ex-husband," Sadler said. "That's the way she wanted it."

"Nothing to her daughter?"

"Only if Dennis predeceased Tinka. In that case, a trust was set up for the child."

"Did Dennis know this?" Meyer asked.

"I have no idea."

"Was a copy of the will sent to him?"

"Not by me."

"How many copies did you send Tinka?"

"Two. The original was kept in our office safe."

"Did she *request* two copies?"

"No. But it's our general policy to send two copies of any will to the testator. Most people like to keep one at home for easy reference, and the other in a safe deposit box. At least, that's been our experience."

"We went over Tinka's apartment pretty thoroughly, Mr. Sadler. We didn't find a copy of any will."

"Then perhaps she *did* send one to her ex-husband. That wouldn't have been at all unusual."

"Why not?"

"Well, they're on very good terms, you know. And, after all, he *is* the only real beneficiary. I imagine Tinka would have wanted him to know."

"Mmm," Meyer said. "How large an estate is it?"

"Well, there's the painting."

"What do you mean?"

"The Chagall."

"I still don't understand."

"The Chagall painting. Tinka bought it many years ago, when she first began earning top money as a model. I suppose it's worth somewhere around fifty thousand dollars today."

"That's a sizable amount."

"Yes," Sadler said. He was in his shorts now, and he was putting on his black gloves and exhibiting signs of wanting to get out on the court. Meyer ignored the signs.

"What about the rest of the estate?" he asked.

"That's it," Sadler said.

"That's what?"

"The Chagall painting *is* the estate, or at least the substance of it. The rest consists of household furnishings, some pieces of jewelry, clothing, personal effects—none of them worth very much."

"Let me get this straight, Mr. Sadler. It's my understanding that Tinka Sachs was earning somewhere in the vicinity of a hundred and fifty thousand dollars a year. Are you telling me that all she owned of value at her death was a Chagall painting valued at fifty thousand dollars?"

"That's right."

"How do you explain that?"

"I don't know. I wasn't Tinka's financial adviser. I was only her lawyer."

"As her lawyer, did you ask her to define her estate when she asked you to draw this will?"

"I did."

"How did she define it?"

"Essentially as I did a moment ago."

"When was this, Mr. Sadler?"

"The will is dated March twenty-fourth."

"March twenty-fourth? You mean just last month?"

"That's right."

"Was there any specific reason for her wanting a will drawn at that time?"

"I have no idea."

"I mean, was she worried about her health or anything?"

"She seemed in good health."

"Did she seem frightened about anything? Did she seem to possess a foreknowledge of what was going to happen?"

"No, she did not. She seemed very tense, but not frightened."

"Why was she tense?"

"I don't know."

"Did you ask her about it?"

"No, I did not. She came to me to have a will drawn. I drew it."

"Had you ever done any legal work for her prior to the will?"

"Yes. Tinka once owned a house in Mavis County. I handled the papers when she sold it."

"When was that?"

"Last October."

"How much did she get for the sale of the house?"

"Forty-two thousand, five hundred dollars."

"Was there an existing mortgage?"

"Yes. Fifteen thousand dollars went to pay it off. The remainder went to Tinka."

"Twenty . . ." Meyer hesitated, calculating. "Twenty-seven thousand, five hundred dollars went to Tinka, is that right?"

"Yes."

"In cash?"

"Yes."

"Where is it, Mr. Sadler?"

"I asked her that when we were preparing the will. I was concerned about estate taxes, you know, and about who would inherit the money she had realized on the sale of the house. But she told me she had used it for personal needs."

"She had spent it?"

"Yes." Sadler paused. "Mr. Meyer, I only play here two afternoons a week, and I'm very jealous of my time. I was hoping . . ."

"I won't be much longer, please bear with me. I'm only trying to find out what Tinka did with all this money that came her way. According to you, she didn't have a penny of it when she died."

"I'm only reporting what she told me. I listed her assets as she defined them for me."

"Could I see a copy of the will, Mr. Sadler?"

"Certainly. But it's in my safe at the office, and I won't be going back there today. If you'd like to come by in the morning . . ."

"I'd hoped to get a look at it before—"

"I assure you that I've faithfully reported everything in

the will. As I told you, I was only her lawyer, not her financial adviser."

"Did she *have* a financial adviser?"

"I don't know."

"Mr. Sadler, did you handle Tinka's divorce for her?"

"No. I began representing her only last year, when she sold the house. I didn't know her before then, and I don't know who handled the divorce."

"One last question," Meyer said. "Is anyone else mentioned as a beneficiary in Tinka's will, other than Dennis or Anna Sachs?"

"They are the only beneficiaries," Sadler said. "And Anna only if her father predeceased Tinka."

"Thank you," Meyer said.

Back at the squadroom, Meyer checked over the typewritten list of all the personal belongings found in Tinka's apartment. There was no listing for either a will or a bankbook, but someone from Homicide had noted that a key to a safety deposit box had been found among the items on Tinka's workdesk. Meyer called Homicide to ask about the key, and they told him it had been turned over to the Office of the Clerk, and he could pick it up there if he was interested and if he was willing to sign a receipt for it. Meyer was indeed interested, so he went all the way downtown to the Office of the Clerk, where he searched through Tinka's effects, finding a tiny red snap-envelope with the safety deposit box key in it. The name of the bank was printed on the face of the miniature envelope. Meyer signed out the key and then—since he was in the vicinity of the various court buildings, anyway—obtained a court order authorizing him to open the safety deposit box. In the company of a court official, he went uptown again by subway and then ran through a pouring rain, courtesy of the vernal equinox, to the First Northern National Bank on the corner of Phillips and Third, a few blocks from where Tinka had lived.

A bank clerk removed the metal box from a tier of similar boxes, asked Meyer if he wished to examine the contents in private, and then led him and the court official to a small room containing a desk, a chair, and a chained ballpoint pen. Meyer opened the box.

There were two documents in the box. The first was a letter from an art dealer, giving appraisal of the Chagall painting. The letter stated simply that the painting had been examined, that it was undoubtedly a genuine Chagall, and that it could be sold at current market prices for anywhere between forty-five and fifty thousand dollars.

The second document was Tinka's will. It was stapled inside lawyer's blueback, the firm name Sadler, McIntyre and Brooks printed on the bottom of the binder, together with the address, 80 Fisher Street. Typewritten and centered on the page was the legend LAST WILL AND TESTAMENT OF TINKA SACHS. Meyer opened the will and began reading:

LAST WILL AND TESTAMENT
of
TINKA SACHS

I, Tinka Sachs, a resident of this city, county, and state, hereby revoke all wills and codicils by me at any time heretofore made and do hereby make, publish and declare this as and for my Last Will and Testament.

FIRST: I give, devise and bequeath to my former

husband, DENNIS R. SACHS, if he shall survive me, and, if he shall not survive me, to my trustee, hereinafter named, all of my property and all of my household and personal effects including without limitation, clothing, furniture and furnishings, books, jewelry, art objects, and paintings.

SECOND: If my former husband Dennis shall not survive me, I give, devise and bequeath my said estate to my Trustee hereinafter named, IN TRUST NEVERTHELESS, for the following uses and purposes:

(1) My Trustee shall hold, invest and re-invest the principal of said trust, and shall collect the income therefrom until my daughter, ANNA SACHS, shall attain the age of twenty-one (21) years, or sooner die.

(2) My Trustee shall, from time to time: distribute to my daughter ANNA before she has attained the age of twenty-one (21) so much of the net income (and the net income of any year not so distributed shall be accumulated and shall, after the end of such year, be deemed principal for purposes of this trust) and so much of the principal of this trust as my Trustee may in his sole and unreviewable discretion determine for any purposes deemed advisable or convenient by said Trustee, provided, however, that no principal or income in excess of an aggregate amount of Five Thousand Dollars ($5,000) in any one year be used for the support of the child unless the death of the child's father, DENNIS R. SACHS, shall have left her financially unable to support herself. The decision of my Trustee with respect

to the dates of distribution and the sums to be distributed shall be final.

(3) If my daughter, ANNA shall die before attaining the age of twenty-one (21) years, my Trustee shall pay over the then principal of the trust fund and any accumulated income to the issue of my daughter, ANNA, then living, in equal shares, and if there be no such issue then to those persons who would inherit from me had I died intestate immediately after the death of ANNA.

THIRD: I nominate, constitute and appoint my former husband, DENNIS R. SACHS, Executor of this my Last Will and Testament. If my said former husband shall predecease me or shall fail to qualify or cease to act as Executor, then I appoint my agent and friend, ARTHUR G. CUTLER, in his place as successor or substitute executor and, if my former husband shall predecease me, as TRUSTEES of the trust created hereby. If my said friend and agent shall fail to qualify or cease to act as Executor or Trustee, then I appoint his wife, LESLIE CUTLER, in his place as successor or substitute executor and/or trustee, as the case may be. Unless otherwise provided by law, no bond or other security shall be required to permit any Executor or Trustee to qualify or act in any jurisdiction.

The rest of the will was boilerplate. Meyer scanned it quickly, and then turned to the last page where Tinka had signed her name below the words "IN WITNESS WHEREOF, I sign, seal, publish and declare this as my Last Will and Testament" and where, below that, Harvey Sadler, William

McIntyre and Nelson Brooks had signed as attesting witnesses. The will was dated March twenty-fourth.

The only thing Sadler had forgotten to mention—or perhaps Meyer hadn't asked him about it—was that Art Cutler had been named trustee in the event of Dennis Sachs's death.

Meyer wondered if it meant anything.

And then he calculated how much money Tinka had earned in eleven years at a hundred and fifty thousand dollars a year, and wondered again why her only possession of any real value was the Chagall painting she had drenched with blood on the night of her death.

Something stank.

Nine

He had checked and rechecked his own findings against the laboratory's reports on the burned wreckage, and at first only one thing seemed clear to Paul Blaney. Wherever Steve Carella had been burned to death, it had not been inside that automobile. The condition of the corpse was unspeakably horrible; it made Blaney queasy just to look at it. In his years as medical examiner, Blaney had worked on cases of thermic trauma ranging from the simplest burns to cases of serious and fatal exposure to flame, light, and electric energy—but these were the worst fourth-degree burns he had ever seen. The body had undoubtedly been cooked for hours: The face was unrecognizable, all of the features gone, the skin black and tight, the single remaining cornea opaque, the teeth undoubtedly loosened and then lost in the fire; the skin on the torso was brittle and split; the hair had been burned away, the flesh completely gone in many places, showing dark red-brown skeletal muscles and charred brittle bones. Blaney's internal examination revealed pale, cooked involuntary muscles, dull and shrunken viscera. Had the body been reduced to its present condition inside that car, the fire would have had to rage for hours. The lab's report indicated that the automobile, ignited by an explosion of gasoline, had burned with extreme intensity, but only briefly. It was Blaney's contention that the body had been burned elsewhere, and then put into the automobile to simulate death there by explosion and subsequent fire.

Blaney was not paid to speculate on criminal motivation, but he wondered now why someone had gone to all this trouble, especially when the car fire would undoubtedly have been hot enough to eliminate adequately and forever any intended victim. Being a methodical man, he continued to probe. His careful and prolonged investigation had nothing to do with the fact that the body belonged to a policeman, or even to a policeman he had known. The corpse on the table was not to him a person called Steve Carella; it was instead a pathological puzzle.

He did not solve that puzzle until late Friday afternoon.

Bert Kling was alone in the squadroom when the telephone rang. He lifted the receiver.

"Detective Kling, 87th Squad," he said.

"Bert, this is Paul Blaney."

"Hello, Paul, how are you?"

"Fine, thanks. Who's handling the Carella case?"

"Meyer's in charge. Why?"

"Can I talk to him?"

"Not here right now."

"I think this is important," Blaney said. "Do you know where I can reach him?"

"I'm sorry, I don't know where he is."

"If I give it to you, will you make sure he gets it sometime tonight?"

"Sure," Kling said.

"I've been doing the autopsy," Blaney said. "I'm sorry I couldn't get back to you people sooner, but a lot of things were bothering me about this, and I wanted to be careful. I didn't want to make any statements that might put you on the wrong track, do you follow?"

"Yes, sure," Kling said.

"Well, if you're ready, I'd like to trace this for you step by step. And I'd like to say at the onset that I'm absolutely convinced of what I'm about to say. I mean, I know how important this is, and I wouldn't dare commit myself on guesswork alone—not in a case of this nature."

"I've got a pencil," Kling said. "Go ahead."

"To begin with, the comparative conditions of vehicle and cadaver indicated to me that the body had been incinerated elsewhere for a prolonged period of time, and only later removed to the automobile where it was found. I now have further evidence from the lab to support this theory. I sent them some recovered fragments of foreign materials that were embedded in the burned flesh. The fragments proved to be tiny pieces of wood charcoal. It seems certain now that the body was consumed in a *wood* fire, and not a gasoline fire such as would have occurred in the automobile. It's my opinion that the victim was thrust headfirst into a fireplace."

"What makes you think so?"

"The upper half of the body was severely burned, whereas most of the pelvic region and all of the lower extremities are virtually untouched. I think the upper half of the body was pushed into the fireplace and kept there for many hours, possibly throughout the night. Moreover, I think the man was murdered *before* he was thrown into the fire."

"Before?"

"Yes, I examined the air passages for possible inhaled

soot, and the blood of carboxyhemoglobin. The presence of either would have indicated that the victim was alive during the fire. I found neither."

"Then how *was* he killed?" Kling asked.

"That would involve guesswork," Blaney said. "There's evidence of extradural hemorrhage, and there are also several fractures of the skull vault. But these may only be postmortem fractures resulting from charring, and I wouldn't feel safe in saying the victim was murdered by a blow to the head. Let's simply say he was dead before he was incinerated, and leave it at that."

"Then why was he thrown into the fire?" Kling asked.

"To obliterate the body beyond recognition."

"Go on."

"The teeth, as you know, were missing from the head, making dental identification impossible. At first I thought the fire had loosened them, but upon further examination, I found bone fragments in the upper gum. I now firmly believe that the teeth were knocked out of the mouth before the body was incinerated, and I believe this was done to further prevent identification."

"What are you saying, Blaney?"

"May I go on? I don't want any confusion about this later."

"Please," Kling said.

"There was no hair on the burned torso. Chest hair, underarm hair and even the upper region of pubic hair had been singed away by the fire. Neither was there any hair on the scalp, which would have been both reasonable and obvious had the body been thrust into a fireplace headfirst, as I surmise it was. But upon examination, I was able to find surviving hair roots in the subcutaneous fat below the dermis on the torso and arms, even though the shaft and epithelial sheath had been destroyed. In other words, though the fire had consumed whatever hair had once existed on the torso and arms, there was nonetheless evidence that hair *had been growing there.* I could find no such evidence on the victim's scalp."

"What do you mean?"

"I mean that the man who was found in that automobile was bald to begin with."

"What?"

"Yes, nor was this particularly surprising. The atrophied internal viscera, the distended aorta of the heart, the abundant fatty marrow, large medullary cavities, and dense compact osseous tissue all indicated a person well on in years. Moreover, it was my initial belief that only one eye had survived the extreme heat—the right eye—and that it had been rendered opaque whereas the left eye had been entirely consumed by the flames. I have now carefully examined that left socket and it is my conclusion that there had not been an eye in it for many many years. The optic nerve and tract simply do not exist, and there is scar tissue present which indicates removal of the eye long before—"

"Cyclops," Kling said. "Oh my God, it's Cyclops!"

"Whoever it is," Blaney said, "it is *not* Steve Carella."

He lay naked on the floor near the radiator.

He could hear rain lashing against the window panes, but the room was warm and he felt no discomfort. Yesterday, the girl had loosened the handcuff a bit, so that it no longer was clamped so tightly on his wrist. His nose was still swollen, but the throbbing pain was gone now, and the girl had washed his cuts and promised to shave him as soon as they were healed.

He was hungry.

He knew that the girl would come with food the moment it grew dark; she always did. There was one meal a day, always at dusk, and the girl brought it to him on a tray and then watched him while he ate, talking to him. Two days ago, she had showed him the newspapers, and he had read them with a peculiar feeling of unreality. The picture in the newspapers had been taken when he was still a patrolman. He looked very young and very innocent. The headline said he was dead.

He listened for the sound of her heels now. He could hear nothing in the other room; the apartment was silent. He wondered if she had gone, and felt a momentary pang. He glanced again at the waning light around the edges of the window shades. The rain drummed steadily against the glass. There was the sound of traffic below, tires hushed on rain-swept streets. In the room, the gloom of dusk spread into the corners. Neon suddenly blinked against the drawn shades. He waited, listening, but there was no sound.

He must have dozed again. He was awakened by the sound of the key being inserted in the door lock. He sat upright, his left hand extended behind him and manacled to the radiator, and watched as the girl came into the room. She was wearing a short silk dressing gown belted tightly at the waist. The gown was a bright red, and she wore black high-heeled pumps that added several inches to her height. She closed the door behind her, and put the tray down just inside the door.

"Hello, doll," she whispered.

She did not turn on the overhead light. She went to one of

the windows instead and raised the shade. Green neon rain-snakes slithered along the glass pane. The floor was washed with melting green, and then the neon blinked out and the room was dark again. He could hear the girl's breathing. The sign outside flashed again. The girl stood near the window in the red gown, the green neon behind her limning her long legs. The sign went out.

"Are you hungry, doll?" she whispered, and walked to him swiftly and kissed him on the cheek. She laughed deep in her throat, then moved away from him and went to the door. The Llama rested on the tray alongside the coffeepot. A sandwich was on a paper plate to the right of the gun.

"Do I still need this?" she asked, hefting the gun and pointing it at him.

Carella did not answer.

"I guess not," the girl said, and laughed again, that same low throaty laugh that was somehow not at all mirthful.

"Why am I alive?" he said. He was very hungry, and he could smell the coffee deep and strong in his nostrils, but he had learned not to ask for his food. He had asked for it last night, and the girl had deliberately postponed feeding him, talking to him for more than an hour before she reluctantly brought the tray to him.

"You're not alive," the girl said. "You're dead. I showed you the papers, didn't I? You're dead."

"Why didn't you really kill me?"

"You're too valuable."

"How do you figure that?"

"You know who killed Tinka."

"Then you're better off with me dead."

"No." The girl shook her head. "No, doll. We want to know how you found out."

"What difference does it make?"

"Oh, a lot of difference," the girl said. "He's very concerned about it, really he is. He's getting very impatient. He figures he made a mistake someplace, you see, and he wants to know what it was. Because if *you* found out, chances are somebody else will sooner or later. Unless you tell us what it was, you see. Then we can make sure nobody else finds out. Ever."

"There's nothing to tell you."

"There's plenty to tell," the girl said. She smiled. "You'll tell us. Are you hungry?"

"Yes."

"Tch," the girl said.

"Who was that in the burned car?"

"The elevator operator. Messner." The girl smiled again. "It was my idea. Two birds with one stone."

"What do you mean?"

"Well, I thought it would be a good idea to get rid of Messner just in case he was the one who led you to us. Insurance. And I also figured that if everybody thought you were dead, that'd give us more time to work on you."

"If Messner was my source, why do you have to work on me?"

"Well, there are a lot of unanswered questions," the girl said. "Gee, that coffee smells good, doesn't it?"

"Yes," Carella said.

"Are you cold?"

"No."

"I can get you a blanket if you're cold."

"I'm fine, thanks."

"I thought, with the rain, you might be a little chilly."

"No."

"You look good naked," the girl said.

"Thank you."

"I'll feed you, don't worry," she said.

"I know you will."

"But about those questions, they're really bothering him, you know. He's liable to get bugged completely and just decide the hell with the whole thing. I mean, I like having you and all, but I don't know if I'll be able to control him much longer. If you don't cooperate, I mean."

"Messner was my source," Carella said. "He gave me the description."

"Then it's a good thing we killed him, isn't it?"

"I suppose so."

"Of course, that still doesn't answer those questions I was talking about."

"What questions?"

"For example, how did you get the name? Messner may have given you a description, but where did you get the name? Or the address, for that matter?"

"They were in Tinka's address book. Both the name *and* the address."

"Was the description there, too?"

"I don't know what you mean."

"You know what I mean, doll. Unless Tinka had a *description* in that book of hers, how could you match a name to what Messner had told you?" Carella was silent. The girl smiled again. "I'm *sure* she didn't have descriptions of people in her address book, did she?"

"No."

"Good, I'm glad you're telling the truth. Because we found the address book in your pocket the night you came busting in here, and we know damn well there're no descriptions of people in it. You hungry?"

"Yes, I'm very hungry," Carella said.

"I'll feed you, don't worry," she said again. She paused. "How'd you know the name and address?"

"Just luck. I was checking each and every name in the book. A process of elimination, that's all."

"That's another lie," the girl said. "I wish you wouldn't lie to me." She lifted the gun from the tray. She held the gun loosely in one hand, picked up the tray with the other, and then said, "Back off."

Carella moved as far back as the handcuff would allow. The girl walked to him, crouched, and put the tray on the floor.

"I'm not wearing anything under this robe," she said.

"I can see that."

"I thought you could," the girl said, grinning, and then rose swiftly and backed toward the door. She sat in the chair and crossed her legs, the short robe riding up on her thighs. "Go ahead," she said, and indicated the tray with a wave of the gun.

Carella poured himself a cup of coffee. He took a quick swallow, and then picked up the sandwich and bit into it.

"Good?" the girl asked, watching.

"Yes."

"I made it myself. You have to admit I take good care of you."

"Sure," Carella said.

"I'm going to take even better care of you," she said. "Why'd you lie to me? Do you think it's nice to lie to me?"

"I didn't lie."

"You said you reached us by luck, a process of elimination. That means you didn't know who or what to expect when you got here, right? You were just looking for someone in Tinka's book who would fit Messner's description."

"That's right."

"Then why'd you kick the door in? Why'd you have a gun in your hand? See what I mean? You knew who he was *before* you got here. You knew he was the one. How?"

"I told you. It was just luck."

"Ahh, gee, I wish you wouldn't lie. Are you finished there?"

"Not yet."

"Let me know when."

"All right."

"I have things to do."

"All right."

"To *you,*" the girl said.

Carella chewed on the sandwich. He washed it down with a gulp of coffee. He did not look at the girl. She was jiggling her foot now, the gun hand resting in her lap.

"Are you afraid?" she asked.

"Of what?"

"Of what I might do to you."

"No. Should I be?"

"I might break your nose all over again, who knows?"

"That's true, you might."

"Or I might even keep my promise to knock out all your teeth." The girl smiled. "*That* was my idea, too, you know, knocking out Messner's teeth. You people can make identifications from dental charts, can't you?"

"Yes."

"That's what I thought. That's what I told him. *He* thought it was a good idea, too."

"You're just *full* of good ideas."

"Yeah, I have a lot of good ideas," the girl said. "You're not scared, huh?"

"No."

"I would be, if I were you. Really, I would be."

"The worst you can do is kill me," Carella said. "And since I'm already dead, what difference will it make?"

"I like a man with a sense of humor," the girl said, but she did not smile. "I can do worse than kill you."

"What can you do?"

"I can corrupt you."

"I'm incorruptible," Carella said, and smiled.

"Nobody's incorruptible," she said. "I'm going to make you *beg* to tell us what you know. Really. I'm warning you."

"I've told you everything I know."

"Uh-uh," the girl said, shaking her head. "Are you finished there?"

"Yes."

"Shove the tray away from you."

Carella slid the tray across the floor. The girl went to it, stooped again, and picked it up. She walked back to the chair and sat. She crossed her legs. She began jiggling her foot.

"What's your wife's name?" she asked.

"Teddy."

"That's a nice name. But you'll soon forget it soon enough."

"I don't think so," Carella said evenly.

"You'll forget her name, and you'll forget her, too."

He shook his head.

"I promise," the girl said. "In a week's time, you won't even remember your *own* name."

The room was silent. The girl sat quiet, still except for the jiggling of her foot. The green neon splashed the floor, and then blinked out. There were seconds of darkness, and then the light came on again. She was standing now. She had left the gun on the seat of the chair and moved to the center of the room. The neon went out. When it flashed on again, she had moved closer to where he was manacled to the radiator.

"What would you like me to do to you?" she asked.

"Nothing."

"What would you like to do to me?"

"Nothing," he said.

"No?" she smiled. "Look, doll."

She loosened the sash at her waist. The robe parted over her breasts and naked belly. Neon washed the length of her body with green, and then blinked off. In the intermittent flashes, he saw the girl moving—as though in a silent movie—toward the light switch near the door, the open robe flapping loose around her. She snapped on the overhead light, and then walked slowly back to the center of the room, and stood under the bulb. She held the front of her robe open, the long pale white sheath of her body exposed, the red silk covering her back and her arms, her fingernails tipped with red as glowing as the silk.

"What do you think?" she asked. Carella did not answer. "You want some of it?"

"No," he said.

"You're lying."

"I'm telling you the absolute truth," he said.

"I could make you forget her in a minute," the girl said. "I know things you never dreamed of. You want it?"

"No."

"Just try and get it," she said, and closed the robe and

tightened the sash around her waist. "I don't like it when you lie to me."

"I'm not lying."

"You're naked, mister, don't tell *me* you're not lying." She burst out laughing and walked to the door, opening it, and then turned to face him again. Her voice was very low, her face serious. "Listen to me, doll," she said. You are *mine,* do you understand that? I can do whatever I want with you, don't you forget it. I'm promising you right here and now that in a week's time you'll be crawling on your hands and knees to me, you'll be licking my feet, you'll be *begging* for the opportunity to tell me what you know. And once you tell me, I'm going to throw you away, doll, I'm going to throw you broken and cracked in the gutter, doll, and you're going to wish, believe me, you are just going to *wish* it was you they found dead in that car, believe me." She paused. "Think about it," she said, and turned out the light and went out of the room.

He heard the key turning in the lock.

He was suddenly very frightened.

Ten

The car had been found at the bottom of a steep embankment off Route 407. The road was winding and narrow, a rarely used branch connecting the towns of Middlebarth and York, both of which were serviced by wider, straighter highways. 407 was an oiled road, potholed and frost-heaved, used almost entirely by teenagers searching for a nighttime necking spot. The shoulders were muddy and soft, except for one place where the road widened and ran into the approach to what had once been a gravel pit. It was at the bottom of this pit that the burned vehicle and its more seriously burned passenger had been discovered.

There was only one house on Route 407, five and a half miles from the gravel pit. The house was built of native stone and timber, a rustic affair with a screened back porch overlooking a lake reportedly containing bass. The house was surrounded by white birch and flowering forsythia. Two dogwoods flanked the entrance driveway, their buds ready to burst. The rain had stopped but a fine mist hung over the lake, visible from the turn in the driveway. A huge oak dripped clinging raindrops onto the ground. The countryside was still. The falling drops clattered noisily.

Detectives Hal Willis and Arthur Brown parked the car at the top of the driveway, and walked past the dripping oak to the front door of the house. The door was painted green with a huge brass doorknob centered in its lower panel and a brass knocker centered in the top panel. A locked padlock still hung in a hinge hasp and staple fastened to the door. But the hasp staple had been pried loose of the jamb, and there were deep gouges in the wood where a heavy tool had been used for the job. Willis opened the door, and they went into the house.

There was the smell of contained woodsmoke, and the stench of something else. Brown's face contorted. Gagging, he pulled a handkerchief from his back pocket and covered his nose and mouth. Willis had backed away toward the door again, turning his face to the outside air. Brown took a quick look at the large stone fireplace at the far end of the room, and then caught Willis by the elbow and led him outside.

"Any question in your mind?" Willis asked.

"None," Brown said. "That's the smell of burned flesh."

"We got any masks in the car?"

"I don't know. Let's check the trunk."

They walked back to the car. Willis took the keys from the ignition and leisurely unlocked the trunk. Brown began searching.

"Everything in here but the kitchen sink," he said. "What the hell's this thing?"

"That's mine," Willis said.

"Well, what is it?"

"It's a hat, what do you think it is?"

"It doesn't look like any hat I've ever seen," Brown said.

"I wore it in a plant couple of weeks ago."

"What were you supposed to be?"

"A foreman."

"Of what?"

"A chicken market."

"That's *some* hat, man," Brown said, and chuckled.

"That's a good hat," Willis said. "Don't make fun of my hat. All the ladies who came in to buy chickens said it was a darling hat."

"Oh, no question," Brown said. "It's a cunning hat."

"Any masks in there?"

"Here's *one.* That's all I see."

"The canister with it?"

"Yeah, it's all here."

"Who's going in?" Willis said.

"I'll take it," Brown said.

"Sure, and then I'll have the N.A.A.C.P. down on my head."

"We'll just have to chance that," Brown said, returning Willis's smile. "We'll just have to chance it, Hal." He pulled the mask out of its carrier, found the small tin of antidim compound, scooped some onto the provided cloth, and wiped it onto the eyepieces. He seated the facepiece on his chin, moved the canister and head harness into place with an upward, backward sweep of his hands, and then smoothed the edges of the mask around his face.

"Is it fogging?" Willis said.

"No, it's okay."

Brown closed the outlet valve with two fingers and exhaled, clearing the mask. "Okay," he said, and began walking toward the house. He was a huge man, six feet four inches tall and weighing two hundred and twenty pounds, with enormous shoulders and chest, long arms, big hands. His skin was very dark, almost black, his hair was kinky and cut close to his scalp, his nostrils were large, his lips were thick. He looked like a Negro, which is what he was, take him or leave him. He did not at all resemble the white man's pretty concept of what a Negro *should* look like, the image touted in a new wave of magazine and television ads. He looked like himself. His wife Caroline liked the way he looked, and his daughter Connie liked the way he looked, and—more important—*he* liked the way he looked, although he didn't look so great at the moment with a mask covering his face and hoses running to the canister resting at the back of his neck. He walked into the house and paused just inside the door. There were parallel marks on the floor, beginning at the jamb and running vertically across the room. He stooped to look at the marks more closely. They were black and evenly spaced, and he recognized them immediately as scuff marks. He rose and followed the marks to the fireplace, where they ended. He did not touch anything in or near the open mouth of the hearth; he would leave that for the lab boys. But he was convinced now that a man wearing shoes, if nothing else, had been dragged across the room from the door to the fireplace. According to what they'd learned yesterday, Ernest Messner had been incinerated in a wood-burning fire. Well, there had certainly been a wood-burning fire in this room, and the stink he and Willis had encountered when entering was sure as hell the stink of burned human flesh. And now there were heel marks leading from the door to the fireplace. Circumstantially, Brown needed nothing more.

The only question was whether the person cooked in this particular fireplace was Ernest Messner or somebody else.

He couldn't answer that one, and anyway his eyepieces were beginning to fog. He went outside, took off the mask, and suggested to Willis that they drive into either Middlebarth or York to talk to some real estate agents about who owned the house with the smelly fireplace.

Elaine Hinds was a small, compact redhead with blue eyes and long fingernails. Her preference ran to small men, and she was charmed to distraction by Hal Willis, who was the shortest detective on the squad. She sat in a swivel chair behind her desk in the office of Hinds Real Estate in Middlebarth, and crossed her legs, and smiled, and accepted Willis's match to her cigarette, and graciously murmured, "Thank you," and then tried to remember what question he had just asked her. She uncrossed her legs, crossed them again, and then said, "Yes, the house on 407."

"Yes, do you know who owns it?" Willis asked. He was not unaware of the effect he seemed to be having on Miss Elaine Hinds, and he suspected he would never hear the end of it from Brown. But he was also a little puzzled. He had for many years been the victim of what he called the Mutt and Jeff phenomenon, a curious psychological and physiological reversal that made him irresistibly attractive to very big girls. He had never dated a girl who was shorter than five-nine in heels. One of his girl friends was five-eleven in her stockinged feet, and she was hopelessly in love with him. So he could not now understand why tiny little Elaine Hinds seemed so interested in a man who was only five feet eight inches tall, with the slight build of a dancer and the hands of a Black Jack dealer. He had, of course, served with the Marines and was an expert at judo, but Miss Hinds had no way of knowing that he was a giant among men, capable of breaking a man's back by the mere flick of an eyeball—well, almost. What then had caused her immediate attention? Being a conscientious cop, he sincerely hoped it would not impede the progress of the investigation. In the meantime, he couldn't help noticing that she had very good legs and that she kept crossing and uncrossing them like an undecided virgin.

"The people who own that house," she said, uncrossing her legs, "are Mr. and Mrs. Jerome Brandt, would you like some coffee or something? I have some going in the other room."

"No, thank you," Willis said. "How long have—"

"Mr. Brown?"

"No, thank you."

"How long have the Brandts been living there?"

"Well, they haven't. Not really."

"I don't think I understand," Willis said.

Elaine Hinds crossed her legs, and leaned close to Willis, as though about to reveal something terribly intimate. "They bought it to use as a summer place," she said. "Mavis County is a marvelous resort area, you know, with many lakes and streams and with the ocean not too far from any point in the county. We're supposed to have less rainfall per annum than—"

"When did they buy it, Miss Hinds?"

"Last year. I expect they'll open the house after Memorial Day, but it's been closed all winter."

"Which explains the broken hasp on the front door," Brown said.

"Has it been broken?" Elaine said. "Oh, dear," and she uncrossed her legs.

"Miss Hinds, would you say that many people in the area knew the house was empty?"

"Yes, I'd say it was common knowledge, do you enjoy police work?"

"Yes, I do," Willis said.

"It must be terribly exciting."

"Sometimes the suspense is unbearable," Brown said.

"I'll just *bet* it is," Elaine said.

"It's my understanding," Willis said, glancing sharply at Brown, "that 407 is a pretty isolated road, and hardly ever used. Is that correct?"

"Oh, yes," Elaine said. "Route 126 is a much better connection between Middlebarth and York, and of course the new highway runs past both towns. As a matter of fact, most people in the area *avoid* 407. It's not a very good road, have you been on it?"

"Yes. Then, actually, anyone living around here would have known the house was empty, and would also have known the road going by it wasn't traveled too often. Would you say that?"

"Oh, yes, Mr. Willis, I definitely *would* say that," Elaine said.

Willis looked a little startled. He glanced at Brown, and then cleared his throat. "Miss Hinds, what sort of people are the Brandts? Do you know them?"

"Yes, I sold the house to them. Jerry's an executive at IBM."

"And his wife?"

"Maxine's a woman of about fifty, three or four years younger than Jerry. A lovely person."

"Respectable people, would you say?"

"Oh, yes, *entirely* respectable," Elaine said. "My goodness, of *course* they are."

"Would you know if either of them were up here Monday night?"

"I don't know. I imagine they would have called if they

were coming. I keep the keys to the house here in the office, you see. I have to arrange for maintenance, and it's necessary—"

"But they didn't call to say they were coming up?"

"No, they didn't." Elaine paused. "Does this have anything to do with the auto wreck on 407?"

"Yes, Miss Hinds, it does."

"Well, how could Jerry or Maxine be even *remotely* connected with that?"

"You don't think they could?"

"Of course not. I haven't seen them for quite some time now, but we did work closely together when I was handling the deal for them last October. Believe me, you couldn't find a sweeter couple. That's unusual, especially with people who have their kind of money."

"Are they wealthy, would you say?"

"The house cost forty-two thousand five hundred dollars. They paid for it in cash."

"Who'd they buy it from?" Willis asked.

"Well, you probably wouldn't know her, but I'll bet your wife would."

"I'm not married," Willis said.

"Oh? *Aren't* you?"

"Who'd they buy it from?" Brown asked.

"A fashion model named Tinka Sachs. Do you know her?"

If they had lacked, before this, proof positive that the man in the wrecked automobile was really Ernest Messner, they now possessed the single piece of information that tied together the series of happenings and eliminated the possibility of reasonable chance or coincidence:

1) Tinka Sachs had been murdered in an apartment on Stafford Place on Friday, April ninth.

2) Ernest Messner was the elevator operator on duty there the night of her murder.

3) Ernest Messner had taken a man up to her apartment and had later given a good description of him.

4) Ernest Messner had vanished on Monday night, April twelfth.

5) An incinerated body was found the next day in a wrecked auto on Route 407, the connecting road between Middlebarth and York, in Mavis County.

6) The medical examiner had stated his belief that the body in the automobile had been incinerated in a wood fire elsewhere and only later placed in the automobile.

7) There was only one house on Route 407, five and a half miles from where the wrecked auto was found in the gravel pit.

8) There had been a recent wood fire in the fireplace of that house, and the premises smelled of burned flesh. There were also heel marks on the floor, indicating that someone had been dragged to the fireplace.

9) The house had once been owned by Tinka Sachs, and was sold only last October to its new owners.

It was now reasonable to assume that Tinka's murderer knew he had been identified, and had moved with frightening dispatch to remove the man who'd seen him. It was also reasonable to assume that Tinka's murderer knew of the empty house in Mavis County and had transported Messner's body there for the sole purpose of incinerating it beyond recognition, the further implication being that the murderer had known Tinka at least as far back as last October when she'd still owned the house. There were still a few unanswered questions, of course, but they were small things and nothing that would trouble any hard-working police force anywhere. The cops of the 87th wondered, for example, who had killed Tinka Sachs, and who had killed Ernest Messner, and who had taken Carella's shield and gun from him and wrecked his auto, and whether Carella was still alive, and where?

It's the small things in life that can get you down.

Those airline schedules kept bothering Kling.

He knew he had been taken off the case, but he could not stop thinking about those airline schedules, or the possibility that Dennis Sachs had flown from Phoenix and back sometime between Thursday night and Monday morning. From his apartment that night, he called Information and asked for the name and number of the hotel in Rainfield, Arizona. The local operator connected him with Phoenix Information, who said the only hotel listing they had in Rainfield was for the Major Powell on Main Street, was this the hotel Kling wanted? Kling said it was, and they asked if they should place the call. He knew that if he was eventually suspended, he would lose his gun, his shield and his salary until the case was decided, so he asked the operator how much the call would cost, and she said it would cost two dollars and ten cents for the first three minutes, and sixty-five cents for each additional minute. Kling told her to go ahead and place the call, station to station.

The man who answered the phone identified himself as Walter Blount, manager of the hotel.

"This is Detective Bert Kling," Kling said. "We've had a murder here, and I'd like to ask you some questions, if I may. I'm calling long distance."

"Go right ahead, Mr. Kling," Blount said.

"To begin with, do you know Dennis Sachs?"

"Yes, I do. He's a guest here, part of Dr. Tarsmith's expedition."

"Were you on duty a week ago last Thursday night, April eighth?"

"I'm on duty *all* the time," Blount said.

"Do you know what time Mr. Sachs came in from the desert?"

"Well, I couldn't rightly say. They usually come in at about seven, eight o'clock, something like that."

"Would you say they came in at about that time on April eighth?"

"I would say so, yes."

"Did you see Mr. Sachs leaving the hotel at any time that night?"

"Yes, he left, oh, ten-thirty or so, walked over to the railroad station."

"Was he carrying a suitcase?"

"He was."

"Did he mention where he was going?"

"The Royal Sands in Phoenix, I'd reckon. He asked us to make a reservation for him there, so I guess that's where he was going, don't you think?"

"Did you make the reservation for him personally, Mr. Blount?"

"Yes, sir, I did. Single with a bath, Thursday night to Sunday morning. The rates—"

"What time did Mr. Sachs return on Monday morning?"

"About six a.m. Had a telegram waiting for him here, his wife got killed. Well, I guess you know that, I guess that's what this is all about. He called the airport right away, and then got back on the train for Phoenix, hardly unpacked at all."

"Mr. Blount, Dennis Sachs told me that he spoke to his ex-wife on the telephone at least once a week. Would you know if that was true?"

"Oh, sure, he was always calling back east."

"How often, would you say?"

"At least once a week, that's right. Even more than that, I'd say."

"How much more?"

"Well . . . in the past two months or so, he'd call her three, maybe four times a week, something like that. He spent a hell of a lot of time making calls back east, ran up a pretty big phone bill here."

"Calling his wife, you mean."

"Well, not only her."

"Who else?"

"I don't know who the other party was."

"But he *did* make calls to other numbers here in the city?"

"Well, *one* other number."

"Would you happen to know that number offhand, Mr. Blount?"

"No, but I've got a record of it on our bills. It's not his wife's number because I've got that one memorized by heart, he's called it regular ever since he first came here a year ago. This other one is new to me."

"When did he start calling it?"

"Back in February, I reckon."

"How often?"

"Once a week, usually."

"May I have the number, please?"

"Sure, just let me look it up for you."

Kling waited. The line crackled. His hand on the receiver was sweating.

"Hello?" Blount said.

"Hello?"

"The number is SE—I think that stands for Sequoia—SE 3-1402."

"Thank you," Kling said.

"Not at all," Blount answered.

Kling hung up, waited patiently for a moment with his hand on the receiver, lifted it again, heard the dial tone, and instantly dialed SE 3-1402. The phone rang insistently. He counted each separate ring, four, five, six, and suddenly there was an answering voice.

"Dr. Levi's wire," the woman said.

"This is Detective Kling of the 87th Squad here in the city," Kling said. "Is this an answering service?"

"Yes, sir, it is."

"Whose phone did you say this was?"

"Dr. Levi's."

"And the first name?"

"Jason."

"Do you know where I can reach him?"

"I'm sorry, sir, he's away for the weekend. He won't be back until Monday morning." The woman paused. "Is this in respect to a police matter, or are you calling for a medical appointment?"

"A police matter," Kling said.

"Well, the doctor's office hours begin at ten Monday morning. If you'd care to call him then, I'm sure—"

"What's his home number?" Kling asked.

"Calling him there won't help you. He really is away for the weekend."

"Do you know where?"

"No, I'm sorry."

"Well, let me have his number, anyway," Kling said.

"I'm not supposed to give out the doctor's home number. I'll try it for you, if you like. If the doctor's there—which I know he isn't—I'll ask him to call you back. May I have your number, please?"

"Yes, it's Roxbury 2, that's RO 2-7641."

"Thank you."

"Will you please call me in any event, to let me know if you reached him or not?"

"Yes, sir, I will."

"Thank you."

"What did you say your name was?"

"Kling, Detective Bert Kling."

"Yes, sir, thank you," she said, and hung up.

Kling waited by the phone.

In five minutes' time, the woman called back. She said she had tried the doctor's home number and—as she'd known would be the case all along—there was no answer. She gave him the doctor's office schedule and told him he could try again on Monday, and then she hung up.

It was going to be a long weekend.

Teddy Carella sat in the living room alone for a long while after Lieutenant Byrnes left, her hands folded in her lap, staring into shadows of the room and hearing nothing but the murmur of her own thoughts.

We now know, the lieutenant had said, that the man we found in the automobile definitely wasn't Steve. He's a man named Ernest Messner, and there is no question about it, Teddy, so I want you to know that. But I also want you to know this doesn't mean Steve is still alive. We just don't know anything about that yet, although we're working on it. The only thing it *does* indicate is that at least he's not for certain dead.

The lieutenant paused. She watched his face. He looked back at her curiously, wanting to be sure she understood everything he had told her. She nodded.

I knew this yesterday, the lieutenant said, but I wasn't sure, and I didn't want to raise your hopes until I had checked it out thoroughly. The medical examiner's office gave this top priority, Teddy. They still haven't finished the autopsy on the Sachs case because, well, you know, when we thought this was Steve, well, we put a lot of pressure on them. Anyway, it isn't. It isn't Steve, I mean. We've got Paul Blaney's word for that, and he's an excellent man, and we've also got the corroboration—what? Corroboration, did you get it? the corroboration of the chief medical examiner as well. So now I'm sure, so I'm telling you. And about the other, we're working on it, as you know, and as soon as we've got anything, I'll tell you that, too. So that's about all, Teddy. We're doing our best.

She had thanked him and offered him coffee, which he refused politely, he was expected home, he had to run, he hoped she would forgive him. She had shown him to the door, and then walked past the playroom, where Fanny was watching television, and then past the room where the twins were sound asleep and then into the living room. She turned out the lights and went to sit near the old piano Carella had bought in a secondhand store downtown, paying sixteen dollars for it and arranging to have it delivered by a furniture man in the precinct. He had always wanted to play the piano, he told her, and was going to start lessons—you're never too old to learn, right, sweetheart?

The lieutenant's news soared within her, but she was fearful of it, suspicious: Was it only a temporary gift that would be taken back? Should she tell the children, and then risk another reversal and a second revelation that their father was dead? "What does that mean?" April had asked, "Does dead mean he's never coming back?" And Mark had turned to his sister and angrily shouted, "Shut up, you stupid dope!" and had run to his room where his mother could not see his tears.

They deserved hope.

They had the right to know there was hope.

She rose and went into the kitchen and scribbled a note on the telephone pad, and then tore off the sheet of paper and carried it out to Fanny. Fanny looked up when she approached, expecting more bad news, the lieutenant brought nothing but bad news nowadays. Teddy handed her the sheet of paper, and Fanny looked at it:

Wake the children.
Tell them their father
may still be alive.

Fanny looked up quickly.

"Thank God," she whispered, and rushed out of the room.

Eleven

The patrolman came up to the squadroom on Monday morning, and waited outside the slatted rail divider until Meyer signaled him in. Then he opened the gate and walked over to Meyer's desk.

"I don't think you know me," he said. "I'm Patrolman Angieri."

"I think I've seen you around," Meyer said.

"I feel funny bringing this up because maybe you already know it. My wife said I should tell you, anyway."

"What is it?"

"I only been here at this precinct for six months, this is my first precinct, I'm a new cop."

"Um-huh," Meyer said.

"If you already know this, just skip it, okay? My wife says maybe you don't know it, and maybe it's important."

"Well, what is it?" Meyer asked patiently.

"Carella."

"What about Carella?"

"Like I told you, I'm new in the precinct, and I don't know all the detectives by name, but I recognized him later from his picture in the paper, though it was a picture from when he was a patrolman. Anyway, it was him."

"What do you mean? I don't think I'm with you, Angieri."

"Carrying the doll," Angieri said.

"I still don't get you."

"I was on duty in the hall, you know? Outside the apartment. I'm talking about the Tinka Sachs murder."

Meyer leaned forward suddenly. "Yeah, go ahead," he said.

"Well, he come up there last Monday night, it must've been five-thirty, six o'clock, and he flashed the tin, and went inside the apartment. When he came out, he was in a hell of a hurry, and he was carrying a doll."

"Are you telling me Carella was at the Sachs apartment last Monday night?"

"That's right."

"Are you sure?"

"Positive." Angieri paused. "You *didn't* know this, huh? My wife was right." He paused again. "She's *always* right."

"What did you say about a doll?"

"A doll, you know? Like kids play with? Girls? A big doll. With blonde hair, you know? A *doll.*"

"Carella came out of the apartment carrying a child's doll?"

"That's right."

"Last Monday night?"

"That's right."

"Did he say anything to you?"

"Nothing."

"A doll," Meyer said, puzzled.

* * *

It was nine a.m. when Meyer arrived at the Sachs apartment on Stafford Place. He spoke briefly to the superintendent of the building, a man named Manny Farber, and then took the elevator up to the fourth floor. There was no longer a patrolman on duty in the hallway. He went down the corridor and let himself into the apartment, using Tinka's own key, which had been lent to the investigating precinct by the Office of the Clerk.

The apartment was still.

He could tell at once that death had been here. There are different silences in an empty apartment, and if you are a working policeman, you do not scoff at poetic fallacy. An apartment vacated for the summer has a silence unlike that one that is empty only for the day, with its occupants expected back that night. And an apartment that has known the touch of death possesses a silence unique and readily identifiable to anyone who has ever stared down at a corpse. Meyer knew the silence of death, and understood it, though he could not have told you what accounted for it. The disconnected humless electrical appliances; the unused, undripping water taps; the unringing telephone; the stopped unticking clocks; the sealed windows shutting out all street noises; these were all a part of it, but they only contributed to the whole and were not its sum and substance. The real silence was something only felt, and had nothing to do with the absence of sound. It touched something deep within him the moment he stepped through the door. It seemed to be carried on the air itself, a shuddering reminder that death had passed this way, and that some of its frightening grandeur was still locked inside these rooms. He paused with his hand on the doorknob, and then sighed and closed the door behind him and went into the apartment.

Sunlight glanced through closed windows, dust beams silently hovered on the unmoving air. He walked softly, as though reluctant to stir whatever ghostly remnants still were here. When he passed the child's room, he looked through the open door and saw the dolls lined up in the bookcase beneath the windows, row upon row of dolls, each dressed differently, each staring back at him with unblinking glass eyes, pink cheeks glowing, mute red mouths frozen on the edge of articulation, painted lips parted over even plastic teeth, nylon hair in black, and red, and blonde, and the palest silver.

He was starting into the room when he heard a key turning in the front door.

The sound startled him. It cracked into the silent apartment like a crash of thunder. He heard the tumblers falling, the sudden click of the knob being turned. He moved into the child's room just as the front door opened. His eyes swept the room—bookcases, bed, closet, toy chest. He could hear heavy footsteps in the corridor, approaching the room. He threw open the closet door, drew his gun. The footsteps were closer. He eased the door toward him, leaving it open just a crack. Holding his breath, he waited in the darkness.

The man who came into the room was perhaps six feet two inches tall, with massive shoulders and a narrow waist. He paused just inside the doorway, as though sensing the presence of another person, seemed almost to be sniffing the air for a telltale scent. Then, visibly shrugging away his own correct intuition, he dismissed the idea and went quickly to the bookcases. He stopped in front of them and began lifting dolls from the shelves, seemingly at random, bundling them into his arms. He gathered up seven or eight of them, rose, turned toward the door, and was on his way out when Meyer kicked open the closet door.

The man turned, startled, his eyes opening wide. Foolishly, he clung to the dolls in his arms, first looking at Meyer's face, and then at the Colt .38 in Meyer's hand, and then up at Meyer's face again.

"Who are you?" he asked.

"Good question," Meyer said. "Put those dolls down, hurry up, on the bed there."

"What . . . ?"

"Do as I say, mister!"

The man walked to the bed. He wet his lips, looked at Meyer, frowned, and then dropped the dolls.

"Get over against the wall," Meyer said.

"Listen, what the hell . . . ?"

"Spread your legs, bend over, lean against the wall with your palms flat. Hurry up!"

"All right, take it easy." The man leaned against the wall. Meyer quickly and carefully frisked him—chest, pockets, waist, the insides of his legs. Then he backed away from the man and said, "Turn around, keep your hands up."

The man turned, his hands high. He wet his lips again, and again looked at the gun in Meyer's hand.

"What are you doing here?" Meyer asked.

"What are *you* doing here?"

"I'm a police officer. Answer my—"

"Oh. Oh, okay," the man said.

"What's okay about it?"

"I'm Dennis Sachs."

"Who?"

"Dennis—"

"Tinka's husband?"

"Well, her ex-husband."

"Where's your wallet?"

"Right here in my—"

"Don't reach for it! Bend over against that wall again, go ahead."

The man did as Meyer ordered. Meyer felt for the wallet and found it in his right hip pocket. He opened it to the driver's license. The name on the license was Dennis Robert Sachs. Meyer handed it back to him.

"All right, put your hands down. What are you doing here?"

"My daughter wanted some of her dolls," Sachs said. "I came back to get them."

"How'd you get in?"

"I have a key. I used to live here, you know."

"It was my understanding you and your wife were divorced."

"That's right."

"And you still have a key?"

"Yes."

"Did she know this?"

"Yes, of course."

"And that's all you wanted here, huh? Just the dolls."

"Yes."

"Any doll in particular?"

"No."

"Your daughter didn't specify any particular doll?"

"No, she simply said she'd like some of her dolls, and she asked if I'd come get them for her."

"How about *your* preference?"

"*My* preference?"

"Yes. Did *you* have any particular doll in mind?"

"Me?"

"That's right, Mr. Sachs. You."

"No. What do you mean? Are you talking about *dolls*?"

"That's right, that's what I'm talking about."

"Well, what would I want with any *specific* doll?"

"That's what *I'd* like to know."

"I don't think I understand you."

"Then forget it."

Sachs frowned and glanced at the dolls on the bed. He hesitated, then shrugged and said, "Well, is it all right to take them?"

"I'm afraid not."

"Why not? They belong to my daughter."

"We want to look them over, Mr. Sachs."

"For what?"

"I don't know for what. For *anything*."

Sachs looked at the dolls again, and then he turned to Meyer and stared at him silently. "I guess you know this has been a pretty bewildering conversation," he said at last.

"Yeah, well, that's the way mysteries are," Meyer answered. "I've got work to do, Mr. Sachs. If you have no further business here, I'd appreciate it if you left."

Sachs nodded and said nothing. He looked at the dolls once again, and then walked out of the room, and down the corridor, and out of the apartment. Meyer waited, listening. The moment he heard the door close behind Sachs, he sprinted down the corridor, stopped just inside the door, counted swiftly to ten, and then eased the door open no more than an inch. Peering out into the hallway, he could see Sachs waiting for the elevator. He looked angry as hell. When the elevator did not arrive, he pushed at the button repeatedly and then began pacing. He glanced once at Tinka's supposedly closed door, and then turned back to the elevator again. When it finally arrived, he said to the operator, "What took you so long?" and stepped into the car.

Meyer came out of the apartment immediately, closed the door behind him, and ran for the service steps. He took the steps down at a gallop, pausing only for an instant at the fire door leading to the lobby, and then opening the door a crack. He could see the elevator operator standing near the building's entrance, his arms folded across his chest. Meyer came out into the lobby quickly, glanced back once at the open elevator doors, and then ran past the elevator and into the street. He spotted Sachs turning the corner up the block, and broke into a run after him. He paused again before turning the corner. When he sidled around it, he saw Sachs getting into a taxi. There was no time for Meyer to go to his own parked car. He hailed another cab and said to the driver, just like a cop, "Follow that taxi," sourly reminding himself that he would have to turn in a chit for the fare, even though he knew Petty Cash would probably never reimburse him. The taxi driver turned for a quick look at Meyer, just to see who was pulling all this cloak and dagger nonsense, and then silently began following Sachs's cab.

"You a cop?" he asked at last.

"Yeah," Meyer said.

"Who's that up ahead?"

"The Boston Strangler," Meyer said.

"Yeah?"

"Would I kid you?"

"You going to pay for this ride, or is it like taking apples from a pushcart?"

"I'm going to pay for it," Meyer said. "Just don't lose him, okay?"

It was almost ten o'clock, and the streets were thronged with traffic. The lead taxi moved steadily uptown and then crosstown, with Meyer's driver skillfully following. The city was a bedlam of noise—honking horns, grinding gears, squealing tires, shouting drivers and pedestrians. Meyer leaned forward and kept his eye on the taxi ahead, oblivious to the sound around him.

"He's pulling up, I think," the driver said.

"Good. Stop about six car lengths behind him." The taxi meter read eighty-five cents. Meyer took a dollar bill from his wallet, and handed it to the driver the moment he pulled over to the curb. Sachs had already gotten out of this cab and was walking into an apartment building in the middle of the block.

"Is this all the city tips?" the driver asked. "Fifteen cents on an eighty-five-cent ride?"

"The city, my ass," Meyer said, and leaped out of the cab. He ran up the street, and came into the building's entrance alcove just as the inner glass door closed behind Sachs. Meyer swung back his left arm and swiftly ran his hand over every bell in the row on the wall. Then, while waiting for an answering buzz, he put his face close to the glass door, shaded his eyes against the reflective glare, and peered inside. Sachs was nowhere in sight; the elevators were apparently around the corner of the lobby. A half-dozen answering buzzes sounded at once, releasing the lock mechanism on the door. Meyer pushed it open, and ran into the lobby. The floor indicator over the single elevator was moving, three, four, five—and stopped. Meyer nodded and walked out to the entrance alcove again, bending to look at the bells there. There were six apartments on the fifth floor. He was studying the names under the bells when a voice behind him said, "I think you're looking for Dr. Jason Levi."

Meyer looked up, startled.

The man standing behind him was Bert Kling.

Dr. Jason Levi's private office was painted an antiseptic white, and the only decoration on its walls was a large, easily readable calendar. His desk was functional and unadorned, made of grey steel, its top cluttered with medical journals and books, X-ray photographs, pharmaceutical samples, tongue depressors, prescription pads. There was a no-nonsense look about the doctor as well, the plain face topped with leonine white hair, the thick-lensed spectacles, the large cleaving nose, the thin-lipped mouth. He sat behind his desk and looked first at the detectives and then at Dennis Sachs, and waited for someone to speak.

"We want to know what you're doing here, Mr. Sachs," Meyer said.

"I'm a patient," Sachs said.

"Is that true, Dr. Levi?"

Levi hesitated. Then he shook his massive head. "No," he said. "That is not true."

"Shall we start again?" Meyer asked.

"I have nothing to say," Sachs answered.

"Why'd you find it necessary to call Dr. Levi from Arizona once a week?" Kling asked.

"Who said I did?"

"Mr. Walter Blount, manager of the Major Powell Hotel in Rainfield."

"He was lying."

"Why would he lie?"

"I don't *know* why," Sachs said. "Go ask *him.*"

"No, we'll do it the easy way," Kling said. "Dr. Levi, *did* Mr. Sachs call you from Arizona once a week?"

"Yes," Levi said.

"We seem to have a slight difference of opinion here," Meyer said.

"Why'd he call you?" Kling asked.

"Don't answer that, Doctor!"

"Dennis, what are we trying to hide. She's dead."

"You're a doctor, you don't have to tell them anything. You're like a priest. They can't force you to—"

"Dennis, she is dead."

"Did your calls have something to do with your wife?" Kling asked.

"No," Sachs said.

"Yes," Levi said.

"Was *Tinka* your patient, Doctor, is that it?"

"Yes."

"Dr. Levi, I *forbid* you to tell these men anything more about—"

"She was my patient," Levi said. "I began treating her at the beginning of the year."

"In January?"

"Yes. January fifth. More than three months ago."

"Doctor, I swear on my dead wife that if you go ahead with this, I'm going to ask the A.M.A. to—"

"Nonsense!" Levi said fiercely. "Your wife is dead! If we can help them find her killer—"

"You're not helping them with anything! All you're doing is dragging her memory through the muck of a criminal investigation."

"Mr. Sachs," Meyer said, "whether you know it or not,

her memory is already in the muck of a criminal investigation."

"Why did she come to you, Doctor?" Kling asked. "What was wrong with her?"

"She said she had made a New Year's resolution, said she had decided once and for all to seek medical assistance. It was quite pathetic, really. She was so helpless, and so beautiful, and so alone."

"I *couldn't* stay with her any longer!" Sachs said. "I'm not made of iron! I couldn't handle it. That's why we got the divorce. It wasn't my fault, what happened to her."

"No one is blaming you for anything," Levi said. "Her illness went back a long time, long before she met you."

"What was this illness, Doctor?" Meyer asked.

"Don't tell them!"

"Dennis, I *have* to—"

"You *don't* have to! Leave it the way it is. Let her live in everyone's memory as a beautiful exciting woman instead of—"

Dennis cut himself off.

"Instead of what?" Meyer asked.

The room went silent.

"Instead of what?" he said again.

Levi sighed and shook his head.

"Instead of a drug addict."

Twelve

In the silence of the squadroom later that day, they read Dr. Jason Levi's casebook:

January 5

The patient's name is Tina Karin Sachs. She is divorced, has a daughter aged five. She lives in the city and leads an active professional life, which is one of the reasons she was reluctant to seek assistance before now. She stated, however, that she had made a New Year's resolution, and that she is determined to break the habit. She has been a narcotics user since the time she was seventeen, and is now addicted to heroin.

I explained to her that the methods of withdrawal which I had thus far found most satisfactory were those employing either morphine or methadone, both of which had proved to be adequate substitutes for whatever drugs or combinations of drugs my patients had previously been using. I told her, too, that I personally preferred the morphine method.

She asked if there would be much pain involved. Apparently she had once tried cold-turkey withdrawal and had found the attempt too painful to bear. I told her that she would experience withdrawal symptoms—nausea, vomiting, diarrhea, lacrimation, dilation of pupils, rhinorrhea, yawning, gooseflesh, sneezing, sweating—with either method. With morphine, the withdrawal would be more severe, but she could expect relative comfort after a week or so. With methadone, the withdrawal would be easier, but she might still feel somewhat tremulous for as long as a month afterward.

She said she wanted to think it over, and would call me when she had decided.

January 12

I had not expected to see or hear from Tinka Sachs again, but she arrived here today and asked my receptionist if I could spare ten minutes. I said I could, and she was shown into my private office, where we talked for more than forty-five minutes.

She said she had not yet decided what she should do, and wanted to discuss it further with me. She is, as she had previously explained, a fashion model. She receives top fees for her modeling and was now afraid that treatment might entail either pain or sickness which would cause her to lose employment, thereby endangering her career. I told her that her addiction to heroin had made her virtually careerless anyway, since she was spending much of her income on the purchase of drugs. She did not particularly enjoy this observation, and quickly rejoin that she thoroughly relished all the fringe benefits of modeling—the fame, the recognition, and so on. I asked her if she really enjoyed anything but heroin, or really thought of anything but heroin, and she became greatly agitated and seemed about to leave the office.

Instead, she told me that I didn't know what it was like,

and she hoped I understood she had been using narcotics since she was seventeen, when she'd first tried marijuana at a beach party in Malibu. She had continued smoking marijuana for almost a year, never tempted to try any of "the real shit" until a photographer offered her a sniff of heroin shortly after she'd begun modeling. He also tried to rape her afterwards, a side effect that nearly caused her to abandon her beginning career as a model. Her near-rape, however, did not dissuade her from using marijuana or from sniffing heroin every now and then, until someone warned her that inhaling the drug could damage her nose. Since her nose was part of her face, and her face was part of what she hoped would become her fortune, she promptly stopped the sniffing process.

The first time she tried injecting the drug was with a confirmed addict, male, in a North Hollywood apartment. Unfortunately, the police broke in on them, and they were both arrested. She was nineteen years old at the time, and was luckily released with a suspended sentence. She came to this city the following month, determined never to fool with drugs again, hoping to put three thousand miles between herself and her former acquaintances. But she discovered, almost immediately upon arrival, that the drug was as readily obtainable here as it was in Los Angeles. Moreover, she began her association with the Cutler Agency several weeks after she got here, and found herself in possession of more money than she would ever need to support both herself *and* a narcotics habit. She began injecting the drug under her skin, into the soft tissue of her body. Shortly afterwards, she abandoned the subcutaneous route and began shooting heroin directly into her veins. She has been using it intravenously ever since, has for all intents and purposes been hopelessly hooked since she first began skin-popping. How, then, could I expect to cure her? How could she wake up each morning without knowing that a supply of narcotics was available, in fact accessible? I explained that hers was the common fear of all addicts about to undergo treatment, a reassurance she accepted without noticeable enthusiasm.

I'll think about it, she said again, and again left. I frankly do not believe she will ever return again.

January 20

Tinka Sachs began treatment today.

She has chosen the morphine method (even though she understands the symptoms will be more severe) because she does not want to endanger her career by a prolonged withdrawal, a curious concern for someone who has been endangering her career ever since it started. I had previously explained that I wanted to hospitalize her for several months, but she flatly refused hospitalization of any kind, and stated that the deal was off if that was part of the treatment. I told her that I could not guarantee lasting results unless she allowed me to hospitalize her, but she said we would have to hope for the best because she wasn't going to admit herself to any damn hospital. I finally extracted from her an agreement to stay at home under a nurse's care at least during the first several days of withdrawal, when the symptoms would be most severe. I warned her against making any illegal purchases and against associating with any known addicts or pushers. Our schedule is a rigid one. To start, she will receive 1/4 grain of morphine four times daily—twenty minutes before each meal. The doses will be administered hypodermically, and the morphine will be dissolved in thiamine hydrochloride.

It is my hope that withdrawal will be complete within two weeks.

January 21

I have prescribed Thorazine for Tinka's nausea, and belladonna and pectin for her diarrhea. The symptoms are severe. She could not sleep at all last night. I have instructed the nurse staying at her apartment to administer three grains of Nembutal tonight before Tinka retires, with further instructions to repeat 11/2 grains if she does not sleep through the night.

Tinka has taken excellent care of her body, a factor on our side. She is quite beautiful and I have no doubt she is a superior model, though I am at a loss to explain how photographers can have missed her obvious addiction. How did she keep from "nodding" before the cameras? She has scrupulously avoided marking either her lower legs or her arms, but the insides of her thighs (she told me she does not model either lingerie or bathing suits) are covered with hit marks.

Morphine continues at 1/4 grain four times daily.

January 22

I have reduced the morphine injections to 1/4 grain twice daily, alternating with 1/8 grain twice daily. Symptoms are still severe. She has cancelled all of her sittings, telling the agency she is menstruating and suffering cramps, a complaint they have apparently heard from their models before. She shows no desire to eat. I have begun prescribing vitamins.

January 23

The symptoms are abating. We are now administering 1/8 grain four times daily.

January 24

Treatment continuing with 1/8 grain four times daily. The nurse will be discharged tomorrow, and Tinka will begin coming to my office for her injections, a procedure I am heartily against. But it is either that or losing her entirely, and I must go along.

January 25

Started one grain codeine twice daily, alternating with 1/8 grain morphine twice daily. Tinka came to my office at eight-thirty, before breakfast, for her first injection. She came again at twelve-thirty, and at six-thirty. I administered the last injection at her home at eleven-thirty. She seems exceptionally restless, and I have prescribed 1/2 grain of phenobarbital daily to combat this.

January 26

Tinka Sachs did not come to the office today. I called her apartment several times, but no one answered the telephone. I did not dare call the modeling agency lest they suspect she is undergoing treatment. At three o'clock, I spoke to her daughter's governess. She had just picked the child up at the play-school she attends. She said she did not know where Mrs. Sachs was, and suggested that I try the agency. I called again at midnight. Tinka was still not home. The governess said I had awakened her. Apparently, she saw nothing unusual about her employer's absence. The working arrangement calls for her to meet the child after school and to spend as much time with her as is necessary. She said that Mrs. Sachs is often gone the entire night, in which case she is supposed to take the child to school in the morning, and then call for her again at two-thirty. Mrs. Sachs was once gone for three days, she said.

I am worried.

February 4

Tinka returned to the office again today, apologizing profusely, and explaining that she had been called out of town on an assignment; they were shooting some new tweed fashions and wanted a woodland background. I accused her of lying, and she finally admitted that she had not been out of town at all, but had instead spent the past week in the apartment of a friend from California. After further questioning, she conceded that her California friend is a drug addict, is in fact the man with whom she was arrested when she was nineteen years old. He arrived in the city last September, with very little money, and no place to live. She staked him for a while, and allowed him to live in her Mavis County house until she sold it in October. She then helped him to find an apartment on South Fourth, and she still sees him occasionally.

It was obvious that she had begun taking heroin again.

She expressed remorse, and said that she is more than ever determined to break the habit. When I asked if her friend expects to remain in the city, she said that he does, but that he has a companion with him, and no longer needs any old acquaintance to help him pursue his course of addiction.

I extracted a promise from Tinka that she would never see this man again, nor try to contact him.

We begin treatment again tomorrow morning. This time I insisted that a nurse remain with her for at least two weeks.

We will be starting from scratch.

* * *

February 9

We have made excellent progress in the past five days. The morphine injections have been reduced to 1/8 grain four times daily, and tomorrow we begin alternating with codeine.

Tinka talked about her relationship with her husband for the first time today, in connection with her resolve to break the habit. He is apparently an archaeologist working with an expedition somewhere in Arizona. She is in frequent touch with him, and in fact called him yesterday to say she had begun treatment and was hopeful of a cure. It is her desire, she said, to begin a new life with him once the withdrawal is complete. She knows he still loves her, knows that had it not been for her habit they would never have parted.

She said he did not learn of her addiction until almost a year after the child was born. This was all the more remarkable since the baby—fed during pregnancy by the bloodstream of her mother, metabolically dependent on heroin—was quite naturally an addict herself from the moment she was born. Dennis, and the family pediatrician as well, assumed she was a colicky baby, crying half the night through, vomiting, constantly fretting. Only Tinka knew that the infant was experiencing all the symptoms of cold-turkey withdrawal. She was tempted more than once to give the child a secret fix, but she refrained from doing so, and the baby survived the torment of forced withdrawal only to face the subsequent storm of separation and divorce.

Tinka was able to explain the hypodermic needle Dennis found a month later by saying she was allergic to certain dyes in the nylon dresses she was modeling and that her doctor had prescribed an antihistamine in an attempt to reduce the allergic reaction. But she could not explain the large sums of money that seemed to be vanishing from their joint bank account, nor could she explain his ultimate discovery of three glassine bags of a white powder secreted at the back of her dresser drawer. She finally confessed that she was a drug addict, that she had been a drug addict for close to seven years and saw nothing wrong with it so long as she was capable of supporting the habit. He goddamn well knew she was earning most of the money in this household, anyway, so what the fuck did he want from her?

He cracked her across the face and told her they would go to see a doctor in the morning.

In the morning, Tinka was gone.

She did not return to the apartment until three weeks later, disheveled and bedraggled, at which time she told Dennis she had been at a party with three colored musicians from a club downtown, all of them addicts. She could not remember what they had done together. Dennis had meanwhile consulted a doctor, and he told Tinka that drug addiction was by no means incurable, that there were ways of treating it, that success was almost certain if the patient— Don't make me laugh, Tinka said. I'm hooked through the bag and back, and what's more I like it, now what the hell do you think about that? Get off my back, you're worse than the monkey!

He asked for the divorce six months later.

During that time, he tried desperately to reach this person he had taken for a wife, this stranger, who was nonetheless the mother of his child, this driven animal whose entire life seemed bounded by the need for heroin. Their expenses were overwhelming. She could not let her career vanish because without her career she could hardly afford the enormous amounts of heroin she required. So she dressed the part of the famous model, and lived in a lavishly appointed apartment, and rode around town in hired limousines, and ate at the best restaurants, and was seen at all the important functions—while within her the clamor for heroin raged unabated. She worked slavishly, part of her income going toward maintaining the legend that was a necessary adjunct of her profession, the remainder going toward the purchase of drugs for herself and her friends.

There were always friends.

She would vanish for weeks at a time, lured by a keening song she alone heard, compelled to seek other addicts, craving the approval of people like herself, the comradeship of the dream society, the anonymity of the shooting gallery where scars were not stigmata and addiction was not a curse.

He would have left her sooner but the child presented a serious problem. He knew he could not trust Anna alone with her mother, but how could he take her with him on archaeological expeditions around the world? He realized that if Tinka's addiction were allowed to enter the divorce proceedings, he would be granted immediate custody of the child. But Tinka's career would automatically be ruined, and who knew what later untold hurt the attendant publicity could bring to Anna? He promised Tinka that he would not introduce the matter of her addiction if she would allow him to hire a responsible governess for the child. Tinka readily agreed. Except for her occasional binges, she considered herself to be a devoted and exemplary mother. If a governess would make Dennis happy and keep this sordid matter of addiction out of the proceedings, she was more than willing to go along with the idea. The arrangements were made.

Dennis, presumably in love with his wife, presumably

concerned about his daughter's welfare, was nonetheless content to abandon one to eternal drug addiction, and the other to the vagaries and unpredictabilities of living with a confirmed junkie. Tinka, for her part, was glad to see him leave. He had become a puritanical goad, and she wondered why she'd ever married him in the first place. She supposed it had had something to do with the romantic notion of one day kicking the habit and starting a new life.

Which is what you're doing now, I told her.

Yes, she said, and her eyes were shining.

February 12

Tinka is no longer dependent on morphine, and we have reduced the codeine intake to one grain twice daily, alternating with 1/2 grain twice daily.

February 13

I received a long-distance call from Dennis Sachs today. He simply wanted to know how his wife was coming along and said that if I didn't mind he would call once a week—it would have to be either Friday or Saturday since he'd be in the desert the rest of the time—to check on her progress. I told him the prognosis was excellent, and I expressed the hope that withdrawal would be complete by the twentieth of the month.

February 14

Have reduced the codeine to 1/2 grain twice daily, and have introduced thiamine twice daily.

February 15

Last night, Tinka slipped out of the apartment while her

nurse was dozing. She has not returned, and I do not know where she is.

February 20

Have been unable to locate Tinka.

March 1

Have called the apartment repeatedly. The governess continues to care for Anna—but there has been no word from Tinka.

March 8

In desperation, I called the Cutler Agency today to ask if they have any knowledge of Tinka's whereabouts. They asked me to identify myself, and I said I was a doctor treating her for a skin allergy (Tinka's own lie!). They said she had gone to the Virgin Islands on a modeling assignment and would not be back until the twentieth of March. I thanked them and hung up.

March 22

Tinka came back to my office today.

The assignment had come up suddenly, she said, and she had taken it, forgetting to tell me about it.

I told her I thought she was lying.

All right, she said. She had seized upon the opportunity as a way to get away from me and the treatment. She did not know why, but she had suddenly been filled with panic. She knew that in several days, a week at most, she would be off even the thiamine—and then what would there be? How could she possibly get through a day without a shot of *something*?

Art Cutler had called and proposed the St. Thomas

assignment, and the idea of sun and sand had appealed to her immensely. By coincidence, her friend from California called that same night, and when she told him where she was going he said that he'd pack a bag and meet her down there.

I asked her exactly what her connection is with this "friend from California," who now seems responsible for two lapses in her treatment. What lapse? she asked, and then swore she had not touched anything while she was away. This friend was simply *that,* a good friend.

But you told me he is an addict, I said.

Yes, he's an addict, she answered. But he didn't even *suggest* drugs while we were away. As a matter of fact, I think I've kicked it completely. That's really the only reason I came here, to tell you that it's not necessary to continue treatment any longer. I haven't had anything, heroin or morphine or *anything,* all the while I was away. I'm cured.

You're lying, I said.

All right, she said. If I wanted the truth, it was her California friend who'd kept her out of prison those many years ago. He had told the arresting officers that he was a pusher, a noble and dangerous admission to make, and that he had forced a shot on Tinka. She had got off with the suspended sentence while he'd gone to prison; so naturally she was indebted to him. Besides, she saw no reason why she shouldn't spend some time with him on a modeling assignment, instead of running around with a lot of faggot designers and photographers, not to mention the lesbian editor of the magazine. Who the hell did I think I was, her keeper?

I asked if this "friend from California" had suddenly struck it rich.

What do you mean? she said.

Well, isn't it true that he was in need of money and a place to stay when he first came to the city?

Yes, that's true.

Then how can he afford to support a drug habit and also manage to take a vacation in the Virgin Islands? I asked.

She admitted that she paid for the trip. If the man had saved her from a prison sentence, what was so wrong about paying his fare and his hotel bill?

I would not let it go.

Finally, she told me the complete story. She had been sending him money over the years, not because he asked her for it, but simply because she felt she owed something to him. His lie had enabled her to come here and start a new life. The least she could do was send him a little money every now and then. Yes, she had been supporting him ever since he arrived here. Yes, yes, it was she who'd invited him along on the trip; there had been no coincidental phone call from him that night. Moreover, she had not only paid for *his* plane fare and hotel bill, but also for that of his companion, whom she described as "an extremely lovely young woman."

And no heroin all that while, right?

Tears, anger, defense.

Yes, there had been heroin! There had been enough heroin to sink the island, and she had paid for every drop of it. There had been heroin morning, noon, and night. It was amazing that she had been able to face the cameras at all, she had blamed her drowsiness on the sun. That needle had been stuck in her thigh constantly, like a glittering glass cock! Yes, there had been heroin, and she had loved every minute of it! What the hell did I want from her?

I want to cure you, I said.

* * *

March 23

She accused me today of trying to kill her. She said that I had been trying to kill her since the first day we met, that I know she is not strong enough to withstand the pains of withdrawal, and that the treatment will eventually result in her death.

Her lawyer has been preparing a will, she said, and she would sign it tomorrow. She would begin treatment after that, but she knew it would lead to her ultimate death.

I told her she was talking nonsense.

March 24

Tinka signed her will today.

She brought me a fragment of a poem she wrote last night:

When I think of what I am
And of what I might have been,
I tremble.
I fear the night.
Throughout the day,
I rush from dragons conjured in the dark.
Why will they not

I asked her why she hadn't finished the poem. She said she couldn't finish it until she knew the outcome herself. What outcome do you want? I asked her.

I want to be cured, she said.

You *will* be cured, I told her.

March 25

We began treatment once more.

* * *

March 27

Dennis Sachs called from Arizona again to inquire about his wife. I told him she had suffered a relapse but that she had begun treatment anew, and that we were hoping for complete withdrawal by April 15th at the very latest. He asked if there was anything he could do for Tinka. I told him that the only person who could do anything for Tinka was Tinka.

March 28

Treatment continues.
1/4 grain morphine twice daily.
1/8 grain morphine twice daily.

March 30

1/8 grain morphine four times daily.
Prognosis good.

March 31

1/8 grain morphine twice daily.
One grain codeine twice daily.

April 1

Tinka confessed today that she has begun buying heroin on the sly, smuggling it in, and has been taking it whenever the nurse isn't watching. I flew into a rage. She shouted "April Fool!" and began laughing.

I think there is a chance this time.

April 2

One grain codeine four times daily.

* * *

April 3

One grain codeine twice daily.
1/2 grain codeine twice daily.

April 4

1/2 grain codeine four times daily.

April 5

1/2 grain codeine twice daily, thiamine twice daily.

April 6

Thiamine four times daily. Nurse was discharged today.

April 7

Thiamine three times daily.
We are going to make it!

April 8

Thiamine twice daily.

April 9

She told me today that she is certain the habit is almost kicked. This is my feeling as well. The weaning from hypodermics is virtually complete. There is only the promise of a new and rewarding life ahead.

That was where the doctor's casebook ended because that was when Tinka Sachs was murdered.

Meyer glanced up to see if Kling had finished the page. Kling nodded, and Meyer closed the book.

"He took two lives from her," Meyer said. "The one she was ending, and the one she was beginning."

That afternoon Paul Blaney earned his salary for the second time in four days. He called to say he had completed the post-mortem examination of Tinka Sachs and had discovered a multitude of scars on both upper front thighs. It seemed positive that the scars had been caused by repeated intravenous injections, and it was Blaney's opinion that the dead girl had been a drug addict.

Thirteen

She had handcuffed both hands behind his back during one of his periods of unconsciousness, and then had used a leather belt to lash his feet together. He lay naked on the floor now and waited for her arrival, trying to tell himself he did not need her, and knowing that he needed her desperately.

It was very warm in the room, but he was shivering. His skin was beginning to itch but he could not scratch himself because his hands were manacled behind his back. He could smell his own body odors—he had not been bathed or shaved in three days—but he did not care about his smell or his beard, he only cared that she was not here yet, what was keeping her?

He lay in the darkness and tried not to count the minutes.

The girl was naked when she came into the room. She did not put on the light. There was the familiar tray in her hands, but it did not carry food any more. The Llama was on the left-hand side of the tray. Alongside the gun were a small cardboard box, a book of matches, a spoon with its handle bent back toward the bowl, and a glassine envelope.

"Hello, doll," she said. "Did you miss me?"

Carella did not answer.

"Have you been waiting for me?" the girl asked. "What's the matter, don't you feel like talking?" She laughed her mirthless laugh. "Don't worry, baby," she said. "I'm going to fix you."

She put the tray down on the chair near the door, and then walked to him.

"I think I'll play with you awhile," she said. "Would you like me to play with you?"

Carella did not answer.

"Well, if you're not even going to talk to me, I guess I'll just have to leave. After all, I know when I'm not—"

"No, don't go," Carella said.

"Do you want me to stay?"

"Yes."

"Say it."

"I want you to stay."

"That's better. What would you like, baby? Would you like me to play with you a little?"

"No."

"Don't you like being played with?"

"No."

"What do you like, baby?"

He did not answer.

"Well, you have to tell me," she said, "or I just won't give it to you."

"I don't know," he said.

"You don't know what you like?"

"Yes."

"Do you like the way I look without any clothes on?"

"Yes, you look all right."

"But that doesn't interest you, does it?"

"No."

"What *does* interest you?"

Again, he did not answer.

"Well, you *must* know what interests you. Don't you know?"

"No, I don't know."

"Tch," the girl said, and rose and began walking toward the door.

"Where are you going?" he asked quickly.

"Just to put some water in the spoon, doll," she said soothingly. "Don't worry. I'll be back."

She took the spoon from the tray and walked out of the room, leaving the door open. He could hear the water tap running in the kitchen. Hurry up, he thought, and then thought, No, I don't need you, leave me alone, goddamn you, leave me alone!

"Here I am," she said. She took the tray off the seat of the chair and then sat and picked up the glassine envelope. She emptied its contents into the spoon, and then struck a match and held it under the blackened bowl. "Got to cook it up," she said. "Got to cook it up for my baby. You getting itchy for it, baby? Don't worry, I'll take care of you. What's your wife's name?"

"Teddy," he said.

"Oh my," she said, "you still remember. That's a shame." She blew out the match. She opened the small box on the tray, and removed the hypodermic syringe and needle from it. She affixed the needle to the syringe, and depressed the plunger to squeeze any air out of the cylindrical glass tube. From the same cardboard box, which was the original container in which the syringe had been marketed, she took a piece of absorbent cotton, which she placed over the milky white liquid in the bowl of the spoon. Using the cotton as a filter, knowing that even the tiniest piece of solid matter would clog the tiny opening in the hypodermic needle, she drew the liquid up into the syringe, and then smiled and said, "There we are, all ready for my doll."

"I don't want it," Carella said suddenly.

"Oh, honey, please, don't lie to me," she said calmly. "I *know* you want it, what's your wife's name?"

"Teddy."

"Teddy, tch, tch, well, well," she said. From the cardboard box, she took a loop of string, and then walked to Carella and put the syringe on the floor beside him. She looped the piece of string around his arm, just above the elbow joint.

"What's your wife's name?" she asked.

"Teddy."

"You want this, doll?"

"No."

"Oooh, it's very good," she said. "We had some this afternoon, it was very good stuff. Aren't you just aching all over for it, what's your wife's name?"

"Teddy."

"Has she got tits like mine?"

Carella did not answer.

"Oh, but that doesn't interest you, does it? All that interests you is what's right here in this syringe, isn't that right?"

"No."

"This is a very high-class shooting gallery, baby. No eyedroppers here, oh no. Everything veddy veddy high-tone. Though I don't know how we're going to keep ourselves in junk now that little Sweetass is gone. He shouldn't have killed her, he really shouldn't have."

"Then why did he?"

"I'll ask the questions, doll. Do you remember your wife's name?"

"Yes."

"What is it?"

"Teddy."

"Then I guess I'll go. I can make good use of this myself." She picked up the syringe. "Shall I go?"

"Do what you want to do."

"If I leave this room," the girl said, "I won't come back until tomorrow morning. That'll be a long long night, baby. You think you can last the night without a fix?" She paused. "Do you want this or not?"

"Leave me alone," he said.

"No. No, no, we can't leave you alone. In a little while, baby, you are going to tell us everything you know, you are going to tell us exactly how you found us, you are going to tell us because if you don't we'll leave you here to drown in your own vomit. Now what's your wife's name?"

"Teddy."

"No."

"Yes. Her name is Teddy."

"How can I give you this if your memory's so good?"

"Then don't give it to me."

"Okay," the girl said, and walked toward the door. "Good-night, doll. I'll see you in the morning."

"Wait."

"Yes?" The girl turned. There was no expression on her face.

"You forgot your tourniquet," Carella said.

"So I did," the girl answered. She walked back to him and removed the string from his arm. "Play it cool," she said. "Go ahead. See how far you get by playing it cool. Tomorrow morning you'll be rolling all over the floor when I come in." She kissed him swiftly on the mouth. She sighed deeply. "Ahh," she said, "why do you force me to be mean to you?"

She went back to the door and busied herself with putting the string and cotton back into the box, straightening the book of matches and the spoon, aligning the syringe with the other items.

"Well, good night," she said, and walked out of the room, locking the door behind her.

Detective Sergeant Tony Kreisler of the Los Angeles Police Department did not return Meyer's call until nine o'clock that Monday night, which meant it was six o'clock on the Coast.

"You've had me busy all day long," Kreisler said. "It's tough to dig in the files for these ancient ones."

"Did you come up with anything?" Meyer asked.

"I'll tell you the truth, if this hadn't been a homicide you're working on, I'd have given up long ago, said the hell with it."

"What've you got for me?" Meyer asked patiently.

"This goes back twelve, thirteen years. You really think there's a connection?"

"It's all we've got to go on," Meyer said. "We figured it was worth a chance."

"Besides, the city paid for the long-distance call, right?" Kreisler said, and began laughing.

"That's right," Meyer said, and bided his time, and hoped that *Kreisler's* city was paying for *his* call, too.

Well, anyway," Kreisler said, when his laughter had subsided, "you were right about that arrest. We picked them up on a violation of Section 11500 of the Health and Safety Code. The girl's name wasn't Sachs then, we've got her listed as Tina Karin Grady, you suppose that's the same party?"

"Probably her maiden name," Meyer said.

"That's what I figure. They were holed up in an apartment in North Hollywood with more than twenty-five caps of H, something better than an eighth of an ounce, not that it makes any difference out here. Out here, there's no minimum quantity constituting a violation. Any amount that can be analyzed as a narcotic is admissible in court. It's different with you guys, I know that."

"That's right," Meyer said.

"Anyway, the guy was a mainliner, hit marks all over his arms. The Grady girl looked like sweet young meat, it was tough to figure what she was doing with a creep like him. She claimed she didn't know he was an addict, claimed he'd invited her up to the apartment, got her drunk, and then forced a shot on her. There were no previous marks on her body, just that one hit mark in the crook of her el—"

"Wait a minute," Meyer said.

"Yeah, what's the matter?"

"The *girl* claimed he'd forced the shot on her?"

"That's right. Said he got her drunk."

"It wasn't the *man* who alibied her?"

"What do you mean?"

"Did the man claim he was a pusher and that he'd forced a fix on the girl?"

Kreisler began laughing again. "Just catch a junkie who's willing to take a fall as a pusher. Are you kidding?"

"The girl told her doctor that the man alibied her."

"Absolute lie," Kreisler said. "*She* was the one who did all the talking, convinced the judge she was innocent, got off with a suspended sentence."

"And the man?"

"Convicted, served his time at Soledad, minimum of two, maximum of ten."

"Then *that's* why she kept sending him money. Not because she was indebted to him, but only because she felt guilty as hell."

"She deserved a break," Kreisler said. "What the hell, she was a nineteen-year-old kid. How do you know? Maybe he *did* force a blast on her."

"I doubt it. She'd been sniffing the stuff regularly and using pot since she was seventeen."

"Yeah, well, we didn't know that."

"What was the man's name?" Meyer asked.

"Fritz Schmidt."

"Fritz? Is that a nickname?"

"No, that's his square handle. Fritz Schmidt."

"What's the last you've got on him?"

"He was paroled in four. Parole Office gave him a clean bill of health, haven't had any trouble from him since."

"Do you know if he's still in California?"

"Couldn't tell you."

"Okay, thanks a lot," Meyer said.

"Don't mention it," Kreisler said, and hung up.

There were no listings for Fritz Schmidt in any of the city's telephone directories. But according to Dr. Levi's casebook, Tinka's "friend from California" had only arrived here in September. Hardly expecting any positive results, Meyer dialed the Information operator, identified himself as a working detective, and asked if she had anything for a Mr. Fritz Schmidt in her new listings.

Two minutes later, Meyer and Kling clipped on their holsters and left the squadroom.

The girl came back into the room at nine-twenty-five. She was fully clothed. The Llama was in her right hand. She closed the door gently behind her, but did not bother to switch on the overhead light. She watched Carella silently for several moments, the neon blinking around the edges of the drawn shade across the room. Then she said, "You're shivering, baby."

Carella did not answer.

"How tall are you?" she asked.

"Six-two."

"We'll get some clothes to fit you."

"Why the sudden concern?" Carella asked. He was sweating profusely, and shivering at the same time, wanting to tear his hands free of the cuffs, wanting to kick out with his lashed feet, helpless to do either, feeling desperately ill and knowing the only thing that would cure him.

"No concern at all, baby," she said. "We're dressing you because we've got to take you away from here."

"Where are you taking me?"

"Away."

"Where?"

"Don't worry," she said. "We'll give you a nice big fix first."

He felt suddenly exhilarated. He tried to keep the joy from showing on his face, tried not to smile, hoping against hope that she wasn't just teasing him again. He lay shivering on the floor, and the girl laughed and said, "My, it's rough when a little jolt is overdue, isn't it?"

Carella said nothing.

"Do you know what an overdose of heroin is?" she asked suddenly.

The shivering stopped for just a moment, and then began again more violently. Her words seemed to echo in the room, do you know what an overdose of heroin is, overdose, heroin, do you, do you?

"Do you?" the girl persisted.

"Yes."

"It won't hurt you," she said. "It'll *kill* you, but it won't hurt you." She laughed again. "Think of it, baby. How many addicts would you say there are in this city? Twenty thousand, twenty-one thousand, what's your guess?"

"I don't know," Carella said.

"Let's make it twenty thousand, okay? I like round numbers. Twenty thousand junkies out there, all hustling around and wondering where their next shot is coming from, and here we are about to give you a fix that'd take care of seven or eight of them for a week. How about that? That's real generosity, baby."

"Thanks," Carella said. "What do you think," he started, and stopped because his teeth were chattering. He waited. He took a deep breath and tried again. "What do you think you'll . . . you'll accomplish by killing me?"

"Silence," the girl said.

"How?"

"You're the only one in the world who knows who we are or where we are. Once you're dead, silence."

"No."

"Ah, *yes*, baby."

"I'm telling you no. They'll find you."

"Uh-uh."

"Yes."

"How?"

"The same way I did."

"Uh-uh. Impossible."

"If *I* uncovered your mistake—"

"There *was* no mistake, baby." The girl paused. "There was only a little girl playing with her doll."

The room was silent.

"We've got the doll, honey. We found it in your car, remember? It's a very nice doll. Very expensive, I'll bet."

"It's a present for my daughter," Carella said. "I told you—"

"You weren't going to give your daughter a *used* doll for a present, were you? No, honey." The girl smiled. "I happened to look under the doll's dress a few minutes ago. Baby, it's all over for you, believe me." She turned and opened the door. "Fritz," she yelled to the other room, "come in here and give me a hand."

The mailbox downstairs told them Fritz Schmidt was in apartment 34. They took the steps up two at a time, drawing their revolvers when they were on the third floor, and then scanning the numerals on each door as they moved down the corridor. Meyer put his ears to the door at the end of the hall. He could hear nothing. He moved away from the door, and then nodded to Kling. Kling stepped back several feet, bracing himself, his legs widespread. There was no wall opposite the end door, nothing to use as a launching support for a flat-footed kick at the latch. Meyer used Kling's body as the support he needed, raising his knee high as Kling shoved him out and forward. Meyer's foot connected. The lock sprang and the door swung wide. He followed it into the apartment, gun in hand, Kling not three feet behind him. They fanned out the moment they were inside the room. Kling to the right, Meyer to the left.

A man came running out of the room to the right of the large living room. He was a tall man with straight blond hair and huge shoulders. He looked at the detectives and then thrust one hand inside his jacket and down toward his belt. Neither Meyer nor Kling waited to find out what he was reaching for. They opened fire simultaneously. The bullets caught the man in his enormous chest and flung him back against the wall, which he clung to for just a moment before falling headlong to the floor. A second person appeared in the doorway. The second person was a girl, and she was very big, and she held a pistol in her right hand. A look of panic was riding her face, but it was curiously coupled with a fixed smile, as though she'd been expecting them all along and was ready for them, was in fact welcoming their arrival.

"Watch it, she's loaded!" Meyer yelled, but the girl swung around swiftly, pointing the gun into the other room instead, aiming it at the floor. In the split second it took her to turn and extend her arm, Kling saw the man lying trussed near the radiator. The man was turned away from the door, but Kling knew instinctively it was Carella.

He fired automatically and without hesitation, the first time he had ever shot a human being in the back, placing the shot high between the girl's shoulders. The Llama in her hand went off at almost the same instant, but the impact of Kling's slug sent her falling halfway across the room, her own bullet going wild. She struggled to rise as Kling ran into the room. She turned the gun on Carella again, but Kling's foot struck her extended hand, kicking the gun up as the second shot exploded. The girl would not let go. Her fingers were still tight around the stock of the gun. She swung it back a third time and shouted, "Let me *kill* him, you bastard!" and tightened her finger on the trigger.

Kling fired again.

His bullet entered her forehead just above the right eye. The Llama went off as she fell backward, the bullet spanging against the metal of the radiator and then ricocheting across the room and tearing through the drawn window shade and shattering the glass behind it.

Meyer was at his side.

"Easy," he said.

Kling had not cried since that time almost four years ago when Claire was killed, but he stood in the center of the neon-washed room now with the dead and bleeding girl against the wall and Carella naked and shivering near the radiator, and he allowed the hand holding the pistol to drop limply to his side, and then he began sobbing, deep bitter sobs that racked his body.

Meyer put his arm around Kling's shoulders.

"Easy," he said again. "It's all over."

"The doll," Carella whispered. "Get the doll."

Fourteen

The doll measured thirty inches from the top of her blonde head to the bottoms of her black patent-leather shoes. She wore white bobby sox, a ruffled white voile dress with a white nylon underslip, a black velveteen bodice, and a ruffled lace bib and collar. What appeared at first to be a simulated gold brooch was centered just below the collar.

The doll's trade name was Chatterbox.

There were two D-size flashlight batteries and one 9-volt transistor battery in a recess in the doll's plastic belly. The recess was covered with a flesh-colored plastic top that was kept in place by a simple plastic twist-lock. Immediately above the battery box there was a flesh-colored, open plastic grid that concealed the miniature electronic device in the doll's chest. It was this device after which the doll had been named by its creators. The device was a tiny recorder.

The brooch below the doll's collar was a knob that activated the recording mechanism. To record, a child simply turned the decorative knob counterclockwise, waited for a single beep signal, and began talking until the beep sounded again, at which time the knob had to be turned once more to its center position. In order to play back what had just been recorded, the child had only to turn the knob clockwise. The recorded message would continue to play back over and over again until the knob was once more returned to the center position.

When the detectives turned the brooch-knob clockwise, they heard three recorded voices. One of them belonged to Anna Sachs. It was clear and distinct because the doll had been in Anna's lap when she'd recorded her message on the night of her mother's murder. The message was one of reassurance. She kept saying over and over again to the doll lying across her lap. "Don't be frightened, Chatterbox, please don't be frightened. It's nothing, Chatterbox, don't be frightened," over and over again.

The second voice was less distinct because it had been recorded through the thin wall separating the child's bedroom from her mother's. Subsequent tests by the police laboratory showed the recording mechanism to be extremely sensitive for a device of its size, capable of picking up shouted words at a distance of twenty-five feet. Even so, the second voice would not have been picked up at all had Anna not been sitting very close to the thin dividing wall. And, of course, especially toward the end, the words next door had been screamed.

From beep to beep, the recording lasted only a minute and a half. Throughout the length of the recording, Anna talked reassuringly to her doll. "Don't be frightened, Chatterbox, please don't be frightened. It's nothing, Chatterbox, don't be frightened." Behind the child's voice, a running counterpoint of horror, was the voice of Tinka Sachs, her mother. Her words were almost inaudible at first. They presented only a vague murmur of faraway terror, the sound of someone repeatedly moaning, the pitiable rise and fall of a voice imploring—but all without words because the sound had been muffled by the wall between the rooms. And then, as Tinka became more and more desperate, as her killer followed her unmercifully around the room with a knife blade, her voice became louder, the words became more distinct. "Don't! Please don't!" always behind the child's soothing voice in the foreground, "Don't be frightened, Chatterbox, please don't be frightened," and her mother shrieking, "Don't! Please don't! Please," the voices intermingling, "I'm bleeding, please, it's nothing, Chatterbox, don't be frightened, Fritz, stop, please, Fritz, stop, stop, oh please, it's nothing, Chatterbox, don't be frightened."

The third voice sounded like a man's. It was nothing more than a rumble on the recording. Only once did a word come through clearly, and that was the word "Slut!" interspersed between the child's reassurances to her doll, and Tinka's weakening cries for mercy.

In the end, Tinka shouted the man's name once again, "Fritz!" and then her voice seemed to fade. The next word she uttered could have been a muted "please," but it was indistinct and drowned out by Anna's "Don't cry, Chatterbox, try not to cry."

The detectives listened to the doll in silence, and then watched while the ambulance attendants carried Carella out on one stretcher and the still-breathing Schmidt out on another.

"The girl's dead," the medical examiner said.

"I know," Meyer answered.

"Who shot her?" one of the Homicide cops asked.

"I did," Kling answered.

"I'll need the circumstances."

"Stay with him," Meyer said to Kling. "I'll get to the hospital. Maybe that son of a bitch wants to make a statement before he dies."

I didn't intend to kill her.

She was happy as hell when I came in, laughing and joking because she thought she was off the junk at last.

I told her she was crazy, she would never kick it.

I had not had a shot since three o'clock that afternoon, I was going out of my head. I told her I wanted money for a fix, and she said she couldn't give me money any more, she said she wanted nothing more to do with me or Pat, that's the name of the girl I'm living with. She had no right to hold out on me like that, not when I was so sick. She could see I was ready to climb the walls, so she sat there sipping her goddamn iced tea, and telling me she was not going to keep me supplied any more, she was not going to spend half her income keeping me in shit. I told her she owed it to me. I spent four years in Soledad because of her, the little bitch, she owed it to me! She told me to leave her alone. She told me to get out and leave her alone. She said she was finished with me and my kind. She said she had kicked it, did I understand, she had kicked it!

Am I going to die?

I

I picked

I picked the knife up from the tray.

I didn't intend to kill her, it was just I needed a fix, couldn't she see that? For Christ's sake, the times we used to have together. I stabbed her, I don't know how many times.

Am I going to die?

The painting fell off the wall, I remember that.

I took all the bills out of her pocketbook on the dresser, there was forty dollars in tens. I ran out of the bedroom and dropped the knife someplace in the hall, I guess, I don't even remember. I realized I couldn't take the elevator down, that much I knew, so I went up to the roof and crossed over to the next building and got down to the street that way. I bought twenty caps with the forty dollars. Pat and me got very high afterwards, very high.

I didn't know Tina's kid was in the apartment until tonight, when Pat accidentally tipped to the goddamn talking doll.

If I'd known she was there, I might have killed her, too. I don't know.

Fritz Schmidt never got to sign his dictated confession because he died seven minutes after the police stenographer began typing it.

The lieutenant stood by while the two Homicide cops questioned Kling. They had advised him not to make a statement before Byrnes arrived, and now that he was here they went about their routine task with dispatch. Kling could not seem to stop crying. The two Homicide cops were plainly embarrassed as they questioned him, a grown man, a cop no less, crying that way. Byrnes watched Kling's face, and said nothing.

The two Homicide copes were called Carpenter and

Calhoun. They looked very much alike. Byrnes had never met any Homicide cops who did not look exactly alike. He supposed it was a trademark of their unique specialty. Watching them, he found it difficult to remember who was Carpenter and who was Calhoun. Even their voices sounded alike.

"Let's start with your name, rank, and shield number," Carpenter said.

"Bertram Kling, detective/third, 74579."

"Squad?" Calhoun said.

"The Eight-Seven." He was still sobbing. The tears rolled down his face endlessly.

"Technically, you just committed a homicide, Kling."

"It's excusable homicide," Calhoun said.

"Justifiable," Carpenter corrected.

"Excusable," Calhoun repeated. "Penal Law 1054."

"Wrong," Carpenter said. "Justifiable, P.L. 1055. 'Homicide is justifiable when committed by a public officer in arresting a person who has committed a felony and is fleeing from justice.' *Just*ifiable."

"Was the broad committing a felony?" Calhoun asked.

"Yes," Kling said. He nodded. He tried to wipe the tears from his eyes. "Yes. Yes, she was." The tears would not stop.

"Explain it."

"She was . . . she was ready to shoot Carella. She was trying to kill him."

"Did you fire a warning shot?"

"No. Her back was turned to me and she was . . . she was leveling the gun at Carella, so I fired the minute I came into the room. I caught her between the shoulders, I think. With my first shot."

"Then what?"

Kling wiped the back of his hand across his eyes. "Then she . . . she started to fire again, and I kicked out at her hand, and the slug went wild. When she . . . when she got ready to fire the third time, I . . . I . . ."

"You killed her," Carpenter said flatly.

"Justifiable," Calhoun said.

"Absolutely," Carpenter agreed.

"I said so all along," Calhoun said.

"She'd already committed a felony by abducting a police officer, what the hell. And then she fired two shots at him. If that ain't a felony, I'll eat all the law books in this crumbly state."

"You got nothing to worry about."

"Except the Grand Jury. This has to go to the Grand Jury, Kling, same as if you were an ordinary citizen."

"You still got nothing to worry about," Calhoun said.

"She was going to kill him," Kling said blankly. His tears suddenly stopped. He stared at the two Homicide cops as though seeing them for the first time. "Not again," he said. "I couldn't let it happen again."

Neither Carpenter nor Calhoun knew what the hell Kling was talking about. Byrnes knew, but he didn't particularly feel like explaining. He simply went to Kling and said, "Forget those department charges I mentioned. Go home and get some rest."

The two Homicide cops didn't know what the hell *Byrnes* was talking about, either. They looked at each other, shrugged, and chalked it all up to the eccentricities of the 87th.

"Well," Carpenter said. "I guess that's that."

"I guess that's that," Calhoun said. Then, because Kling

seemed to have finally gotten control of himself, he ventured a small joke. "Stay out of jail, huh?" he said.

Neither Byrnes nor Kling even smiled.

Calhoun and Carpenter cleared their throats and walked out without saying good night.

She sat in the darkness of the hospital room and watched her sedated husband, waiting for him to open his eyes, barely able to believe that he was alive, praying now that he would be well again soon.

The doctors had promised to begin treatment at once. They had explained to her that it was difficult to fix the length of time necessary for anyone to become an addict, primarily because heroin procured illegally varied in its degree of adulteration. But Carella had told them he'd received his first injection sometime late Friday night, which meant he had been on the drug for slightly more than three days. In their opinion, a person psychologically prepared for addiction could undoubtedly become a habitual user in that short a time, if he was using pure heroin of normal strength. But they were working on the assumption that Carella had never used drugs before and had been injected only with narcotics acquired illegally and therefore greatly adulterated. If this was the case, anywhere between two and three weeks would have been necessary to transform him into a confirmed addict. At any rate, they would begin withdrawal (if so strong a word was applicable at all) immediately, and they had no doubt that the cure (and again they apologized for using so strong a word) would be permanent. They had explained that there was none of the addict's usual psychological dependence evident in Carella's case, and then had gone on at great length about personality disturbances, and tolerance levels, and physical dependence—and then one of the doctors suddenly and quietly asked whether or not Carella had ever expressed a prior interest in experimenting with drugs.

Teddy had emphatically shaken her head.

Well, fine then, they said. We're sure everything will work out fine. We're confident of that, Mrs. Carella. As for his nose, we'll have to make a more thorough examination in the morning. We don't know when he sustained the injury, you see, or whether or not the broken bones have already knitted. In any case, we should be able to reset it, though it may involve an operation. Please be assured we'll do everything in our power. Would you like to see him now?

She sat in the darkness.

When at last he opened his eyes, he seemed surprised to see her. He smiled and then said, "Teddy."

She returned the smile. She touched his face tentatively.

"Teddy," he said again, and then—because the room was dark and because she would not see his mouth too clearly—he said something which she was sure she misunderstood.

"That's your name," he said. "I didn't forget."

FOLIOTHÈQUE
Collection dirigée par
Bruno Vercier
Maître de conférences
à l'Université de
la Sorbonne Nouvelle-Paris III

Marguerite Duras

Le ravissement de Lol V. Stein

par Madeleine Borgomano

Madeleine Borgomano

présente

Le ravissement de Lol V. Stein

de Marguerite Duras

Gallimard

Madeleine Borgomano est maître de conférences à l'université d'Aix-en-Provence. Spécialiste de Marguerite Duras, elle a aussi publié des études sur J. M. G. Le Clézio, sur la nouvelle en France au XXe siècle et sur la littérature d'Afrique noire.

LISTE DES ABRÉVIATIONS

A.	*L'amant*, éd. de Minuit.
A.A.	*L'amante anglaise*, Gallimard.
A.C.	*L'amant de la Chine du Nord*, Gallimard, « Folio ».
Am.	*L'amour*, Gallimard, « Folio ».
A.M.A.	*L'après-midi de Monsieur Andesmas*, Gallimard.
C.	*Le camion*, éd. de Minuit.
D.d.	*Détruire, dit-elle*, éd. de Minuit.
E.V.C.	Édition vidéographique critique, ministère des Relations extérieures.
F.G.	*La femme du Gange*, Gallimard.
H.	*Hiroshima mon amour*, Gallimard, « Folio ».
Lieux	*Les lieux de Marguerite Duras*, éd. de Minuit.
M.C.	*Moderato cantabile*, éd. de Minuit.
P.	*Les parleuses*, éd. de Minuit.
S.B.	*Savannah Bay*, éd. de Minuit.
V.C.	*Le vice-consul*, Gallimard, « L'imaginaire ».
Y.V.	*Les yeux verts*, Gallimard.

Pour *Le ravissement de Lol V. Stein*, les numéros de page entre parenthèses renvoient à l'édition Folio, n° 810. Le titre a souvent été abrégé ainsi : le *Ravissement*.

Sauf indication contraire, les mots figurant en italique dans les citations sont soulignés par nous-même.

INTRODUCTION

Il faut se perdre. Je ne sais pas. Tu apprendras. Je voudrais une indication pour me perdre. Il faut être sans arrière-pensée, se disposer à ne plus reconnaître rien de ce qu'on connaît...
(V.C., p. 9)[1].

Ne rien savoir de Lol était la connaître déjà. On pouvait, me parut-il, en savoir moins encore, de moins en moins sur Lol V. Stein (p. 81).

1. Cet ordre surprenant, émanant d'une voix anonyme, est donné dès les premiers mots du *Vice-consul*, à la mendiante indienne.

Suggérer au lecteur qu'il lui faudrait chercher à « se perdre », en épigraphe à une étude critique dont la fonction devrait être celle d'un guide, paraît paradoxal et tout aussi paradoxale l'apologie de l'ignorance.

Mais *Le ravissement de Lol V. Stein* n'est pas un roman ordinaire et le jeu des paradoxes voudrait frayer la voie à une approche tâtonnante et non conventionnelle, où le lecteur consente à se laisser « ravir », à entreprendre, bien au-delà d'une simple lecture, une expérience intérieure risquée.

À ce « ravissement » du lecteur, s'attache pourtant, peut-être, un réel danger : « La mort et la douleur sont la toile d'araignée du texte et malheur au lecteur complice qui succombe à son charme : il peut y rester pour de vrai[2]. »

2. Julia Kristeva, *Soleil noir, dépression et mélancolie*, Gallimard, p. 237. Voir aussi Dossier, p. 185-186.

Il est évident que l'écriture de Marguerite Duras possède, surtout dans ce roman, des pouvoirs ensorcelants. Mais elle construit aussi ses garde-fous, qu'il faut apprendre à lire. Ce qui justifie l'existence du texte critique, s'il se propose, tout en évitant « la crécelle théorique » (*P.*, p. 225), de permettre au lecteur de frôler les gouffres sans y tomber, d'écouter la voix des sirènes sans suivre leur appel mortel, de consentir au ravissement et à la perdition, mais pas tout à fait « pour de vrai ».

I MARGUERITE DURAS JUSQU'AU « RAVISSEMENT DE LOL V. STEIN »

1. UN ROMAN CHARNIÈRE

Paru en 1964 et déjà considéré, dix ans après sa parution, comme un « roman charnière[1] », le *Ravissement* reste un livre essentiel ; le plus controversé, probablement, mais l'un des romans les plus fascinants et les plus originaux du XXe siècle, l'un des plus magiques et des plus mystérieux aussi.

Le *Ravissement* ne ressemble guère à d'autres romans (malgré quelques rapprochements, intéressants mais souvent contestables)[2]. Il ne s'inscrit nettement dans aucun courant, aucune école littéraire[3] ; il reste possible, pourtant, de le rattacher à ce courant

1. Michel Grisolia, *Le Nouvel Observateur*, octobre 1973.

2. Voir Dossier, « Intertextualité », p. 195 *sq.* Le *Ravissement* a souvent été rapproché, en particulier, de *Nadja*, d'André Breton, livre phare du surréalisme.

3. Voir, cependant, *infra*, « Intertextualité », p. 137 *sq.*

moderne, issu du rêve de Flaubert, pris vraiment à la lettre : écrire « un livre sur rien[1] ».

Par contre, le *Ravissement* manifeste des affinités avec les mouvements d'idées contemporains mettant en question l'homogénéité du sujet humain, à la suite, en particulier des découvertes de la psychanalyse[2].

Cependant, bien des éléments du *Ravissement* se trouvaient en germe dans les écrits antérieurs de Duras (romans et nouvelles, scénarios, pièces de théâtre). Le *Ravissement* en rassemble et en condense les thèmes essentiels : un certain goût pour l'abandon, la perte, la mort ; des identités incertaines et des rôles interchangeables ; des glissements entre réel et fantasme. Le *Ravissement* soumet ces thèmes à toutes sortes de distorsions et de métamorphoses. Il apparaît alors à la fois comme un aboutissement et comme une origine.

1. *Flaubert*, Lettre à Louise Colet, 16 janvier 1852. Voir R. E. Reinton, « *Le ravissement de Lol V. Stein :* un livre sur rien ? ». « Rien » est l'un des mots obsessionnels du *Ravissement*.

2. Voir *infra*, p. 103 *sq*. et Dossier, p. 177 *sq*.

PLACE DU ROMAN DANS L'HISTOIRE DE L'ŒUVRE

Marguerite Duras est déjà très connue, en tant qu'écrivain et aussi en tant que scénariste, avant la publication du *Ravissement*, en 1964. Son premier roman, *Les impudents*, à vrai dire passé inaperçu, date de 1943. *Un barrage contre le Pacifique*, en 1950, véritable roman des origines, son premier succès, a même manqué de peu le prix Goncourt[3]. *Moderato cantabile*[4], en 1958, a atteint cinq cent mille exemplaires. Et, en 1960, le film d'Alain Resnais, *Hiroshima mon amour*, dont elle a écrit le scénario, a fait de Duras une vedette.

3. Voir l'étude de M. Th. Ligot, « Foliothèque », n° 18, 1992.

4. Voir l'étude de Madeleine Borgomano, éd. Bertrand-Lacoste, « Parcours de lecture », 1990.

Après *Moderato cantabile*, Marguerite Duras a publié une pièce de théâtre, *Les viaducs de la Seine-et-Oise*, inspirée par une affaire criminelle (ce texte, remanié, deviendra en 1967 *L'amante anglaise*), et deux romans, *Dix heures et demie du soir en été*, en 1960, et *L'après-midi de Monsieur Andesmas*, en 1962.

UNE VOIX, UNE MUSIQUE

Dans le scénario d'*Hiroshima mon amour*, et dans ses romans, depuis *Moderato cantabile*, Marguerite Duras a trouvé sa voix. Cette « musique[1] » très personnelle la distingue nettement de tous ses contemporains. Musique indéfinissable, bien sûr. Mais si reconnaissable qu'elle a souvent été imitée et parodiée. Musique qualifiable : une extrême simplicité de vocabulaire et de syntaxe, qui sera peu à peu poussée jusqu'au plus grand dénuement, mais qui, dans les années soixante, reste encore trouée d'images fulgurantes ; un art de l'ellipse et du non-dit, qui laisse l'essentiel se jouer entre les lignes, entre les mots. Un mépris des liaisons et des subordinations, un goût pour la juxtaposition et le fragmentaire. Ces derniers traits expliquent peut-être pourquoi une écriture aussi simple peut paraître à certains difficile, voire illisible.

1. Ou « musica », en référence au titre d'une pièce de Duras, *La musica*.

2. L'ÉCRITURE DU ROMAN

« Je suis dans l'incapacité de vous dire comment j'ai écrit *Le ravissement de Lol V. Stein*[1]. »

À lire cette phrase et à en croire l'auteur(e)[2] elle-même (et qui d'autre croire, en l'occurrence ?), Lol serait une sorte de météorite tombée on ne sait d'où et l'écriture du roman se serait faite, à une période difficile et solitaire de sa vie, dans une totale obscurité et une très grande peur.

Certes, l'écriture, la vraie, surgit toujours, selon Marguerite Duras, du plus profond de « l'ombre interne » (*P.*, p. 50). Mais le *Ravissement* émerge d'un lieu plus mystérieux encore et plus enfoui.

1. *Marguerite Duras à Montréal*, p. 23. Voir Dossier, p. 158.

2. Les Québécois utilisent couramment « auteure » ou « écrivaine » pour révéler le féminin que l'emploi indifférencié d'« auteur » ou « écrivain » masque (ou noie). Je les suivrai, en gardant mes distances : « auteur(e) », « écrivain(e) ».

Marguerite Duras réactive donc, en parlant de son écriture, les mythes, antiques et romantiques, d'une inspiration, sinon divine et sacrée, du moins « donnée » et échappant à la maîtrise de l'auteur.

Elle s'oppose ainsi à la conception d'une écriture maîtrisée, travaillée, générée même parfois par des calculs ou des techniques, qui est, à la même époque, celle des « nouveaux romanciers ». La question est complexe. Mais les critiques qui avaient rattaché Duras au courant du Nouveau Roman, parce qu'il est commode de classer les écrivains par catégories, semblent bien avoir commis une double erreur. De fait, Duras n'a jamais appartenu à ce « groupe » (pour autant qu'il ne soit pas fictif). Mais surtout, malgré une commune remise en question des formes traditionnelles du roman, Marguerite Duras affirme ne rien « organiser » (*P.*, p. 119), et opère la déconstruction du récit en se fondant sur les charmes du romanesque le plus conventionnel.

UN MODÈLE DE LOL ?

« Je ne sais pas d'où vient Lola Valérie Stein[1]. » Le personnage principal du *Ravissement* émerge, lui aussi, de l'ombre. Duras suggère pourtant l'existence d'un « modèle » de Lol, dès 1964, dans une interview télévisée[2]. Elle revient sur cette origine de son personnage en 1988 : « Lol V. Stein était une jeune malade que m'avait confiée, un dimanche, sur ma demande, le médecin-chef de l'asile psychiatrique de Villejuif[3]. »

1. « La couleur des mots », voir Dossier, p. 158.

2. Interview partiellement retranscrite dans le Dossier, p. 156.

3. *Outside 2*, p. 215.

Mais cette jeune malade sans mémoire semble avoir été seulement un mannequin, une forme vide autour d'une absence, à l'intérieur de laquelle Duras a introduit le personnage imaginaire, tout aussi insaisissable, de Lol. L'opération a quelque chose de magique : Lol serait-elle un zombie ?

Cette forme qui dessine une absence est aussi une forme sans histoire : la jeune malade ne pouvait rien raconter, ayant oublié l'histoire de sa vie. Le bal du roman n'est rien d'autre que celui de la rencontre avec Duras.

Le plus souvent, Duras affirme ignorer l'origine de son personnage : « Je ne l'ai jamais vue, Lol V. Stein [...] je mourrai sans doute sans savoir exactement qui c'est » (*Lieux*, p. 99).

Marguerite Duras, par ses confidences et ses affirmations contradictoires, nous apprend beaucoup sur les mécanismes mystérieux de l'écriture, ou, du moins, de son écriture.

Duras met ces mécanismes en scène au sein même de la diégèse — du monde — de son roman. Jacques Hold, le narrateur fasciné par Lol V. Stein et qui tente de reconstituer son histoire, reproduit, sous une identité masculine, le rapport de Marguerite Duras avec la jeune malade. Néanmoins, il n'est pas présenté comme un écrivain, mais comme un médecin et surtout comme un homme fasciné et amoureux.

Dans *Le vice-consul*, roman publié en 1964, un an seulement après le *Ravissement*, et qui appartient au même cycle[1], Marguerite Duras introduit, comme une sorte de double de Jacques Hold, cette fois explicitement désigné comme écrivain, Peter Morgan. L'écrivain est montré en train d'« inventer » un personnage, la mendiante indienne, à partir d'une « vraie » mendiante amnésique qui erre dans les rues de Calcutta, et d'une anecdote qui lui a été racontée (*V.C.*, p. 29, 156, 179-183).

1. Voir Dossier, p. 169.

Ces représentations de l'invention de Jacques Hold et de l'écriture de Peter Morgan apparaissent comme très éclairantes pour rendre compte de l'écriture de Duras (même si le choix de personnages masculins dans le rôle de l'écrivain interdit toute équivalence simple, provoque des distorsions et transforme les significations)[2].

2. Voir Dossier p. 181-194.

Écrire pourrait être aussi une tentative pour répondre à des questions semblables : « Quoi dire à la place de [...] ce qu'elle ne dira pas ? [...] à la place de ce qui a disparu de toute mémoire ? » (*V.C.*, p. 75). Ou encore : « Comment la retrouver dans le passé ? rassembler même sa folie ? séparer sa folie de la folie, son rire du rire... ? » (*V.C.*, p. 183).

L'INSPIRATRICE D'ANNE-MARIE STRETTER

Si l'origine de Lol reste indécise, Duras évoque, par contre, très fréquemment, le « modèle » de l'autre personnage féminin, la « ravisseuse », Anne-Marie Stretter, qui réapparaîtra de façon obsessive dans la suite de l'œuvre durassienne. Ce modèle, très nettement identifié, était « un des personnages dominants de [son] enfance », une femme réelle, qu'elle raconte avoir vue souvent de loin. La fascination que cette femme du monde, rousse aux yeux clairs, exerçait sur l'enfant, son aura de transgression, de mystère et de mort, serait née des rumeurs qui la rendaient responsable du suicide d'un très jeune amant[1].

Cette femme a été pour la jeune Marguerite Donnadieu « comme la foudre ou la foi ». Son apparition troublante, lointaine et ravageuse, a inspiré la scène originelle du *Ravissement*, même si A.M.S.[2] se trouve le plus souvent fortement liée à l'espace indochinois, où vivait Marguerite Donnadieu[3], espace étranger au monde du *Ravissement*. Il est vrai que Duras déclare aussi, plus tard, qu'Anne-Marie Stretter « vient du Nord ».

Si le modèle de Lol reste très flou, l'inspiratrice d'Anne-Marie Stretter est affirmée comme bien réelle. Dans *Les yeux verts*, Marguerite Duras donne des garanties, en reproduisant la lettre que lui a écrite la femme de son souvenir quand elle s'est reconnue dans les livres. Le rapport de la fiction et de la réalité, de l'écriture et du « réel » est ici suggéré dans toute sa complexité.

1. Voir Dossier, p. 158.

2. Initiales par lesquelles Anne-Marie Stretter va souvent être désignée dans la suite de l'œuvre.

3. Voir Dossier, « Biographie », p. 151.

TATIANA, LOL ET HÉLÈNE LAGONELLE

Une autre filiation, plus incertaine, n'est devenue manifeste que très tardivement.

Tatiana Karl, l'amie d'enfance de Lol, le seul témoin du bal, pourrait bien s'apparenter à Hélène Lagonelle, personnage de *L'amant* (1984) et de *L'amant de la Chine du Nord* (1991), textes déclarés autobiographiques : Tatiana aurait alors, elle aussi, son origine dans les souvenirs d'enfance de l'écrivain(e).

De même que Tatiana est l'amie d'enfance de Lol, Hélène Lagonelle était l'amie de pension de « la petite ». Elles dansaient ensemble dans le préau de la même manière. Comme Tatiana, Hélène se promenait nue, exhibant innocemment un corps et des seins très beaux[1]. Tatiana peut apparaître comme une façon de ressusciter, secrètement, la belle jeune fille morte très jeune. En même temps, les sonorités de son nom rapprocheraient plutôt Hélène Lagonelle de Lol[2]. Lol et Tatiana, il est vrai, apparaissent bien souvent comme des doubles[3].

ÉCRIRE

Notons enfin que l'auteur(e) — comme les critiques — voit dans le *Ravissement* un tournant : « J'ai l'impression quelquefois que j'ai commencé à écrire avec ça, avec *Le ravissement de Lol V. Stein*, avec *L'amour* et *La femme du Gange...* » (*Lieux*, p. 90). « Quelque chose a été franchi, là, mais qui m'a échappé... » (*Lieux*, p. 101).

Les éventuelles « sources » des personnages ou de l'histoire, même fournies par l'auteur(e), ne constituent nullement des explications, mais des hypothèses, des pistes

1. Dans *L'amant*, Marguerite Duras parle avec exaltation du corps d'Hélène : « Je suis exténuée par la beauté du corps d'Hélène Lagonelle [...]. Ce corps est sublime [...]. Les seins sont comme je n'en ai jamais vu. [...] Elle est impudique, Hélène Lagonelle, elle ne se rend pas compte, elle se promène toute nue dans les dortoirs. Ce qu'il y a de plus beau de toutes les choses données par Dieu, c'est ce corps d'Hélène Lagonelle... » (*A.*, p. 89).

2. Marguerite Duras déclare, dans « Duras tout entière... », *Le Nouvel Observateur*, 14-20 novembre 1986, qu'Hélène Lagonelle est « évidemment » Lol V. Stein.

3. Voir *infra*, p. 95 *sq.*

ouvertes à l'imagination. La constatation de Duras : « Quelque chose m'a échappé », est essentielle. « Qu'est-ce qui m'est arrivé ? Je ne comprends pas très bien. C'est comme ça, écrire[1]. »

1. Voir Dossier, p. 158.

Dans le *Ravissement*, l'écriture de Duras se transforme profondément, acquiert cette dimension absolument originale, cette magie ouvrant des « champs magnétiques[2] » qui appellent la coopération du lecteur et déclenchent la multitude des interprétations.

2. Peter Handke, « La sorcière », *Le Monde*, 19 novembre 1992.

Marguerite Duras nous y invite elle-même : « Elle est à vous, Lol V. Stein [...] Lol V. Stein, c'est ce que vous en faites... » (*Lieux*, p. 101). Elle ajoute même, provocante, comme souvent : « Lol V. Stein, c'est ma prostitution. »

3. LA PART DU LIVRE À FAIRE PAR LE LECTEUR

Le ravissement de Lol V. Stein est ainsi livré à ses lecteurs par son auteur(e) même. Il n'en résulte pas que ce lecteur soit en droit d'en faire tout ce qu'il veut.

Il existe des limites à l'interprétation[3], comme le montre Umberto Eco, convaincu, pourtant, que le texte est « un tissu de non-dit », « un mécanisme paresseux [...] qui requiert des mouvements coopératifs actifs et conscients de la part du lecteur[4] ».

3. Umberto Eco, *Les limites de l'interprétation*, Grasset, 1990.

4. Umberto Eco, *Lector in fabula*, Grasset, 1979-1985, p. 66.

Ces limites sont fixées par le texte lui-même, considéré comme un ensemble structuré au sein duquel rien n'est isolable puisque toute signification naît du système de relations. Une interprétation non arbitraire se doit de prendre en compte la littéralité même du texte, mais aussi sa totalité.

Le *Ravissement* est un texte tout particulièrement incomplet : sa structure même repose sur les relations entre l'acte de narration (qui est aussi quête d'un savoir sur Lol) et ce « ravissement », structure intersubjective qui échappe largement au discours[1]. Ce roman exige beaucoup plus de ses lecteurs qu'un roman plus « classique », plus conforme aux normes et aux attentes ordinaires.

De plus, le *Ravissement* ne peut que très difficilement s'isoler complètement de l'œuvre entière de Duras. Il en va de même chez la plupart des grands écrivains. Mais l'œuvre de Marguerite Duras présente l'originalité d'être un « ensemble » très continu, une « totalité[2] ». Lieux, personnages, éléments narratifs sont sans cesse repris, modulés, transformés, dans un réseau mouvant profondément original.

Aussi, pour apporter une aide au lecteur, cette étude se voudra-t-elle à la fois rigoureusement « textuelle » et « intertextuelle » : le *Ravissement* sera lu avec les autres livres de Marguerite Duras, ceux qui l'ont précédé, mais aussi ceux qui lui ont succédé.

1. Voir *infra*, en particulier p. 93 et 105 *sq*.

2. Ces mots sont empruntés aux textes durassiens, en particulier à *L'amour*, « suite » du *Ravissement*.

II LES SEUILS DU ROMAN

1. UN TITRE À FAIRE RÊVER

Le titre est le véritable « seuil[1] » du roman ; il appartient également au dehors et au dedans. Carte d'identité, il joue aussi souvent un rôle d'appât commercial. « Le ravissement de Lol V. Stein », par son étrangeté et son opacité, dédaigne cette séduction facile. Duras, il est vrai, a longtemps voulu fuir à tel point les succès populaires qu'en 1981 (27 novembre), pour la sortie de son film, *L'Homme Atlantique*[2], elle faisait passer dans *Le Monde* un avertissement aux spectateurs, leur demandant « d'éviter complètement de voir [ce film] et même de le fuir ».

Cependant *Le ravissement de Lol V. Stein* est aussi un titre « à ravir », à faire rêver. Marguerite Duras a beau déclarer : « Le mot dont j'ai le plus horreur [...] c'est le mot *rêve*. Je n'ai jamais rêvé, c'est pour cela que j'ai écrit[3] ; elle n'en joue pas moins avec la faculté de rêve de son lecteur dans ce titre énigmatique qui produit du sens, comme le travail du rêve décrit par Freud, dans l'ambivalence, le déplacement et la condensation[4].

1. Gérard Genette, *Seuils*, Le Seuil, coll. « Poétique », 1987.

2. Film, il est vrai, composé en partie de plans noirs.

3. « Work and words », *E.V.C.*, p. 63.

4. S. Freud, *L'interprétation des rêves*, 1926, PUF.

RAVISSEMENT ?

Ravissement ? Rapt[1] ou enchantement ? Violence ou transport délicieux ? Lol est-elle emportée au septième ciel, dans une sorte d'extase (la ravie, comme « le ravi » des crèches provençales)[2], ou volée, frustrée ? Qui est la ravisseuse, qui est la ravie ?

Le mot « ravissement » n'apparaît jamais ailleurs que dans le titre du roman, un peu hors texte, donc. Ce signifiant, dont les signifiés sont multiples et presque contradictoires, reste très énigmatique. Il pourrait occuper assez bien la place vide de ce « mot-absence » (p. 48) qu'il aurait fallu trouver pour désigner (« faire résonner ») une expérience indicible de Lol[3], liée au bal de T. Beach.

Écoutons un lecteur prestigieux du roman, Jacques Lacan : « Du ravissement — ce mot nous fait énigme. Est-il objectif ou subjectif à ce que Lol V. Stein le détermine ? »

« Ravie. On évoque l'âme, et c'est la beauté qui opère. [...] Ravisseuse est bien aussi l'image que va nous imposer cette figure de blessée, exilée des choses, qu'on n'ose pas toucher, mais qui vous fait sa proie. [...] Cet art suggère que la ravisseuse est Marguerite Duras, nous les ravis[4]. »

Ce qu'exhiberait alors ce titre serait la démarche même d'un texte qui à la fois révèle, raconte et met en œuvre la fascination, dite ici « ravissement ».

Ce serait aussi la demande de l'auteur à son lecteur « modèle », cette demande qui se perçoit dans la structure même du roman : « laissez-vous ravir ».

1. « Ce livre devait s'appeler " Enlèvement ". J'ai voulu, dans ravissement, conserver l'équivoque » (*Lettres françaises*, 30 avril-6 mai 1964). *International Herald Tribune* traduit « The Kidnapping of Lol V. Stein », 4 mars 1996 ! (La traduction admise est « The Ravishing of Lol V. Stein ».)

2. Santon provençal, représenté les deux bras ouverts, en extase devant l'Enfant Jésus.

3. Voir *infra*, « Le mot-trou », p. 105.

4. Jacques Lacan, « Hommage fait à Marguerite Duras du *Ravissement de Lol V. Stein* », *Cahiers Renaud-Barrault*, décembre 1963, p. 7.

LE NOM DE LOL

Quant au nom propre qui « détermine » (au sens grammatical) ce ravissement, il accentue encore son caractère énigmatique. Il se prête aux jeux verbaux et s'offre au « délire[1] » des interprétations. Ce nom semble créé pour donner des « ailes » à l'imagination.

Lol : prénom réversible, où s'amorce le « mouvement symétrique et inverse » dont nous verrons qu'il est la dynamique même du texte.

Au centre, un 0 — zéro ? — symbole du néant, du « rien » au cœur de Lol, encadré de deux L / ailes. Lol, « en allée loin de vous et de l'instant » (p. 13), s'envole autour de ce vide central : « si constamment envolée de sa vie vivante » (p. 166). Équivalent spatial du personnage, le Casino[2] « au centre de T. Beach, d'une blancheur de lait, immense oiseau posé, ses *deux ailes* régulières bordées de balustrades... » (p. 176). Lol, prénom symétrique, clos sur lui-même, évoque aussi la forme à trois termes du triangle[3].

Lol, nous dira-t-on, n'était jamais tout à fait là (p. 13). Dans le roman, elle revient à elle, parfois, et se nomme « Lola », son prénom d'enfance, peut-être, car Tatiana l'appelle ainsi quand elle la retrouve (p. 74). « Lola » est un diminutif espagnol de Dolorès, dont le sens, tacite (« douleurs »), n'est pas non plus indifférent.

Le « a » (marque d'hispanité, mais plus encore de féminité, en français aussi) est soustrait — ravi ? — du prénom. Voilà Lol qui « rime avec fol [...] amputée de son fémi-

1. Terme à prendre ici « littéralement et dans tous les sens ».

2. Raynalle Udris propose de lire aussi « Casino », comme « quasi-no » (presque rien), *op. cit.*, p. 169.

3. Voir *infra*, p. 120.

nin[1] » : « il manquait déjà quelque chose à Lol pour être — elle dit : là. [...] C'était peut-être en effet le cœur de Lol V. Stein qui n'était pas — elle dit : là » (p. 12-13).

O : « l » suivi de « o » : « l'eau », mais avec une ouverture : dans le prénom, le « o » n'est pas fermé ; l'eau fuit, échappe à toute prise : « au collège, on se la disputait bien qu'elle vous fuît dans les mains comme l'eau » (p. 13).

1. Mireille Calle-Grüber, « L'amour fou, femme fatale. Marguerite Duras », in *L'Icosathèque*, Minard, *Revue des lettres modernes*, n°s 94-99, 1964, p. 38.

V., OU LE NOM CACHÉ DE VALÉRIE

V : initiale de Valérie. Jacques Hold décline le nom complet de Lol, comme un signe de connivence, la première fois où il se trouve seul avec Lol : « Lola Valérie Stein. » Elle répond « Oui » (p. 113). Dans le reste du roman, le prénom de Valérie reste caché : un blanc dans le nom de Lol. Et son nom mutilé est celui qu'elle choisit de « se donn[er] » (p. 189).

Pourtant, ce prénom secret de Valérie établit une continuité dans l'œuvre durassienne, en créant des liens avec *L'après-midi de Monsieur Andesmas*, roman paru juste un an avant le *Ravissement*, en 1962. Lol, grâce à ce nom, trouve une sœur intertextuelle dans la très blonde[2] Valérie Andesmas, l'absente du roman, la ravisseuse de Michel Arc, l'abandonneuse de Monsieur Andesmas, son père impotent qui l'attend en vain, tout un long après-midi sur une terrasse.

Mais un point isole le V initial, mutile Valérie, donne au nom ainsi formé un air américain, tout en y installant, de manière redondante, le vide et l'absence.

2. La blondeur extrême éblouit et rend presque invisible.

Ce *V.* fonctionne aussi en continuité (alphabétique) avec les autres initiales qui jalonnent le texte, marquant ses lieux : *S.* (Tahla), *T.* (Beach), *U.* (Bridge), Lol *V.* Stein. Comme si c'était à Lol que conduisait ce chemin tracé par les noms confondus des lieux et des personnages, ainsi qu'à la fin d'*Hiroshima mon amour* :

« Elle. Hi-ro-shi-ma. C'est ton nom.

« Lui. C'est mon nom, oui [...]. Ton nom à toi est Nevers. Ne-vers-en-Fran-ce » (*H.*, p. 124).

Ou dans la préface de *Savannah Bay* : « Savannah Bay, c'est toi » (*S.B.*, p. 7).

LE NOM DE STEIN

STEIN : La consonance allemande du nom contraste avec le prénom espagnol et les noms anglais des lieux et du personnage de Michael Richardson, mais s'accorde avec le nom de Tatiana Karl, son double textuel.

Peut-on jouer aux anagrammes ? STEIN : NI EST. Négation de l'être. Lol n'est pas... Dénégation : nier ? SI NET : Lol est une obsédée de l'ordre. SINTE : (sainte Lol !) mais non sans une faute.

Si le nom de Lol est étrange, on ne peut que trouver plus étrange encore qu'elle porte, systématiquement répété dans le *Ravissement*, le nom de Stein. Nom de son père, conservé, à l'encontre de la coutume sociale (son mari se nomme Jean Bedford) et contre la coutume de l'univers durassien

(Anne Desbaresdes, Claire Lannes, Anne-Marie Stretter portent le nom de leur mari)[1].

Il est tentant de signaler ici, à propos du « nom du père », que Marguerite Duras a rejeté, elle, le nom paternel de Donnadieu, qu'elle tient, écrit-elle, « en horreur » (*P.*, p. 23). Il n'est pas question de donner une explication biographique (tentante ici, pourtant), mais seulement de montrer à quel point le nom de Stein ouvre une inépuisable réserve de sens.

1. Dans le *Ravissement*, Lol n'est pas seule à conserver le nom du père. Tatiana, son amie, reste toujours « Tatiana Karl » et n'est jamais désignée par le nom de son mari « Beugner ».

Stein est aussi un nom propre récurrent dans les textes durassiens après le *Ravissement*. Nom germanique, certes, mais surtout nom associé, dans l'univers durassien, à la judéité. Peu importe que cela soit vrai ou non dans le monde extérieur. Les linguistes disent que les noms propres n'ont pas de signifié, qu'ils désignent seulement et identifient. Au contraire, chez Duras, les noms « ne nomme[nt] pas » (p. 113), et n'identifient pas non plus, mais ils entrent dans un réseau de significations.

Par son nom de Stein, Lol inaugure une longue lignée durassienne de Juifs, du Stein de *Détruire, dit-elle* à Aurélia Steiner, personnage éponyme de trois films, et à Yann Andréa « Steiner ».

Le Juif, explicitement présent dans l'œuvre de Duras depuis *Détruire, dit-elle* (1969) et *Abahn Sabana David* (1970), est une figure symbolique porteuse de la douleur et des horreurs de notre époque. « Dans ma vie, déclare Marguerite Duras, il y a d'abord l'enfance, puis l'adolescence [...] Et puis tout à coup, sans prévenir, comme la foudre, les Juifs. Pas d'âge adulte : les Juifs massacrés. 1944. [...] Le peuplement de mes livres est juif [...]. Mais les Juifs de mes romans, de mes films, ils se taisent comme moi » (*Le monde extérieur, Outside*, p. 30-31).

Certes, la dimension juive de Lol V. Stein est discrète, silencieuse, justement, et ne pouvait guère se percevoir au moment de la parution du roman.

« — Lol V. Stein, juive.

« — Oui, juive, je crois. Je crois que je ne me pose pas la question dans le livre. Le vice-consul aussi était juif », écrit M. Duras en 1980 (*Y. V.*, p. 76).

Mais la dimension judaïque des personnages durassiens, qui prendra une importance essentielle dans la suite de l'œuvre, reste encore, dans le *Ravissement*, une virtualité en suspens. *Le ravissement de Lol V. Stein* serait alors un prélude à cette « musique sur le nom de Stein » dont l'arrivée foudroyante est annoncée aux derniers mots de *Détruire, dit-elle* (*D.d.*, p. 123).

PIERRE

Il faut aussi traduire le mot étranger : STEIN = PIERRE. Ce nom semble relier Lol à Pierre Beugner, mari de Tatiana, avec lequel pourtant elle n'a, semble-t-il, de relation que mondaine. Mais, au-delà de la clôture du roman, ce nom établit des corrélations.

Avec les romans antérieurs : Pierre, mari volage de Maria, et amant de son amie Claire, dans *Dix heures et demie du soir en été*. Avec des textes postérieurs : « Peter » Morgan, l'écrivain du *Vice-consul* [1], « Pierre » Lannes, mari de Claire, la meurtrière de *L'amante anglaise*.

Mais bien plus essentiel apparaît un autre écho, explicité en 1991 seulement, par

1. Cf. *supra*, p. 17.

L'amant de la Chine du Nord. Pierre se révèle avoir été le nom du « frère aîné », déjà doté, dans *L'amant*, d'une dimension criminelle : « l'assassin de la nuit du chasseur » (*A.*, p. 67)[1]. La révélation de ce prénom ouvre une relecture de bien des textes antérieurs.

PIERRE : ce mot n'est pas seulement un nom propre. Son signifié ouvre aussi sur un réseau significatif dans les textes durassiens, où se profile le danger de la pétrification[2]. Désir impossible : « Comme toi j'ai désiré avoir une inconsolable mémoire, une mémoire d'ombres et de pierre », dit la Française d'*Hiroshima* à son amant japonais. C'est bien aussi cette « mémoire de pierre » que cherchent les textes de Duras à propos de l'Holocauste. Mais ils ne peuvent s'écrire que sur « la mémoire de l'oubli[3] ».

Ainsi, dans le nom même de Lol se mêlent et se contrarient des références indirectes à deux éléments de nature opposée, l'eau et la pierre. Ce qui peut suggérer déjà son être contradictoire.

Il serait présomptueux et absurde d'attacher à ces jeux du signifiant des significations trop précises et définies, de leur assigner des enjeux de vérité. Mais il est essentiel de les faire jouer et de montrer ainsi comment se construit la complexité d'une œuvre et même d'un livre : tressages, tissages, réseaux subtils. Le *Ravissement* ouvre bien pour nous l'espace du rêve, et débouche sur des lectures « illimitées[4] ».

1. Allusion au film de Charles Laughton, *La nuit du chasseur* (voir *Y.V.*, p. 60). « Chasseur » qualifie les deux frères.

2. Voir Madeleine Borgomano, *Une lecture des fantasmes*, Cistre, 1985, p. 84 *sq.*

3. *Marguerite Duras à Montréal*, *op. cit.*, p. 41.

4. Expression empruntée à un titre durassien, *Agatha ou les Lectures illimitées.*

2. INCIPIT

Après le titre, le commencement du livre — premiers mots, premières pages — est un autre seuil essentiel. Il permet au lecteur d'entrer dans le « monde » du roman, un monde qui, pour ressembler, bien sûr, au monde extérieur, n'en est pas moins un univers fictif très autonome dont les éléments n'ont aucune existence avant les premières phrases, ou incipit.

De plus, cet incipit offre souvent des règles, un code pour le déchiffrement du texte qui va suivre, un peu comme l'ouverture d'un opéra en annonce les motifs et les tonalités.

UNE FICHE D'IDENTITÉ ?

Le premier paragraphe du *Ravissement* paraît d'abord extrêmement simple. Il présente une fiche d'identité du personnage éponyme : localisation, origines, famille. Fiche sèche, comme celle qu'on remplit en entrant dans un pays étranger, ou celle établie sur un « cas » médical.

Les renseignements très ordinaires donnés sur le personnage semblent annoncer un roman classique, voire même « réaliste », situer le personnage en répondant aux questions : qui ? quand ? où ? Mais ils sont livrés avec un peu trop de concision et de sécheresse.

Le texte est au passé composé (temps du présent) et au présent. Si ces « temps » sont bien ceux d'une fiche, ils ne sont pas ceux du roman réaliste, qui, généralement, éloigne et ordonne les événements dans un récit au passé simple.

« DIT-IL », OU LE ROMAN COMME DISCOURS DU NARRATEUR

Ce présent est associé à l'acte de narration : présent de l'énonciation, moment où le narrateur, désigné encore uniquement par « je », raconte l'histoire. À la différence du roman réaliste, le narrateur, ici, au lieu de s'effacer, se déclare dès les premiers mots, et se pose aussi comme personnage, en disant « Elle a un frère [...] je ne l'ai jamais vu... » (p. 11).

Il joue donc d'emblée ce double rôle que signale, tout en le masquant, l'emploi du « je ». Il est, en même temps, le sujet du verbe « raconter » (et, par là, il se situe dans un monde qui englobe le monde de l'« histoire », un autre monde), et le sujet des verbes d'action (ici « voir » ou plutôt « ne pas voir ») qui le situent aussi dans le monde des personnages dont il parle.

Position double, et dominante, à ne jamais perdre de vue en lisant le roman. Devant tout ce que dit le narrateur, il s'agit de toujours rétablir un présupposé : « moi, narrateur, je dis que... ». Tout ce qui est raconté devient alors subordonné à cette parole, dépendant totalement d'elle. Rien n'est donné comme « vérité », tout n'est qu'opinion. Non pas de l'auteur, qui ne prend jamais directement la parole, mais du narrateur même.

En conséquence, le lecteur n'accède jamais à Lol qu'à travers cette parole, ce filtre (ou « philtre » peut-être aussi bien). Cette constatation relativise aussitôt toute interprétation : le « cas » Lol ne nous est, après tout, accessible qu'à travers ce que choisit d'en dire le narrateur, et selon sa perspective. Ce qui rejoint l'une des constantes de l'écriture durassienne, la répétition de la formule du discours, qui se manifestera très ouvertement dans le titre « Détruire, dit-elle ». Mais, dans le *Ravissement*, ce serait « Lol, dit-il ».

UN NARRATEUR IGNORANT

Ce narrateur est d'abord sujet de verbes négatifs : le frère de Lol, il ne l'a jamais vu ; sur l'enfance, il n'a rien entendu dire. Il détient un pouvoir sur le discours et peut construire à son gré le personnage, mais il se présente cependant comme essentiellement ignorant. « Je parle de Lol », dit-il, mais « sur Lol je ne sais rien ». Cette position paradoxale est une des clés du roman.

Le monde que met en place cet étrange narrateur est constitué d'un seul personnage présent, actuel, Lol V. Stein, auquel vient ensuite s'ajouter Tatiana Karl, « sa meilleure amie ». Les autres personnages évoqués sont morts ou absents : le père, le frère, les parents. La fiche établit alors une curieuse identité, percée de trous, « une identité de nature indécise qui pourrait se nommer de noms indéfiniment différents... » (p. 41).

Après lecture, même superficielle, du roman, cette fiche apparaît comme plus étrange encore. En effet, ni du père ni du frère il ne sera plus jamais question. Ces mentions deviennent alors très problématiques, car elles contreviennent à une règle du langage romanesque : les détails mentionnés devraient, pour correspondre aux attentes du lecteur ordinaire, avoir une nécessité dans le récit, se trouver au moins liés à d'autres.

Bien sûr, la mention de la profession du père peut se trouver justifiée dans le cadre d'une interprétation sociocritique du texte[1].

Par contre, le frère ne sert vraiment à rien (fonctionnellement), sinon peut-être à établir des liens, très discrets, entre Lol et d'autres héroïnes durassiennes, passées, comme Suzanne, du *Barrage*, ou futures, comme Agatha, et avec Duras elle-même.

Les informations données sur le personnage ne sont donc qu'en apparence créatrices d'une illusion de réalité. Minées par l'ignorance avouée du narrateur, elles sont en fait sans aucune consistance. Qui ? Une femme dotée d'un nom étrange et composite. Quand ? On ne sait, la seule référence étant la coïncidence entre le moment de la vie du personnage et celui du récit par le narrateur. Où ? S. Tahla ne se trouve sur aucune carte. C'est le nom d'une ville imaginaire[2].

1. Voir « Lol et les autres », *infra*, p. 82 *sq*.

2. Voir *infra*, p. 63.

« JE CHERCHE QUI EST CETTE FEMME[3] »

3. *L'amante anglaise*, p. 62.

La fiche inaugurale est le véritable incipit. Mais il est possible de donner à ce terme une plus grande extension et de prendre en compte l'ensemble du premier « chapitre ».

Le terme « chapitre » n'est qu'une commodité. Le roman n'est pas vraiment découpé en chapitres, seulement en segments séparés par des blancs. Des ruptures nettes apparaissent pourtant, chaque fois qu'un segment commence au milieu de la page, découpant dix-huit unités irrégulières, que je nommerai chapitres (faute de mieux !) (p. 11, 23, 32, 37, 52, 58, 67, 75, 88, 111, 120, 122, 127, 141, 162, 165, 183, 187). Mais d'autres blancs introduisent des subdivisions secondaires, « séquences » (unités nommables du récit : le bal, la rencontre, le voyage).

Le premier « chapitre » (p. 11-22) serait alors découpé par les blancs en trois « séquences » : le passé de Lol, les hésitations du narrateur, le bal de T. Beach.

« J'INVENTE »

La séquence centrale (p. 12-13) est particulièrement importante, en ce qu'elle révèle le rôle et la position du narrateur, toujours aussi anonyme et indéfini, mais masculin.

Il est le sujet d'une volonté forte, qui va animer le roman tout entier : celle de « connaître » Lol V. Stein, sur laquelle il mène une véritable enquête. Le roman n'est donc pas donné comme l'histoire de Lol, mais comme l'histoire d'une enquête sur Lol.

Le *Ravissement* s'insère par là dans une forme privilégiée du roman moderne, qui a souvent substitué l'enquête à la quête, héritée de l'épopée et du conte, que racontait le roman « classique ».

Les dix-neuf années précédentes, « je ne *veux* pas les connaître », « je *vais* [...] *chercher* [Lol], je la *prends* » (terme qu'il ne faudra pas oublier) « là où je crois *devoir* le faire » (p. 14) : le désir qui entraîne le récit est d'abord celui du narrateur.

Mais d'un narrateur qui multiplie les marques de son ignorance. Négations, interrogations, médiations : les informations sur Lol résultent des dires de Tatiana, témoin incertain : Tatiana « ne croit pas », « aurait tendance à croire », « croyait » : ses déclarations se situent sur le plan de la croyance, de l'opinion, pas sur le plan du « savoir ». De plus, l'informatrice principale est finalement récusée : « Je ne crois plus à rien de ce que dit Tatiana, je ne suis convaincu de rien », « ce faux-semblant que raconte Tatiana » *(ibid.)*.

Le narrateur, alors, n'a plus qu'à « inventer » : « je raconterai *mon histoire* de Lol V. Stein » *(ibid.)*.

LOL, OU « LE CŒUR INACHEVÉ »

La première séquence évoque quelques traces de la jeunesse de Lol, racontées au narrateur par Tatiana ; la danse dans le préau sur les airs « démodés » d'une « émission-souvenir[1] ».

La seconde séquence raconte les fiançailles de Lol avec le riche et oisif Michael Richardson et la « folle passion » qu'elle lui portait. En même temps, le narrateur, aidé de Tatiana, tente de construire un portrait de Lol, de lui

1. Cet épisode sera repris, trente ans plus tard, dans *L'amant de la Chine du Nord* : « la petite » danse avec son amie de pension, Hélène Lagonelle.

attribuer des « qualités » qui feraient d'elle un personnage de récit. Mais Lol échappe à ceux qui veulent la « prendre » ou la « comprendre ». Lol n'est « pas pareille » (p. 13). Vue de l'extérieur, elle frappe par son « indifférence », « jamais elle n'avait paru souffrir ou être peinée » (p. 12), et par son « absence ». Tatiana trouve des explications à cet état, pose un diagnostic : « maladie », « crise ». Lol serait, « depuis toujours », une malade.

Mais ce diagnostic est donné par le narrateur comme un « faux-semblant ». Lui, il se refuse à « remonter » dans le passé et récuse, donc, la « différence » originelle : Lol, pour lui, n'est pas « anormale » depuis son enfance. Mais sa « croyance » n'est nullement pure, elle non plus : il choisit de ne percevoir Lol qu'en fonction de lui-même : « je la prends [...] au moment où elle me paraît commencer à bouger pour venir à ma rencontre » (p. 14).

Ainsi Lol reste-t-elle, pour le lecteur aussi, à distance, insaisissable « être de fuite » (comme Albertine pour le narrateur proustien), déclenchant déjà son désir d'interprétation.

3. LE BAL DE T. BEACH

De toute la jeunesse de Lol, seul surnage, élu par le narrateur comme le commencement de l'histoire, là où « [il] croi[t] devoir [la prendre] », « ce fameux bal de T. Beach », susceptible d'avoir joué un « rôle prépondérant [...] dans la maladie de Lol » (p. 14).

UN PASSÉ PAS SI SIMPLE

Le récit, en contraste avec le présent du début, adopte le passé simple du roman classique comme temps de base, temps des actions principales : « Michael Richardson se tourna vers Lol et l'invita à danser pour la dernière fois » (p. 17) ; « Alors elles virent : la femme entrouvrit les lèvres [...], dans la surprise émerveillée de voir le nouveau visage de cet homme... » (p. 18) ; « Lol cria » (p. 22) ; « Lol les suivit des yeux à travers les jardins. Quand elle ne les vit plus, elle tomba par terre, évanouie » *(ibid.)*.

L'emploi du passé simple « suppose un monde construit, élaboré, détaché, réduit à des lignes significatives [...], il est l'expression d'un ordre, et par conséquent d'une euphorie », écrivait Barthes[1].

Dans le cas du bal de T. Beach, les premiers qualificatifs utilisés par Barthes, surtout « détaché », sont parfaitement adaptés. Il y a construction, ou reconstruction, par le narrateur, tentative de mettre de l'ordre. Mais ce n'est qu'une tentative, donnée comme telle et non pas vraiment aboutie : le récit reste plein d'incertitudes, émaillé de points d'interrogation.

---

1. Roland Barthes, *Le degré zéro de l'écriture*, Le Seuil, coll. « Points », p. 26.

Avec ce passé simple, jouent, comme il est grammaticalement normal, les temps de l'imparfait, construisant une sorte de second plan. Le plus-que-parfait domine largement, produisant un effet de recul dans le temps et de reconstitution d'un passé achevé, toujours déjà perdu : « Lol resta toujours là où l'événement l'avait trouvée lorsque Anne-Marie Stretter était entrée, derrière les plantes vertes du bar » (p. 20).

En contraste avec la rapidité sommaire et lacunaire des quatre premières pages, balayant dix-neuf années, le récit (huit pages pour quelques heures) se fait très lent, accordant au bal, contrairement à l'opinion de Tatiana, une importance extrême, en faisant vraiment l'origine de l'histoire de Lol : car il s'agit de l'événement même ici nommé « ravissement ».

Un événement en deux temps : la nuit du bal, puis l'aurore et « la fin ».

LA NUIT, LA DANSE

La nuit du bal est le moment même d'un premier « ravissement ». Elle est découpée comme une scène de théâtre, par l'entrée de deux femmes (la mère et la fille) qui franchissent la porte de la salle de bal (p. 14) et la sortie de la femme la plus âgée avec le fiancé de Lol, par une porte que Lol tente de maintenir fermée (p. 22). Entre-temps, le bal se déroule à huis clos.

Au vide initial : « La piste s'était vidée lentement. Elle fut vide » (p. 15), répond le vide final : « Le bal apparut presque vide » (p. 20). Tout au long de la nuit, ce vide persistera, laissant seuls (semble-t-il), sur la piste illuminée, les deux danseurs éblouis. Dans la salle, derrière les plantes vertes, deux spectatrices fascinées, Lol, la fiancée délaissée et son amie Tatiana.

« Ravissement » : le mot se déploie en significations multiples. Il peut dénommer les deux « coups de foudre » réciproques.

Michael Richardson, « pâli », « devenu différent » (p. 17), invite la femme « dans une émotion si intense qu'on prenait peur à l'idée qu'il aurait pu être éconduit » (p. 18). Silencieux, sourd et aveugle, il est entré dans un « ravissement » de somnambule. La femme, dans sa « surprise émerveillée », « sa gaucherie soudaine », « son expression abêtie », « figée par la rapidité du coup » (p. 18-19), partage ce « ravissement » de la passion soudaine.

La stupeur des nouveaux amants s'inscrit rigoureusement dans le stéréotype du coup de foudre, de l'amour fou, avec comme un écho racinien :

« Je le vis, je rougis, je pâlis à sa vue ;
Un trouble s'éleva dans mon âme éperdue ;
Mes yeux ne voyaient plus, je ne pouvais parler ;
Je sentis tout mon corps et transir et brûler[1]. »

1. Racine, *Phèdre*, I, 3.

Étrangement, le « ravissement » de Lol V. Stein prend la même forme de saisissement extrême : « frappée d'immobilité » (p. 15), sans souffrance, elle « guettait l'événement, couvait son immensité, sa précision d'horlogerie [...] fascinée » (p. 17-18).

Mais cette fascination-là paraît d'un tout autre ordre, même si elle est interprétable, en apparence, comme un traumatisme, un désespoir d'amour. Car le « ravissement de Lol » désigne aussi l'arrachement, l'enlèvement dont elle est la victime. La voici, en effet, dépouillée de ce fiancé qu'elle aimait, disait-on, d'une « folle passion » (p. 13).

L'autre femme : Anne-Marie Stretter

Le « portrait » de Lol, lacunaire, ne retenait que des caractères moraux, tous aussitôt mis en doute. Par contre, Anne-Marie Stretter est décrite exclusivement par ses caractères physiques, son apparence. Son corps, grand et maigre, ses mouvements, sa grâce, ses vêtements, son regard, ses cheveux roux. Les qualificatifs sont élogieux : élégance, grâce, ossature « admirable » (à qui les attribuer ? Le narrateur ne peut que rapporter la rumeur publique, ce que « on » pense). « Était-elle belle ? » (p. 16).

C'est une femme « âgée », accompagnée d'une fille adulte qui lui ressemble. Mais elle est douée de cette qualité que Duras nommera « la splendeur de l'âge[1] ».

Le texte présente cette « voleuse » comme pleine d'assurance : « elle se voulait ainsi faite et vêtue » (p. 15), « une audace pénétrée d'elle-même, semblait-il, seule, la faisait tenir debout » (p. 16). Sa beauté reste incertaine, mais elle possède un intense pouvoir de séduction : au premier regard, elle provoque le « désarroi » de Michael Richardson, son « changement » (p. 17) et le commencement d'une « nouvelle histoire ».

1. Préambule de *Savannah Bay*, à propos de l'actrice Madeleine Renaud.

Une danse macabre ?

Mais, à bien lire la description de cette femme (p. 15-16), apparaissent des traits qui, comme son élégance, « inqui[ètent] » : « charpente [...] dure », « maigreur » où se devine « l'ossature », « grâce [...] ployante

[...] d'oiseau mort », « fourreau » — terme évoquant une arme qui sera repris dans le fantasme de mise à nu : « d'autres seins apparaissent, blancs, sous le fourreau noir » (p. 50). Dans le même registre on peut encore noter : « noir », « non-regard », « décoloration presque pénible de la pupille ». Quelque soupçon se dessine : serait-ce un squelette habillé ? S'agirait-il d'une danse macabre ? Comme pourraient le suggérer encore les « violons, enfermés dans des boîtes funèbres » (p. 21).

Une « femme fatale » ?

Anne-Marie Stretter est donc présentée (même si le terme, comme d'ailleurs celui de « ravissement », reste totalement absent du texte) comme une « femme fatale », autre stéréotype très actif, surtout au cinéma. Et la scène du bal, vue de loin, cadrée par la piste de danse et la lumière, avec sa lenteur cérémonielle, ses acteurs exceptionnels, est semblable à une scène de cinéma.

Mais les éléments macabres du texte suggèrent qu'il faut prendre aussi l'expression « femme fatale » littéralement : celle qui exerce une séduction irrésistible, qui rend « fou » d'amour, mais surtout, celle qui tue, « une donneuse de mort[1] ». Séductrice de Michael Richardson au premier regard, sans l'avoir cherché, elle devient « ravisseuse », et par là « meurtrière » de Lol, presque sans le savoir, semant sur son passage, comme par inadvertance, la folie et une forme de mort[2]. Méduse ? Gorgone ?

1. « La couleur des mots », p. 22. Voir Dossier, p. 158.

2. Hélène Cixous a de très belles formules pour décrire A.M.S. : « C'est une sorte de soleil très noir : au centre il y a la dame, celle qui draine tous les désirs dans tous les livres. De texte en texte, ça s'engouffre, il y a un gouffre. C'est un corps de femme qui ne se connaît pas lui-même, mais qui sait quelque chose dans le noir, qui sait le noir, qui sait la mort » (Hélène Cixous et Michel Foucault, « À propos de Marguerite Duras, *Cahiers Renaud-Barrault*, n° 89, octobre 1975, p. 14).

L'AURORE

Le bal pourtant s'achève, avec « l'aurore », l'arrêt de la musique et le « vide » revenu (p. 20). Le « ravissement » de Lol alors connaît un deuxième temps et prend des significations nouvelles, sur lesquelles le premier récit reste encore peu explicite.

Aucun des trois personnages ne paraît savoir « comment sortir de la nuit » (p. 21). Tous les trois, comme Michael Richardson, semblent « cherch[er] dans la salle quelque signe d'éternité » *(ibid.)*.

« Il aurait fallu murer le bal », rêvera Lol dix ans après (p. 49). Mais déjà son « sourire », s'il avait été vu, aurait pu être un « signe d'éternité » : car Lol ne souffre pas, « la souffrance n'avait pas trouvé en elle où se glisser » (p. 19). Elle veut que continue l'extase de la nuit. Un leurre, en fait, car, si Lol est fascinée par la contemplation du couple, eux l'ignorent, ne la voient pas et ne sont fascinés que l'un par l'autre. Il y a malentendu.

L'arrivée de la mère de Lol, ses cris injurieux, l'intrusion d'un corps étranger brisent l'enchantement, remettent le temps en mouvement, dénoncent aussi le malentendu. Lol crie. De déchirement[1]. Les nouveaux amants sortent en ignorant ses cris et ses gesticulations et Lol, qui alors seulement, quand elle ne les voit plus, se sent totalement exclue, « tomb[e] évanouie » : dernière forme, radicale, du « ravissement », la syncope.

1. Comme criera le vice-consul, chassé du bal.

Déconstruction des stéréotypes

L'histoire du bal pourrait être lue comme une réitération de plusieurs stéréotypes, moules prêts à recevoir une pensée toute faite.

Le mythe de l'amour fou, « inventé » par la littérature occidentale[1], puis galvaudé dans les romans et les chansons « de quatre sous », ne cesse de renaître de ses cendres.

1. Voir Denis de Rougemont, *L'amour et l'Occident.*

Ces « mythes » ne restent pas l'apanage de la paralittérature : ils règlent et ont réglé les comportements de la plupart des gens, et continuent à fournir les repères des « idées reçues » et des jugements de valeur courants.

L'œuvre de Duras s'en alimente volontiers elle aussi, ce qui explique bien des rejets de critiques méprisants.

Mais ces « idées reçues », cette mythologie, elle leur fait subir un traitement décapant, les subvertit et les « déconstruit ». Lol n'est qu'en apparence victime de l'amour fou : en fait, comme nous le verrons, elle vit tout autre chose.

Une déesse ? une sorcière ?

Le stéréotype de la « femme fatale » connaît lui aussi une forme de déconstruction. Non seulement parce qu'il est tiré, nous l'avons vu, plus que dans son usage courant, vers la mort, mais parce que le personnage, très mystérieux, d'Anne-Marie Stretter est doté de caractères qui en font presque une sorte de déesse.

« Elle se voulait ainsi faite et vêtue, et elle l'était à son souhait, irrévocablement » (p. 15-16). Ces mots lui supposent non seulement une position de sujet, mais une autonomie totale : en somme, elle se veut telle qu'elle est, se fait elle-même, comme Dieu. Autocréation réussie : elle est « pleine de grâce[1] ». Le monde extérieur, à part sa fille (qu'elle oublie vite) et Michael Richardson, semble ne pas exister pour elle, son regard est un « non-regard » : elle paraît autosuffisante.

En même temps, il est aussi suggéré qu'elle pourrait être une incarnation de l'ange du mal : elle « portait ces inconvénients comme les emblèmes d'une obscure négation de la nature » (p. 15). Ou encore une forme ambivalente de la « femme éternelle », dangereuse séductrice, et pourtant mère aussi, accompagnée de sa fille, son double.

Elle se trouve encore reliée, par les images du texte, aux éléments naturels, comme les sorcières qu'affectionne Marguerite Duras[2]. Le feu, avec lequel les sorcières pactisent, dit-on, colore sa chevelure : « elle était teinte en roux[3] ». Le feu, ambivalent, menace aussi de la brûler, comme il a brûlé tant de sorcières : n'est-elle pas déjà « brûlée de rousseur » (p. 16) ?

En même temps, et dans la même phrase, elle se trouve associée à l'élément le plus contraire, l'eau, la mer, puisqu'elle est nommée, très poétiquement, « Ève marine ».

Ainsi se voit-elle prise par le texte dans un réseau de traits contradictoires : en pleine « intelligence avec la nature » (comme les sor-

1. Y aurait-il même sacrilège, par évocation discrète de l'*Ave Maria* : « Je vous salue Marie, pleine de grâce » ?

2. Voir, en particulier, *Les lieux*, p. 12-13.

3. Dans *India Song*, la caméra s'attarde longuement sur la perruque rousse d'A. M. S.

cières, dont elle a aussi le pouvoir magique d'attraction), elle la nie pourtant obscurément. Vivante, dans son éclat, elle est aussi habitée par la mort : « Rien ne pouvait plus arriver à cette femme, pensa Tatiana, plus rien, rien. Que sa fin » *(ibid.)*.

Le personnage d'Anne-Marie Stretter est tissé de contradictions. Complexe, fascinant, il est déjà prêt à émigrer vers bien d'autres livres, d'autres films, avant de finir, « tuée » par sa créatrice[1].

1. Marguerite Duras raconte à Xavière Gauthier l'état de deuil où elle se trouvait après la fin du tournage d'*India Song* : « Que j'avais tué A. M. Stretter, qu'elle était morte, cette chose-là les autres s'en sont emparé lorsqu'ils ont vu le film. [...] Quelqu'un a dit ça : elle est comme en deuil depuis trois semaines, elle a tué A. M. S. » (*Marguerite Duras*, Albatros, 1975, p. 76).

Peines d'amour perdues

La déconstruction des stéréotypes se manifeste bien davantage encore dans le comportement de la victime, l'héroïne du roman, Lol.

Lol est « fascinée » (p. 18), « frappée d'immobilité » (p. 15), tout autant que son fiancé. Mais pas de la même manière, et pas du tout selon les modalités convenues. « Fascinée » est un mot à prendre, comme souvent, à la lettre : Lol se trouve dans un état quasi hypnotique, en transe. Or, le « coup de foudre », ce sont les autres qui le vivent, à ses dépens. Sa manière de « guetter l'événement », comme si elle avait été « l'agent même non seulement de sa venue mais de son succès » (p. 18), reste d'abord stupéfiante.

Selon les critères de l'amour-passion, Lol aurait dû éprouver des sentiments, souffrir, mourir peut-être. « Chagrin d'amour dure toute la vie... »

Or Lol, immobile et souriante, ne souffre pas, ne paraît pas souffrir, pendant le bal, de la trahison de son fiancé : « cette vision [...] ne par[ut] pas s'accompagner chez Lol de souffrance » (p. 17).

Le texte insiste sur cette réaction incroyable et incompréhensible. C'est seulement quand elle voit se dessiner « la fin » que Lol paraît retrouver un comportement « normal », ou, du moins, attendu.

L'« étrange omission de la douleur » (p. 24) est au cœur du « cas » de Lol, au cœur de son mystère aussi et des interprétations qu'il suscite. C'est par là qu'elle fascine Jacques Hold et c'est pour tenter de capter le secret de Lol qu'il entreprend son récit. Mais c'est aussi par cette étrangeté qu'au-delà de son histoire, elle fascine les lecteurs.

UN POINT DE VUE EXTERNE ET DISTANT

Cependant, il ne faudrait pas perdre de vue le caractère relatif et incertain de ce récit et des images proposées pour l'« événement » du bal.

Le bal est raconté par un narrateur qui n'en a pas été témoin et qui fait appel, comme informateur principal, à Tatiana, seule spectatrice du bal, qui « n'avait pas quitté Lol » et se trouvait à côté d'elle, derrière les plantes vertes.

Tatiana a vu ce qu'a vu Lol. Mais certainement pas de la même manière. De plus, le récit est fait par Tatiana au narrateur dix ans après l'événement. Ses interprétations ne sont que des reconstructions d'un souvenir, des suppositions.

À maintes reprises, le narrateur rappelle cette médiation : « pense Tatiana » (p. 16), « Tatiana l'avait trouvé pâli », « Tatiana la trouva elle-même changée » (p. 17), « Tatiana l'avait [...] vu agir avec sa nouvelle façon » (p. 18), « Tatiana avait compris » (p. 19). Tout repose donc sur ce témoignage unique et contestable, auquel doit se fier le narrateur, bien qu'il le récuse avant même de le rapporter : « Je ne crois plus à rien de ce que dit Tatiana » (p. 14).

Ces couches intermédiaires de subjectivité signalent ouvertement l'impossible accès à un « réel », même fictif. Le roman ne permet jamais au lecteur, du moins au lecteur attentif aux signes du texte, de s'abandonner à l'« illusion de réalité ». Même si, dans le récit du bal, le « je » du narrateur s'est provisoirement effacé, il reste à l'arrière-plan. Et ce « dit-il » implique un « croit-il » : le narrateur, sujet du discours, est aussi le sujet du point de vue dominant.

Les trois personnages principaux, eux, sont résolument et exclusivement perçus de l'extérieur. Lol était physiquement proche de Tatiana ; mais elle lui était toujours restée très incompréhensible (dit-elle). Et, durant le bal, avant le cri, elle ne parle jamais et ne manifeste rien.

Michael Richardson n'était guère connu de Tatiana et, au bal, elle ne le voit que de loin. Anne-Marie Stretter est plus lointaine encore : une apparition, certes, qu'elle regarde intensément. Mais une totale inconnue, dont elle ne s'approche jamais.

De ces effets de distance il résulte que le récit du bal est un récit hypothétique, incertain et que les personnages, perçus de l'extérieur et de loin, restent parfaitement opaques. Cette opacité fascine : tous les pouvoirs du roman découlent de cette réalité insaisissable, qui agit sur le lecteur comme Lol sur son entourage : « on se la disputait bien qu'elle vous fuît dans les mains comme l'eau parce que le peu que vous reteniez d'elle valait la peine de l'effort » (p. 13). Cette phrase sur le caractère évasif de Lol pourrait s'appliquer aussi bien au texte de ce roman « si mystérieux parce qu'il est irréductible »[1].

1. Maurice Blanchot, « La communauté des amants » (à propos de *La maladie de la mort*), in *La communauté inavouable*, éd. de Minuit, 1983, p. 49.

III UNE CONSTRUCTION COMPLEXE

La construction du *Ravissement* est complexe : plusieurs structures se superposent, coexistent et parfois se contrarient. Le roman peut donc être lu à différents niveaux, ce qui amène à lui reconnaître des sens pluriels, souvent indécidables : il n'est en rien « monologique ».

Pour découvrir la construction d'un roman (à défaut de sa « structure », terme trop ambitieux car il implique la prise en compte de toutes les relations entre les éléments d'un texte, sans exception), une méthode différentielle, inspirée des analyses structurales, paraît irremplaçable. Elle part des points de changement, d'articulation du texte, de ses ruptures.

---

1. L'INTRUSION DU NARRATEUR DANS L'HISTOIRE

L'incipit du *Ravissement* nous invite à considérer le discours du narrateur, sans cesse ramené au premier plan, comme essentiel pour la construction du sens (fût-il insaisissable) dans ce texte. Aussi est-ce au niveau de la narration que se manifeste la plus importante rupture dans le texte.

Les sept premiers « chapitres » du *Ravissement* (p. 11-75) se déroulent selon les codes perceptibles dès les premières pages : présence permanente et explicite du narrateur, mais seulement au niveau du discours, comme une voix sans identité et sans visage ; incertitudes et hésitations de son discours : le narrateur ne « sait » rien ; il mène une enquête et instaure, entre lui et Lol, une série de relais ou de médiations : Tatiana, la mère de Lol, son mari Jean Bedford, la gouvernante, et sa propre imagination. Le texte, au présent quand il s'agit du discours (comme il se doit), est au passé simple quand il devient récit.

Le personnage principal, et presque unique, de ce roman est Lol V. Stein. Le narrateur reconstitue son histoire de façon globalement chronologique.

Mais au début du huitième chapitre (p. 75), la situation du narrateur change brusquement. Cette transformation est annoncée aux derniers mots du chapitre précédent : « Tatiana présente à Lol Pierre Beugner, son mari, et Jacques Hold, un de leurs amis, la distance est couverte, moi » (p. 74). Ce « moi » (« nom propre du locuteur[1] ») introduit le narrateur dans le monde des personnages. Au lieu de rester une voix abstraite et anonyme, il joue alors deux rôles très différents dans le récit, dont il devient à la fois producteur et acteur.

1. Benveniste, *Problèmes de linguistique générale*, t. II, « L'antonyme et le pronom en français moderne », Gallimard, coll. « Tel », p. 200.

En tant que personnage, il acquiert une identité : un nom, un métier : médecin, un passé et une relation avec les autres personnages : « Je suis l'amant de Tatiana Karl » (p. 75).

Les premiers mots du huitième chapitre entrent aussi en corrélation avec l'incipit du roman, la « fiche » de Lol. Ils offrent au lecteur une fiche d'identité semblable et aussi sèche qui le renseigne sur Jacques Hold. Cette fiche d'identité diffère de celle de Lol par la première personne, et par la présence d'une donnée « en trop » : « Je suis l'amant de Tatiana Karl. » Une information aussi privée sur la vie intime est généralement tenue secrète. Mais cette relation adultère va être essentielle pour l'intrigue, en définissant la position de Jacques Hold dans les divers « triangles ». La fiche se trouve ainsi donnée comme un élément du matériel romanesque, une façon un peu désinvolte de présenter rapidement le « personnel du roman ».

En répétant, avec des variations, le début du roman, ce passage coupe le récit en deux parties : avant et après la rencontre de Lol et de Jacques Hold. La narration, elle, reste continue (car il est évident que Jacques Hold a déjà rencontré Lol quand il commence à raconter son histoire).

Cependant, la narration change de modalité : le passé simple disparaît. Le récit est fait, à partir de là, au présent et parfois au passé composé, qui reste un temps du présent.

Le présent (devenu aussi banal dans le roman actuel que le passé simple dans le roman classique) produit cependant une tout autre impression. Comme si les faits et leur narration étaient simultanés, simultanéité qui ne peut être que fictionnelle. Et même, comme s'ils étaient contemporains du moment de la lecture, sans cesse inachevés, offrant ainsi une place encore vide au lecteur. « Le présent dans lequel advient l'action devient un territoire extrêmement instable suspendu entre des moments du temps, des points de l'espace et aussi entre les frontières psychologiques sûres[1]. »

---

1. Michael Sheringham, « Knowledge and Repetition in *Le ravissement de Lol V. Stein* », p. 124 (ma traduction).

Dans le *Ravissement*, le présent s'accorde aussi avec cette affirmation du narrateur, restée assez étrange : « la présence de son adolescence dans cette histoire risquerait d'atténuer un peu aux yeux du lecteur *l'écrasante actualité* de cette femme dans ma vie » (p. 14).

À partir du moment où Jacques Hold entre dans l'histoire de Lol, il tend à « abandonner la position de narrateur comme sujet de la connaissance » pour acquérir « la position de protagoniste comme sujet du désir[2] ».

2. Michael Sheringham, *op. cit.*, p. 134.

Ainsi le roman est-il d'abord découpé et structuré par sa narration même, jeu de construction destiné aux « yeux du lecteur ».

2. LE TEXTE TRAVERSÉ

UNE IDENTITÉ RÉPÉTÉE

Il faut pourtant nuancer et relativiser ce découpage trop simple, en deux « parties » : rien, dans le *Ravissement*, n'est jamais simple.

Le lecteur retrouve, avec surprise, la fiche d'identité de Lol qui ouvrait le roman, répétée, mot pour mot, pendant le récit de la première réception que donne Lol, le soir, chez elle (p. 102). La fiche fait intrusion en plein cœur d'une conversation qu'elle vient interrompre, on ne sait pas pourquoi. Une information s'y trouve ajoutée qui concerne le frère absent de Lol : « il vit à Paris, elle ne parle pas de ce seul parent ». Alors pourquoi le texte en parle-t-il ? Y aurait-il un lien avec les « oiseaux sauvages de sa vie » (p. 145) qui parfois traversent Lol ? Comme Lol, « sous le coup », le texte « s'immobilise » un instant, « travers[é] de part en part[1] ». Mais, après ce trou étrange, le texte se referme aussitôt et continue son cours.

1. Voir M. Borgomano, *Une lecture des fantasmes*, « Les oiseaux menaient loin... », p. 15 *sq.*

Dans ce « frère » et ces « oiseaux », aussi curieusement inutiles et inexplicables dans le récit, il est possible de reconnaître ce que Charles Mauron nommait « métaphores obsédantes[2] » et que Pierre Glaudes appelle « scrupules, si l'on veut bien conserver à ce mot son sens étymologique : petite pierre pointue qui gêne la marche »[3].

Par ces « scrupules » se manifesterait la présence souterraine de ce que les psychanalystes désignent comme une « autre scène », celle où se jouent les désirs et les pulsions de l'inconscient. Une lecture, « flot-

2. Charles Mauron, *Des métaphores obsédantes aux mythes personnels*, José Corti, 1962.

3. Pierre Glaudes, « Le contre-texte », in *Littérature*, n° 90, mai 1990, Larousse, p. 88.

tante » comme l'attention requise des analystes, permet alors de repérer ces « trous » dans le signifiant des textes et de découvrir des fantasmes récurrents[1].

1. Voir définition, *infra*, p. 58-59.

Mais cette lecture, passionnante, porte nécessairement sur l'ensemble d'une œuvre et non sur un seul texte. Elle reste aussi très dépendante de la subjectivité du critique et ne peut avoir de valeur que relative.

JACQUES HOLD, LE RAVISSEUR

Revenons à notre premier découpage que confirment d'autres indices, d'autres échos du texte. À cette phrase du début : « Je vais [...] la chercher, je la prends, là où je crois devoir le faire, au moment où elle me paraît commencer à bouger pour venir à ma rencontre... » (p. 14) répond : « la distance est couverte » (p. 74). Ainsi se trouve confirmée la prétention du narrateur : toute l'histoire de Lol depuis le bal, il la conçoit comme orientée vers lui, par lui. C'est lui, en somme, qui lui donne un sens, et d'abord littéralement : en tout cas, c'est ce qu'il dit, et il est le seul à détenir la parole.

Son nom, alors, devient significatif. Jacques Hold, prénom français, nom anglais. *To hold* ne se traduit-il par « tenir », « détenir », « se saisir de », écho, encore, à « je la prends » ? Cette prise pouvant devenir piège : « Mes mains deviennent le piège dans lequel l'immobiliser... » (p. 107). Jacques Hold, qui croit « tenir » l'histoire en la racontant (nonobstant l'aveu de son ignorance), l'empêcher, en somme, de devenir « illimitée ». Jacques, qui croit se saisir de Lol, « ravisseur » lui aussi ? ou désirant l'être.

Mais le rapport de Jacques Hold avec l'histoire de Lol n'est pas si simple. Le terme « contaminé » pourrait rendre compte de l'effet-retour de l'histoire et de son personnage, Lol, sur son narrateur même.

Si Jacques Hold « prend », Lol, elle aussi, « veut » et « prend » :

« Je suis dans la nuit de T. Beach. C'est fait[1]. Là, on ne donne rien à Lol V. Stein. Elle prend. J'ai encore envie de fuir.

« — Mais qu'est-ce que vous voulez ?

« Elle ne sait pas.

« — Je veux, dit-elle » (p. 112).

Deux désirs s'affrontent ou se conjuguent alors dans l'« histoire[2] » : celui du narrateur qui veut reconstituer le cheminement de Lol, s'approcher d'elle et la prendre ; celui de Lol qui veut, d'une « volonté farouche » (p. 71).

Mais que veut-elle ? « Voir » (p. 105), « revoir » (p. 174), être « remplacée » (p. 50) dans « l'éviction souhaitée de sa propre personne » (p. 124)[3] ?

Si insaisissable que soit le désir de Lol, il finit par entraîner Jacques Hold dans son orbite, jusqu'à « une complète identification avec la position de Lol[4] ». Ce qui l'amène à une sorte de dédoublement, de détachement de lui-même, où, sans cesser d'employer le « je » en tant que narrateur, il se désigne à la troisième personne comme personnage : « Je me souviens : l'homme vient tandis qu'elle s'occupe de sa chevelure... » (p. 65).

Par ce passage à la troisième personne — la non-personne, selon Benveniste, « l'absent »,

1. Dans d'autres romans de Duras, et déjà dans *Moderato cantabile*, cette formule signifie « faire l'amour », ou plutôt toujours déjà l'avoir fait.

2. « L'histoire » : terme que Duras emploie de façon insistante dans la présentation de la quatrième page de couverture.

3. Voir *infra*, p. 115 *sq*.

4. Raynalle Udris, *Welcome Unreason*, *op. cit.*, p. 46.

selon les grammairiens arabes —, Jacques Hold s'anéantit lui-même comme sujet du discours, donc de la narration.

3. DES RÉPÉTITIONS STRUCTURANTES / DÉSTRUCTURANTES

L'articulation capitale du roman est donc marquée par une répétition formelle (la forme de la fiche), mais elle se situe surtout au niveau de l'énonciation. D'autres répétitions, parfois textuelles, mais surtout narratives (des scènes, des situations), se superposent et articulent d'autres niveaux d'une construction plus musicale que narrative.

LE BAL RECOMMENCÉ

Le bal constitue le premier « leitmotiv » du roman, toujours aussi insaisissable : « reconstitution » (p. 46) de Lol reconstituée par Jacques Hold. Impossible, pour l'une comme pour l'autre, éternellement inachevée, « sans fin » (p. 155).

Des échos du bal résonnent aussi dans le texte : la danse des collégiennes dans le préau (p. 85), celle des invités à la soirée de Lol (p. 153 *sq.*).

Le bal — selon Jacques Hold — « tremblait au loin, ancien, seule épave d'un océan maintenant tranquille » (p. 45). Il « reprend un peu de vie » au cours de l'errance de Lol dans les rues de S. Tahla. Dans des pages essentielles (p. 46-51), le narrateur tente d'approcher le désir de Lol, en reconstruisant le bal et sa fin fantasmée par Lol.

Après la station de Lol dans le champ de seigle, « la lumière du bal s'est cassée d'un seul coup » (p. 67). Cette « lumière » — à la fois réelle, le bal est un « navire de lumière » (p. 49), et métaphorique — reparaît quand Lol rend visite à Tatiana. Le bal resurgit alors sous la forme d'un mot, un peu magique, répété par Tatiana elle-même : « ce bal, ce bal, la folle, l'aimait-elle toujours ? Oui » (p. 73).

Lors de la soirée chez les Bedford, le bal est évoqué dans la conversation entre Tatiana et Lol, encore par Tatiana : « Ce bal ! Oh ! Lol, ce bal ! » (p. 98), « Ce bal a été aussi celui de Tatiana » (p. 100). C'est la seule occasion où le bal apparaît dans un discours rapporté et non dans une reconstruction indirecte.

Quand il la rencontre dans un salon de thé (p. 129-140), Jacques Hold répète à Lol le récit de Tatiana qui, dans la chambre de l'Hôtel des Bois, lui a raconté encore une fois « avec beaucoup de détails » le bal « où Lol, dit-on, a perdu la raison » (p. 135).

Dans le train qui emmène Lol et Jacques Hold à T. Beach, le bal revient encore, au futur, cette fois : « Le bal sera au bout du voyage, il tombera comme château de cartes comme en ce moment le voyage lui-même. Elle revoit sa mémoire-ci pour la dernière fois de sa vie, elle l'enterre » (p. 175).

À T. Beach, en compagnie de Jacques Hold, Lol descend vers le Casino du bal, y entre, rit de ne pas trouver ce qu'elle cherchait (p. 179), même dans la salle du bal. Jacques Hold, essayant « d'accorder [...] [s]on regard au sien », commence à se « souvenir, à chaque seconde davantage, de son souvenir » (p. 180). Dans l'hallucination d'une fusion avec Lol, il croit voir directement le bal. Pourtant, il constate aussi : « Aucune trace, aucune, tout a été enseveli » (p. 181). Ainsi le bal de T. Beach, son premier temps de jouissance extasiée pendant la danse, se voit annulé, vidé de sa substance par ce retour dans son lieu même.

Il ne reste plus alors qu'à « inventer » « la fin sans fin, le commencement sans fin de Lol V. Stein » (p. 184). Et cette fin indéfinie se noue dans une scène imaginaire, rêve diurne de Lol.

LE CHAMP DE SEIGLE : MISE EN SCÈNE DU FANTASME

La scène du champ de seigle, comme celle du bal, se répète dans le texte et contribue à le structurer.

D'abord racontée par Lol elle-même à Jacques Hold (p. 115), elle est revécue à plusieurs reprises par Lol, avec la complicité de Jacques Hold qui assure à Lol une sorte de présence fantomatique dans la chambre même (p. 120, 125). Elle est ensuite racontée en détail à Lol par Jacques Hold (p. 131) ; puis revécue encore (p. 132), imitée (imparfaitement) ensuite par la scène entre Lol et Jacques Hold à l'hôtel de

T. Beach (p. 187-189). Enfin, c'est l'amorce de cette scène qui achève le roman : Lol « dormait dans le champ de seigle, fatiguée, fatiguée par notre voyage » (p. 191).

Cette scène, intimement liée à celle du bal (sa suite et sa fin), en diffère pourtant profondément. Elle n'est pas la reconstruction, dans la mémoire et l'imagination, d'un lieu et d'un moment passés mais « réels » (le bal) et d'un événement non moins réel (le « ravissement » comme rapt). Elle apparaît comme exactement opposée : aménagement d'un événement réel (la station dans le champ de seigle) à la place d'une scène non réelle, imaginée par Lol, une « minute pensée de sa vie » (p. 47) : le geste inachevé de dénudation d'A.M.S.

Couchée dans le champ de seigle, Lol retrouve une « place » analogue à sa place de spectatrice du bal, et surtout analogue à la place qu'elle aurait désiré occuper dans la scène imaginaire de l'aurore, en plus modeste : « Une place est à prendre, qu'elle n'a pas réussi à avoir à T. Beach, il y a dix ans. Où ? Elle ne vaut pas cette place d'opéra de T. Beach. Laquelle ? Il faudra bien se contenter de celle-ci pour arriver enfin à se frayer un passage, à avancer un peu plus vers cette rive lointaine où ils habitent, les autres » (p. 60-61)[1]. Tel est le fantasme de Lol, sur lequel il nous faudra plusieurs fois revenir.

1. Voir *infra*, « Le cinéma de Lol V. Stein », p. 110.

Voici la définition du fantasme proposée par le *Vocabulaire de la psychanalyse* : « Scénario imaginaire où le sujet est présent et qui figure, de façon plus ou moins déformée par les processus défensifs, l'accomplissement d'un désir et, en dernier ressort, d'un désir inconscient[1]. »

Nous verrons aussi que le scénario de Lol s'apparente à l'un de ces « fantasmes originaires », « structures fantasmatiques typiques que la psychanalyse retrouve comme organisant la vie psychique, quelles que soient les expériences personnelles des sujets[2] ».

Cette définition convient si littéralement au scénario inventé par Lol, dans le *Ravissement*, qu'il en paraîtrait exemplaire si Marguerite Duras ne déclarait pas son désintérêt et son refus de la psychanalyse : « Je ne les lis pas, leurs trucs[3]. » (Rejet aisément interprétable comme une « dénégation », c'est-à-dire une affirmation de fait, inconsciente et d'autant plus forte.)

Mais le psychanalyste Lacan déclare qu'il faut « se rappeler, avec Freud, qu'en sa matière, l'artiste toujours le précède ». À quoi il ajoute cet hommage ambigu : « Marguerite Duras s'avère savoir sans moi ce que j'enseigne[4]. »

1. Laplanche et Pontalis, *Vocabulaire de la psychanalyse*, PUF, 1967, p. 152 et 157.

2. *Ibid.*, p. 257.

3. *Marguerite Duras à Montréal*, *op. cit.*, p. 61.

4. Lacan, « Hommage... », p. 9. Voir Dossier, p. 177-178, pour un extrait plus complet.

Le texte du roman, reproduisant l'obsession de Lol, s'enroule autour de ce bal et de ses deux moments, sans jamais l'atteindre. Par cette construction obsessionnelle, en spirale, se trouvent mis à mal aussi bien la progression linéaire d'un récit classique que l'espace et le temps.

AUTRES RÉPÉTITIONS

Outre ce système majeur de répétition, le récit se plaît encore à raconter des événements eux-mêmes itératifs ; l'errance de Lol à travers les rues de S. Tahla (p. 39-51, 52-57) ; les scènes mondaines, visites, réceptions (p. 75-87, 88-110, 141-161) ; les rencontres de Jacques Hold avec Lol (p. 11-119, 129-140, 165-190).

La phrase : « Morte peut-être », glissant d'un personnage à l'autre, se répète plusieurs fois. Crainte ? ou désir ? : Lol entend « isolément » ces mots dits par Tatiana devant sa maison (p. 38). Le narrateur voit une « relation » entre ces mots entendus et l'invention de Lol de sortir dans les rues (p. 39). Lol les reprend, sous forme de question à Tatiana, à propos de Michael Richardson : « Il est mort peut-être ? » (p. 101), puis d'Anne-Marie Stretter : « Elle est morte ? » (p. 102), et enfin d'elle-même, comme une phrase que se seraient dite en dansant les amants du bal : « J'ai entendu : peut-être qu'elle va mourir » (p. 104).

La répétition est inscrite au cœur même du roman comme au cœur « inachevé » de Lol : elle prend la place du vide.

4. LA RÉPÉTITION DANS L'ÉCRITURE

La répétition se manifeste aussi dans l'écriture même, au niveau des mots, des phrases. C'est une constante de l'écriture du roman sur laquelle il serait fastidieux de revenir en détail, mais qui est très sensible à tous les détours du texte et dès les premières pages :

« *Était-ce le cœur qui n'était pas là ?* Tatiana aurait tendance à croire que *c'était peut-être en effet le cœur* de Lol V. Stein *qui n'était pas* — elle dit : *là* » (p. 13). « *Rien* ne pouvait plus arriver [...], plus *rien, rien* » (p. 16). « Lol *le regardait, le regardait* changer » (p. 17) ; « combien c'était ennuyeux et *long, long* d'être Lol V. Stein » (p. 24). « Elle désire *suivre. Suivre* puis *surprendre,* menacer de *surprise* » (p. 55). « Ce temps [...], il le perdait bien, il *marchait, marchait.* Chacun de ses pas s'ajoute en Lol, *frappe, frappe* juste, au même endroit, le clou de chair » (p. 56).

« Ce redoublement omniprésent des mots agit comme une double négation, éloignant et intensifiant à la fois sa propre évanescence[1]. » Il crée un rythme de vagues. La mer, presque absente du paysage, bat à l'arrière-plan du texte, comme dans l'esprit de Lol, pour qui la mer n'est jamais loin : « elle dit que la mer n'est pas loin de la villa qu'elle habitait à U. Bridge. Tatiana a un sursaut : la mer est à deux heures de U. Bridge » (p. 82).

1. Verena Andermatt, « Rodomontages of *Le ravissement de Lol V. Stein* », *Modern French Fiction,* n° 57, Yale French Studies, 1979.

Ces répétitions correspondent aussi, de façon complexe et contradictoirement interprétable, au désir de Lol : « dans cette enceinte largement ouverte à son seul regard, elle *recommence* le passé, elle l'ordonne, sa véritable demeure, elle la range » (p. 46). « Lol rêve d'un autre temps où la même chose qui va se produire se produirait différemment. Autrement. Mille fois. Partout. Ailleurs » (p. 187) ; « elle aurait voulu que tout recommence » (p. 189).

On voit qu'à la fin de l'histoire, la répétition est exprimée — peut-être provisoirement ? — au mode conditionnel irréel. Cette transformation, qui fait passer le recommencement de la fin du bal du présent (hallucination ? vision ? folie ?) à l'irréel (désir ? souhait ? reconnu comme impossible, irréalisable), pourrait suggérer que Lol, justement, ne devient pas folle, qu'au contraire même, elle pourrait être revenue à la plus banale normalité.

Ainsi s'enroule et se déroule une spirale complexe, construction et déconstruction à la fois, piège où le lecteur se trouve pris presque autant que Lol.

IV ESPACE ET TEMPORALITÉ

1. LES DÉPLACEMENTS DE LOL, ORIENTATION DE L'ESPACE

L'histoire de Lol semble être structurée par ses déplacements, seule donnée visible. L'espace où elle bouge n'est donc pas utilisé comme un décor, ni pour produire une illusion de réalité, mais à titre d'élément fondamental de la construction du sens.

Ces mouvements restent souvent inexplicables, dépourvus de causalité, puisque personne n'accède à l'intériorité de Lol : c'est le narrateur qui « invent[e] les chaînons qui [lui] manquent dans l'histoire de Lol V. Stein » (p. 37), « chaînons » des motivations et des causes, ceux-là mêmes qui permettent d'ordinaire de construire une histoire cohérente.

S. TAHLA

Tout commence à S. Tahla, où Lol est née, une ville au nom aussi étrange que celui de Lol. Marguerite Duras établit une équivalence : « L'histoire de Lol V. Stein, qui est l'histoire de S. Thala *[sic]*[1], c'est une seule et même chose » (*Lieux*, p. 96).

« S. Tahla », dépourvu de référent géographique, pourrait faire écho au nom de Tallahassee, capitale de la Floride. Comme s'il en était un diminutif. Si S. Tahla n'est jamais localisée, son espace, ses jardins, la proximité de la mer, les noms anglais pourraient évoquer les petites villes, basses et végétales, de Floride ou, tout aussi bien, celles de la côte est des États-Unis.

Toutefois, quand Duras parle de S. Tahla, elle la situe tantôt explicitement « en Angleterre[2] », tantôt sur les plages de l'Atlantique : à T. Beach, « la plage est vaseuse, on se baigne plus loin, à des kilomètres » (p. 183), « la mer [...] laisse derrière elle des marécages bleus de ciel » (p. 182). Ces lieux « relèvent d'une mer du Nord[3], la mer de [s]on enfance aussi, des mers... illimitées » (*Lieux*, p. 84).

L'incohérence géographique est totale : les « mers de son enfance » étaient asiatiques. Mais un « glissement » s'est opéré, comme il sera dit explicitement dans *La femme du Gange*, l'un des avatars du *Ravissement* : « là-bas a glissé. Il est ici » (*F.G.*, p. 124).

Les incertitudes délibérées de la géographie durassienne se retrouvent tout au long de son

1. Marguerite Duras a oublié l'orthographe du nom dans le *Ravissement*, et l'a confondue avec l'orthographe utilisée dans *L'amour*.

2. Interview télévisée avec Paul Seban, 1964 ; voir Dossier, p. 156.

3. Le *Ravissement* a été écrit à Trouville, dans l'appartement des Roches Noires acheté depuis peu par M. Duras.

œuvre et manifestent, en apparence, un refus du réalisme traditionnel et un basculement vers la subjectivité.

Pour les personnages les lieux ne prennent sens que par rapport à la perception qu'ils en ont, dans le système de relations et de hiérarchies que construisent leurs désirs.

Le lecteur lui aussi est amené, en particulier par les lacunes du texte, à s'approprier cet espace, en y projetant ses propres références et repères.

Duras déclare aussi n'avoir découvert que bien plus tard un rapprochement musical, pourtant apparemment évident : S. Tahla / Thalassa (la mer, en grec).

Ce rapport à une mer peut-être nordique vient probablement aussi d'une confusion avec *L'amour* ou *La femme du Gange*. Dans *L'amour* (1971), qu'on peut envisager comme une suite du *Ravissement*[1], l'orthographe du mot glisse aussi. « S. Tahla » y devient « S. Thala », se rapprochant (même dans la forme de son nom) de la mer au bord de laquelle la ville, cette fois, est située. Quant au film *La femme du Gange*, dont *L'amour* est, d'une certaine façon, l'adaptation filmique, il a été tourné justement sur ces plages du Nord, à Trouville.

1. Mais *L'amour* ne peut être réduit à cette fonction.

Même si S. Tahla n'existe nulle part ailleurs que dans le monde fictif du *Ravissement*, sa description, vague, fait preuve d'un pseudo-réalisme : « centre [...] étendu, moderne à rues perpendiculaires », « quartier résidentiel [...] à l'ouest » s'étendant jusqu'à la forêt, faubourgs industriels « de l'autre côté », dans lesquels est « enclavée » la maison de Lol (p. 40). La ville a subi des transformations depuis la jeunesse de Lol et Tatiana (p. 77).

Cette cartographie très banale, aisément généralisable, établit un arrière-plan rassurant, quoique dénué de caractères distinctifs. Sur ce décor s'inscrit une autre ville, totalement fantasmatique, propre à Lol, dans laquelle elle entraîne peu à peu Jacques Hold, orientée selon des pôles invisibles qui construisent une géographie radicalement différente.

La géographie durassienne, toujours largement fictive, ne subvertit pas ouvertement les règles d'une représentation « réaliste » du monde, elle les fait sournoisement déraper, vers un monde largement fantasmatique. Elle crée des villes imaginaires auxquelles, par un effet de lecture, elle parvient à donner une existence très intense, peut-être en partie grâce à leur récurrence, avec variations, dans les textes successifs.

ENTRE S. TAHLA ET T. BEACH, UN VOYAGE ANÉANTI

Le premier déplacement de Lol, mouvement actif dont elle est le sujet, la conduit de S. Tahla à T. Beach, lieu du bal et du ravissement, salle de spectacle vide et illuminée dans la nuit.

Après le bal, les verbes de mouvement sont employés au passif : « Lol, raconte Mme Stein, fut ramenée à S. Tahla » (p. 23). Lol cesse, pendant dix ans, de se comporter en sujet actif de sa propre histoire. Son premier voyage vers T. Beach se trouve annulé : Lol se retrouve à S. Tahla sans même en avoir eu conscience. Il s'est produit une lacune spatiale dans son histoire, un « trou ». Lol est restée dans l'enclos lumineux du bal, où le temps aussi s'est arrêté. Elle « fait la morte » (p. 37).

Quand elle recommence à « bouger » (p. 39), il lui faut revenir à ce lieu, à ce point, pour combler la lacune et reprendre son chemin. Elle se dirige donc de nouveau vers T. Beach, secrètement, mais obstinément.

RÉPÉTITION DU MOUVEMENT

Tout se passe alors comme si les mouvements de Lol s'organisaient, plus ou moins délibérément, comme une répétition. Les déplacements de Lol pourraient se comparer à ceux d'un pendule, oscillant d'un pôle à l'autre, de S. Tahla à T. Beach et de T. Beach à S. Tahla.

Un troisième lieu s'interpose pourtant : U. Bridge, où Lol, toujours passive, est emmenée par Jean Bedford, le premier homme venu, rencontré dans la rue, qu'elle a épousé « sans passer par la sauvagerie d'un choix » (p. 31).

U. Bridge, où elle est pourtant restée dix ans, ne laisse aucune trace en Lol. Elle y aurait vécu comme une « dormeuse debout » (p. 33), saisie dans les « glaces de l'hiver » (p. 34) ; quand elle essaie d'en parler, elle confond tout (p. 82). Le passage à U. Bridge peut être considéré comme une boucle insignifiante. Le sens du mot « bridge » (pont) et la forme même du « U » confortent cette interprétation[1]. Le retour à l'origine, à S. Tahla, annule le séjour à U. Bridge.

1. Notons qu'aux États-Unis, un « U-turn », virage sur place, est une manœuvre généralement interdite.

Ce retour est accompli avec la volonté de Lol, qui a raison de l'hésitation de son mari et se déclare « très heureuse » (p. 35) de reprendre la maison de ses parents, sa maison natale. En choisissant ce retour, Lol est donc redevenue active, a retrouvé une position de sujet. Mais c'est seulement pour mettre en branle son mouvement de balancier, un « déplacement machinal » (p. 45) dans les rues de S. Tahla.

Son « errance bienheureuse » (p. 42) se change un jour en une recherche nettement orientée : suivre l'homme entrevu (p. 56-57) jusqu'au rendez-vous de l'Hôtel des Bois ; retrouver Tatiana, la revoir. Aux autres ces mouvements de Lol paraissent erratiques, étranges et suspects. Elle ne cherche pas à les justifier. Seul Jacques Hold comprend peu à peu qu'elle se dirige à nouveau vers T. Beach, lieu de son « ravissement », et que la station dans le champ de seigle (qu'il est seul à connaître) n'est pour elle qu'un équivalent dégradé, un substitut de T. Beach[1].

1. Voir *supra*, p. 58.

La « place » dans le champ de seigle apparaît bien comme la première étape dans la réparation de cette lacune dans l'itinéraire d'une vie. Une grande cohérence (excessive, peut-être) se manifeste dans la démarche de Lol, qui reste invisible aux autres pour lesquels son comportement peut paraître dévoyé — « une vicieuse » (p. 46), dit Tatiana, qui pourtant ignore son comportement de « voyeuse ». Mais elle, Lol, se croit au contraire (au moins momentanément) en route pour retrouver « la rive des autres gens » (ici, une histoire continue, sans hiatus) ; donc pour redevenir, à leurs yeux, et peut-être aux siens, « normale ».

LA QUÊTE DE LOL

Le mouvement de Lol, après la première scène dans le champ de seigle, s'accélère et se transforme en une vraie quête. Elle cherche activement Tatiana, lui rend visite, l'invite par deux fois et lui « ravit » son amant, Jacques Hold (p. 111-118). Lol a repris sa vie en main, elle est redevenue pleinement un sujet actif. « Despotique, irrésistiblement, elle veut » (p. 112).

Alors, une première fois, elle retourne, seule, à T. Beach (p. 152), mais sans aller « sur la plage », sans quitter la gare (p. 166). Cette première fois, T. Beach n'est encore qu'un reflet : « Je ne voyais pas directement la mer. Je la voyais devant moi dans une glace sur un mur » (p. 152). Mais y a-t-il une différence essentielle entre la réalité et son reflet ? Et toute la réalité ne finit-elle pas par devenir, aux yeux de Lol, puis, par contamination, de Jacques Hold, un « miroir qui ne reflétait rien » (p. 124) ?

Lol entraîne enfin Jacques Hold avec elle à T. Beach, où ils revisitent le Casino, la salle de bal, la plage. Finalement, ils entrent ensemble dans une chambre d'hôtel où « il n'y a plus eu de différence entre elle et Tatiana Karl » (p. 189).

Ce voyage pourrait être la réalisation du désir impérieux de Lol, l'aboutissement du projet qu'elle poursuit depuis qu'elle s'est « réveillée », l'annulation de la lacune, la réparation de la perte de T. Beach. C'est probablement ce que Lol voulait, ou croyait vouloir.

Mais la fin du roman dément cette interprétation. Lol n'a pas réussi à reprendre le chemin des autres gens. Le roman s'achève sur la reprise du mouvement pendulaire. De retour à S. Tahla, Lol revient encore vers le champ de seigle. Le mal n'est pas réparé, le mouvement n'est pas arrêté. Lol n'est pas guérie. Elle s'endort dans le champ, « fatiguée, fatiguée par notre voyage » (p. 191).

Ce sommeil pourrait signifier aussi le retour à l'état glaciaire de U. Bridge. C'est ce que suggère la lecture de *L'amour*[1].

1. Voir *infra*, p. 142-143, et Dossier, p. 170-171.

UNE PROGRESSION RIGOUREUSEMENT PARALLÈLE ET INVERSE

Ces déplacements, qui rythment « ce qui se voit » de l'histoire de Lol, restent largement immotivés. Leur caractère mystérieux — « cette absence, comme c'était impressionnant, et c'est sans doute ça qui intéresse Jacques Hold » (p. 156) — anime toute l'entreprise d'enquête de Jacques Hold, toute l'écriture du roman et, au-delà, toutes ses lectures.

Jacques Hold les reconstitue et les interprète à sa manière, celle d'un homme — « Comment savez-vous ces choses-là sur Lol [...] : comment les savez-vous à la place d'une femme ? » demande Tatiana (p. 151) —, celle d'un amoureux fasciné, mais rationnel et désireux d'emprise. Il ne dissimule d'ailleurs pas que ce qu'il raconte, c'est seulement ce qu'il est « arrivé à croire »

Sommeil, inachevé

(p. 46). Le lecteur se trouve, à son tour, happé par ce mystère : que veut Lol ? Que fait Lol ?

Une formule, lisible dans le roman, offre, sinon une explication, du moins une description satisfaisante des relations de Lol avec l'espace, de ses mouvements. Cette formule apparaît dans la reconstruction de l'obsession de Lol, tentant d'imaginer la scène qui aurait suivi la fin du bal, rapportée au conditionnel, puisqu'il s'agit d'une spéculation de Jacques Hold : « Le corps long et maigre de l'autre femme serait apparu peu à peu. Et *dans une progression rigoureusement parallèle et inverse*, Lol aurait été remplacée par elle auprès de l'homme de T. Beach » (p. 49-50).

« Une progression rigoureusement parallèle et inverse », telle est bien la « forme-sens[1] » du mouvement qui anime toute l'histoire et tout le récit. Forme paradoxale, inquiétante, comme Lol : le mouvement ainsi décrit s'annule lui-même et ne peut guère aboutir qu'à cet « anéantissement de velours » (p. 50) dont Lol rêve. C'est aussi une forme qui anime le mouvement de Lol presque malgré elle, largement à son insu : une forme surgie de son inconscient, peut-être une forme du délire ou de la folie.

Ce mouvement me paraît donner aussi une forme à la temporalité du roman et aux relations entre les personnages.

1. Henri Meschonnic, *Pour la poétique*, I, Gallimard, coll. « Le chemin », 1970, p. 176.

2. UN « TEMPS PUR, D'UNE BLANCHEUR D'OS »

Dans le *Ravissement*, le temps devient une matière aussi malléable que l'espace. Lol semble en faire ce qu'elle veut, tout en aboutissant toujours à « rien ».

L'histoire de Lol n'est pas orientée et soutenue par une chronologie ordinaire. Le temps « chronique » (comme dit Benveniste)[1], celui des horloges et des calendriers, y tient peu de place. Les rares repères relèvent d'une chronologie purement interne. Le fonctionnement du temps chronique s'accorde ainsi à celui de l'espace : un « fond » tout à fait conforme aux normes, mais fictif, non moins détaché de l'Histoire que l'espace l'est de la géographie. Et, sur ce « fond », les mouvements transgressifs d'un temps fantasmatique.

1. Benveniste, *Problèmes de linguistique générale*, *op. cit.*, « Le langage et l'expérience humaine », p. 70.

DE RARES REPÈRES CHRONOLOGIQUES

L'histoire de Lol, considérée indépendamment de sa narration, se déroule selon une chronologie précise, quoique détachée de tout référent.

La nuit lumineuse du bal

Au bal de T. Beach, Lol a « dix-neuf ans » (p. 12). Ses fiançailles « doivent » avoir duré six mois.

Le bal se prolonge une nuit, jusqu'à l'arrivée de « l'aurore » qui sépare brutalement Lol du couple qu'elle regarde. C'est une nuit pendant laquelle le temps s'arrête dans le « ravissement », pour Lol, comme pour les deux danseurs éblouis.

Mais, en même temps, ce temps arrêté s'écoule à toute allure. « Tatiana avait vu comme ils avaient vieilli [...] tous les trois, ils avaient pris de l'âge à foison, des centaines d'années, de cet âge, dans les fous, endormi » (p. 19-20). « Nous avions tous un âge énorme, incalculable. Tu étais la plus vieille », dira Tatiana à Lol (p. 104).

Le bal prend fin avec l'aurore, malgré les cris et les supplications de Lol (p. 22). Mais c'est une « fin sans fin » (p. 184), une fin, pour elle, inaccomplie, inachevée.

Les glaces de l'hiver

Lol reste enfermée « quelques semaines » (p. 23), répétant « combien c'était ennuyeux et long, long d'être Lol V. Stein » (p. 24).

Mariée « au mois d'octobre », elle part avec son mari pour U. Bridge où elle séjourne « dix ans » (p. 32). Dix ans de sommeil et d'ordre « glacé ». Dix ans de conformisme encouragé par son mari. Dix ans de « rien » : « [...] ne s'occupait-elle à *rien* à U. Bridge ? À *rien*. Mais encore ? Elle ne savait dire comment, *rien* » (p. 45).

Quand Lol revient à S. Tahla, le temps, pour elle, semble n'avoir pas passé : « elle [est] restée maladivement jeune » (p. 29). L'ordre et « la propreté » avaient pris « la place du temps » (*A.A.*, p. 144).

Le temps de l'éveil

Après son éveil (p. 39), le mouvement qu'entreprend Lol la promène dans le temps, autant et de la même manière que dans l'espace : « le déplacement machinal de son corps » (p. 45) la pousse à « toujours aller et venir d'un bout à l'autre du temps » (p. 107), dans « un affolement régulier et vain de tout son être » (p. 47).

Le texte, alors, cessant de suivre sagement, quoique sur un rythme variable, le cours linéaire du temps chronique, se livre lui aussi à des va-et-vient. Technique romanesque banale du récit rétrospectif (« flashback » au cinéma, « analepse » dans le vocabulaire de G. Genette).

Mais ici, les analepses sont répétitives et retournent toutes, comme la pensée de Lol, au même moment : celui de la fin du bal. Ou plus exactement, et plus étrangement, à un moment qui n'a jamais eu lieu, un « trou » dans le passé, un « spectacle inexistant, invisible » (p. 63).

Dans ce mouvement, le présent se trouve comme annihilé : ainsi, les rendez-vous entre Lol et Jacques Hold sont occupés exclusivement à des retours à diverses couches, plus ou moins proches du passé. « Ces scènes sont comme des plis dans le tissu narratif[1]. »

1. M. Sheringham, *op. cit.*, p. 129.

En attendant la fin du monde

Le phénomène de va-et-vient se reproduit jusqu'à la fin du roman, sans jamais s'achever : « Lol rêve d'un autre temps où la même chose qui va se produire se produirait différemment. Autrement. Mille fois. Partout. Ailleurs. Entre d'autres... » (p. 187).

Et, en attendant cette « fin du monde » (p. 47), elle se retrouve dans le champ de seigle, d'où elle peut (ne pas) voir ce « spectacle inexistant », qu'elle rêve comme un arrêt du temps.

DEUX TEMPORALITÉS SUPERPOSÉES

Cette reconstitution chronologique de l'histoire de Lol ne rend pas compte du télescopage temporel qu'opère le récit qui juxtapose deux temporalités, tout aussi subjectives : celle de l'enquête de Jacques Hold, et celle de la quête, circulaire, de Lol.

La grande rupture, qui se produit dans le texte quand le narrateur pénètre dans l'histoire comme protagoniste (p. 75), transforme le rapport du récit au temps de l'histoire. Au cours des premiers chapitres, le récit, le plus souvent très sommaire, balayait largement de longues durées : les dix-neuf ans de jeunesse (en trois pages), les dix années de U. Bridge (en trois pages) résumées dans la formule, quasi elliptique et presque caricaturale : « Dix ans de mariage passèrent » (p. 34).

Quand Lol revient à S. Tahla et se rapproche du narrateur, le rythme se ralentit beaucoup. La durée du séjour de Lol à S. Tahla, jusqu'à la rencontre, reste vague, mais n'excède pas quelques mois, qui occupent quarante pages du récit.

Tout au long de cette première partie, c'est le temps de la narration qui constitue le présent textuel. Lol est reléguée dans le passé simple du récit, dans une « bulle » séparée par la distance essentielle qui coupe radicalement le monde du conteur du monde du conte.

L'entreprise du narrateur qui réduit le temps vécu par Lol à une épure se trouve justifiée car elle mime l'entreprise même de Lol « rebâtissant » la fin du bal : « Il ne reste de cette minute que son temps pur, d'une blancheur d'os » (p. 47). (Belle formule, qui renvoie cependant un peu à la danse macabre suggérée par la description du bal[1].)

1. Ph. Le Touzé traduit : « temps fossile », *op. cit.*, p. 212.

À partir du moment où se produit la collusion des niveaux de la narration et de l'histoire, tout change. Lol est entrée dans le présent, en cours, inachevé, désordonné, qui redevient opaque, insaisissable. Les deux temporalités tendent à se confondre. Jacques Hold accepte de se laisser « contaminer » par Lol. Il n'y a plus, alors, à proprement parler, d'enquête. Le narrateur entre dans le jeu et collabore à la quête de son héroïne, perdant distance et sécurité : « Qu'elle m'emporte, qu'il en aille enfin différemment de l'aventure désormais, qu'elle me broie avec le reste, je serai servile... » (p. 106).

Pour tous les deux, le temps devient cyclique, tournant dans un cercle irrésistible, « sans fin ».

UN ESPACE-TEMPS ?

Le fantasme de Lol et le texte mimétique de Duras tissent entre espace et temps des liens inextricables. Tout se passe comme si le temps ne pouvait se dissocier de l'espace : le terme « chronotope » employé par Bakhtine[1] donne trop la prééminence au temps. Le *Ravissement* met en jeu un phénomène qui pourrait plutôt se nommer, à la manière de la science (et de la science-fiction !), un « espace-temps ».

1. Voir Henri Mitterand, « Chronotopies romanesques », *Poétique*, n° 81, Le Seuil, février 1990.

Le temps s'y trouve comme enfermé dans l'espace, selon le désir de Lol : « Un ordre rigoureux régnait dans la maison de Lol à U. Bridge [...] presque tel qu'elle le désirait, presque, dans l'espace et dans le temps » (p. 33).

Le moment du bal est figé, « glacé », dans S. Tahla. Lol elle-même : « on aurait dit [...] qu'elle était devenue un désert » (p. 24). La ville n'est pas vraiment « reconnue » (p. 42) par Lol : « elle commença à retourner jour après jour, pas à pas vers son ignorance de S. Tahla » *(ibid.)*. Ignorance, ou méconnaissance, processus de l'inconscient ? Tout au long du texte, ignorance et connaissance sont données comme interactives, ou même équivalentes, avec une valorisation positive pour l'ignorance (p. 81).

Lol se laisse emporter par le vent qui s'engouffre dans sa maison (p. 45), qui s'engouffre en elle aussi, avec « le vent de ce vol » (p. 145) des « oiseaux sauvages de sa vie » (p. 145), ce vent qui finalement « balaie » les salles désertes et vides du Casino à la

vent

blancheur de lait (p. 179) (interprétable aussi comme l'une des métaphores spatiales de Lol).

Tout se passe comme si l'espace de S. Tahla avait gardé, conservé le temps passé, déposé en des couches superposées (pareille expérience du pouvoir de l'espace sur le temps, loin d'être liée à la folie, se révèle tout à fait commune, quoique assez méconnue). Marguerite Duras déclare être le lieu de pareilles expériences : « C'est très rare que je me promène dans mon jardin, à la campagne, ou ici sur la plage, sans que je revoie certaines choses très, enfin, incommensurablement lointaines. Ça m'arrive par bouffées, comme ça. Et je me dis que ce sont les lieux qui la recèlent, cette mémoire... que si on n'offrait pas de résistance culturelle ou sociale, voyez, on y serait perméable » (*Lieux*, p. 96).

Lol, obscurément consciente de ce lien entre espace et temps, tente davantage : elle retourne, avec Jacques Hold, à T. Beach, dans le Casino du bal. Le rideau rouge et les plantes vertes sont toujours là. Mais T. Beach n'a pas les pouvoirs de S. Tahla. Seul, Jacques Hold, conditionné, a une hallucination : « j'ai commencé à me souvenir, à chaque seconde davantage, de son souvenir » (p. 180). Il « voit » le bal passé. Lol, elle, malgré sa volonté, échoue dans sa tentative de « revoir bêtement ce qui ne peut pas se revoir » (p. 181). « Aucune trace, aucune, tout a été enseveli *(ibid.)* ». L'espace-temps reste mystérieux et ne fonctionne pas mécaniquement.

L'espace-temps se confond tout aussi bien avec l'oubli qu'avec la mémoire. Les mots « mémoire » et « oubli » sont utilisés par le *Ravissement* (et plus généralement par les textes durassiens) de façon improbable et souvent paradoxale.

L'histoire de Lol, résumée, paraît bien se ramener à une « recherche du temps perdu », à une entreprise de mémoire. Mais la part relative de l'oubli et de la mémoire y reste indécise. Lol « se souvient-elle ? » (p. 54), et de quoi ?

Déjà dans l'enfance (dit Tatiana) : « Elle donnait l'impression d'endurer dans un ennui tranquille une personne qu'elle se devait de paraître mais dont elle perdait la mémoire à la moindre occasion » (p. 12). Lol vit, peut-être depuis toujours, dans une identité discontinue qui doit se réinventer à chaque moment (seule la mémoire assure la continuité du sujet).

Le collège, l'amitié, la présence de Tatiana au bal, elle a tout oublié ou, du moins, « elle paraissait en avoir une mémoire très atteinte, perdue » (p. 77). Mais : « De l'amour, dit-elle, je me souviens » (p. 98). Cependant : « De la distance invariable du souvenir elle ne dispose plus : elle est là » (p. 43).

Ainsi Lol, qui pourrait sembler tournée vers le passé, ne vit en fait que dans un présent immédiat. Le temps n'a plus pour elle d'épaisseur, le passé ne garde pas ses distances : « De loin, avec des doigts de fée, le souvenir d'une certaine mémoire passe. Elle frôle Lol... » (p. 63).

« Mortelle fadeur de la mémoire de Lol » (p. 182), pareille au « lait brumeux et insipide de [sa] parole » (p. 106). Lol doit, sans cesse, « recommence[r] le passé » (p. 46), tenter de le revivre au présent, donc de le réinscrire dans un espace semblablement structuré. Il ne s'agit alors pas d'accès à un vrai souvenir, mais d'un « transfert », qui le rejoue dans le présent. Lol a donc absolument besoin d'un autre, et Jacques Hold est choisi comme pourrait l'être n'importe qui, pour tenir ce rôle : « Je ne peux plus me passer de vous dans mon souvenir de T. Beach » (p. 167), lui affirme Lol. Jacques Hold, en accompagnant Lol dans son voyage, croit donc l'aider, en partageant sa mémoire : « Voici venue l'heure de mon accès à la mémoire de Lol V. Stein » (p. 175), mais aussi en l'obligeant à « enterrer cette mémoire », à la remplacer par celle du présent où il se trouve avec elle. Il échoue : Lol continue à vouloir que tout recommence.

Rejouer le moment du « ravissement », reconstituer une mémoire de l'oubli, pourrait ressembler à une cure et conduire à une guérison. Mais la reprise du « recommencement » paraît au contraire un inquiétant symptôme. Il est vrai, cependant, que le roman ne s'achève pas, débouche sur une « fin sans fin » (p. 184). Le texte laisse béante une nouvelle lacune temporelle, entre le moment où Lol se retrouve couchée dans le champ de seigle, à la dernière page du livre, et le moment incertain où Jacques Hold a commencé à raconter (écrire) son histoire.

Ce vide entre la narration et l'histoire n'est comblé par rien et laisse le champ libre aux hypothèses et aux interprétations[1].

1. Voir *infra*, p. 103 *sq.*

Le navire de lumière

Tout au long du texte, le temps est spatialisé. La scène de ravissement, nous l'avons vu, est liée à un espace vide et à un lieu clos : « navire de lumière » (p. 49) enfermé toute la nuit derrière des « portes » (le terme est répété quatre fois, p. 22).

L'aurore a pour effet d'effacer cette clôture : « La pénombre de l'aurore était la même au-dehors et au-dedans de la salle » (p. 22).

Ces éléments spatiaux, bien plus qu'un décor de l'événement, sont ses constituants essentiels. Comme il apparaît bien quand ils se répètent dans le texte : toutes les métaphores, approches tâtonnantes de l'imaginaire, sont spatiales. Il est vrai, bien sûr, que l'espace, plus concret que le temps, est un meilleur pourvoyeur de métaphores. Mais dans le *Ravissement*, une véritable confusion s'opère entre espace et temps.

« Elle commence à marcher dans le palais fastueux de l'oubli de S. Tahla » (p. 43). Lol cherche « un ailleurs, uniforme, fade et sublime » (p. 44) qui ne se trouve nulle part. Le bal est devenu la « seule épave d'un océan maintenant tranquille » (p. 45). Lol « pénètre » dans l'« enceinte », « sa véritable demeure, elle la range » (p. 46). « Ce qu'elle rebâtit c'est la fin du monde » (p. 47). (Où apparaît explicitement la fusion espace-temps.)

Lol et Tatiana sont « embusquées » (p. 99) dans le bal de T. Beach, devenu une bulle d'espace-temps, Tatiana même y reste « enfoncée » (p. 100).

Dans le désir de Lol, son fantasme impossible, au conditionnel-irréel : « les fenêtres fermées, scellées, le bal muré dans sa lumière nocturne les aurait contenus tous les trois et eux seuls. Lol en est sûre : ensemble ils auraient été sauvés de la venue d'un autre jour, d'un autre, au moins » (p. 47). L'espace, muré, aurait contenu, arrêté le temps, fermé les portes de la nuit. Dans *L'amour*, la femme qui peut être lue comme l'avenir de Lol « marche droite, face au temps, entre ses murs » (*Am.*, p. 102).

« Il aurait fallu murer le bal, en faire ce navire de lumière sur lequel chaque après-midi Lol s'embarque mais qui reste là, dans ce port impossible, à jamais amarré et prêt à quitter, avec ses trois passagers, tout cet avenir-ci dans lequel Lol V. Stein maintenant se tient » (p. 49).

Cette dernière métaphore, véritable mise en scène narrative du fantasme, sera reprise dans le titre du *Navire Night*.

Dans une autre métaphore spatiale, indécise, gouffre, source, tourbillon, s'exprime cette forme durassienne du rêve d'un temps cyclique, de l'éternel retour : Lol « croyait qu'un temps était possible qui se remplit et se vide alternativement, qui s'emplit et se désemplit, puis qui est prêt encore, toujours, à servir, elle le croit encore, elle le croira toujours, jamais elle ne guérira » (p. 159).

L'histoire de Lol V. Stein s'inscrit donc dans un espace-temps presque autonome qu'elle « aménage » (p. 103) au gré de son désir. Malgré le « dépeuplement » (p. 115) grandissant provoqué par ce « rêve si fort » (p. 106), Lol rencontre les autres, dont elle va troubler la tranquillité « à jamais » (p. 71) en tentant de les entraîner dans la ronde sans issue de ce rêve, et peut-être même de les transformer.

V LOL ET LES AUTRES

Les relations entre Lol V. Stein, mystérieuse au premier plan, et les autres personnages, dessinent les contours d'une petite société et proposent sur elle un discours critique.

1. UNE SOCIÉTÉ BOURGEOISE « QUELCONQUE »

La société dans laquelle évolue Lol, aussi vaguement localisée que S. Tahla, n'est pas davantage située dans le temps historique. Ressentie, par défaut, comme contemporaine par le lecteur des années soixante, elle peut l'être encore presque autant par celui des années quatre-vingt-dix.

De cette imprécision « émerge une société quelconque[1] », aisément généralisable, dont

1. *Moderato cantabile*, p. 95.

le roman ne prélève qu'une toute petite couche : un groupe appartenant à la bourgeoisie aisée (p. 28, 72).

Tous les personnages masculins sont dotés d'une profession : le père de Lol était professeur d'université (p. 102) ; son mari, ingénieur dans une usine d'aviation (p. 29), est aussi violoniste ; Pierre Beugner et Jacques Hold font partie « du corps médical » (p. 75).

Ces précisions sans aucune fonction diégétique jouent seulement le rôle d'indices sociaux, au même titre que les grandes maisons entourées de parcs, la gouvernante des enfants, les « heures habituelles des visites » (p. 72), les vacances à T. Beach, le bal du Casino.

Un seul de ces hommes est différent : l'ex-fiancé de Lol, le « riche » (p. 28) Michael Richardson, « fils unique de grands propriétaires terriens » (p. 12), est « sans emploi » (p. 102). Son oisiveté de « rentier » en fait un survivant d'une époque antérieure. Elle le prédispose aussi aux grandes aventures, à la façon d'un héros romantique : allant jusqu'au bout de sa passion, il vend tous ses biens et part rejoindre Anne-Marie Stretter aux Indes (p. 30). En se distinguant du modèle masculin commun, il se trouve en parfait accord avec l'univers durassien, où « ne faire rien » est à la fois une situation fréquente et une sorte d'idéal.

Les femmes, comme il se doit dans ce milieu, ne travaillent pas, ne font, justement, « rien ». Elles ont « du temps libre, beaucoup » (p. 95). Tatiana le consacre à son amant, pratiquant un adultère sans amour (p. 60), que son mari semble tolérer (p. 90).

Par ces traits — choix d'un cadre peu défini et d'une société oisive, du moins jamais présentée dans ses activités — le roman de Marguerite Duras s'apparente au roman et même à la tragédie classiques, dont la préoccupation n'était en rien une description « réaliste » de la société qui aurait détourné l'attention de l'essentiel : une situation morale.

Certes, Lol V. Stein ne ressemble guère à la princesse de Clèves, mais le *Ravissement*, en dépit de son extrême modernité, ou post-modernité, rejoint davantage le récit-épure de Mme de Lafayette que le roman descriptif « balzacien ».

Ce classicisme, relativement peu soucieux du social, fait aussi du *Ravissement* un texte à part dans le déroulement de l'œuvre. Les autres romans de Duras, à l'époque, offrent une perspective plus large et plus ouvertement critique sur la société. *Moderato cantabile* oscille entre les deux extrémités du boulevard de la Mer, mais transfère au Café du Port, dans la zone des chantiers navals, le pôle attirant. *Le vice-consul* opposera au « petit cercle » de l'ambassade le personnage fascinant de la mendiante indienne. Rien de tel dans le *Ravissement*, qui se cantonne dans le petit monde de Lol V. Stein.

« ON-DIT »

Si la société est à peine décrite dans le roman, son discours, omniprésent, accompagne tout événement, en une constante « rumeur, au loin » (p. 81).

Le pronom « on » se rencontre avec une fréquence inhabituelle dans un texte écrit.

« On », sujet de verbes de parole ou d'évaluation (p. 23, 31, 38, 41, etc.), renvoie à un ensemble indéfini et non identifiable. Il inclut les voix indistinctes de l'entourage de Lol, ses proches (p. 24, 25), ou son mari : « Elle mentit et on la crut [...]. On la plaignit tendrement... » (p. 66). Jean Bedford, attaché aux apparences (p. 142, 143), se fond souvent dans la voix sans visage du « on ».

Mais « on » englobe aussi la ville entière : « L'histoire de la jeune fille il [Jean Bedford] la connaissait, comme toute la bourgeoisie de la ville » (p. 28). Le bal de T. Beach s'est changé en légende : dix ans après, le gardien du Casino « reconnaît mademoiselle Lola Stein » (p. 182). Le mariage de Lol aussi : « Leur histoire s'ébruita — S. Tahla n'était pas assez grande pour se taire et avaler l'aventure... » (p. 30).

Cette présence souterraine, permanente, de la rumeur manifeste la forte pression sociale qui s'exerce sur Lol, devenue, bien malgré elle, un personnage public : plus que personne, elle doit sauver les apparences. Lol vit dans une « virtualité irréprochable » (p. 70). (Ce qualificatif la rapproche d'Anne-Marie Stretter, dans *Le vice-consul* : « Rien ne se voit, c'est ce que j'appelle irréprochable... », *V.C.*, p. 100.)

UN VAUDEVILLE

Le roman tend à devenir, dans certaines scènes, une véritable comédie, voire un vaudeville. Rien de commun avec la satire féroce, très explicite, qui se manifestait à l'égard des cérémonials de la bourgeoisie, dans le « chapitre du saumon » de *Moderato cantabile* [1]. Le *Ravissement* abandonne les déclarations explicites pour un jeu subtil de situations, surtout dans les chapitres des mondanités, au centre du roman (p. 75-161). Cet aspect-là du texte est rarement souligné par les critiques, qui oublient volontiers l'ironie durassienne, son « désespoir gai[2] ».

La première soirée chez les Bedford (p. 88-110) offre un bon exemple de scène traitée en comédie, par le télescopage des niveaux de savoir.

Lol, qui « joue avec [le] feu » (p. 103), est la seule à détenir toutes les clés. Jacques Hold, voyeur, puis complice tacite, n'est qu'un demi-savant. Tatiana, manipulée, « ne s'aperçoit de rien » (p. 91).

Déplacements, gestes et regards sont réglés comme un ballet que rythment les exercices « très aigus » (p. 89) du violon de Jean Bedford.

Le lecteur installé, avec Jacques Hold, dans une position de voyeur, a le plaisir de connaître en partie le dessous des cartes en même temps que celui d'un certain suspense : il lui faut attendre la scène suivante pour comprendre que Lol aménageait, aux dépens de Tatiana, l'espace de son fantasme.

À travers ce jeu de cache-cache, la mondanité se manifeste comme un ballet de dupes, dont l'ordonnance visible n'est qu'une apparence trompeuse. De fait, il est réglé par le

1. *Moderato cantabile*, chap. VII, p. 91. Voir étude du roman, M. Borgomano, éd. Bertrand Lacoste, p. 75.

2. Marguerite Duras, « La voie du gai désespoir », *Outside*, Albin Michel, 1981, p. 170-179. Voir aussi Liesbeth Kortalis Altès, « L'ironie ou le savoir de l'amour et de la mort », *RSH*, 1986-2, nº 202, p. 139.

mensonge et la trahison généralisés. Ce jeu social comique, mais cruel, le texte le montre en actes, sans commentaires.

Le manège et les mensonges de Lol ne peuvent se réduire à un adultère de vaudeville. Cependant la satire sociale apparaît comme l'une des significations plurielles du roman, qui ne deviendrait fausse qu'à se vouloir exclusive.

Cette scène installe Jacques Hold, en tant qu'acteur (avec la collaboration de Lol), dans une position de spectateur-voyeur, celle même de Lol au bal de T. Beach, sous la fenêtre de l'Hôtel des Bois et dans le scénario de son désir. Lol l'a donc amené à prendre sa place. Et Jacques Hold en tant que narrateur contraint le lecteur à prendre à son tour cette place. Le récit est performatif : il fait ce qu'il dit, met en acte cela même qu'il raconte.

Ainsi la scène satirique se trouve-t-elle aussi profondément en accord avec le fantasme de Lol et les enjeux essentiels du roman.

2. DE L'AUTRE CÔTÉ DU FLEUVE

En donnant à la société bourgeoise la forme diffuse d'un discours anonyme et d'un regard omniprésent, en démontant les ressorts de sa comédie, le roman construit un système d'opposition. D'un côté, le corps social tout entier, « on » ; de l'autre, Lol, toute seule : « un peu gênée mais amusée de se trouver de l'autre côté du large fleuve qui la séparait de ceux de S. Tahla, du côté où ils n'étaient pas » (p. 42).

CONFORMISME, GLACIATION

Cependant, la différence entre Lol et les autres évolue considérablement au cours du récit. La transformation a lieu en trois temps, marqués par les événements qui font rupture, le bal, la rencontre de Jacques Hold.

Avant le bal, Lol est jugée « pas pareille » (p. 13). Sa différence échappe aux mots : « une part d'elle-même [...] toujours en allée loin de vous et de l'instant. Où ? Dans le rêve adolescent ? Non, répond Tatiana, non, on aurait dit dans rien encore, justement, rien » *(ibid.)*. Mais ce creux, ce vide au cœur reste une interprétation de la seule Tatiana.

La « folle passion » de Lol pour Michael Richardson avait paru rendre Lol plus « normale ». Sa réaction après le bal, jugée excessive, avait semblé aussi très « explicable » : Lol « payait maintenant, tôt ou tard cela devait arriver, l'étrange omission de sa douleur durant le bal » (p. 24).

Le « désespoir[1] » de Lol, peu convenable, était apparu conforme au mythe romanesque de l'amour fou, et par là récupérable, voire même admirable, à condition toutefois de ne pas sortir du cadre de ce mythe : « On devait ne jamais guérir tout à fait de la passion » (p. 76).

Un deuxième temps commence alors où Lol, en se mariant, se rapproche sensible-

1. « Jean Bedford croit m'avoir sauvée du désespoir, je ne l'ai jamais démenti » (p. 137).

ment des autres. À partir de là, le conformisme le plus radical l'emporte chez Lol : elle paraît oublier et chercher à faire oublier aux autres à la fois sa différence originelle et sa brève incursion dans les désordres de l'amour. Dans un « effacement continuel », une « virtualité constante et silencieuse », elle impose à tous un « ordre rigoureux », approchant « de la perfection » (p. 33).

« L'agencement des chambres, du salon était la réplique fidèle de celui des vitrines de magasin, celui du jardin dont Lol s'occupait de celui des autres jardins de U. Bridge. Lol imitait, mais qui ? les autres, tous les autres, le plus grand nombre possible d'autres personnes » (p. 34).

Ce goût « de commande », Lol le conserve en aménageant sa maison de S. Tahla, « d'une propreté méticuleuse et d'une ordonnance rectiligne » (p. 90). Elle l'adopte aussi dans ses tenues. « La rigueur de son manteau gris, ses robes sombres au goût du jour » (p. 41) lui donnent une « sage raideur de pensionnaire grandie » (p. 147). Elle se coiffe d'un « chignon serré au-dessus de la nuque » *(ibid.)*. Lol cherche à passer inaperçue, à disparaître : « On dirait qu'elle veut faire comme les autres, dit Tatiana, se ranger » (p. 128).

Les métaphores de cet « ordre glacé » manifestent clairement une évaluation négative de Jacques Hold et, probablement, de l'auteur(e). Lol est devenue une « dormeuse debout » (p. 33) prise dans les « glaces de l'hiver » (p. 34), elle « fait la morte » (p. 37). Au-delà du comportement particulier de

Lol, ce jugement de valeur très critique atteint la société bourgeoise qui exige de ceux, et surtout de celles, qui veulent y être acceptées, de s'enterrer dans cette « glaciation » (p. 61).

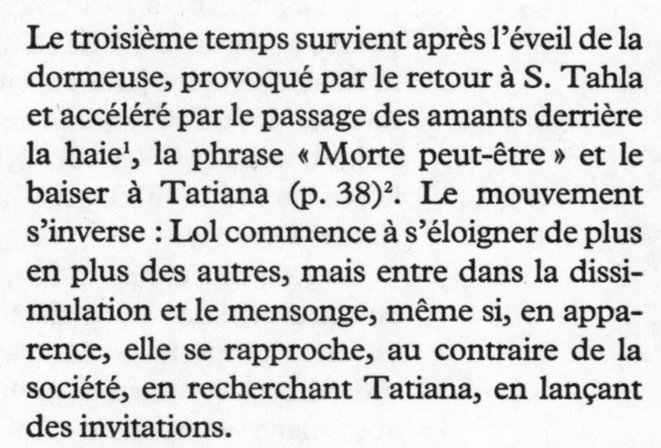

LE CRAQUEMENT DES GLACES DE L'HIVER

Le troisième temps survient après l'éveil de la dormeuse, provoqué par le retour à S. Tahla et accéléré par le passage des amants derrière la haie[1], la phrase « Morte peut-être » et le baiser à Tatiana (p. 38)[2]. Le mouvement s'inverse : Lol commence à s'éloigner de plus en plus des autres, mais entre dans la dissimulation et le mensonge, même si, en apparence, elle se rapproche, au contraire de la société, en recherchant Tatiana, en lançant des invitations.

Pourtant, tous ses gestes deviennent de scandaleuses infractions aux normes convenues. Suivre un inconnu (p. 54-57) ; se coucher dans un champ de seigle pour devenir voyeuse (p. 62-65), même si elle est une voyeuse qui ne voit rien ; mentir à son mari (p. 66), puis à Tatiana ; « choisir » un homme, le « ravir », en lui déclarant ouvertement son désir (p. 112) ; l'enlever à Tatiana et pourtant « [le] supplie[r]; [le] conjure[r] » (p. 117) de ne pas quitter Tatiana, d'accepter d'introduire le regard de Lol dans son intimité avec Tatiana.

La « rive lointaine où ils habitent, les autres » (p. 61) ne cesse de s'éloigner : « certains lut-

1. Encore une scène où Lol, cachée, entend et voit.

2. Voir *La Belle au Bois Dormant*, *infra*, p. 140, et Dossier, p. 195.

teraient [...] retourneraient chez eux en courant [...]. Mais c'est la dernière peur apprise de Lol... » (p. 63).

Délivrée de la « peur apprise », ressort du conformisme, Lol semble agir à la seule écoute de son propre désir. Et nous retrouvons, comme forme-sens de son rapport à la société, le « mouvement parallèle et inverse » d'annulation[1].

1. Voir *supra*, p. 69.

On pourrait alors considérer qu'en dépréciant les normes bourgeoises et en valorisant les transgressions de Lol, le roman prêche, discrètement, pour un individualisme radical, une forme d'anarchie, ou d'« utopie[2] ».

2. M. Duras, « La destruction, la parole » : « Je suis en pleine utopie », p. 52.

Cette lecture serait en accord avec le refus global de la société, souvent affirmé par Duras (*P.*, p. 151) et ses personnages, qui culmine dans le vœu de la vieille dame du *Camion* : « Que le monde aille à sa perte. »

Pourtant, il faut la nuancer. Car Lol, dans le *Ravissement*, est aussi une malade. La seule alternative au conformisme serait-elle la folie ?

3. LES HOMMES ET LES FEMMES

Le corps social, opposé à Lol dans le système du roman, tient un discours homogène. Mais, par ailleurs, il se structure nettement en deux catégories : les hommes, les femmes.

Les personnages masculins exercent une fonction et sont ainsi pourvus d'une situation sociale dont les femmes sont dépourvues. Pour le reste, ils sont très peu individualisés. Leurs traits physiques inexistants et leur comportement les rendent tous pareils : des « coureurs ». Jean Bedford trompe sa femme « avec les très jeunes ouvrières de son usine » (p. 33). Jacques Hold : « Sur les femmes jeunes et belles, il se retournait, s'arrêtait parfois, vulgaire » (p. 54). Et Lol se souvient que son fiancé « courait », lui aussi, « après toutes les femmes » (p. 52).

Peu importe alors que les deux hommes ne se ressemblent en rien *(ibid.)*, ils sont prêts à jouer, pour Lol, le même rôle : Lol « choisit » Jacques Hold, d'« un choix exempt de toute préférence » (p. 113), en raison de ses relations avec Tatiana : il est un substitut, un tenant-lieu.

Les femmes étant toutes socialement dépendantes (femmes de...), le mariage (de raison) est leur ancrage. Jean Bedford « disait aimer sa femme » (p. 33), « croit [la] protéger » (p. 144), mais protège surtout sa propre tranquillité. (« Bed », le lit ; « ford », le gué, l'endroit où la rivière est basse : le nom du mari de Lol symbolise bien sa conception du mariage bourgeois.) Pierre Beugner, beaucoup moins dévalorisé, « porte à Tatiana un amour revenu de bien des épreuves, sentiment qu'il traîne mais qu'il traînera jusqu'à la mort... » (p. 155). Il veille attentivement sur sa femme : « Dans la vie de Tatiana, l'impérieuse obligation première et dernière à laquelle il n'est pas question qu'elle se dérobe un jour, c'est de revenir toujours, Pierre Beugner est son retour, sa trêve, sa seule constance » *(ibid.)*. Leur maison « a résisté à tous les vents » *(ibid.)*.

Lol, au contraire, n'est en rien installée. Son mariage n'a rien de solide, elle se laisse porter par le « vent[1] ».

1. Voir *infra*, p. 132.

Jacques Hold, célibataire, malgré sa liaison avec Tatiana, reste disponible pour toutes les aventures. Distinct du lot commun, il peut remplacer l'exceptionnel Michael Richardson jusqu'à se fondre en lui.

LOL ET LES AUTRES FEMMES

Face à ces hommes sans visages, les personnages féminins sont dotés de traits physiques marqués. Il est vrai que le discours du roman, attribué à Jacques Hold, reflète son goût des corps féminins ; mais la répartition des traits distinctifs (aux hommes les fonctions sérieuses, aux femmes le corps et les vêtements) est aussi le reflet des valeurs sociales conventionnelles.

À ne considérer que leur apparence, les personnages féminins constituent deux groupes. D'un côté Lol et Anne-Marie Stretter, maigres, longues, aux cheveux clairs. De l'autre Tatiana, au corps voluptueux et au tout petit visage triangulaire noyé sous une chevelure noire. Toutes les trois se ressemblent cependant par leurs yeux très clairs.

« La masse noire de [sa] chevelure vaporeuse et sèche » (p. 58) distingue fortement Tatiana des deux autres femmes[2]. Ces cheveux noirs, trop lourds, sous lesquels elle apparaît nue à Lol, sont aussi comme l'emblème d'une évidente sensualité.

2. En 1986, Marguerite Duras intitule un de ses livres *Les yeux bleus cheveux noirs*.

Anne-Marie Stretter, « brûlée de rousseur », est aussi une sorcière, dotée d'une sensualité plus secrète, liée au feu. Tandis que Lol, « si blonde » (p. 114), reste invisible : « Il ne sera jamais question de la blondeur de Lol » (p. 79). Et pourtant, Lol est réduite aussi à cette abstraction, sa blondeur : « Tout à coup la blondeur n'a plus été pareille, elle a bougé » (p. 122)[1]. La blondeur, c'est aussi un trou dans le texte.

Le corps de Tatiana, « habill[é] d'une peau d'or » (p. 74), la distingue tout autant. Son mouvement est « charnel » (p. 79) : « elle se dirige vers lui, dans ce déhanchement circulaire, très lent, très doux, qui la fait à tout moment de sa marche l'objet d'une flatterie caressante, secrète, et sans fin, d'elle-même » (p. 58). Comme ses cheveux, ses seins sont trop lourds (p. 65). « Ce corps d'adultère » (p. 58), « Son corps de fille, sa plaie [...], il appelle le paradis perdu de son unité [...], il n'est entier que dans un lit d'hôtel » (p. 79).

À l'opposé, le corps de Lol est « raidi par l'observation d'un effacement constant [...], corps de pensionnaire grandie » (p. 114). « As-tu remarqué [...] ce corps, de Lol, à côté du mien comme il est mort, comme il ne dit rien ? » observe Tatiana (p. 160). Si Jacques Hold reconnaît à Lol un corps « long et beau » (p. 114) (assez semblable au « corps long et maigre » (p. 49) d'Anne-Marie Stretter), il la présente aussi d'une façon curieusement péjorative : « La bonne femme est voûtée, maigre, dans sa robe noire » (p. 111).

1. Autre parenté avec Valérie Andesmas, dont la blondeur éblouit et creuse un vide, dans *L'après-midi de Monsieur Andesmas.*

Tatiana exerce une séduction d'ordre sexuel ; Anne-Marie Stretter et Lol V. Stein attirent tout autrement, de façon presque magique, par leur mystère.

Les différences d'âge organisent autrement les équivalences : Lol et Tatiana ont le même âge. Lol est restée « maladivement jeune » (p. 29), « noyé[e] dans la douceur d'une enfance interminable qui surnage à fleur de chair » (p. 177).

Anne-Marie Stretter, dès le bal où elle est accompagnée d'une fille déjà grande, est beaucoup plus âgée. Dix ans après, selon Tatiana, « elle est vieille » (p. 102).

Mais la dynamique du récit tend à atténuer toutes ces différences et à faire de ces rivales non des mères et des filles, mais des sœurs, ou même des doubles. Anne-Marie Stretter remplace Lol au cours du bal et conserve cette place dans son fantasme : elles sont devenues interchangeables.

Les mots du texte annihilent aussi les différences d'âge. Lol est comparée à « une femme [...] très âgée » qui « regarde [...] ses enfants s'éloigner » (p. 18). Et Tatiana constate : « Nous avions tous un âge énorme, incalculable. Tu étais la plus vieille » (p. 104). Lol est devenue une « émigrée centenaire de sa jeunesse » (p. 99).

Lol et Tatiana portent, comme la femme du bal, des robes noires, « qui les font [...] moins différentes l'une de l'autre, peut-être, aux yeux des hommes » (p. 147). « Aux yeux des hommes », et en particulier de Jacques Hold, les voici même confondues « dans la dilution nocturne, d'une féminité pareillement rejointe en moi » (p. 92). Serait-ce la vieille antienne « machiste » : « Toutes pareilles » ?

Et, dans le lit d'hôtel de T. Beach, où Lol prend la place de la femme du bal, « il n'y a plus eu de différence entre elle [Lol " si savante "] et Tatiana Karl » (p. 189). Lol elle-même se donne deux noms : « Tatiana Karl et Lol V. Stein » *(ibid.)*.

Ainsi les femmes du roman, « mal désignée[s] » (p. 123), « coulée[s] dans une identité de nature indécise qui pourrait se nommer de noms indéfiniment différents » (p. 41), peuvent aisément jouer, volontairement ou non, le jeu du « remplacement ». Seul importe le rôle, non l'actrice.

Se trouve déniée, ou tout au moins problématisée, dans ce glissement, la construction « réaliste » de personnages différenciés et identifiés. Mais, au-delà, est mise en question la notion même d'identité distincte, aussi bien dans sa continuité que dans sa spécificité.

Le « remplacement », ébranlement de l'identité, se produit surtout pour les femmes. Mais, par contagion, il atteint aussi au moins Jacques Hold. En entrant dans le jeu de Lol, il est amené à partager un moment sa différence, en perdant sa propre identité : « le souvenir d'un mort inconnu me revient : il va servir l'éternel Richardson, l'homme de T. Beach, on se mélangera à lui, pêle-mêle tout ça ne va faire qu'un, on ne va plus reconnaître qui de qui, ni avant, ni après, ni pendant, on va se perdre de vue » (p. 113).

RELATIONS SEXUELLES

Les relations entre personnages s'organisent en profondeur autour du nœud des rapports sexuels. Leur forte présence dans le *Ravissement* donne au roman une dimension érotique.

Un érotisme au masculin puisque Jacques Hold, narrateur, est aussi le détenteur du point de vue dominant. On peut s'étonner de ce détour, voire même, dans une optique féministe, s'en scandaliser. Mais, si l'on tient compte de la signature féminine de l'auteur, la perspective change et il devient possible de considérer ce dispositif comme mise en scène ironique d'une situation. Mise en crise aussi, comme il apparaît clairement si l'on met en série toutes les scènes érotiques pour en lire les transformations signifiantes.

Le roman présente, directement ou indirectement, plusieurs scènes proprement érotiques. La scène de la fin du bal (construction imaginaire par Lol) réinventée par Jacques Hold (p. 50). La première scène de l'Hôtel des Bois, entrevue à distance par Lol (p. 65), puis évoquée par elle à Jacques Hold (p. 115). La deuxième rencontre entre Jacques Hold et Tatiana dans le même hôtel, après l'aveu de Lol, racontée deux fois : d'abord récit direct du narrateur (p. 122-126), elle est racontée de nouveau par Jacques Hold à Lol dans le salon de thé (p. 134-136). Un troisième rendez-vous avec Tatiana (p. 162-164), une scène brièvement évoquée par Jacques Hold dans le train

(p. 167) et, enfin, la scène de l'hôtel de T. Beach, entre Jacques Hold et Tatiana (p. 187-189), sont aussi des récits directs.

Sur un fond d'analogie, ces scènes révèlent des différences qui manifestent une transformation significative du personnage masculin.

Présence du tiers

Scènes intimes, dans une chambre en apparence fermée, elles accueillent toutes un tiers, qui voit, ou, au moins, sait. Ce qui est montré, c'est l'amour (sous sa forme sexuelle), mais ce qui est en jeu, c'est le « voir » et le « savoir ». Et, sur ce plan, Lol apparaît comme dominante : lors de la première rencontre, elle est seule à savoir qu'elle voit. La révélation à Jacques Hold de son intrusion le bouleverse (p. 116). La deuxième fois, Jacques Hold est dans le secret : le savoir est partagé et devient une complicité, dont Tatiana, qui, elle, ne sait rien, est exclue. La complicité et l'exclusion s'intensifient encore quand Jacques Hold raconte à Lol ce qu'elle ne pouvait pas voir, ni savoir, la rapprochant ainsi de la scène d'amour. Lors du troisième rendez-vous, la situation reste la même, mais Lol, présente sous la fenêtre, s'est aussi introduite dans la chambre, elle rend Jacques Hold impuissant (p. 163) et Tatiana, désespérée, sent sa présence : « C'est Lol ? [...] C'est notre petite Lola ? » Dans la scène suivante, déplacée dans un autre hôtel, Lol est dans la chambre et dans le lit. Mais est-ce bien elle ? « Qui est là dans le lit ? Qui, croit-elle ? » (p. 187). « Il n'y a plus eu de différence entre elle et Tatiana Karl sauf [...] dans les deux noms qu'elle se donnait : Tatiana Karl et Lol V. Stein » (p. 189).

Le regard

À l'intérieur même des scènes, le regard joue un rôle primordial : le regard fasciné du témoin redouble le regard de l'amant. Michael Richardson « en reste là ; ébloui » par la blancheur des seins découverts (p. 50). Dans le récit de Jacques Hold à Lol, « il la regarde » est répété quatre fois en un seul paragraphe. Le regard devient si intense qu'il finit par ne rien voir (« ébloui ») : « Il la regarde jusqu'à perdre de vue l'identité de chaque forme, de toutes les formes et même du corps entier » (p. 134). Le regard de l'amant ébloui s'est fait l'équivalent de celui de Lol, « dévorant un spectacle inexistant, invisible » (p. 63). Ils « regardent bien le vide[1] ».

Par contre, dans la scène de T. Beach, c'est Lol, inquiète, qui suit des yeux Jacques Hold « comme un inconnu » (p. 187). Lui « la caresse sans la regarder » (p. 188). Un changement s'est opéré : l'homme a renoncé à voir et, en partie, à savoir. Il a lâché prise.

1. *Détruire, dit-elle*, p. 54.

La « mise à nu »

L'acte capital, à chaque fois, est une « mise à nu » (p. 50). La formule, surprenante, rappelle fâcheusement la « mise à mort ». Elle s'accorde avec la violence, presque cruelle, qui anime le récit de ces scènes, une violence plus textuelle que diégétique, qui culmine dans la deuxième rencontre, celle où Jacques Hold connaît la présence de Lol. « Sans lui faire grâce d'aucune approche, Jacques Hold rejoignit Tatiana Karl. Jacques Hold posséda Tatiana Karl sans merci. Elle [Tatiana] n'opposa aucune résistance, ne dit rien, ne refusa rien, s'émerveilla d'une telle possession » (p. 123). La relation sexuelle est bien désignée, avec insistance, comme « possession » : « Tout à l'heure, tout à l'heure, je posséderai toute Tatiana Karl, complètement, jusqu'à sa fin » (p. 91). La posséder, et l'achever : il s'agit de maîtrise — redoublée par le savoir non partagé —, non d'amour. Car les mots d'amour : « Tatiana je t'aime, je t'aime Tatiana » (p. 123) s'adressent à une femme « mal désignée ». Et Tatiana ne s'y trompe pas :

« [...] tout à coup, interdite, dans l'orient pernicieux des mots [...].

« — Ah ces mots, tu devrais te taire, ces mots, quel danger » (p. 124-125). Le mot, ici dit par méprise, c'est le mot « amour ».

Quand Jacques Hold raconte la scène à Lol, il révèle mieux encore l'événement qui se produit, comme dans la nuit du bal : « l'amour changé de mains, de nom, d'erreur » (p. 101). « Il cache le visage de Tatiana sous les draps et ainsi il a son corps décapité sous la main, à son aise entière » (p. 134). Tatiana « décapitée » est privée de regard et réduite au silence : « Il faut de nouveau faire taire Tatiana sous le drap » (p. 135). On pourrait croire à un viol, à une immolation. Mais il s'agit aussi de remplacement, encore partiel, d'effacement de l'identité : « Ce n'est pas moi, n'est-ce pas, Tatiana sous le drap, la tête cachée ? » demande Lol. « C'est pour vous », répond Jacques Hold (p. 136).

La scène racontée dans le train est aussi violente, ou violents sont les mots pour la dire : « Son corps chaud et bâillonné je m'y enfonce, heure creuse pour Lol, heure éblouissante de son oubli, je me greffe, je pompe le sang de Tatiana. Tatiana est là, pour que j'y oublie Lol V. Stein. Sous moi, elle devient lentement exsangue » (p. 167). Décapitation, vampirisme : l'amour, selon Jacques Hold, est dévoration et annihilation de l'autre, même si « leur plaisir fut grand et partagé » (p. 123). Car au sadisme de l'un répond le masochisme de l'autre, dans une parfaite complémentarité.

UNE MUTATION DU SUJET MASCULIN

La troisième rencontre avec Tatiana, après cette exaltation du plaisir et du pouvoir, est une retombée, un fiasco : « Je n'essaye même pas de la prendre, je sais que je serai impuissant à le faire » (p. 163). Jacques Hold a d'ailleurs perdu sa position de sujet du discours : une saisissante mutation grammaticale l'a fait basculer de la première à la troisième personne : « Je ne sais que faire [...]. Je me caresse. Il parle à Lol V. Stein perdue pour toujours, il la console d'un malheur inexistant qu'elle ignore » (p. 162). Le voici dédoublé, dépersonnalisé : « je » est devenu un autre. Ainsi le pouvoir a été réduit à l'impuissance. Par le seul regard de Lol, tout se trouve déplacé. C'est Tatiana qui « enfouit son visage dans les draps » et « ne sait pas où se mettre elle non plus » (p. 163-164).

Déjà, avant la rencontre de Lol, les amants « ne s'aim[ai]ent pas » et Lol le savait (p. 60). Tatiana avait demandé à Jacques Hold s'il apercevait « une manière possible non d'amour, mais amoureuse » entre eux, plus tard (p. 151). Mais, avec l'intrusion de Lol, Tatiana s'affole : « elle a un vertige et l'idée de sa mort afflue, eau fraîche, qu'elle se répande sur cette brûlure, alors la vérité se fera » (p. 158). Elle a retrouvé « le goût commun, le sucre du cœur » (p. 125).

Jacques Hold, lui, expérimente le mot magique « amour » qu'il ignorait. « J'ai trop d'amour pour cette forme dans le champ, désormais, trop d'amour, c'est fini » (p. 163).

Reste la dernière scène, où Lol a pris la place de Tatiana. Lol, la belle au bois dormant, prend une part étonnamment active à l'acte d'amour : « Après, dans les cris, elle a insulté, elle a supplié, imploré qu'on la reprenne et qu'on la laisse à la fois, traquée, cherchant à fuir de la chambre, du lit, y revenant pour se faire capturer, savante » (p. 189). « Savante » : le « savoir » a changé de main, et de forme, tout autant que l'amour.

Ainsi, le passage de Lol a tout transformé. La conception masculine des relations sexuelles — plaisir sans amour, possession violente de l'autre réduit à la passivité et au silence (« décapitée » : privée de sa tête) — s'est vue ébranlée. L'homme a lâché prise : « Je suis devenu maladroit » (p. 113). Mais « des chemins s'ouvrent » *(ibid.)*. Voici l'amour et la douceur : « Je dessine des fleurs dessus [sur son corps] » (p. 188). Voici l'acceptation des formes plus fluides d'une autre sensualité : « Par son visage et seulement par lui, alors que je le touche avec ma main ouverte de façon de plus en plus pressée et brutale, elle éprouve le plaisir de l'amour » (p. 173). L'acceptation aussi de ce désir triangulaire, inquiétant et risqué.

Bien avant *L'amour*, il est déjà possible de dire de Lol : « Où qu'elle aille, tout se défait » (*A.M.*, p. 75). Ou de voir dans Lol la grande sœur d'Alissa : « Détruire, dit-elle. » Mais en n'oubliant pas que, dans le vocabulaire paradoxal de Duras, « détruire » n'a rien de concret ni de négatif et qu'il s'agit plutôt de faire place nette pour inventer d'autres choses. « Il s'agit pour moi d'une destruction toute intérieure », explique Duras[1].

1. « Ce que parler ne veut pas dire » (*Les Nouvelles littéraires*, 15 avril 1974).

VI. LE FANTASME DE LOL V. STEIN

Le mouvement de tourbillon qui anime le *Ravissement* finit par entraîner même le texte critique. Nous avons tourné autour du fanstasme de Lol sans jamais vraiment l'atteindre. Il faut maintenant plonger dans l'œil du cyclone, l'« ouragan de la nuit » (p. 135).

1. LE SECRET

Le discours de Lol fournit bien peu de lumières. Lol parle peu : « Ses avis étaient rares, ses récits, inexistants » (p. 44). Installée dans un inachèvement généralisé, elle finit rarement ses phrases (p. 27, 93, 146, 175, etc.) : « Mais si un jour, je... — elle cogne sur le mot qu'elle ne trouve pas » (p. 139).

Derrière ce silence, un « secret » se laisse deviner. Est-il volontaire ? « Je vous cache des choses », dit-elle (p. 170 ; cf. aussi p. 108). Jacques Hold le sait, elle garde « un secret [...] que jamais elle ne lui dévoilera » (p. 129).

Ne ressemblerait-il pas plutôt à ce que les psychanalystes nomment « la méconnaissance[1] » ? « Même si Lol disait ce secret, dit Pierre Beugner [médecin], il ne serait peut-être pas celui qu'elle croit, malgré elle, il serait différent » (p. 108).

Tous ces non-dit, ces vides (déjà figurés par les multiples lacunes du nom même de Lol)[2], le roman les thématise dans deux passages qui se répondent, celui du « mot-trou » (p. 48-49), et celui de la phrase « qui crève le sens » (p. 115-116). Manque, vide et impuissance, débordant Lol et son fantasme, se voient alors installés au cœur même du langage.

1. Caractère qui affecte tous les effets de l'inconscient.

2. Voir *supra*, p. 24-25.

LE MOT-TROU

Lol, errant dans les rues de S. Tahla, sent le bal « sort[ir] de ses plis » (p. 46). Elle « progresse [...] dans la reconstitution » de « l'inconnu sur lequel ouvre » la fin du bal de T. Beach, où elle croit n'avoir pu « pénétrer », « faute d'un mot » (p. 48).

Le texte alors s'interrompt pour un couplet délirant sur le « mot-absence ». Ce passage, difficilement attribuable à la pensée de Lol, renverrait plutôt, au-delà même du narrateur, à une intrusion de la voix de l'auteur : « un mot-trou, creusé en son centre d'un trou, de ce trou où tous les autres mots auraient été enterrés » *(ibid.)*.

Tous les verbes sont conjugués au conditionnel (irréel du passé), qui, associé à la négation, confère au « mot » un statut intensifié d'inexistence : « On n'aurait pas pu le dire mais on aurait pu le faire résonner. Immense, sans fin, un gong vide » *(ibid.)*.

Ce mot magique, actif et puissant, littéralement « performatif », « aurait retenu ceux qui voulaient partir, il les aurait convaincus de l'impossible » *(ibid.)*. Dire, alors, ç'aurait été vraiment « faire[1] ».

« Manquant, ce mot, il gâche tous les autres, les contamine, c'est aussi le chien mort de la plage en plein midi, ce trou de chair [...], ce mot, qui n'existe pas, pourtant est là : il vous attend au tournant du langage, il vous défie, il n'a jamais servi, de le soulever, de le faire surgir hors de son royaume percé de toutes parts à travers lequel s'écoulent la mer, le sable, l'éternité du bal dans le cinéma de Lol V. Stein » (p. 48-49).

1. J. L. Austin, *Quand dire, c'est faire*, Le Seuil, 1970.

p. 48

Le texte, contaminé par cette absence, a oublié les règles de la cohérence logique. Il va dans tous les sens, divague, s'égare et mêle tous les domaines, dans un torrent désordonné d'images.

Le creux, la béance au sein du langage ne sont pas donnés seulement comme l'incapacité à s'exprimer d'une femme « pas pareille », « folle » peut-être, mais comme la condition même de tout discours et de toute écriture, leur impuissance, leur vide essentiel. Ce qui renverrait assez bien, malgré toutes les différences, au discours des poètes, depuis Mallarmé, ou même Baudelaire.

En même temps, la forme vide du « mot-trou » est censée « crier » (comme Lol à la fin du bal) au centre même du *Ravissement*, du livre que nous lisons.

Le texte sur ce « mot-absence » repose sur une aporie, une impossibilité logique : dire ce qui ne peut se dire. Il lui faut donc procéder par approximations, frôler le gouffre sans y tomber, quitter la fonction référentielle du langage, celle qui prétend renvoyer aux choses, et laisser jouer la fonction poétique.

Les images les plus diverses se bousculent. « Trou » (répété trois fois), qui devient aussi « tombeau », grâce à « enterrer ». (« Aplanir le terrain, le défoncer, ouvrir des tombeaux où Lol fait la morte... », ainsi Jacques Hold présentait-il son entreprise, p. 37.)

Le mot résonne comme un « gong vide ». Métaphore isolée, dans le *Ravissement*, mais à laquelle fera écho, dans *Le vice-consul*, l'image utilisée pour le mot unique resté dans la bouche de la mendiante folle et muette, mot-trou aussi, vidé de son signifié : « Battambang. Les trois syllabes sonnent avec la même intensité [...] sur un petit tambour trop tendu » (*V.C.*, p. 21).

Le mot manquant « contamine » tous les autres. Le motif de la maladie prolifère dans le *Ravissement*. Et n'est-ce pas déjà une forme de ce que Duras nommera, plus tard, *La maladie de la mort* (1982) ?

Au « chien mort de la plage », très déconcertant dans le contexte, répondra, à la fin du roman, sur la plage de T. Beach, un rassemblement « autour de quelque chose, peut-être un chien mort » (p. 184).

Cette image du chien mort est, dans l'œuvre de Duras, une de ces métaphores récurrentes, de ces « scrupules » dont nous avons parlé[1]. Elle se trouve souvent en relation avec l'image de l'« oiseau mort » (utilisée, dans le *Ravissement*, pour décrire Anne-Marie Stretter, p. 15)[2].

Au fil du texte sur le mot-trou, les images se bousculent de plus en plus et leur violence s'accroît : « trou de chair », « aventures étouffées dans l'œuf, piétinées », « massacres », « inachèvements sanglants ». L'aventure du mot devient une vraie bataille.

Tout le texte du roman s'enroule autour de mots absents, depuis la désinence effacée du féminin de Lol : « la ». Le mot absent désignerait-il la « féminité », cette insaisissable qualité, « ce sexe qui n'en est pas un[3] » ? Lol, nous l'avons vu, bute sans cesse sur des mots qui se dérobent, inexistants, ou impuissants. Le mot « folie », peut-être ? Ou le mot « amour ».

1. Voir *supra*, p. 52.

2. Voir, dans *Emily L.*, l'association répétée du « chien mort » avec un souvenir d'enfance (p. 47, 53, 55, 64, 142).

3. Luce Irigaray, *Ce sexe qui n'en est pas un*, éd. de Minuit, 1977.

chien mort

« Ce qui est beau à pleurer, c'est l'amour. Et plus encore peut-être la folie », déclarait Duras[1].

1. Entretien avec Jean Schuster, *L'Archibras*, nº 2 (reproduit dans A. Vircondelet, *Marguerite Duras*, Seghers, 1972, p. 180).

Quand elle les trouve, ses mots, Lol (comme Duras) les détache, les défait, leur donne autonomie et liberté : « déjà, comme je vous aime », dit Lol à Jacques Hold. « Le mot traverse l'espace, cherche et se pose. Elle a posé le mot sur moi » (p. 133).

Ainsi les mots sont employés « en connaissance de leur prix. Un à un en connaissance de cause [...] en attente d'être dit par une voix [...] qui les transfigure, ou plutôt leur donne leur vrai timbre, leur entière plénitude, leur gloire[2] ». À la manière des poètes.

2. Dominique Noguez, « La gloire des mots », *L'Arc*, nº 98, p. 37.

LA PHRASE QUI CRÈVE LE SENS

À ce mot-fantasme répond, quelques pages plus loin, une phrase bien réelle, mais presque aussi magique, qui entraîne un nouveau délire textuel.

Cette phrase, c'est Lol qui la prononce après avoir avoué à Jacques Hold qu'elle l'avait suivi jusqu'à l'Hôtel des Bois : « Votre chambre s'est éclairée et j'ai vu Tatiana qui passait dans la lumière. Elle était nue sous ses cheveux noirs » (p. 115).

Comme l'aurait fait le mot-absence, « les deux derniers mots surtout sonnent avec une égale et étrange intensité. [...] L'intensité de la phrase augmente tout à coup, l'air a claqué autour d'elle, la phrase éclate, elle crève le sens. Je l'entends avec une force assourdissante et je ne la comprends pas, je ne comprends même plus qu'elle ne veut rien dire » (p. 116).

Jacques Hold reçoit cette phrase, unique aveu du rêve de Lol, comme une révélation du vide : « Le vide est statue. Le socle est là : la phrase » *(ibid.)*. Cette phrase, si simple en apparence, provoque, par tout ce qu'elle présuppose et implique, une distorsion, une dissociation entre les signifiants, vidés, et leurs signifiés isolés, sans attaches. Ce divorce entraîne une vision surréaliste : « Tatiana sort d'elle-même, se répand par les fenêtres ouvertes [...], boue, liquide, marée de nudité » *(ibid.)*.

Au contraire de Lol V. « Stein », pétrifiée, figée dans les glaces de l'hiver, Tatiana nue, liquéfiée, se répand comme une « boue ».

MENSONGE ET FAUSSE MONNAIE

Traduire ce délire textuel en langage rationnel serait un véritable contresens. Ici, le texte « ment ». Du moins imite-t-il le « mensonge » (p. 86, 95) de Lol, redit avec insistance. Lol a « une façon personnelle et capitale de mentir » (p. 106), une façon séduisante aussi : « Je désire comme un assoiffé boire le lait brumeux et insipide de la parole qui sort de Lol V. Stein, faire partie de la chose mentie par elle » (p. 106).

Il apparaît clairement qu'il ne s'agit en rien ici du mensonge ordinaire et qu'il n'entre dans ce mot aucune forme de jugement moral. Lol « ment » comme elle « est silencieuse » (p. 48), « faute d'un mot ». « Lol n'est [...] ni Dieu ni personne » *(ibid.)*.

Mais Lol pourrait bien se trouver, sans le savoir, dans cette défiance même vis-à-vis du langage qui affecte si profondément la philosophie contemporaine sous sa forme « post-moderne ».

« Moi seul de tous ces faussaires, je sais, je ne sais pas », déclare Jacques Hold. « Faussaires », qui font circuler la « fausse monnaie » du langage et de la littérature, déjà dénoncée par Baudelaire[1], dans un texte avec lequel joue Derrida en utilisant le langage d'une manière glissante et subversive, certes philosophique, mais très apparentée à celle, poétique, de Marguerite Duras : « L'inviolabilité des personnages [...] dit donc la (non-) vérité de la littérature, disons le secret *de* la littérature : ce que la fiction littéraire nous dit du secret, de la (non-) vérité du secret, mais aussi un secret dont la possibilité assure la possibilité de la littérature[2]. »

1. Baudelaire, « La fausse monnaie », in *Spleen de Paris*.

2. Jacques Derrida, *Donner le temps*, I, *La fausse monnaie*, Galilée, 1991, p. 194.

---

2. LE DÉSIR DE LOL

LE CINÉMA DE LOL V. STEIN : UNE CATHARSIS ?

Si Lol ne peut exprimer directement son désir, elle récuse pourtant l'interprétation courante du bal de T. Beach : « Autour de moi [...] on s'est trompé sur les raisons » (p. 103 ; cf. aussi p. 76).

À la question réitérée : « Que désiriez-vous ? » Lol donne deux fois la même réponse laconique : « Les voir » (p. 103,

105). Seul Jacques Hold semble l'entendre et sinon la comprendre, du moins lui faire écho en reprenant le verbe « voir » : « Je vois tout. Je vois l'amour même » (p. 105). Il croit alors entrer, avec elle, « dans la nuit de T. Beach » (p. 112).

Le désir de Lol passe par le regard ; il prend la forme d'un spectacle[1]. Son « scénario[2] » emprunte des éléments à la scène du bal. Le décor : fermé, vide, lumineux dans la nuit. Les personnages : trois, regroupés en deux acteurs et une voyeuse. Un « ravissement » commun et pourtant dissocié : à l'extase passionnelle du couple répond une extase bien plus abstraite du seul regard.

Ces éléments, déplacés et radicalisés, sont transférés à la scène de mise à nu, que Lol voit, presque par hasard, réalisée dans le champ de seigle et qu'elle travaille ensuite à remettre activement en scène.

L'« opéra de T. Beach » (p. 60) s'est dégradé en « cinéma » (p. 47). L'opéra, animé de musique, de couleurs, reste une imitation vivante de la vie[3]. Le cinéma, images-leurres, avoue bien plus son caractère artificiel. L'écran lumineux de la fenêtre simule un cadrage rigoureux et mutilant : le buste des amants se voit « *coupé* à la hauteur du ventre » (p. 64).

Marguerite Duras est coutumière de telles métaphores de destruction pour qualifier le cinéma[4]. Elle met l'accent, verbalement plus que filmiquement, sur l'effet de coupure du cadrage. Mais, surtout, elle pense le cinéma, et en particulier son cinéma, comme un moyen de « détruire[5] ». Détruire les livres : « Dans *La femme du*

1. Voir *supra*, p. 57 59.

2. Revoir, p. 58-59, la définition du fantasme.

3. Dans le scénario, écrit par Duras, du film de Gérard Jarlot, *Une aussi longue absence* (1961), des airs d'opéra restent, pour un clochard amnésique, la seule trace de son passé. Et, dans *Hiroshima mon amour*, le ton et la diction adoptés au début du film sont ceux d'un récitatif d'opéra.

4. Voir M. Borgomano, *L'écriture filmique de Marguerite Duras*, p. 22-27.

5. Voir *supra*, p. 103, à propos de « destruction ».

Gange, trois livres sont embarqués, massacrés. » (Le *Ravissement* est l'un de ces livres.) Détruire les personnages obsessionnels, comme Anne-Marie Stretter, « tuée » par *India Song*. Mais « détruire », dans le vocabulaire durassien, n'est pas un verbe seulement négatif, c'est aussi faire le vide : « Je voudrais détruire la connaissance pour la remplacer par le vide[1]. »

Ces rapprochements intertextuels éclairent la forme cinématographique donnée au fantasme de Lol.

Cependant le verbe « voir », dans le désir de Lol, reste souvent sans objet. Le regard de Lol est « opaque » (p. 91) ou, au contraire, « transparent » (p. 155) : « Je les vois [ses yeux] : une transparence me regarde. [...] La transparence m'a traversé, je la vois encore, buée maintenant, elle est allée vers autre chose de plus vague, sans fin, elle ira vers autre chose que je ne connaîtrai jamais » (p. 155). Opacité ou transparence : les yeux de Lol ne regardent, en fait, rien, sinon, au-delà du spectacle invisible, le vide[2].

Projeter son fantasme sous forme de spectacle est une démarche qui pourrait tenir de la « catharsis », ressort de la tragédie classique, déjà définie par Aristote comme « purgation des passions » par le spectacle de leur représentation. L'histoire de Lol serait-elle racinienne[3] ?

Cependant, il y a une différence notable : Lol est elle-même le metteur en scène, et, d'une certaine façon, l'auteur du scénario. Il manque alors les médiations qui permettraient la « purgation ».

La psychanalyse a repris le terme de « catharsis ». Elle est considérée comme « une

1. « La destruction, la parole », entretien avec Rivette et Narboni, *Cahiers du cinéma*, n° 217, novembre 1969, p. 52.

2. Lol inaugure par là le cycle des femmes durassiennes. Comme Elizabeth Alione, dans *Détruire, dit-elle* : « Elle regarde le vide, dit Stein. C'est la seule chose qu'elle regarde. Mais bien. Elle regarde bien le vide » (*D.d.*, p. 54).

3. Michèle Druon, « Mise en scène et catharsis de l'amour dans *Le ravissement de Lol V. Stein*, de Marguerite Duras », *The French Review*, vol. LVIII, n° 3, février 1985.

des dimensions de toute psychanalyse », « reviviscence intense de certains souvenirs, s'accompagnant d'une décharge émotionnelle plus ou moins orageuse[1] ».

L'histoire de Lol peut être lue comme une cure analytique. Lol serait atteinte d'une névrose, à la fois traumatique (consécutive au choc du bal) et obsessionnelle. « Maladie » assez courante. « Tout le monde fait des névroses », déclare Duras[2].

Les divers incidents de S. Tahla amènent Lol d'abord à une remémoration de son traumatisme, puis à une tentative active d'« acting out[3] ». Aidée (?) par l'action de Jacques Hold et le relatif transfert[4] qu'il lui permet.

Mais, malgré Jacques Hold, ce que fait Lol reste une analyse « sauvage », dont le nom même exprime bien les limites et les dangers. « Il n'est nullement souhaitable, écrivait Freud, que le patient *mette en acte* au lieu de se souvenir[5]. »

Cette mise en acte sauvage risque aussi de déboucher sur une répétition infinie, comme le suggère la dernière vision du roman (p. 191).

VOIR L'AMOUR SE FAIRE : UNE SCÈNE PRIMITIVE

Si la forme du scénario fantasmatique est névrotique, son contenu est aussi très troublant, comme le montre l'effet produit sur Jacques Hold par la phrase : « [Tatiana] nue sous ses cheveux noirs » (p. 115).

1. *Vocabulaire de la psychanalyse, op. cit.*

2. « La destruction la parole », p. 54.

3. Passage à l'acte, actuation. Le terme anglais est en général préféré.

4. Le *Vocabulaire de la psychanalyse, op. cit.*, propose comme définition du transfert : « Processus par lequel les désirs inconscients s'actualisent sur certains objets [notamment] dans le cadre de la relation analytique. » Il s'agit d'un « déplacement », d'une « substitution de la personne du médecin à une personne antérieurement connue » (Freud).

5. Cité par le *Vocabulaire de la psychanalyse, op. cit.*, p. 8. Souligné par Freud.

L'expérience du « ravissement », pendant le bal, est celle d'un paradoxe réalisé (un oxymore[1] vécu) : dépouillée de son amour, transféré sur une autre, Lol s'en trouve « ravie ». Car elle opère, elle aussi, un transfert : sa jouissance provient non plus de « vivre l'amour » ou de « faire l'amour », mais de « voir l'amour ». Cependant, cette jouissance n'est pas achevée et la laisse dans un manque extrême (le mode irréel) : « ç'aurait été pour toujours, pour sa tête et pour son corps, leur plus grande douleur et leur plus grande joie confondues... » (p. 48).

1. Figure de rhétorique unissant deux mots contradictoires.

voir

La scène fantasmatique de dénudation est une tentative (vaine : « elle attend en vain, elle crie en vain », p. 51) de mener cette jouissance à son terme. Elle cherche à entrer au cœur de l'intimité du couple d'amants, tout en en restant absente.

voyeurer

Elle imagine le commencement de la scène d'amour : « Michael Richardson [...] commence à dévêtir une autre femme que Lol et lorsque d'autres seins apparaissent, blancs, sous le fourreau noir, il en reste là : ébloui... » (p. 50). Le scénario s'arrête, comme le bal, avant sa fin : « Cet arrachement très ralenti de la robe d'Anne-Marie Stretter, cet anéantissement de velours de sa propre personne, Lol n'a jamais réussi à le mener à son terme » *(ibid.)*.

Le fantasme devient alors une mise à nu incomplète (les seins seulement, le sexe reste interdit) et éternellement inachevée. Lenteur extrême, solennité, noir et blanc, nudité donnent au fantasme une tonalité fortement onirique[2].

2. Dans la séquence initiale d'*Hiroshima mon amour*, deux corps nus, coupés et à peine visibles, s'enlacent sur un récitatif d'opéra.

Le texte, mimant l'inconscient (un personnage fictif ne peut avoir d'inconscient !), fonctionne vraiment comme le langage des rêves, sur les jeux du signifiant. Il laisse jouer un mot absent : « dérober ». Ce terme caché (qui se « dérobe »), mais d'autant plus actif qu'il est plus méconnu, permet de glisser, par pure homonymie, du vol dont Lol est victime, à l'arrachement de la « robe » noire.

Le spectacle impossible dont rêve Lol évoque fortement « la scène primitive (ou originaire) » freudienne, « un élément qui manque rarement dans le trésor des fantasmes inconscients qu'on peut découvrir chez tous les névrosés et probablement chez tous les enfants des hommes[1] ». Dans cette scène (peu importe que l'expérience ait été réelle ou purement imaginaire, ce qui est d'ailleurs le plus souvent impossible à déterminer), le jeune enfant est témoin, en secret, des rapports sexuels de ses parents. De la même manière, dans le fantasme de Lol se trouvent associés le regard du sujet voyeur et son exclusion. Les trois acteurs de cette scène pourront se voir incarnés par toutes sortes de figures différentes, au gré des fantasmes.

1. Freud, cité par le *Vocabulaire de la psychanalyse*, *op. cit.*, article « Scène originaire », p. 432.

Or, Anne-Marie Stretter, lors du bal, apparaît comme une figure maternelle : âgée, accompagnée d'une fille déjà grande qui lui ressemble (et donc ressemble aussi à Lol). Elle est aussi une mauvaise mère, qui oublie totalement sa fille. La violence (paternelle dans la scène primitive) est déplacée[2] sur l'aurore, qui arrive « avec une brutalité inouïe » (p. 46), et sur Lol elle-même, qui

2. Le « déplacement » est l'un des mécanismes essentiels de l'inconscient, sensible, en particulier, dans le travail du rêve.

renverse sa mère « très fort » (p. 22). Lol n'aurait fait que reconnaître (inconsciemment) ce fantasme dans l'événement de T. Beach, mise en scène éblouissante de son exclusion. Sa maladie remonterait alors, comme le pense Tatiana, bien au-delà du bal. Atteinte d'une forme de dépression mélancolique, elle serait incapable d'autre chose que d'une incessante répétition.

Cette explication est aussi une banalisation : Lol rejoint un sort bien commun.

3. CETTE ÉTRANGE OMISSION DE LA DOULEUR

Le plus « étrange », dans l'histoire de Lol, c'est peut-être l'« omission » de tout sentiment.

Absence de douleur, comme le confirme Tatiana : « Je suis ton seul témoin. Je peux le dire : non. Tu leur souriais. Tu ne souffrais pas » (p. 99).

Disparition de l'amour même : « Je n'ai plus aimé mon fiancé dès que la femme est entrée. [...] Quand je dis que je ne l'aimais plus, je veux dire que vous n'imaginez pas jusqu'où on peut aller dans l'absence d'amour » (p. 137-138). « Lol ne pense plus à cet amour. Jamais. Il est mort jusqu'à son odeur d'amour mort » (p. 50). Lol, « cette revenante tranquille d'un amour si grand, si fort » (p. 80), est « indifférente », « sans une larme » même à la mort de sa mère (p. 32). Pour elle tout « est pareil » (p. 139, 150)[1].

1. Comment ne pas penser, malgré toutes les évidentes différences, à *L'étranger* de Camus, répétant : « ça m'est égal » ? Lol est aussi, dans le sens camusien, une « étrangère ».

Le sentiment semble généralement étranger à Lol. Elle rejette violemment « la plainte sentimentale, boueuse » de sa mère à la fin du bal (p. 22). Et elle se trouve « embarrassée » par « les restes qui traînent partout dans le monde, qui tournent, ce déchet à moitié rongé par les rats déjà, la douleur de Tatiana » (p. 159) (qui soupçonne la trahison) ; « partout le sentiment », pense-t-elle, féroce, « on glisse sur cette graisse » *(ibid.)*.

Cette indifférence la rend profondément différente et inquiétante. S'il s'agit d'un symptôme, il est beaucoup plus grave que les autres, et suggérerait une psychose, forme, cette fois, de la folie.

À moins que cette indifférence ne soit lue comme un détachement conquis, une forme d'ataraxie : « Dans un certain état toute trace de sentiment est chassée » (p. 140). Car Lol parle de son « bonheur » (p. 108, 109), Jacques Hold voit dans ses yeux « une joie barbare, folle » (p. 129) et quelque chose aussi qui pourrait être de la jalousie, quand il lui déclare qu'il ne peut pas se passer de Tatiana : « Elle réprime une souffrance très grande dans laquelle elle ne sombre pas » (p. 132).

Les émotions de Lol ne sont pas sentimentales mais sauvages, à la façon d'un instinct animal. C'est du moins ce que suggère l'une des métaphores les plus surprenantes et les plus poétiques du *Ravissement* : « Lol a un accent que je ne lui connaissais pas encore [...]. La bête séparée de la forêt dort, elle rêve de l'équateur de la naissance, dans un frémissement, son rêve solaire pleure » (p. 117)[1].

1. Dans une lecture intertextuelle, on pourrait rapprocher Lol de la panthère noire en cage, de la nouvelle « Le boa », in *Des journées entières dans les arbres* (nouvelles).

UNE IDENTITÉ DE NATURE INDÉCISE

À l'absence de sentiment s'ajoute la perte d'identité, autre symptôme, dont la manifestation la plus flagrante se produit à l'hôtel de T. Beach, où Lol dit d'elle-même : « Qui c'est ? » (p. 188) et finit par se donner deux noms : « Tatiana Karl et Lol V. Stein » (p. 189). Lol n'est « ni Dieu, ni personne » (p. 49 ; cf. aussi p. 47). Elle n'est « pour ainsi dire personne de conséquent » (p. 161). « Elle se croit coulée dans une identité de nature indécise qui pourrait se nommer de noms indéfiniment différents » (p. 41).

Lol propage la perte d'identité, par contamination. Sur les lieux mêmes : « Sa présence fait la ville pure, méconnaissable » (p. 43) ; « Elle raconte en fait le dépeuplement d'une demeure avec sa venue » (p. 82). Et sur les êtres, avec le même mot : « Notre dépeuplement grandit » (p. 113). Et : « Pour la première fois mon nom prononcé ne nomme pas » *(ibid.)*, observe Jacques Hold, d'abord effrayé.

Cet évidement des identités facilite le glissement des personnages. Pour « expliquer » le bal, Lol déclare : « C'est un remplacement. [...] Je n'étais plus à ma place. Ils m'ont emmenée. Je me suis retrouvée sans eux. [...] Je ne comprends pas qui est à ma place » (p. 138).

Dans l'histoire de Lol, il n'est guère question de « personnes », mais de « places » qui peuvent être occupées par n'importe qui, ou presque.

Le « fantasme » de Lol peut alors s'exprimer dans un vocabulaire mathématique[1]. « Elle avait oublié la vieille algèbre des peines d'amour » (p. 19). Algèbre : une abstraction rationnelle, où les « peines d'amour », codifiées, seraient enfermées dans les théorèmes de la société ou des mythes qu'elle produit. Pourtant, en pratiquant les remplacements et les déplacements, en effaçant les identités au profit des rôles, Lol V. Stein vit bien dans un univers algébrique[2].

Mais « la vieille algèbre des peines d'amour » est aussi un système fondé sur le chiffre deux, où le tiers ne peut être qu'exclu. La société n'admet, en théorie du moins, que des couples : Lol et Michael Richardson, ou Michael Richardson et Anne-Marie Stretter. Jacques Hold et Tatiana, ou Lol et Jacques Hold. Le « ou » est exclusif. Et le tiers apporte la peine.

À la place de cette algèbre, Lol vit une figure géométrique, projetée dans l'espace, et bien moins conventionnelle : « Elle se voit, et c'est là sa pensée véritable, à la même place, dans cette fin, toujours, au centre d'une *triangulation*[3] dont l'aurore et eux deux sont les termes éternels » (p. 47). *L'amour* inscrira sur le sable le triangle dessiné par la marche des trois personnages anonymes (dont l'un est l'avenir de Lol).

Lors de la remémoration du bal, le troisième « terme » du triangle n'est pas la ravisseuse, mais « l'aurore » qui intervient « avec une brutalité inouïe » (p. 46) pour

1. La mère de Marguerite Donnadieu voulait pour elle l'agrégation de mathématiques (*A.*, p. 29-31).

2. Ce caractère mathématique établit une ressemblance avec *L'année dernière à Marienbad.*

3. Il faut remarquer que le terme « triangulation » (par opposition à « triangle ») introduit la notion d'action et de mobilité. Il ne s'agit pas d'un triangle figé, mais d'une forme dynamique.

séparer « pour toujours, toujours » Lol du couple. Comme le bal, le fantasme de Lol est nocturne et supporte mal la clarté du jour (et de la raison ?) qu'apporte l'aurore : Lol « est la nuit de T. Beach » (p. 104).

Peu à peu, Lol transforme le triangle. Elle supprime l'aurore et inscrit son désir dans une structure à trois « termes », qui appelle les interprétations.

UNE TRIANGULATION

Le triangle de Lol prend parfois, nous l'avons vu, des airs de vaudeville[1]. Il serait regrettable de l'ignorer et de sacraliser le roman en effaçant son côté littérature « de quatre sous ». Cependant, représenter ces jeux et ces clichés, c'est en même temps mettre à jour leur pouvoir aliénant et, par là, les désamorcer.

Le triangle pourrait aussi apparaître comme une figure de ce que René Girard nomme le désir « triangulaire », « mimétique[2] » : désir selon l'autre, qui a besoin d'un médiateur, forme la plus courante, mais la plus méconnue des désirs humains, que nie le « mensonge romantique » mais que révèlent les grands romans.

Ce désir triangulaire semble bien souvent, en effet, le ressort des actions de nombreux personnages masculins du *Ravissement*. Jean Bedford, par exemple : « on le suspecta [...] d'avoir d'étranges inclinations pour les jeunes filles délaissées, par d'autres rendues folles » (p. 30-31). Ou même Jacques Hold,

1. Voir *supra*, p. 85-87.

2. René Girard, *Mensonge romantique, vérité romanesque*, Grasset, 1961, p. 11-58.

qui oriente son désir selon Tatiana : « ce que je trouve d'intéressant à Lol V. Stein [...], n'est-ce pas elle qui me l'a montré ? » (p. 158), et bien plus encore selon Lol : « Mais qu'est-ce que j'ignore de moi-même à ce point et qu'elle me met en demeure de connaître ? » (p. 105). « Qu'elle me broie avec le reste, je serai servile » (p. 106). « Elle m'a cueilli, m'a pris au nid » (p. 113). « [Son] rêve me contamine » (p. 187).

Mais pourtant, le désir des personnages féminins, contrairement à l'opinion reçue qui fait des femmes les esclaves des « modes », serait bien moins médiatisé, ce qui semble une prise de position féministe discrète. Tatiana est poussée par sa sensualité, les exigences de son corps[1]. Lol, il est vrai, « aime, aime celui qui doit aimer Tatiana. Personne » (p. 133). Elle a besoin de Tatiana dans sa relation avec Jacques Hold. Mais ce n'est pas l'homme aimé par son amie qu'elle veut : c'est leur couple, pour qu'il l'exclue. Et ce désir ne lui est dicté par personne, n'est l'imitation d'aucun autre. Au contraire.

Le triangle du fantasme de Lol évoquerait davantage le triangle œdipien qui lie l'enfant à ses deux parents (ou à leurs équivalents symboliques). « Le complexe d'Œdipe », dans une perspective freudienne, « joue un rôle fondamental dans la structuration de la personnalité et dans l'orientation du désir humain[2] ».

Ces tentatives d'explication, même si elles ont leur pertinence, restent très incomplètes. Le *Ravissement*, surtout s'il est mis en rela-

1. Voir *supra*, p. 93 *sq*.

2. *Vocabulaire de la psychanalyse*, *op. cit.*, p. 80, voir *supra*, « La scène primi-

tion avec le reste de l'œuvre durassienne, ouvre sur des interprétations moins négatives, suggérées déjà par le mot « folie », aux signifiés et aux connotations multiples et contradictoires. « L'absence bien connue de frontière entre la non-folie et la folie ne me dispose pas à accorder une valeur différente aux perceptions et aux idées qui sont le fait de l'une ou de l'autre[1] », écrivait Breton. Le « geste de coupure[2] » qui décide de distinguer la folie de la raison est radicalement culturel, donc relatif.

1. André Breton, *Nadja*, Gallimard, 1964, p. 171.

2. Michel Foucault, *Histoire de la folie*, Plon, 1961.

4. LA FOLIE, QUELLE FOLIE ?

La question « Lol est-elle folle ? » n'a, rigoureusement, aucune pertinence. Lol, « être de papier », est contenue tout entière dans les mots qui la disent, comme tout personnage de fiction. Mais le paradoxe est que les mots, précisément, lui manquent et manquent aussi au texte. Les silences et les lacunes suggèrent alors une profondeur et des secrets impossibles, pourtant, chez un « être de papier ». Et placent le lecteur devant un mystère presque égal à celui d'une personne réelle. Il n'y a là, bien sûr, que rhétorique et effet de lecture. Mais le charme opère et Lol émerge, hologramme vivant à s'y méprendre. Alors, même si elle ne porte que sur cette projection imaginaire, la question de la folie reprend sa pertinence.

LA « FOLIE » DE LOL, COMME MALADIE MENTALE

Tout s'explique, si l'on en croit Tatiana et la voix anonyme de la société, par la « folie » de Lol, comprise au sens de maladie mentale, sous des noms divers que nous avons partiellement évoqués[1]. Il faudrait y ajouter celui d'hystérie, cette forme de névrose supposée propre aux femmes et qui tire son nom du corps féminin[2].

Lol aurait-elle été « incomplète » dès l'enfance (p. 12 et 80), ou rendue folle par le traumatisme du bal ? L'opinion de Tatiana fluctue entre ces deux hypothèses. La seconde est partagée par Jean Bedford (p. 34, 66, 143) et la rumeur publique (p. 24, 31).

Le roman propose le développement assez complet d'un « cas » : antécédents, traumatisme, crise, symptômes, guérison, rechute[3].

Lol fait peur (p. 149), même à Jacques Hold, ses proches vivent dans une « inquiétude [...] constante » (p. 143). Tatiana porte sur cette « folle » des jugements brutaux : « Une vicieuse, dit Tatiana, elle devait toujours penser à la même chose » (p. 46). « C'est notre petite Lola ? [...] Cette dingue ? » (p. 163).

Et pourtant, en même temps, la folie de Lol rassure. Elle confirme les clichés : « On devait ne jamais guérir tout à fait de la passion » (p. 76). Elle apparaît aussi comme une victoire sur le passage du temps : « cette survivance même pâlie de la folie de Lol met en échec l'horrible fugacité des choses, ralentit un peu la fuite insensée des étés passés » (p. 84).

1. « Folie » et « maladie » sont des termes très récurrents dans le roman.

2. Maladie de Dora, dans le cas analysé par Freud, *Fragment d'une analyse d'hystérie : Dora* (1905), in *Cinq psychanalyses*, PUF, 1954. Dora est parfois rapprochée de Lol, voir par ex. Susan Rubin Suleiman, « Nadja, Dora, Lol V. Stein : women, madness and narrative ».

3. On peut lire, dans Raynalle Udris, *Welcome Unreason, op. cit.*, p. 48-50, un résumé complet du « cas ».

Même Jacques Hold s'inquiète : « je me demande jusqu'à la torture, je me demande à quoi m'attendre encore de Lol. À quoi ? Je suis, je serais donc dupé par sa folie même ? » (p. 152).

Lacan aurait livré à Marguerite Duras, un jour, à minuit, dans un sous-sol ce diagnostic : « " Un délire cliniquement parfait[1]. " " Il m'a fait peur, Lacan " », ajoute Duras.

1. « La destruction, la parole », p. 56.

Lol serait donc « folle », selon les critères de S. Tahla (et de Lacan !). Elle le sait et craint le sort qui lui est promis, comme en témoigne ce dialogue avec Jacques Hold :

« — Mais si un jour je... — elle cogne sur le mot qu'elle ne trouve pas — est-ce qu'ils me laisseront me promener ?

« — Je vous cacherai.

« — Ils se tromperont ce jour-là ?

« — Non » (p. 139). Le mot absent, ici, c'est clairement le mot « folie ». *L'amour* semble confirmer le diagnostic et les craintes de Lol (*Am.*, p. 105).

Si Lol est « folle », et quel que soit le sens du terme, toutes les lacunes et les réticences du texte se justifient. Comment parler au nom de la folie, à la place de son silence ? La tentative de Jacques Hold se heurte à l'impossible et contraint le lecteur à la même expérience.

LA FOLIE COMME DÉRAISON

Mais cette « folie », autant que maladie, ne serait-elle pas « déraison » ? Refus de la raison des autres ? de la raison sociale[2] ?

2. Voir R. Udris, *Welcome Unreason, op. cit.*

Lol a tenté la voie de l'intégration. Elle s'est ensevelie vivante sous les « glaces » de l'hiver. « Dormeuse debout », elle a « fait la morte ». Et c'est justement cette phrase, « morte peut-être », autant que le retour à S. Tahla, qui l'a sortie des « tombeaux » (p. 37).

Il est tentant, avec les lectrices féministes, de lire là aussi une métaphore de l'ensevelissement des femmes, réduites, comme Lol, à une « virtualité irrépprochable », interdites d'accès à un désir autre et imprévisible. La transgression de Tatiana, l'adultère, reste dans les normes et bénéficie d'indulgence, du moins pour celles qui, comme Tatiana justement, tiennent « à faire comme si la chose était secrète » (p. 118).

Mais l'« incongruité[1] » de Lol est très différente et beaucoup plus subversive : « Elle sait quand même que certains lutteraient — elle hier encore — qu'ils retourneraient chez eux en courant dès qu'un reste de raison les ferait se surprendre dans ce champ » (p. 63).

Le profond désir de Lol, c'est, comme l'écrit Lacan, « être à trois[2] ». Rien moins qu'une autre modalité d'amour et de rapports sociaux, plus ouverte et plus imprévisible aussi. Des relations sans exclusive, « sans préférence ». Une véritable « utopie[3] ».

Lol, cependant, ne va pas très loin dans cette direction : elle en reste à une sorte d'aménagement, peu satisfaisant, de l'adultère mondain : « Lol n'évolue qu'en elle-même, c'est tout », déclare Marguerite Duras[4]. Peut-être parce que Jacques Hold,

1. Lol se trouve apparentée avec Anne Desbaresdes, dans *Moderato cantabile* : « Si son incongruité la dévore, elle ne peut s'imaginer » (*M.C.*, p. 93).

2. « Hommage », p. 12.

3. « La destruction, la parole », p. 54.

4. Cité par Michèle Druon, « Mise en scène et catharsis de l'amour », *op. cit.*, p. 388.

tout en l'accompagnant dans son voyage, tente aussi de l'entraîner vers des chemins mieux balisés, les siens. Et parce que Lol « est débordée par l'aboutissement, même inaccompli, de son désir » (p. 131). Lol ne fait qu'ouvrir une voie, où s'engouffreront ses sœurs plus audacieuses, dans l'avenir de l'œuvre : Anne-Marie Stretter, dans *Le vice-consul*, Alissa, dans *Détruire, dit-elle*.

« Des fous », dit Duras, « les asiles en sont pleins partout. Moi, ça me rassure profondément. Ça prouve bien que le monde est insupportable... [...] C'est un espoir que j'exprime là. Qu'il y ait de plus en plus de fous[1]. » Vœu provocant et fortement contestable, car il tend à n'opérer, dans la folie, aucune distinction. Mais qui montre l'impact de cette Lol, dont le silence est comme un écho du grand silence de la folie[2].

1. « La destruction, la parole », p. 54.

2. M. Foucault, *op. cit.*, p. 9.

LE VENTRE DE DIEU

Au-delà, encore, de cette mise en cause des conventions sociales, de cette tentative, avortée, de redistribution des cartes, le *Ravissement* a été lu aussi comme un livre religieux ou même mystique[3].

3. Voir Dossier, p. 189 *sq.*

Il est vrai que l'on remarque, dans le roman, une surprenante récurrence du mot « Dieu », dans des contextes insolites. Ainsi, tentant de « murer le bal », d'arrêter le temps, Lol, impuissante, déchirée, « n'est ni Dieu ni personne » (p. 49). Michael Richardson, commençant à « dévêtir une autre femme que Lol [...] en reste là ; ébloui, un

Dieu lassé par cette mise à nu, sa tâche unique » (p. 50). Jacques Hold, dans son « émotion très violente », demande « l'aide de Dieu » (p. 120).

« Dieu » semble pourtant utilisé comme un mot, ou de façon métaphorique et un peu dérisoire[1]. Sauf dans une déclaration étrange que Lol fait à Jacques Hold, dans le train qui les emmène vers T. Beach, en évoquant son précédent voyage : « La mer était dans la glace de la salle d'attente [...]. Vous n'étiez pas du tout dans la ville, même avant. Si je croyais en vous comme les autres croient en Dieu je pourrais me demander pourquoi vous, à quoi ça rime ? Pourtant la plage était vide autant que si elle n'avait pas été finie par Dieu » (p. 171-172). Un monde d'avant la Création, un Dieu qui n'a pas fini sa tâche et qui reste figé dans un geste inachevé, infiniment associé au vide.

1. On lira aux derniers mots de *L'amour* : « le bruit vous savez ?... de Dieu ?... ce truc ?... » (*Am.*, p. 131). Voir le commentaire de Danielle Bajomée, *Duras, ou la Douleur* (*op. cit.*, p. 76, 77). La formule choquante de Duras se voit rapprochée du commentaire de Lévi-Strauss sur Marcel Mauss, à propos du « mana », manière familière d'évoquer le sacré.

Une autre phrase étonnante décrit l'éveil de Lol : « Puis un jour ce corps infirme remue dans le ventre de Dieu » (p. 51). « Le ventre de Dieu », formule sacrilège, certes : Dieu serait-il devenu femme ? Lol cherche le retour à un grand tout maternel et féminisé, au sein duquel elle va pouvoir revivre, au moins quelques jours.

Revivre, cependant, c'est être « remplacée », perdre son identité, dans l'écartèlement du triangle impossible. Au cœur du désir de Lol, « rien », le vide. Désir « fou » ou désir mystique ?

Le style du *Ravissement* use fréquemment de formules paradoxales. Lol est « devenue un désert » (p. 24). Elle cherche un « ailleurs

[...] fade et sublime [...], adorable à son âme » (p. 44). « ç'aurait été [...] leur plus grande douleur et leur plus grande joie confondues... » (p. 48). Elle regarde « un spectacle [...] invisible » (p. 63).

Ces paradoxes définissent un mode de connaissance privilégié. Lol retourne « vers son ignorance de S. Tahla » (p. 42). Jacques Hold a une révélation : « je sais : je ne sais rien [...] : ne rien savoir de Lol était la connaître déjà » (p. 81). « Il la console d'un malheur inexistant et qu'elle ignore » (p. 162). « Puisque je sais [...] qu'elle m'est inconnaissable, on ne peut pas être plus près d'un être humain que je le suis d'elle » (p. 166). Et Lol lui déclare : « Je ne vous aime pas cependant je vous aime » (p. 169).

Ils attendent alors : « la fin sans fin [...] de Lol V. Stein » (p. 184).

Ce jeu des paradoxes (proche des jeux du style de Lacan — calqués sur le fonctionnement de l'inconscient — ou des jeux rhétoriques des philosophes post-modernes)[1] agace souvent les lecteurs en mal de certitudes. Il peut aussi être rapproché des expressions de certains mystiques affrontés à la « déchirante impossibilité » de dire l'indicible : « Je meurs de ne pas mourir », écrivait Thérèse d'Avila[2].

Mais le « vide » désiré évoque aussi tout autant les philosophies orientales, en particulier le taoïsme, qui envisagent le Vide tout autrement que notre pensée occidentale et lui accordent une valeur positive.

1. Voir *supra*, p. 110.

2. Ph. Le Touzé, « Désir, transition et vide ». Voir Dossier, p. 189-191.

Cette référence aux philosophies orientales paraît très excentrique par rapport à l'univers du *Ravissement*. Elle le devient beaucoup moins si l'on considère l'ensemble de la pensée durassienne telle qu'elle se dégage de ses romans et films, mais aussi de tout le péritexte déclaratif.

« Dans l'optique chinoise, le Vide n'est pas, comme on pourrait le supposer, quelque chose de vague et d'inexistant, mais un élément éminemment dynamique et agissant » ; « le Vide est un pivot », « un signe privilégié » par rapport auquel se définissent les autres signes[1]. La peinture chinoise est axée sur le vide.

1. François Cheng, *Vide et plein, le langage pictural chinois*, Le Seuil, 1979, p. 21.

Le *Ravissement*, fiction centrée sur la fracture du désir et du langage impuissant à le dire, déclenche des interprétations illimitées dont le jeu miroitant constitue les sens pluriels du roman. Le texte, à prendre ici comme « tissu » et comme « pratique signifiante[2] », ne peut se réduire à un sens stable et unique. La pluralité des significations se trouve programmée par le roman lui-même.

2. Roland Barthes, « Texte (théorie du) », in *Encyclopaedia universalis*.

VII MOTIFS ET MÉTAPHORES

Les phrases du *Ravissement* ont toujours l'air de chercher un mot-trou, calquant la quête insatisfaite de Jacques Hold, elle-même écho de la poursuite que mène Lol d'« un ailleurs [...] fade et sublime » (p. 44) qui ne cesse de lui échapper. Dans une cohérence presque trop parfaite, le roman pratique, jusqu'en sa syntaxe même, une politique du leurre.

S'il se trouve ainsi doté d'une ouverture où peuvent s'engouffrer les interprétations, il prête aussi à une autre forme de « dé-lire » : la poursuite des métaphores, des motifs récurrents et des réseaux signifiants qu'ils dessinent. Le texte devient véritablement une « chambre d'échos » où les mots, puisqu'il y a quand même des mots (à la place, peut-être, du silence ?), résonnent comme « un gong vide » (p. 48).

Le problème alors, pour la critique, est d'effleurer ces motifs, de les « traverser », sans les restructurer à sa façon, ce qui serait à la fois les trahir et les transformer[1]. Il y faudrait « des doigts de fée », comme dit précisément le texte même : « De loin, avec des doigts de fée, le souvenir d'une certaine mémoire passe » (p. 63).

1. R. Barthes, *S/Z*, Le Seuil, p. 18.

1. LA BÊTE CHANTEUSE

Dans un article très lacanien, Duras est comparée à « la sphinge », « celle que Sophocle appelle, on l'oublie, " la bête chanteuse, de la famille des sirènes ", celle qui pose à Œdipe l'énigme, mais qui, loin d'être " un puits de science ", est présentée comme " attendant sans cesse les mots qui l'attendraient, en un long chant, continu et allusif "[2] ».

Les textes de Duras devraient peut-être être lus à haute voix. Leur vrai caractère, oral et musical, masqué par l'écrit, devient alors sensible, comme il apparaît clairement dans les films, et déjà, juste avant le *Ravissement*,

2. Christiane Rabant, « La Bête chanteuse », *L'ARC*, n° 58, numéro spécial *Jacques Lacan*, 1974, p. 16.

dans le récitatif qui ouvre *Hiroshima mon amour.* Le narrateur y redevient une voix vivante et la musique est la matière même du style. On pourrait dire du *Ravissement* ce que Duras dit des *Parleuses* : « Ce n'est pas un livre qu'on lit, c'est un livre qu'on écoute[1]. »

Cette musique un peu verlainienne des phrases fait écho aux motifs musicaux du *Ravissement.* Pas de piano, comme dans *Moderato cantabile* et, plus tard, dans *Nathalie Granger.* L'opéra est absent comme terme d'une métaphore, souvenir fantasmé d'un oubli. C'est le violon qui accompagne le *Ravissement* et lui donne sa tonalité un peu grinçante.

Les violons du bal, leur présence ne devient sensible que dans leur disparition. Les amants, « n'entendant pas qu'il n'y avait plus de musique », s'étaient rejoints « comme des automates » quand ils voient les musiciens passer devant eux « en file indienne, leurs violons, enfermés dans des boîtes funèbres » (p. 21). La musique fait partie intégrante du spectacle ; quand elle cesse, avec l'aurore, le jour se lève sur « la fin du monde ».

Les exercices de violon du mari de Lol rythment la soirée. Le violon « s'insinue » (p. 114). Lol l'écoute plus que les paroles. Ambivalence de ce violon. Il retient Lol et la rappelle à l'ordre. Mais il est signe aussi d'un ordre douloureusement conquis : « exercices [...] sur double corde [...] très aigus » (p. 89), ils rendent sensibles une souffrance très secrète, mais très maîtrisée : « Leur frénésie monotone est éperdument musicale, chant

1. « Ce que parler ne veut pas dire », entretien avec J. L. Ézine, *Les Nouvelles littéraires*, 16 avril 1974.

de l'instrument même » *(ibid.)*. Quand le violon « se retire » (comme à la fin du bal), il a creusé un gouffre : « il laisse derrière lui les cratères ouverts du souvenir immédiat » (p. 118).

Présence/absence, le violon fait partie du « ravissement » : signe vide, il ne signifie pas. Comme la musique elle-même, il existe seulement, « éperdument ».

2. UNE CHAMBRE D'ÉCHOS

Les métaphores, comme en poésie, empruntent souvent leur comparant aux éléments, instaurant ainsi une continuité entre le monde fictif et l'univers cosmique[1].

Le texte baigne dans la liquidité et laisse partout s'engouffrer l'air. Ces milieux instables conviennent à Lol, qui, à la fois « vous fuit dans les mains comme l'eau » (p. 13) et se voit « constamment envolée de sa vie vivante » (p. 166)[2].

1. Voir, bien sûr, les études de Bachelard.

2. Voir *supra*, « Le nom de Lol », p. 24-25.

LE VENT QUI S'ENGOUFFRE

Lol paraît être le jouet du vent. Ainsi, dans les rues de S. Tahla, le soir où Jean Bedford la rencontre, « elle avançait, mais ni plus ni moins que le vent qui s'engouffre là où il trouve du champ » (p. 28), « happée pardevant elle, droit » (p. 39). Et quand elle commence à bouger, c'est que « de l'air s'engouffre dans sa maison, la dérange, elle en est chassée » (p. 45). L'air et le vent deviennent le contraire de l'ordre glacé, mais aussi de la solidité (dont, par contre, participe Tatiana, ou du moins son mariage : « leur maison est solide plus qu'une autre, elle a résisté à tous les vents », p. 155). Lol est comme un espace vide, ouvert de toutes parts : « Elle s'immobilise sous le coup d'un passage en elle, de quoi ? de versions inconnues, sauvages, des oiseaux sauvages de sa vie, qu'en savons-nous ? qui la traversent de part en part, s'engouffrent ? puis le vent de ce vol s'apaise ? » (p. 145-146)[1].

Lol, toujours, reste passive. Le vent « dérange », « traverse », mais surtout, de façon presque obsessive, « le vent s'engouffre ». L'association insistante de ces deux mots suggère, encore, le vide au cœur de Lol. Mais creuse ce « trou de chair » (p. 48) en un « gouffre » angoissant, évocateur de désastres : « des chairs se déchirent, saignent, se réveillent » (p. 131). Et, pendant le voyage vers T. Beach : Lol « a été à côté de moi séparée de moi, gouffre et sœur » (p. 166)[2].

1. Pour les oiseaux, voir *supra*, p. 52.

2. Réminiscence baudelairienne ? « Le gouffre » et « L'invitation au voyage » : « Mon enfant, ma sœur... »

LA MER DANS UNE GLACE

Les métaphores qui évoquent Lol sont en majorité empruntées au domaine aquatique. Pendant son sommeil de U. Bridge, l'eau dont elle est faite se fige en glace. Lol est « morte », mais à la façon de Blanche-Neige, de la Belle au Bois Dormant, ou encore de la belle héroïne de *La nuit des temps*[3]. Quand Lol s'éveille, l'eau se remet à circuler en elle.

3. Barjavel, *La nuit des temps*, Presses de la Cité, 1969.

Les yeux de Lol, « d'*eau morte* et de *vase* mêlées » (p. 83), « *noyé[s]* dans la douceur d'une enfance interminable qui *surnage* à fleur de chair » (p. 177), contaminent Jacques Hold dont « le sang [est] *noyé*, le cœur de *vase* » (p. 111). Leur transparence se change en « *buée* » (p. 155). Sa parole est un « *lait* brumeux et insipide » (p. 106). « Elle se croit *coulée* dans une identité de nature indécise » (p. 41). « Elle *baigne* dans la joie. Les signes de celle-ci [...] sortent *par flots* d'elle-même tout entière » (p. 165) ; un « large *fleuve* [...] la séparait de ceux de S. Tahla » (p. 42).

Surtout, Lol est inséparable de la mer. Pourtant, S. Tahla, celui du *Ravissement*, n'est pas au bord de la mer. Marguerite Duras l'associe à ce milieu marin : « Les différents lieux de Lol V. Stein sont tous des lieux maritimes » (*Lieux*, p. 84). Dans cette déclaration Duras pense davantage à *L'amour* et surtout au film *La femme du Gange*. Mais elle fait aussi la même erreur que Lol, celle qui fait sursauter Tatiana : « elle dit que la mer n'est pas loin de la villa qu'elle habitait à U. Bridge. Tatiana a un sursaut : la mer est à deux heures de U. Bridge » (p. 82).

Cette erreur est comme une percée du désir de Lol, inlassablement tourné vers la mer, qui lui est rendue une première fois, mais seulement dans un miroir : « Je ne voyais pas directement la mer. Je la voyais devant moi dans une glace sur un mur. J'ai éprouvé une très forte tentation d'y aller, d'aller voir » (p. 152)[1]. Scène crépusculaire,

1. Le jeu phonique induit par la langue française, « mer/mère », est évidemment bien tentant, d'autant que le motif de la maternité est aussi partout sous-jacent.

opposée à la scène de l'aurore. La mer revient avec la nuit. Mais ce n'est pas une vraie mer, seulement un reflet inaccessible : Lol se trouve séparée d'elle par une glace, comme il advient dans la schizophrénie. Le mot « glace », préféré au mot « miroir », fait un sinistre écho aux « glaces » de l'hiver qui enfermaient le sommeil de Lol, et préfigure sa plongée dans un nouveau sommeil aux derniers mots du roman.

Car la mer n'affleure que très rarement dans ce texte, qui laisse plutôt émerger des signes de son absence. Ainsi, le nom répété de T. Beach. « Beach », la plage. Et « T » ? L'initiale de Tahla, de « thalassa » ? Tandis que le « S » de S. Tahla pourrait signifier *sea*, la mer, en anglais, cette fois. Jeux de mots incomplets, énigmes, rébus de la sphinge. La mer se cache. À la fin, quand on pourrait croire que Lol l'a enfin rejointe, en même temps qu'elle aurait comblé son désir, la mer d'abord se retire : « la mer, elle baisse, baisse, laisse derrière elle des marécages bleus de ciel » (p. 182). Puis elle revient, mais pour apporter mort et confusion : « la mer monte enfin, elle noie les marécages bleus les uns après les autres, progressivement et avec une lenteur égale ils perdent leur individualité et se confondent avec la mer [...]. La mort des marécages emplit Lol d'une tristesse abominable, elle attend, la prévoit, la vit. Elle la reconnaît » (p. 185-186). « Vase », « marécages », Lol lit sa propre histoire dans le sort de ces marécages.

AUTRES MÉTAPHORES

Quelques autres métaphores surprenantes trouent le texte de leur fulguration, sans construire de figures : on pense aux images surréalistes.

Ainsi, à la « marche de prairie » des deux femmes du bal (p. 16) répond « la vaste et sombre prairie de l'aurore » qui interrompt l'hallucination de Jacques Hold (p. 181), tandis que Lol est mêlée à « une lumière verte qui divague et s'accroche partout dans des myriades de petits éclatements aveuglants » (p. 165).

Ainsi l'étrange présence des minéraux, et même du minerai, contrepoids à la légèreté de Lol, mais signe aussi d'une matière résistante et impénétrable : « son passé devenu de fer-blanc » (p. 32), son corps « lourd, plombé » (p. 53), le « champ immense mais aux limites d'acier » de son mensonge (p. 106), le « minerai de chair » de ses yeux (p. 165).

Et, pour terminer cette promenade sans dessein parmi les motifs et les métaphores (semblable, en somme, à l'errance de Lol dans les rues de S. Tahla), je citerai de nouveau l'image plus éblouissante, tout à fait isolée dans le texte, malgré les échos assourdis que lui font quelques adjectifs, « joie barbare » (p. 129), « oiseaux sauvages de sa vie » (p. 145) : « Lol a un accent que je ne lui connaissais pas encore, plaintif et aigu[1]. La bête séparée de la forêt dort, elle rêve de l'équateur de sa naissance, dans un frémissement, son rêve solaire pleure » (p. 117). Voici Lol brusquement devenue « panthère

1. Remarquons l'harmonie avec les exercices de violon.

noire des marécages palétuviens » qui se meurt de sécheresse sur un sol de ciment (comme l'animal sauvage enfermé au zoo de la nouvelle « Le boa »)[1] et rattachée ainsi, très secrètement, à l'univers de l'enfance de Duras.

1. In *Des journées entières dans les arbres.*

Il s'agissait seulement, dans cette partie un peu excentrique, de nous laisser guider par « l'orient pernicieux des mots » (p. 124), quitte, comme Lol, avant la mendiante, à y perdre un peu « le nord ».

VIII INTERTEXTUALITÉ

1. RENCONTRES ET DIALOGUES

L'originalité du *Ravissement* n'exclut pas des rencontres de divers types avec des textes multiples.

De rares critiques, surtout au moment de la publication du roman, ont souligné ses ressemblances avec des textes parus dans un passé proche[2]. À l'examen, elles se révèlent n'être, le plus souvent, que de vagues parentés.

2. Voir Dossier, p. 197-199 *sq.*

Cependant, le *Ravissement* s'inscrit, de toute évidence, dans des courants littéraires et philosophiques, sans pourtant se réclamer d'eux directement. Il se trouve profondément lié à son temps par cette « autre réalité formelle », située « entre la langue et le style », que Barthes nomme l'« écriture » :

« acte de solidarité historique », « compromis entre une liberté et un souvenir[1] ».

Le dialogue explicite avec d'autres textes récents est inexistant dans le *Ravissement*, même si les errances de Lol V. Stein dans S. Tahla peuvent rappeler celles de Nadja dans les rues de Paris, ou si le jeu des leurres de la mémoire et des répétitions évoque *L'année dernière à Marienbad*[2]. On a même pu voir un caractère proustien dans ce roman qui, il est vrai, est aussi une recherche du temps perdu, et qui a été écrit dans l'un des hauts lieux proustiens, Trouville. Mais ces analogies plutôt floues relèvent davantage de l'« air du temps » que d'influences directes ou de rencontres profondes.

1. Roland Barthes, *Le degré zéro de l'écriture*, Le Seuil, coll. « Points », p. 14-16.

2. Voir Dossier, p. 198-199.

ISEULT OU EURYDICE

Le *Ravissement*, solidaire de son époque par son écriture, dialogue plutôt avec le texte beaucoup plus ancien et plus diffus des légendes et des mythes. Ce dialogue est d'ailleurs une autre forme de rencontre avec les grands livres du XXe siècle pour lesquels une intertextualité complexe avec les mythes est constitutive. Le jeu intertextuel ne prend jamais, dans le roman de Duras, le caractère systématique qu'il a chez Joyce, répétant, dans *Ulysse*, la structure de l'*Odyssée*, ni celui, non moins systématique, mais plus dissimulé encore, choisi par Robbe-Grillet construisant *Les gommes* sur le mythe d'Œdipe, ou par Butor édifiant *L'emploi du temps* sur l'histoire de Caïn et d'Abel.

Les allusions, dans le *Ravissement*, restent indirectes, souvent implicites : l'intertextualité légendaire sert plutôt de fond diffus.

L'une des références les plus explicites se reproduit deux fois dans le roman : « l'étendard blanc des amants dans leur premier voyage » (p. 81). La première fois l'étendard « flotte toujours sur la ville obscurcie », accompagnant la tristesse vespérale de Tatiana. À la fin du dîner chez Lol, il devient problématique : « qui sait ? » pense Jacques Hold, en voyant souffrir Tatiana, « peut-être, l'étendard blanc des amants du premier voyage passera-t-il très près de ma maison » (p. 158).

« L'étendard blanc des amants » évoque la légende de Tristan et Iseult, remémorée avec quelque méprise : le signe d'Iseult la blonde à Tristan est une voile blanche, qui, changée en voile noire dans le traître discours de l'autre Iseult « aux blanches mains », provoque la mort des amants. Lol aussi « est blanche d'une blancheur nue » (p. 112) et Jacques Hold remarque sa main. Laquelle des Iseult évoque alors Lol ? « La blonde », victime du philtre et morte d'amour fou ? Ou l'autre, la trahie et la traîtresse ?

Le *Ravissement* laisse flotter, à l'arrière-plan de l'histoire de Lol, ce beau conte d'amour et de mort, source possible du mythe de l'amour fou. Mais comme la mémoire d'une ancienne histoire oubliée, dont les motifs s'entremêlent et glissent. Ou comme un regret, peut-être, des temps mythiques où pouvaient naître de telles histoires et exister de telles amours.

Plus lointaine encore, et bien moins explicite, se profile l'histoire d'Orphée et d'Eurydice. Comme Orphée, Jacques Hold veut « ouvrir des tombeaux où Lol fait la morte » (p. 37) et tente de la ramener de l'« enfer » de sa folie vers le monde des vivants. Comme Orphée, il échoue.

Dans les deux cas, la belle légende évoquée se trouve métamorphosée, dégradée dans sa version moderne : l'« amour parfait » n'est plus qu'un modèle impossible, la mort est devenue folie.

LA BELLE AU BOIS DORMANT

Plus proches, peut-être, les contes. Surtout *La Belle au Bois Dormant*. Lol, « dormeuse debout » (*sleeping beauty*[1], dans les traductions anglaises), endormie par la mauvaise fée, endormie aussi dans le champ de seigle devant l'hôtel « des Bois », s'éveille grâce au passage et au baiser du « prince charmant[2] », Jacques Hold. Mais quelques jours seulement : elle est rendormie aux derniers mots du roman. Le sommeil reste sa condition, comme celle aussi de bien d'autres héroïnes durassiennes. Sommeil très ambivalent : à la fois condition sociale prescrite — le mari, très conventionnel, de Lol aime son sommeil et cherche à la maintenir endormie. Mais aussi sommeil prêt à devenir subversion délibérée, passivité efficace[3], remise en cause des images féminines[4].

Ces dialogues avec d'autres textes ne prennent jamais une forme savante, ni même

1. C'est le titre anglais du conte.

2. En fait Jacques Hold serait plutôt un prince de second choix, de substitution, mis à la place du « vrai » prince : Michael Richardson, qui, dans la version moderne du conte, ne remplit plus son rôle et fait défaut.

3. « Cette grande passivité qui, à mon avis, s'annonce fondamentale » (*P.*, p. 148).

4. Comme le montre Susan Cohen, dans un chapitre intitulé « Sleeping Beauties » (p. 103-130) consacré aux textes érotiques de Duras.

exacte. Ils jouent sur des approximations, des textes oubliés, désindividualisés, comme les personnages durassiens, devenus échos de légendes. Selon sa propre formule, l'écriture durassienne est « une chambre d'écho » (*P.*, p. 218).

2. AUTO-INTERTEXTUALITÉ

Les corrélations intertextuelles sont, par contre, fondamentales à l'intérieur du grand ensemble de l'œuvre durassienne. Marguerite Duras déclare : « Je l'aime infiniment, cette Lol V. Stein, et je peux pas m'en débarrasser. Elle a pour moi une..., une sorte de grâce inépuisable » (*P.*, p. 160). Pourtant, elle ne lui accorde qu'une place assez modeste, bien différente de la présence envahissante et durable d'Anne-Marie Stretter.

Tout se passe même comme s'il se produisait, dans le déroulement de l'œuvre, pour ces deux personnages féminins, ce mouvement « parallèle et inverse » de remplacement (la forme du « U ») qui anime tout le *Ravissement.* Dans ce premier roman du cycle, Anne-Marie Stretter ne fait que passer, passage déterminant mais bref comme une apparition, tandis que Lol est au premier plan.

« LE VICE-CONSUL »

Dans *Le vice-consul*, qui succède immédiatement au *Ravissement*, Lol disparaît complètement ; Anne-Marie Stretter a pris la première place. Mais apparaît une autre femme, réduite à une telle misère qu'elle a tout perdu, même la parole et la mémoire : la mendiante indienne[1]. Elle n'est pas le personnage principal du roman *Le vice-consul*, seulement celui du livre qu'écrit l'un des personnages, Peter Morgan. Mais elle est présente dès les premiers mots du *Vice-consul :* « Elle marche, écrit Peter Morgan. »

1. Voir Madeleine Borgomano, « L'Histoire de la mendiante indienne », *Poétique*, n° 48, Le Seuil, novembre 1981.

Ce personnage-limite se trouve ainsi mis à la place de Lol : comme Jacques Hold tentant de comprendre Lol et de reconstruire son histoire, Peter Morgan, fasciné par l'extrême dénuement de la mendiante, essaie d'écrire un livre sur elle. Comme Lol, la mendiante marche, comme elle aussi, elle est silencieuse (mais plus radicalement : elle a perdu « sa langue »), comme elle, elle oublie tout. Littéralement, et en dépit de toutes leurs différences de race, de classe, de lieu, il apparaît que la mendiante anonyme remplace Lol V. Stein.

« L'AMOUR »

L'amour (1971) a pris comme titre l'un des mots magiques qui hantaient le *Ravissement*. Mais isoler ce mot dans un titre, ce n'est pas lui donner une présence. D'amour, dans le récit, il n'en est jamais question ; on dirait même que le souvenir en a disparu. Seule reste la folie : le titre est un leurre.

Au contraire de ce qui se passe dans *Le vice-consul*, dans *L'amour*, Anne-Marie Stretter a disparu et Lol revient, mais privée de nom et presque de mémoire, réduite à un état très proche de celui de la mendiante indienne. Ce récit austère se développe sur la forme du triangle, dessiné sur le sable d'une plage par trois personnages qui marchent, deux hommes et une femme. Le lieu, nommé S. Thala, déserté ou peuplé de fantômes, est devenu un espace à la fois largement ouvert sur la mer et concentrationnaire : « Prison dehors les murs... internement volontaire » (*Am.*, p. 51). Plus aucun nom pour les ombres errantes, mais des bribes d'histoire renvoient au *Ravissement*, dont la mémoire rend *L'amour* plus lisible. Aucun événement, sauf, aux tout derniers mots, « progression de l'aurore extérieure » (*Am.*, p. 131).

Lol, selon *L'amour*, s'est rendormie. Malade, elle a été internée et « n'a jamais guéri » (*Am.*, p. 73). Au contraire, sa « folie » semble avoir contaminé « l'ensemble » : « Où qu'elle aille, tout se défait » (*Am.*, p. 75). Même le récit, gagné par la contagion, a tout perdu, son narrateur, sa cohérence, et presque son intelligibilité. Il s'est fait aussi proche que possible du « degré zéro de l'écriture ».

FILMS

Il est remarquable que Marguerite Duras, qui « liquide » ses livres importants en les transcrivant — en les « massacrant » — dans des films[1], n'ait jamais tiré de film du *Ravissement* : « Évidemment, dit-elle à Michelle Porte, je peux montrer Lol V. Stein au cinéma, mais je ne peux la montrer que cachée, quand elle est comme un chien mort sur la plage, recouverte de sable... » (*Lieux*, p. 100).

1. Voir *supra*, p. 111.

C'est donc de *L'amour* et du *Vice-consul* que sont issus *La femme du Gange* et *India Song*.

En 1972, dans *La femme du Gange*, film jamais distribué, voué lui aussi à la perdition, Marguerite Duras filme *L'amour*. Le film donne à S. Thala l'apparence d'une plage du Nord, immense et déserte, où la mer se retire très loin. Si l'on en croit les « didascalies » du livre, cette plage nordique figure aussi, en même temps, les Indes où sont partis les amants du bal : « Où est-ce ? Un quai de douane de là-bas, de la Mésopotamie du Gange, perdu ici à S. Thala ? » (*F.G.*, p. 124). Mais le spectateur du film ne voit qu'un lieu de nulle part.

Le film reprend, en les entremêlant, les histoires déjà racontées dans les trois romans. Rien, ou presque, n'est représenté, sauf les lentes déambulations. Mais on entend, en contrepoint des images, le dialogue de deux voix *off*, des voix féminines, dépourvues de visage et de corps. Ces voix désincarnées communiquent au film une dimension angoissante, une « inquiétante étrangeté[1] », onirique ou fantasmatique. Par là, il figure, sans le représenter, l'univers mental de Lol.

1. Freud, « L'inquiétante étrangeté », Gallimard, coll. « Folio Essais » : « Cette sorte de l'effrayant qui se rattache aux choses familières », qui émane des complexes refoulés et se manifeste fréquemment dans la fiction.

Mais le dialogue des voix apporte tout de même quelque allégement à l'austérité du film. Car, non sans hésitations et lacunes, il évoque les histoires de Lol et d'Anne-Marie Stretter.

Les personnages ont retrouvé leurs noms, mais perdu leur substance. Sont-ils devenus ces fantômes errants ? Ou n'existent-ils plus que dans les fragments « lézardés » des histoires évoquées par des voix fantomatiques, elles aussi ? Les voix *off* évoquent la mort d'Anne-Marie Stretter (*F.G.*, p. 126), un homme affirme la mort de « mademoiselle Stein » (*F.G.*, p. 188).

Lol revient, une dernière fois, invisible, dans un autre film, *India Song* (1975). Elle est renvoyée à l'arrière-plan, de nouveau remplacée par Anne-Marie Stretter. Ce sont toujours des voix *off* qui rappellent l'histoire du bal, comme celle d'un ancien meurtre et, de nouveau, répètent qu'elle n'a jamais guéri. Les images ne la montrent jamais.

Une dernière fois, le nom de Lol se fait entendre dans la bande-son du film *Son nom de Venise dans Calcutta désert*. Il s'agit d'ailleurs de la bande-son d'*India Song*, réutilisée pour un film gageure, où l'image ne montre que des ruines, désertes, et où la bande-son se déroule sur ce spectacle mort de fin du monde. L'histoire de Lol V. Stein se trouve ainsi dépouillée de toute substance, enfouie dans un lointain passé, lézardée, désintégrée.

Peut-être est-ce Lol cette femme en noir qu'on voit quelques instants, immobile et silencieuse, aux dernières images de *Son nom de Venise dans Calcutta désert* ? Lol ou son ombre, dépouillée de toute identité.

Après *India Song*, Lol et son histoire disparaissent des romans et des films, tandis qu'Anne-Marie Stretter, pourtant délibérément tuée par sa créatrice[1], renaît encore de ses cendres, dans *L'amant* et *L'amant de la Chine du Nord.*

1. *Marguerite Duras à Montréal, op. cit.*, p. 33.

CONCLUSION

« [Lol V. Stein] c'est plutôt à vous autres qu'à moi. Le livre a été appréhendé par des gens, si bien que j'en suis dépossédée » (*P.*, p. 188). « Elle est à vous, Lol V. Stein, elle est aux autres... » (*Lieux*, p. 101). Ainsi Marguerite Duras nous livrait-elle son roman et son héroïne, à nous, lecteurs ; tout comme le font, implicitement, tous les écrivains qui publient leurs œuvres. Mais avec cette particularité qu'il s'agit d'une œuvre « ouverte », béante, même. D'un roman « inépuisable », comme son personnage. En mettant en scène l'opération même de sa propre genèse, il « met en abyme[2] » tout aussi bien, l'acte de sa lecture, qui ne peut s'achever.

À relire et relire le *Ravissement*, le lecteur ne cessera de s'apercevoir que s'ouvrent toujours de nouveaux gouffres inaperçus. Cette lec-

2. « Mise en abyme » : figuration en modèle réduit, à l'intérieur d'un récit, d'un constituant de ce récit, ou de sa structure, produisant, comme les reflets multipliés dans les miroirs, des perturbations et des effets de profondeur infinie.

ture, déceptive, ne peut être assouvissante et ne conviendra pas à ceux qui cherchent des messages ou des vérités. Cette lecture, exigeante, lassera les lecteurs paresseux. Si « ravissement » il doit y avoir, encore faut-il le conquérir. Mais aussi ne pas y céder totalement. Garder quelque distance, c'est pratiquer cette liberté à laquelle le roman nous invite. À ce prix, *Le ravissement de Lol V. Stein*, s'il ne prétend pas changer le monde, changera peut-être un peu son lecteur et deviendra pour lui, beaucoup plus qu'un divertissement, une aventure intérieure.

DOSSIER

I. BIOGRAPHIE

La biographie de Marguerite Duras, rien de moins secret, en apparence, puisqu'elle l'étale elle-même au grand jour, de livres en interviews, puisqu'elle en tire des « autobiographies », comme *L'amant*, puis *L'amant de la Chine du Nord*. Pourtant, rien de plus inaccessible, aussi insaisissable que le personnage de Lol V. Stein. Car les éléments de la biographie durassienne ne cessent de se composer, de se recomposer, de se décomposer, comme les éléments de « *l'ensemble* » incertain construit par ses livres. Dont, d'ailleurs, ils ne se distinguent guère, variables, incertains, sujets à des versions diverses et parfois contradictoires. Les biographies de Duras se contentent souvent de répéter ce que Duras dit ou écrit, sans prendre de distance critique, devenant alors paraphrases mytho-biographiques, voire hagiographies. Je ne donnerai ici que quelques repères.

1914 Avril : naissance de Marguerite Donnadieu, à Gia-Dinh, près de Saigon, en Cochinchine, actuel Vietnam.

« Duras » est un pseudonyme, adopté, dit-elle, parce qu'elle tient son nom « dans une telle horreur qu'elle arrive à peine à le prononcer » (*P.*, p. 23-24). Duras n'est donc pas le « nom du père » ; pourtant, le pseudonyme est emprunté à un village du Lot-et-Garonne, région paternelle, où le père serait mort.

Le père de Marguerite, Henri Donnadieu, est professeur de mathématiques. Sa mère, Marie Legrand, originaire du nord de la France, est institutrice. Marguerite est la plus jeune : elle a deux demi-frères, fils d'un premier mariage du père, restés en France, dans le Sud-Ouest, et deux frères, nommés, si l'on en croit *L'amant de la Chine du Nord,* Pierre et « Paulo », « le petit frère différent ».

1918 Mort du père, qui avait été rapatrié en France.

1918-1932 La famille Donnadieu vit en Indochine, à Phnom Penh, Vinh Long, Sadec, au gré des affectations de la mère, institutrice d'école indigène, « un emploi tout à fait parmi les derniers là-bas » (*Lieux*, p. 56).
Marguerite fait ses études secondaires au lycée de Saigon, où elle vit dans une pension pour jeunes filles.
De cette jeunesse indochinoise ont surgi les principaux « motifs » générateurs de l'écriture, sans cesse ressassés :
— le « décor fluvial » et les paysages asiatiques ;
— la famille « en pierre, pétrifiée ».
— l'histoire des barrages ;
— le passage du fleuve et l'histoire de l'amant ;
— le passage d'une mendiante qui « vend son enfant » ;
— la rencontre avec « la Dame ».

1932 Retour en France, avec la mère et le petit frère. Mais ils repartent rapidement en Indochine. Pour elle, la rupture est terrible : « je suis restée à dix-huit ans [...]. Si j'étais morte hier, je serais morte à dix-huit ans » (*Y.*, p. 23). Sur cette partie de sa vie, Marguerite Duras reste beaucoup plus discrète, elle ne la fait pas entrer en littérature.
Études de droit, de sciences politiques, de mathématiques « très... vagues » (« La destruction, la parole », p. 52).

1937 Emploi au ministère des Colonies.

1939 Mariage avec Robert Antelme.

1940 Le premier livre publié, chez Gallimard, au nom de Marguerite Donnadieu (en collaboration *avec* Ph. Roques) s'intitule *L'Empire français*, et célèbre l'empire colonial.
Recrutée au Cercle de la librairie.

1942 Marguerite Duras aménage 5, rue Saint-Benoît (où elle habitera jusqu'à la fin de sa vie et qui sera longtemps un lieu littéraire que fréquenteront Blanchot, Genet, Bataille, Edgar Morin, Merleau-Ponty, Claude Roy, etc.).
Son premier enfant meurt à la naissance.
Le « petit frère » meurt en Indochine.
Rencontre avec Dyonis Mascolo.

1943 Publication du premier roman signé Marguerite Duras, *Les impudents*, chez Plon (repris ensuite par Gallimard).
Entrée dans un réseau de Résistance, où elle rencontre François Mitterrand, qui porte le pseudonyme de Morland.

1944 Publication de *La vie tranquille*, chez Gallimard.
Arrestation, puis déportation de Robert Antelme.

1945 Retrouvé par François Mitterrand, Robert Antelme est ramené de Dachau (voir *La douleur*, journal qui aurait été écrit à l'époque, puis oublié). Robert Antelme publiera, en 1947, *L'espèce humaine*.
6 août 1945 : bombe atomique sur Hiroshima.

1946 Divorce d'avec Robert Antelme. Marguerite Duras vit désormais avec Dyonis Mascolo.

1947 Naissance du fils de Duras, Jean Mascolo.
Marguerite Duras milite activement au parti communiste, dans lequel elle se trouve marginalisée dès 1948.

1950 Publication d'*Un barrage contre le Pacifique*, qui rate de peu le prix Goncourt.

Duras est exclue du parti communiste.
Sa mère rentre en France.

(Après 1950, les publications de Duras, textes, théâtre, films, se succèdent à un rythme très rapide, accompagnées de nombreuses interventions journalistiques. Ne seront notés ici que quelques textes ou films essentiels.)

1955 *Le square*, première pièce de théâtre.

1957 Séparation d'avec Dyonis Mascolo.
Rencontre passionnée avec Gérard Jarlot.
Date probable de la mort de la mère. (M. Duras déclare avoir oublié cette date.)

1958 *Moderato cantabile.*
Achat de la maison de Neauphle-le-Château.

1959 Marguerite Duras est scénariste du film d'Alain Resnais, *Hiroshima mon amour.*

1963 Acquisition d'un appartement aux Roches Noires, à Trouville, où elle écrit le *Ravissement.*

1964 Mars : *Le ravissement de Lol V. Stein.*

1965 *Le vice-consul.*

1968 Participation active aux événements de mai 68.

1969 Premier film réalisé par Duras seule, *Détruire, dit-elle.*

1975 *India Song*, prix de l'Association française des cinémas d'art et d'essai au Festival de Cannes.

Été 1980 Rencontre avec Yann Andréa, jeune homme de vingt-sept ans, qui devient le compagnon de Marguerite Duras.
Événements de Gdansk, en Pologne.
Marguerite Duras rédige, pour *Libération*, une chronique qui deviendra *L'été 80.*

1982 Marguerite Duras, alcoolique depuis longtemps, subit une terrible cure de désintoxication.

1984 *L'amant*, qui obtient le prix Goncourt.

1985 17 juillet : publication dans *Libération* d'un article sur Christine Villemin, « Sublime, forcément sublime, Christine V. ».

1988-1989 Coma grave et longue hospitalisation.

1995 *C'est tout*, dernier livre publié.

1996 Dimanche 3 mars : mort de Marguerite Duras.

II. NAISSANCE DU « RAVISSEMENT »

Sur la genèse du *Ravissement*, les seules traces sont les confidences de Marguerite Duras elle-même, sujettes à variations commes les éléments de sa biographie.

Voici quelques-unes de ses déclarations au fil du temps.

1964 :

Lol, je l'ai écrit très vite, à Trouville, entre juin et octobre 1963. J'étais seule. Je doutais beaucoup de la valeur du livre. J'étais, vis-à-vis de moi-même, dans une sorte de méfiance. Je l'ai écrit comme ça.

Lettres françaises, 30 avril 1964.

1964 encore :

J'avais été très malade... c'était la première fois que j'écrivais sans alcool... C'était très dur... J'avais peur...

Lol V. Stein... je l'ai vue dans un bal de Noël dans un asile psychiatrique des environs de Paris. [...]

Et après... je l'ai revue une fois très longtemps.

[Elle était] comme un automate. Elle m'avait frappée parce qu'elle était belle... et intacte physiquement. D'habitude, les malades sont très marqués. Elle, elle ne l'était pas du tout.

[Elle avait] trente ans, mais elle paraissait très jeune... [...]

J'ai essayé de la faire parler très longtemps, enfin toute une journée... Elle parlait comme tout le monde, avec une banalité extraordinaire, une banalité remarquable... Elle croyait que j'étais un docteur... Elle parlait pour paraître, être comme tout le monde et plus elle le faisait, plus elle était singulière à mes yeux... C'était très impressionnant...

Transcription des propos tenus en 1964, dans un entretien télévisé avec Paul Seban, *Lectures pour tous*. Repris, en abyme, in *Lire et écrire*, entretien avec Pierre Dumayet (La 7, 1992).

1977 :

Tandis que je l'écrivais, j'ai eu un moment [...] de peur. J'ai crié. Je pense que quelque chose a été franchi, là, mais qui m'a échappé [...], peut-être un seuil d'opacité [...], je suis tombée dans l'opacité plus grande après ; c'est ça qui m'a fait crier, je me souviens de ça, ça ne m'était jamais arrivé avant. J'écrivais, et tout d'un coup j'ai entendu que je criais, parce que j'avais peur. Je ne sais pas très bien de quoi j'avais peur. C'était une peur... apprise aussi, une peur de perdre un peu la tête

Entretien avec Michelle Porte, *Les lieux de Marguerite Duras*, éd. de Minuit, 1977, p. 101.

C'est ça, Lol V. Stein, c'est quelqu'un qui chaque jour se souvient de tout pour la première fois, et ce tout se répète chaque jour, elle s'en souvient chaque jour pour la première fois comme s'il y avait entre les jours de Lol V. Stein des gouffres insondables d'oubli. Elle ne s'habitue pas à la mémoire. Ni à l'oubli, d'ailleurs. Mais elle est encore très enfoncée dans l'écrit. Je ne l'ai jamais vue, Lol V. Stein... vraiment... vous savez. C'est un peu comme des noyés dans l'eau qui reparaissent comme ça à la surface et puis qui replongent. C'est comme ça que je la vois, Lol V. Stein, elle apparaît à la surface des eaux et elle replonge. Mais je mourrai sans doute sans savoir exactement qui c'est. D'habitude, quand je fais un livre, je sais à peu près ce que j'ai fait, j'en suis quand même un peu le lecteur... Là non. Quand j'ai eu fait Lol V. Stein, ça m'a complètement échappé.

Ibid., p. 99.

C'est quand même un livre qui est traduit partout [...] donc ça a traîné dans beaucoup de mains, dans beaucoup de consciences, c'est déjà une prostitution, Lol V. Stein. Mais Lol V. Stein surgissante, alors qu'elle sortait de moi, quand je l'ai vue pour la première fois, je ne la retrouverai plus jamais. Elle est à vous, Lol V. Stein [...] Lol V. Stein, c'est ce que vous en faites.

Ibid., p. 100-101.

1981

L'écriture du *Ravissement* : Je suis dans l'impossibilité totale de vous dire comment ça s'est fait, ça s'est passé. Mais quand je les relis, je suis étonnée, je me dis : « Qu'est-ce qui m'est arrivé ? » Je ne comprends pas très bien. C'est comme ça, écrire.

Marguerite Duras à Montréal, Montréal, éd. Spirale, 1981, p. 23.

Anne-Marie Stretter : C'est comme si tu me demandais pourquoi je l'aime. Je ne sais pas. C'est un des personnages dominants de mon enfance. Je l'ai vraiment connue ; j'ai connu ses filles aussi. Elle était la femme de l'administrateur général du poste de Vinh Long sur le Mékong, et je l'ai vue souvent, j'avais huit ans, je m'en souviens bien. Je ne me suis pas trompée d'ailleurs. Elle était vraiment ce que j'ai dit : elle était étrangère, elle était musicienne, elle était rousse, elle avait les yeux clairs, elle avait beaucoup d'amants. Un de ses amants s'est suicidé. Tout était juste. Les enfants voient bien.

Ibid., p. 33.

1984 :

M. D. Je ne sais pas d'où vient Lola Valérie Stein. Mais je sais qu'Anne-Marie Stretter, c'est Elizabeth Striedter [...].

D. N. Vous avez employé l'expression de « scène primitive », à propos de ce suicide d'un jeune homme qui s'était tué pour elle.

M. D. Oui. [...] Pour la première fois de ma vie, j'entendais dire qu'on pouvait se tuer par amour.

D. N. Est-ce qu'il n'y a pas une autre « scène primitive », celle qui est au cœur du *Ravissement de Lol V. Stein :* le rapt de l'amant de Lol par une femme plus âgée, une femme en noir — par elle, Anne-Marie Stretter ?

M. D. Oui. Anne-Marie Stretter est en plein dans son rôle de donneuse de mort, là.

Entretien avec Dominique Noguez, « La couleur des mots », in *Édition vidéographique critique*, p. 22.

1987 :

Il y a eu Vinh Long [...]. J'avais entre huit et dix ans lorsque c'est arrivé. Comme la foudre ou la foi. C'est arrivé pour ma vie entière. À soixante-douze ans, c'est encore là comme hier : les allées du poste, pendant la sieste, le quartier des Blancs, les avenues désertes bordées de flamboyants. Le fleuve qui dort. Et elle qui passe dans sa limousine noire. S'appelle presque Anne-Marie Stretter. S'appelle Striedter. La femme de l'administrateur général. Ils ont deux enfants. Ils viennent du Laos où elle avait un jeune amant. Il vient de se tuer parce qu'elle était partie de lui. [...]

Je me souviens de la sorte d'émotion qui s'est produite dans mon corps d'enfant : celle d'accéder à une connaissance encore interdite pour moi. [...] Il fallait garder cette connaissance pour moi seule. Dès lors, cette femme est devenue mon secret : Anne-Marie Stretter.

« Vin Long », in *La vie matérielle,* Gallimard, Folio, 1987, p. 30.

III. RÉCEPTION

1. LA PRESSE

Lors de la sortie du *Ravissement*, la presse n'a pas été unanime. Même *Le Monde* publie un article très critique de Jacqueline Piatier, intitulé « Marguerite Duras à l'heure de Marienbad ». (« Le pire article que j'ai eu sur ce livre, c'est quand même Jacqueline Piatier qui l'a écrit dans *Le Monde*, c'est-à-dire une femme », écrira Duras, dans *Les parleuses*, p. 161.)

Selon le titre, il faudrait subir *Le ravissement de Lol V. Stein* comme un charme. Sans cela le livre agace, ennuie. [...]

Jacqueline Piatier, « Marguerite Duras à l'heure de Marienbad », *Le Monde*, 28 avril 1964.

Quelle a été ici l'intention de Marguerite Duras ? Peindre une névrose ou saisir dans un cas poussé à la limite le ressort de la souffrance d'amour féminine ? [...]

C'est une manière de *Belle au Bois Dormant*. [...] Dans les contes de fées modernes, les enchantements ne prennent jamais complètement fin. Ravie à elle-même, Lol V. Stein ne peut plus aimer que par rivale interposée. [...]

Névrose, fascination, obsession d'un passé traumatisant, est-ce que tous ces thèmes ne font pas songer au *Marienbad* de Robbe-Grillet ? [...] Mais M. Duras ne pousse pas jusqu'au bout ce voyage à deux dans l'imaginaire. [...] Ce qui manque le plus dans son livre, c'est la mise en œuvre de la fascination. Elle retombe vite dans son propre univers, assez étroitement circonscrit depuis *Moderato cantabile* à la blessure d'amour. [...] Comme elle est loin de Colette, de sa santé, de son équilibre, de sa lucidité, de son goût de la vie, des êtres, de la nature !

Candide publie un article désinvolte intitulé : « Duras, mais oui, c'est la Piaf du " nouveau roman " » (phrase attribuée à Robbe-Grillet) et sous-titré : « Un ballet d'amibes » (8-15 avril 1964).

Robert Kanters, dans _Le Figaro_, est plus nuancé :

Robert Kanters, *Le Figaro littéraire*, 7 mai 1964.

En lisant *Le ravissement de Lol V. Stein*, on regrette un peu d'abord le fini, l'aisance dans la modulation de *L'après-midi de Monsieur Andesmas* [...]. Mais on ne tarde pas à s'apercevoir que dans ce livre-ci les défauts font partie des qualités [...], les dialogues ne sont là que pour nous faire sentir le contenu des silences [...], les scènes qui semblent maladroitement racontées sont là pour nous suggérer certains manques, certains trous, et finalement un certain vide dont il est important que nous ayons le sentiment, peut-être parce que ce vide est dans notre vie aussi, et que nous non plus nous n'aimons pas trop en prendre une connaissance plus claire.

La Commission de lecture de la Jeunesse indépendante chrétienne féminine (JICF) condamne franchement le roman :

Un chrétien qui sait la hiérarchie des choses ne peut s'empêcher de s'étonner devant la pauvreté de ce volume où l'intelligence et le talent ne suffisent pas à masquer le vide. [...]

Tout est raconté de façon froide et impersonnelle, sans que jamais intervienne le moindre jugement moral. On dirait un exposé clinique. Et cette froideur du ton donne à ce récit extrêmement scabreux une sorte de chasteté que souligne encore la pureté d'une langue très classique. Mais cette étude d'une névrose appartient-elle encore à la littérature ? [...]

Marguerite Duras occupe une place de premier plan dans le roman moderne. On ne peut négliger ses livres [...]. Mais ceux qui ont aimé ses livres précédents seront déçus par celui-ci, quand bien même il répond à « une esthétique nouvelle ».

Le ravissement de Lol V. Stein paraît une œuvre ratée.

Mais beaucoup de critiques, comme Claude Roy, dans *Libération*, Claude Mauriac dans *Le Figaro*, Roger Grenier dans *Elle*, André Delmas dans *La Tribune des nations*, saluent « le plus beau roman de Marguerite Duras ».

Claude Roy fait du roman un éloge dithyrambique, mais en le noyant un peu de comparaisons :

Claude Roy, « Le ravissement de Marguerite Duras », *Libération*, 7 avril 1964.

Le *Ravissement* est une œuvre singulière, de premier abord difficile [...]. Les romans, les nouvelles et les scénarios des films de Marguerite Duras sont des poèmes tragiques où les personnages sont saisis à un moment de crise, qui amplifie et intensifie les traits ordinaires, [...]. Ce ne sont pas des sentiments très exceptionnels. L'auteur du *Square* qui écrit comme personne, sent comme tout le monde, comme avant elle Ovide et Tchekhov, Lucrèce et Kafka, l'Ecclésiaste et Proust. [...]

Marguerite Duras exprime avec une violence et une lenteur implacable ces moments de la vie où nous avons la sensation d'être les spectateurs impuissants, fascinés, terrifiés du destin, cette sorte d'accident, ce ralenti des ruptures et des collisions d'automobiles, des agonies et des tremblements de terre. [...]

« Aucun amour au monde ne peut tenir lieu de l'amour », disait un personnage dans un des premiers romans de Marguerite Duras[1]. Elle n'a jamais, d'ailleurs, dit autre chose. [...] Plus que des romanciers du Nouveau Roman, c'est au Tchekhov des grandes nouvelles métaphysiques [...] que Marguerite Duras s'apparente.

1. *Les petits chevaux de Tarquinia.*

Claude Mauriac fait un éloge du roman plus spécifique, mais assorti de lourds préjugés sur les femmes écrivains.

Voici peut-être le plus beau des romans de Marguerite Duras. Déconcertant et d'une simplicité trompeuse [...].

Ce qui éclate, chez Marguerite Duras, c'est le talent et c'est l'intelligence. Rien n'est plus rare dans la littérature et plus beau qu'une femme écrivain, sachant comprendre et commenter ce que sa sensibilité lui a révélé. L'intelligence est ici au service de l'instinct dont elle décrypte et traduit à mesure les indications.

La technique de ce roman est aussi habile que subtile. Elle fera l'admiration des auteurs dits du « nouveau roman », qui y retrouveront leurs propres préoccupations, mais exprimées d'une manière et sur un ton personnels. [...] Marguerite Duras reste à la superficie des phrases, à la surface des visages. Mais, servie par son talent singulier, elle sait capter dans le miroitement vague des mots et l'indétermination des gestes les mystères remontés des profondeurs.

Claude Mauriac, « *Le ravissement de Lol V. Stein* de Marguerite Duras », *Le Figaro*, 29 avril 1964.

L'article de Madeleine Chapsal, dans *L'Express*, intitulé « Plus loin dans le trouble », témoigne d'une lecture plus approfondie :

Par des chemins [...] qui passent par l'émerveillement, le désespoir, la folie, l'érotisme et une très déchirante tendresse, Marguerite Duras continue d'un roman sur l'autre [...] à cerner [...] de plus en plus ce point brûlant, « ravissant » disent les mystiques [...], à partir duquel flamboie une grande partie de son œuvre et qui est un personnage de femme.

Une figure de femme de plus en plus émouvante et perdue, et de plus en plus irrésistible à mesure qu'elle est plus faible et plus dénuée,

Madeleine Chapsal, « Plus loin dans le trouble », *L'Express*, 2 avril 1964.

comme cette Lol V. Stein qui n'est même plus tout à fait une femme entière, mais une demi-folle, absente aux autres, à elle-même, presque privée de son corps, réduite, à la limite, à un visage, à des yeux. [...]

Comme le furent autrefois les héroïnes d'Anouilh, celles de Marguerite Duras sont des exilées, elles ne craignent pas la mort, elles ne s'intéressent à rien, elles ne veulent que leur désir qui ne peut être qu'un désir d'amour ; ce sont des refusantes, des impies, des êtres qui disent « non », attitude scandaleuse, pour la société presque toujours bourgeoise dont elles sont issues, et qui risque de faire d'elles des objets de dégoût et d'opprobre — risque qui bien souvent les attire plus qu'il ne les effraye. [...]

Étrange démarche que celle de Marguerite Duras [...]. Pour parvenir à la clarté, elle accumule, à plaisir, dirait-on, les voiles, les obscurités, l'ambiguïté et les questions. [...]

Dans la perpétuelle mise en question de ce que l'on sait, de ce que l'on voit, ce que l'on sent, au nom d'une connaissance meilleure et plus vaste qu'on pourrait avoir de tout, et qui est à conquérir, nous avançons, puisqu'il le faut, vers quelque chose, un événement capital. Mais avec quelle peine ! souffrant, comme le narrateur lui même « de l'insuffisance déplorable de notre être à connaître cet événement ».

2. QUELQUES LECTURES

Micheline Tison-Braun liquide le *Ravissement*, en une lecture rapide et plutôt négative, dans un chapitre intitulé « Le cycle de la folie ». Mais ses arguments sont surprenants : elle considère ce roman comme trop classique, voire trop facile :

Le *Ravissement*, contemporain du *Vice-consul*[1], est de facture beaucoup plus traditionnelle ; l'anecdote y tient une grande place, le cadre sécrète peu de poésie ; les personnages et leurs dialogues relèvent de la psychologie, celle de l'adultère courant, corsé de voyeurisme et d'un brin de lesbianisme. La folie de Lol V. Stein est affirmée plutôt qu'étudiée, puisque la majeure partie du roman se déroule entre les deux crises décisives. Seuls les premier et avant-dernier chapitres participent de la poésie et préparent l'accès à l'univers métaphysique. [...]

Les années passent. Lol V. Stein est une morte vivante [...], elle n'aime plus que par procuration. Elle revoit la salle du « bal mort de S. Thala » *[sic]* [...] sans émotion. Elle reconnaît sans ressentir, abolie, anesthésiée, et on apprendra beaucoup plus tard que cette « mortelle fadeur » de sa mémoire préparait la crise définitive. [...] Le reste du récit — les pages intermédiaires — appartiennent au romanesque habituel.

Micheline Tison-Braun, *Marguerite Duras*, Rodopi, Amsterdam, 1984, p. 57-59.

Yvonne Guers-Villate reconnaît au contraire au *Ravissement* complexité et ambiguïté. Elle interprète le roman grâce au thème Éros/Thanatos, mais les équivalences symboliques point par point qu'elle établit sont presque caricaturales :

Dans *Lol* [...], la composition du roman en deux parties [...] de part et d'autre du moment où le narrateur est présenté à Lol et identifié comme personnage principal a [...] une très grande importance. Thanatos règne dans la première ; Éros arrive à vaincre dans la deuxième. La complexité accrue de ce roman provient aussi de l'introduction d'un troisième personnage dans la relation amoureuse du couple. Une série de triangulations en résulte tandis que le rôle de certains s'inverse d'un triangle à un autre.

Yvonne Guers-Villate, *Continuité, discontinuité de l'œuvre durassienne*, éd. de l'université de Bruxelles, 1985, p. 105, D.R.

1. *Le vice-consul* paraît quand même un an après !

Le personnage de Lol, « dormeuse debout », objectifie le thème de l'anéantissement dans l'amour, le romantisme tragique de mourir d'aimer. Les allées du jardin de Lol « pas utilisables » car elles ne mènent nulle part sont allégoriques de son état d'esprit comme l'ordre rigide et froid de sa maison. Ses déambulations à travers sa ville natale traduisent spatialement son cheminement vers Éros. Le leitmotiv de la « mise à nu » qui révélera le corps « dérobé » est symbolique d'une connaissance totale dans l'amour où, avec la robe, tombent toutes les barrières : inhibitions, apparences, masque social. Lol observant les amants derrière la fenêtre de l'hôtel des Bois peut être le symbole d'une médiation d'ordre métaphysique. La tête cachée sous les draps représente la perte de toute identité individuelle dans l'orgasme et l'anonymité du corps dans l'érotisme.

Ibid., p. 111.

Jean Pierrot prend en compte les diverses réactions critiques et élabore des interprétations un peu simplificatrices, mais claires :

[...] la première impression qui se dégage de la lecture de l'œuvre [est] celle d'une étrangeté assez déroutante. Impression confirmée par les premiers commentaires, visiblement embarrassés, qui ont suivi la publication du livre, et qui a continué à prévaloir jusqu'à l'époque actuelle. « On doit croire », écrit par exemple R.-M. Albérès, dans un ouvrage publié en 1971[1], « que Marguerite Duras fait exprès de nous intriguer jusqu'à l'absurde, de nous donner l'impression de comprendre alors que nous ne comprenons pas, ou inversement ». Rejetons, à la différence de ce critique, l'hypo-

Jean Pierrot, *Marguerite Duras*, José Corti, 1986, p. 203-206.

1. R.-M. Albérès, *Le roman d'aujourd'hui*, Albin Michel, 1971, p. 185.

thèse d'une mystification délibérée, dont d'ailleurs on ne comprendrait pas l'intérêt, ou d'une quête intentionnelle de l'hermétisme : il reste qu'on pourra être tenté de reprocher à l'auteur d'avoir cherché à nous intéresser avec un cas pathologique, trop en dehors des normes psychologiques ordinaires pour que nous puissions nous sentir vraiment concernés. [...]

Que la maladie mentale soit la raison essentielle qui permette de rendre compte de la conduite de l'héroïne, telle est en effet l'hypothèse qui paraît s'imposer à la lecture du livre. [...]

Cette narration est conduite de façon assez insolite. [...] Désinvolture de l'auteur par rapport aux règles habituelles du récit, ou volonté de compliquer délibérément le travail du lecteur ? [...]

Il serait bien sûr absurde [...] d'attribuer ces éléments à des négligences ou à la maladresse. Tout ceci est évidemment délibéré et prémédité. En compliquant les modalités de la narration, en exigeant du lecteur qu'il garde un esprit constamment alerté et une attention sans faille, l'auteur s'amuse sans doute [...] à reprendre certains jeux propres au Nouveau Roman. Mais il est évident aussi que cette technique sert les desseins de l'auteur. Le caractère aléatoire et hypothétique de la narration, les zones d'ombre qui subsistent tendent manifestement à renforcer l'impression de mystère et d'étrangeté qui vient du comportement même de l'héroïne.

J. Pierrot tente de restituer au récit « une cohérence peu visible » :

Ibid., p. 210.

Ce que nous raconte *Le ravissement de Lol V. Stein*, c'est donc [...] une « éducation de l'oubli ». Au faux oubli [...] apparent, dans lequel le passé survit caché et continue à développer son influence invisible mais délétère sur le présent, à cette latence si dangereuse au cours de laquelle le temps et la vie sont comme arrêtés, doit être substitué le vrai oubli, l'oubli libérateur, celui qui consiste à revivre une bonne fois son passé pour pouvoir le réinterpréter, l'assimiler à son histoire, et ainsi le liquider.

La tentative d'exorcisme que raconte le *Ravissement* n'a sans doute pas entièrement réussi [...], les réapparitions ultérieures explicites de l'héroïne de *L'amour* et *La femme du Gange* la montreront devenue tout à fait folle.

IV. TEXTES DURASSIENS EN CORRÉLATION AVEC LE « RAVISSEMENT »

Citer des extraits de roman est toujours une opération délicate, à la fois amputation et manipulation, fortement contestable. Les citations suivantes essaient seulement de montrer certaines concordances très sensibles entre les textes durassiens, et espèrent inciter à leur lecture.

1. « LE VICE-CONSUL » (1965)

Dans *Le vice-consul*, qui succède immédiatement au *Ravissement*, Lol V. Stein a disparu. Mais on retrouve, dans une Calcutta très symbolique, Anne-Marie Stretter, dont le portrait est littéralement conforme à celui de la ravisseuse du bal de T. Beach, et son amant, au nom amputé, Michael Richard.

Le vice-consul, Gallimard, « L'imaginaire », p. 92.

Ce soir, à Calcutta, l'ambassadrice Anne-Marie Stretter est près du buffet, elle sourit, elle est en noir, sa robe est à double fourreau de tulle noir [...]. Aux approches de la vieillesse, une maigreur lui est venue qui laisse bien voir la finesse, la longueur de l'ossature. Ses yeux sont trop clairs, découpés comme ceux des statues, ses paupières sont amaigries.

Ibid., p. 109-110.

Au Cercle, les autres femmes parlent d'elle. Que se passe-t-il dans cette existence ? Où la trouver ? On ne sait pas. Elle se plaît dans cette ville de cauchemar. Eau qui dort, cette femme ?

L'histoire de Lol et le bal de T. Beach sont complètement effacés, puisque le récit que fait Michael Richard à Charles Rossett propose une version totalement différente de sa rencontre avec Anne-Marie Stretter, sous le signe de la musique :

— Avant de connaître Anne-Marie Stretter [...] je l'entendais jouer à Calcutta, le soir, sur le boulevard ; ça m'intriguait beaucoup [...] j'étais venu en touriste à Calcutta [...] je ne tenais pas du tout le coup... je voulais repartir dès le premier jour, et... c'est elle, cette musique que j'entendais qui fait [...] que... j'ai pu rester à Calcutta... Je l'ai écoutée plusieurs soirs de suite, posté dans l'avenue Victoria, et puis, un soir, je suis entré dans le parc, les sentinelles m'ont laissé passer, tout était ouvert, je suis entré dans cette pièce où nous étions hier soir. Je me souviens, je tremblais... — il rit —, elle s'est retournée, elle m'a vu, elle a été surprise, mais je ne crois pas qu'elle ait eu peur, voilà comment je l'ai connue.

Ibid., p. 187.

2. « L'AMOUR » (1971)

***L'amour* peut être lu à la fois comme une suite du *Ravissement*, où Lol, devenue folle, errerait sur la plage en suivant « le prisonnier fou qui marche le long de la mer » (*Am.*, p. 13) [Jacques Hold ?] suivie à son tour par « le voyageur » (Michael Richardson ?) sans qu'aucun nom leur soit jamais donné dans le texte.**

S. Thala est devenu le nom de l'espace tout entier :

[Le voyageur] demande :

— S. Thala, c'est mon nom.

— Oui — elle lui explique, montre : — tout, ici, tout c'est S. Thala.

L'amour, Gallimard, Folio, p. 62.

Le hall de l'hôtel ressemble à la salle du bal de T. Beach et au salon de Lol, dégradés et ternis (*Am.*, p. 64). On y

entend « la musique des fêtes mortes de S. Thala » (*Am.*, p. 66), « la musique des fêtes sanglantes, celle de l'hymne de S. Thala, lointaine, très lointaine » (*Am.*, p. 115). Une femme aux cheveux très noirs, « teints en noir » (*Am.*, p. 77), évoque Tatiana et se dénomme « la morte de S.Thala » (*Am.*, p. 78).

L'histoire de Lol est évoquée de façon elliptique :

Le voyageur dit :

— Dix-huit ans...

— Quand pour la première fois vous êtes tombée malade — il ajoute — Après un bal. [...]

— Un bal.

— Oui — il hésite — vous étiez, à ce moment-là, supposée aimer. [...]

— Oui. Après... — elle retourne au temps pur, à la contemplation du sol — après j'ai été mariée avec un musicien, j'ai eu deux enfants — elle s'arrête — ils les ont pris aussi.

Ibid., p. 102-105.

Le voyageur refait avec la femme le voyage qu'avait fait Lol avec Jacques Hold dans le *Ravissement*, mais il est seul à pénétrer dans la salle de bal où « il n'y a plus de bal », pendant qu'elle dort sur le sable (p. 123-124).

3. « INDIA SONG », TEXTE, THÉÂTRE, FILM (1973)

***India Song*, « texte, théâtre, film » est une version du *Vice-consul* dans laquelle l'histoire de Lol V. Stein est réintroduite, à l'arrière-plan : jamais représentée, même de façon épurée et distante, elle est évoquée par les voix *off*, voix sans visage et sans corps, voix de femmes « lentes, douces. Enfermées comme nous dans le lieu. Et intangibles, inaccessibles ».**

Je ne cite que le dialogue des voix, dialogue initial, en omettant la plupart des didascalies qui sont intercalées. Dans le livre, les voix *off* parleraient sur les images d'une « demeure des Indes » déserte (*India Song*, p. 15). Dans le

film, elles accompagnent en contrepoint un lent panoramique sur le tissu rouge foncé de la robe portée par Anne-Marie Stretter pendant la réception.

VOIX 1 : Il l'avait suivie aux Indes.
VOIX 2 : Oui. *(Temps.)*
VOIX 2 : Pour elle il avait tout quitté.
En une nuit.
VOIX 1 : La nuit du bal... ?
VOIX 2 : Oui. [...]
VOIX 1 : C'était elle qui jouait du piano ?
VOIX 2 *(hésite)* : Oui... mais lui aussi...
C'était lui qui, parfois, le soir, jouait au piano cet air de S. Thala... *(Silence.)* [...]
VOIX 1 *(comme lu)* : « Michael Richardson était fiancé à une jeune fille de S. Thala. Lola Valérie Stein. Le mariage devait avoir lieu à l'automne.
Puis il y a eu ce bal.
Ce bal de S. Thala... » *(Silence.)*
VOIX 2 : Elle était arrivée tard à ce bal... au milieu de la nuit...
VOIX 1 : Oui... *(Habillée de noir.)*
Que d'amour, ce bal...
Que de désir...

India Song, Gallimard, « L'imaginaire », p. 14-16.

Dans le film, cette fois à peu près en accord avec le livre, les voix parlent sur un lent travelling montrant l'image d'Anne-Marie Stretter, en peignoir noir, étendue par terre. La caméra s'approche du tissu noir si près que l'écran tout entier devient noir un instant, puis elle s'éloigne pour découvrir Michael Richardson, assis près d'elle, caressant ses cheveux :

VOIX 1 : Où était la jeune fille de S. Thala ? *Pas de réponse.*
VOIX 1 *(comme lu)* : « Derrière les plantes vertes du bar, elle les regarde. *(Temps.)* Ce n'est qu'à l'aurore *(Arrêt.)* quand les amants se dirigèrent vers les portes du bal que Lola Valérie Stein poussa un cri. » [...]

Ibid., p. 36-38.

VOIX 1 : Elle n'a jamais guéri la jeune fille de S. Thala ?

VOIX 2 : Jamais.

VOIX 1 : Ils ne l'ont pas entendue crier?

VOIX 2 : Non.

N'entendaient plus rien.

Ne voyaient plus rien. *(Temps.)*

VOIX 1 : L'ont abandonnée ? *(Temps.)* Tuée ?

VOIX 2 : Oui. *(Temps.)*

VOIX 1 : Ce crime derrière eux...

VOIX 2 *(à peine)* : Oui. *(Silence.)*

VOIX 1 : Que voulait la jeune fille de S. Thala ?

VOIX 2 : LES SUIVRE

LES VOIR

LES AMANTS DU GANGE : LES VOIR

Et le texte commente, assimilant le désir du spectateur à celui de Lol : « C'est ce que nous, nous faisons : voir. » Et il décrit les images que voit le spectateur : « Lentement l'homme s'allonge près du corps endormi. La main continue à caresser le visage, le corps. » C'est ce que nous, nous faisons : voir.

4. « LA FEMME DU GANGE » (FILM, 1972 ; LIVRE, 1973)

Le film *La femme du Gange* apparaît surtout comme l'adaptation de *L'amour*. Mais, en même temps, comme le déclare Duras : « Dans *La femme du Gange*, trois livres sont embarqués, massacrés. C'est-à-dire que l'écriture a cessé. »

Trois livres : *Le Ravissement, Le vice-consul, L'amour*. Les personnages « ont perdu la mémoire. Leur mémoire est maintenant dehors... Des cendres... » (*F.G.*, p. 110).

L'histoire du bal est reprise par les voix *off*, parfois avec les mots de *L'amour* (*F.G.*, p. 113), d'autres fois avec des variantes :

VOIX 2 : Elle est arrivée tard à ce bal... Au milieu de la nuit...

La femme du Gange, Gallimard, p. 122-125.

VOIX 1 : L'autre femme... ?
VOIX 2 : Oui.
Habillée de noir...
Elle est presque vieille déjà. Laide.
Maigre. *(Temps.)*
VOIX 2 *(temps)* : Elle vient des Indes... Des Ambassades...
Elle arrive...
Elle traverse le bal...
Absente... *(Temps.)*
VOIX 1 : Il dit à la jeune fille : « Il faut que j'invite cette femme à danser... ? »
VOIX 2 : C'est ça... *(Silence.)*
VOIX 1 : Ils dansent.
VOIX 1 : Où est la jeune fille ?
VOIX 2 : Derrière les plantes vertes du bar.
Elle regarde...
Elle les regarde... *(Silence.)*
VOIX 1 : La jeune fille sait qu'on va l'assassiner ?
VOIX 2 : Oui.
VOIX 1 : ... qu'on va la tuer ?

Le dialogue des voix est beaucoup plus proche du texte du *Ravissement* auquel il fait des références précises, comme à des archives du film :

VOIX 1 : Il y en avait une... vous savez ?... « *nue sous ses cheveux noirs* »... elle a su toutes ces choses très bien... elles étaient toujours ensemble.

Ibid., p. 133.

VOIX 2 : Ah oui... un nom allemand ?
VOIX 1 : C'est ça...
VOIX 2 : Elle a eu beaucoup d'amants, des propriétés... mariée plusieurs fois...
VOIX 1 : Oui... en dernier... ici... à S. Thala...
VOIX 2 : Oui... à un docteur... *(Silence.)*
VOIX 1 : Elles s'étaient connues au collège..

VOIX 1 : « ... *dans la lumière d'un parasol bleu... les pieds nus sur la pierre de la terrasse... en robe d'été...* ».

Cependant, les phrases en italique ont un statut ambigu. Si « nue sous ses cheveux noirs » est bien une phrase exacte et importante du *Ravissement*, la deuxième phrase n'est qu'une évocation approximative (p. 68, 72). De plus, les italiques ne sont évidemment pas perceptibles par le spectateur.

D'autres transformations interviennent qui rétablissent une continuité en suggérant les chaînons manquants entre le *Ravissement* et *L'amour* :

VOIX 1 : Oui... et cette ambulance est allée la prendre dans le champ de seigle...

Ibid., p. 137.

5. UN SCRIPT PERDU : « LE CINÉMA DE LOL V. STEIN »

***Le ravissement de Lol V. Stein*, contrairement à la plupart des livres de Duras, n'a jamais connu de version filmique.**

Cependant, Marguerite Duras avait publié une ébauche de script, sous le titre « Le cinéma de Lol V. Stein », dans *Art Press International*, n° 24, en janvier 1979. Dans *La vie matérielle*, elle résume de nouveau ce script disparu :

Toutes les femmes de mes livres, quel que soit leur âge, découlent de Lol. C'est-à-dire d'un certain oubli d'elles-mêmes. [...]

Toutes les femmes de cette procession de femmes des livres et des films se ressemblent, depuis *La femme du Gange* jusqu'à ce dernier état de Lol V. Stein, dans ce script que j'ai perdu. Pourquoi j'ai eu l'idée de ce script ? Je ne sais plus. C'est exactement comme une de ces visions que j'avais, pendant la période qui a suivi la cure de désintoxication alcoolique

La vie matérielle, Gallimard, Folio, p. 35-36.

Ça se passait dans la ville. Le casino était éclairé, et le même bal continuait comme s'il n'avait pas cessé depuis vingt ans. Oui, je crois que c'est ça. C'est la répétition du bal de S. Thala, mais à l'échelle théâtrale. Là, on n'avance pas dans la connaissance de Lol V. Stein, c'est fini tout ça. Là elle va mourir. Elle a fini de me hanter, elle me laisse tranquille, je la tue, je la tue pour qu'elle cesse de se mettre sur mon chemin, couchée devant mes maisons, mes livres, à dormir sur les plages par tous les temps, dans le vent, le froid, à attendre, à attendre ça : que je la regarde encore une dernière fois. On célèbre sa folie. Elle est vieille, elle sort du casino sur une chaise à porteur, elle est devenue Chinoise. La chaise est portée par des hommes, sur les épaules, comme un cercueil. Lol V. Stein est très fardée, peinturlurée. Elle ne sait pas ce qui lui arrive. Elle regarde les gens, la ville. Elle a les cheveux teints, elle est fardée comme une putain, elle est détruite, comme on dirait, née. Elle est devenue la plus belle phrase de ma vie : « Ici, c'est S. Thala jusqu'à la rivière, et après la rivière, c'est encore S. Thala. »

V. LACAN ET COMPAGNIE

1. L'HOMMAGE

L'« Hommage fait à Marguerite Duras du *Ravissement de Lol V. Stein* » par Jacques Lacan est l'une des premières interprétations psychanalytiques du roman. Ce patronage illustre désigne le *Ravissement* à l'attention des intellectuels d'avant-garde et des psychocritiques, mais décourage les lecteurs ordinaires par l'hermétisme du style et contribue à faire classer le roman parmi les œuvres difficiles, voire illisibles.

Les préciosités et les obscurités de l'écriture lacanienne me paraissent s'être atténuées avec le temps et il suffit souvent de prendre le texte à la lettre pour en saisir la portée :

La scène dont le roman n'est tout entier que la remémoration, c'est proprement le ravissement de deux en une danse qui les soude, et sous les yeux de Lol, troisième, avec tout le bal, à y subir le rapt de son fiancé par celle qui n'a eu qu'à soudaine apparaître. [...] Ce n'est pas l'événement, mais un nœud qui se refait là. Et c'est ce que ce nœud enserre qui proprement ravit, mais là encore qui ? [...]

Je pense que, même si Marguerite Duras me fait tenir de sa bouche qu'elle ne sait pas dans toute son œuvre d'où Lol lui vient [...], le seul avantage qu'un psychanalyste ait le droit de prendre de sa position [...] c'est de se rappeler avec Freud qu'en sa matière, l'artiste toujours le précède et qu'il n'a donc pas à faire le psychologue là où l'artiste lui fraie la voie.

C'est précisément ce que je reconnais dans le ravissement de Lol V. Stein, où Marguerite Duras s'avère savoir sans moi ce que j'enseigne. [...] Que

Jacques Lacan, « Hommage fait à Marguerite Duras du *Ravissement de Lol V. Stein* », in *Cahiers Renaud-Barrault*, nº 52, décembre 1965. Repris in F. Barat et J. Farges, *Marguerite Duras*, D.R., Albatros, 1975, p. 93-99. D.R.

la pratique de la lettre converge avec l'usage de l'inconscient, est tout ce dont je témoignerai en lui rendant hommage. [...]

Le nœud [...] est à prendre à la première scène, où Lol est de son amant proprement dérobée, c'est-à-dire qu'il est à suivre dans le thème de la robe, lequel ici supporte le fantasme où Lol s'attache le temps d'après, d'un au-delà dont elle n'a pas su trouver le mot, ce mot qui, refermant les portes sur eux trois, l'eût conjointe au moment où son amant eût enlevé la robe, la robe noire de la femme et dévoilé sa nudité. Ceci va-t-il plus loin ? oui, à l'indicible de cette nudité qui s'insinue à remplacer son propre corps. Là tout s'arrête. [...]

Ce qui nous retiendra dans Jacques Hold, c'est qu'il est dans l'être à trois où Lol se suspend, plaquant sur son vide le « je pense » de mauvais rêve qui fait la matière du livre.

Cet être à trois, pourtant, c'est bien Lol qui l'arrange. Et c'est pour ce que le « je pense » de Jacques Hold vient hanter Lol d'un soin trop proche à la fin du roman où il l'accompagne d'un pèlerinage au lieu de l'événement, — que Lol devient folle.

Dont en effet l'épisode porte des signes, mais dont j'entends faire état ici que je le tiens de Marguerite Duras.

C'est que la dernière phrase du roman ramenant Lol dans le champ de seigle, me paraît faire une fin moins décisive que cette remarque. Où se devine la mise en garde contre le pathétique de la compréhension. Être comprise ne convient pas à Lol, qu'on ne sauve pas du ravissement.

Le titre même de ce texte souligne son ambivalence : car Lacan offre, en somme, à Marguerite Duras ce dont elle est pourtant l'auteur(e). Même si Duras elle-même s'extasie sur de pareils transferts — « La plus belle chose qu'on

m'ait dite, à propos de *Lol V. Stein*, c'est un critique, c'est ceci : " *Lol V. Stein* c'est moi qui l'ai écrit " » (*P.*, p. 161) —, la prétention paraît excessive.

2. RÉACTIONS CRITIQUES À L'HOMMAGE DE LACAN

Aussi cet « hommage » a-t-il été très fécond, déclencheur d'écritures, mais très diversement apprécié. Marguerite Duras elle-même l'accueille de façon nuancée : « Qui a sorti Lol V. Stein de son cercueil ? C'est quand même un homme, c'est Lacan », répond-elle à la féministe Xavière Gauthier, dans *Les parleuses*, en 1974 (*P.*, p. 161). Mais, en 1981, à Montréal, elle ajoute :

Quand Lacan dit : « elle sait, cette femme sait... » je ne sais pas quelle est sa phrase... [...] C'est un mot d'homme, de maître. C'est quand même un homme de pouvoir, c'est évident. La référence, c'est lui. « Ce que j'enseigne », elle, cette petite bonne femme, elle le sait. C'est un hommage énorme, mais c'est un hommage qui ricoche sur lui.

Les parleuses, éd. de Minuit, p. 61.

Marcelle Marini dénonce, à juste titre, « l'outrecuidance de ce jugement de Lacan » :

Son article est remarquable en tout ce qu'il dévoile et de la problématique du texte et de sa propre problématique pour laquelle le texte joue comme révélateur. Mais Lacan ne voit pas — sans doute ne peut pas voir — que se figure en ce texte l'impossibilité pour toute femme d'accéder au statut de « sujet » sauf à se mettre au masculin [...] ; que s'y déploie le filet qui enferme le poisson dans la nasse des relations familiales où triomphe la « loi » de l'homme-père.

Marcelle Marini, *Territoires du féminin* avec Marguerite Duras, éd. de Minuit, 1977, p. 32.

Voici une critique du texte de Lacan toute différente, puisqu'elle reproche au maître célèbre d'utiliser le *Ravissement* comme matériau exemplaire de sa propre théorie, sans en faire une véritable lecture :

Le récit que fait Lacan du *Ravissement* produit un scénario beaucoup moins compliqué et ambigu que le roman original de Marguerite Duras : il se transforme en une histoire d'hommage rendu par un homme à une femme aimée, un tribut payé par l'autorité masculine captivée pour captiver la beauté féminine, plutôt évocateur des contes d'amour courtois que l'on peut lire dans *L'Heptaméron* de Marguerite de Navarre, que Lacan cite comme prototype intertextuel du roman de Duras.

Leslie Hill, *Marguerite Duras, Apocalyptic Desires*, Routledge, Londres et New York, 1993, p. 71 (ma traduction). D.R.

Par contre, Susan Rubin Suleiman reconnaît son plein accord avec la lecture de Lacan :

Lacan écrit de Jacques Hold qu'il n'est pas un simple « montreur de machine », mais « l'un de ses ressorts » qui « ne sait pas tout ce qui l'y prend ». [...] Jacques Hold est impliqué par Lol, devient ravi en réinventant son ravissement [...]. Être un montreur de machine, c'est être dehors, observer. C'est être là où se trouvait Breton [par rapport à Nadja], là où Freud désirait être [par rapport à Dora]. Jacques Hold est, et désire être, dedans ; il est rivé à Lol : « Nous voici chevillés ensemble » (p. 113). Le désir de Lol l'a choisi [...] Il la suit dans ses souvenirs.

Susan Rubin Suleiman, « Nadja, Dora, Lol V. Stein : women madness and narrative », in *Discourse in Psychoanalysis and Literature*, éd. par Shlomith Rimmon-Kenan, Methuen, Londres et New York, 1987, p. 142 (ma traduction). D.R.

La critique cite alors la fin de l'analyse de Lacan consacrée au roman de Duras, où il s'agit de la « folie » de Lol (voir *supra*, p. 178), la « traduit » et l'interprète. Selon cette interprétation, Jacques Hold, à la fin du roman, s'approche « trop près » de Lol et ainsi la fait basculer vers la folie. Mais cette « folie » finale, Lacan en laisse la responsabilité à Duras, considérant, selon lui, que la fin du roman est « moins décisive ». Susan R. Suleiman

pense aussi, avec Lacan, que Lol ne devient pas folle, que « rien ne finit à la fin du roman », que « la dernière phrase n'est pas une fin, mais un suspens », et que « le voyage peut continuer ». Finalement, à son avis, la conception « magnifiquement pessimiste et en même temps inspirée et inspirante, totalement moderne et pourtant étonnamment romantique de l'amour et de ses relations avec l'écriture » de Lacan, répond et correspond à une conception identique de Duras.

3. INTERPRÉTATIONS PSYCHANALYTIQUES ET FÉMINISTES

L'hommage de Lacan ouvre le chemin des interprétations psychanalytiques ; les critiques que déclenche cet hommage inaugurent les interprétations « féministes » du *Ravissement*. Les deux tendances se trouvent souvent liées et foisonnent en particulier aux États-Unis. Marguerite Duras y serait devenue l'auteur phare, parmi la « petite poignée » d'écrivains français étudiés : « Dans toutes les universités américaines, il y a quelqu'un qui travaille sur Marguerite Duras », écrit Antoine Compagnon (« The Diminishing Canon of French Literature » [« Le rétrécissement du " canon " de la littérature française »], *Stanford French Review*, vol. 15, 1-2, 1991, p. 104). Et *Le ravissement de Lol V. Stein* serait considéré comme un livre fétiche.

Pour Marcelle Marini, dans *Territoires du féminin*, les romans de Duras, et en particulier le *Ravissement*, constituent, par leur structure et leur écriture mêmes, une forte dénonciation en acte de la condition féminine, leur prise de position est essentiellement féministe. Même si, dans ces textes, « c'est d'un homme avec obstination qu'une femme attend la représentation et le nom de son sexe » et si « sous le regard masculin, une femme s'efface dans son individualité jusqu'à l'anonymat », le féminin s'émancipe des significations qui lui étaient imposées, de la « féminité requise » (comme dans le cas de la phrase de

Lol sur Tatiana nue) et devient alors non-sens et violence sauvage, sorte de « matière incontrôlable qui submergerait le monde entier. Cataclysme pour la civilisation ».

L'Américaine Trista Selous, tout en partageant beaucoup des points de vue du livre de Marcelle Marini, n'est pas de son avis sur l'effet de l'écriture durassienne. Pour elle, la pratique de la réticence à tous les niveaux pousse le lecteur à la poursuite d'un « leurre fétichisé », l'installe dans une position de fascination passive et entretient ainsi l'image traditionnelle et aliénante de « La Femme source et objet du désir de l'homme ». Un lien intertextuel très fort se crée avec la fiction « romantique », dont Duras ne subvertit pas vraiment les modèles :

Je pense que ce que fait Duras est précisément le contraire. Plutôt que de disloquer le modèle, elle le dénude jusqu'au squelette, qui va seul permettre de remettre de la chair sur les os d'une manière spécifique, par le biais du narrataire. C'est là son habileté particulière : elle est capable de pousser le lecteur à adopter cette place et à se concentrer sur le processus de reconstruction de ce que le texte ne fait que suggérer. Elle fait cela en utilisant un langage très clair, simple [...]. Ces histoires d'amour très élémentaires, ce qui leur donne une qualité particulière c'est le fait que le processus de leur reconstruction n'est jamais achevé. L'élément crucial qui transformerait la déduction du lecteur en certitude est construit comme au-delà de la portée du texte, une « lacune » irrémédiable. Duras n'invite pas ses lecteurs à apprendre quelque chose, à comprendre « ce qui est arrivé » et à penser à ce sujet ce qu'ils veulent : elle les invite à ressentir quelque chose à travers un acte d'identification à la place du narrataire.

Trista Selous, *The Other Woman. Feminism and Feminity in the Work of Marguerite Duras*, Yale University Press, New Haven et Londres, p. 239, 1988 (ma traduction). D.R.

Au contraire, d'autres femmes critiques, en particulier Martha Noel Evans et Susan Cohen, sans nier les procédés de fascination du lecteur mis en œuvre par Duras et

leurs risques, jugent indispensable la prise en compte du nom (et donc du sexe) de l'auteur(e), qui transforme radicalement l'effet de ces procédés.

Selon Martha Noel Evans, la menace de folie (ressentie par l'écrivain(e) elle-même) est un des thèmes centraux du roman : il devient alors difficile de distinguer entre « les cris » et « l'écrit », entre le dedans et le dehors. Dans le *Ravissement*, « émerge une mutation clairement définie et radicalement neuve dans une vieille définition de l'écriture des femmes comme prostitution ».

Duras [...] assume une image de la femme, socialement condamnée mais transgressive — dans ce cas, la prostituée. Mais, plutôt que de définir cette condition conformément aux normes traditionnelles, comme un exemple de défiance et de marginalisation, elle retourne la transgression. La prostituée devient celle qui regarde, celle qui choisit, le centre du pouvoir, et, en procédant ainsi, elle définit une nouvelle logique, une nouvelle économie dans l'échange linguistique. Dans *Le ravissement de Lol V. Stein*, comme Duras dévoile et explore l'indécence de l'écriture féminine, elle révèle cette indécence comme un voile pour quelque chose d'autre : « la prostitution cachée du langage ».

Martha Noel Evans, « Marguerite Duras : The Whore », p. 123-156, in *Masks of Tradition, Women and the Politics of Writing in Twentieth-Century France*, Cornell University Press, Ithaca et Londres, 1987, p. 124 (ma traduction). D.R.

La transgression de l'écriture entraîne à la fois Duras et son personnage principal au bord de la folie.

Ibid., p. 20.

Susan Cohen est plus radicale et plus optimiste. Pour elle, le risque de folie ne concerne que les femmes « rendues folles par la privation de récit », tandis que l'accès au discours préserve Duras — et ses héroïnes — de la folie. Elle cite des paroles de Duras elle-même : « Depuis le début de ma vie, le problème pour moi, a été de savoir qui parlait quand je parlais dans mes livres... et s'il y a une invention dans mes livres, elle est là. » Elle constate que « le " quelqu'un " parle à partir d'une " ignorance " originelle, permanente et textuellement productive ».

Le *Ravissement* a une structure narrative rare : un auteur féminin, un « écrivain » narrateur masculin et une protagoniste féminine sur laquelle il prétend centrer son attention. Ce texte mine l'unité d'un simple narrateur interne, dramatise l'effet destructeur du besoin d'un langage unitaire et dépeint son échec essentiel.

Susan Cohen, « Phantasm and Narration in *Le ravissement de Lol. V. Stein* ». *Women and Discourse in the Fiction of Marguerite Duras*, Macmillan, Londres, 1993, p. 34 (ma traduction). D.R.

Le texte raconte deux fantasmes, mais il a un seul narrateur.

Ibid., p. 39.

Seul le narrateur constitue, même de façon fantasmatique, une subjectivité tandis que Lol reste l'objet sans voix du texte. [...] Lol doit rester silencieuse, réduite au silence, pour que le narrateur/écrivain puisse s'approprier son fantasme, sa personne, son histoire. Si l'on se souvient de l'assertion de Freud selon laquelle le mutisme, dans les rêves, est une représentation banale de la mort, et que ce roman est une sorte de rêve fantasmatique, on peut conclure que le silence de Lol, sur lequel la voix cannibale du « je » est fondée, correspond à sa « mort » désirée, encouragée, assurée par lui. [...] Le texte du narrateur, alors, existe au prix du « meurtre » de deux femmes.

Ibid., p. 48.

Voici une autre analyse très claire et juste du roman des positions masculines et féminines dans le *Ravissement* :

Ce qui fait surface dans ces récits d'hommes — mais récits écrits par une femme, mettant donc en scène des fantasmes féminins de pouvoir masculin — c'est le sadisme des personnages masculins. [...] Dans le *Ravissement*, le sadisme de Jacques Hold informe tout le texte et ses relations avec les femmes. Il est nettement visible dans ses gestes avec Tatiana (p. 167), mais il l'est aussi avec Lol (p. 173). Cette scène réapparaît dans deux autres textes de Duras, dans *Le vice-consul* et dans

Catherine Rodgers, « Déconstruction de la masculinité », in *Marguerite Duras*, Actes du Colloque de Cerisy, éd. Écriture, 1994, p. 50-52.

L'homme assis dans le couloir. [...] Si l'érotique durassienne nécessite un mâle à la virilité sadique, sa personnalité, sa position sociale sont par contre de peu d'importance. Ce qui explique peut-être pourquoi les personnages masculins, même quand ils ne sont pas narrateurs, sont si peu décrits. [...]

À côté de ces hommes qui, par leur regard, leur désir. souvent leur sadisme, savent déclencher le désir féminin, se trouvent d'autres personnages masculins qui eux n'éveillent aucun désir, et dont la sexualité est inexistante. D'un côté évoluent des caricatures de l'homme fort, autoritaire, respecté par la société, dont la virilité a été canalisée, neutralisée par cette même société — ce sont souvent les maris des héroïnes durassiennes — et de l'autre côté des hommes démunis dont la masculinité a été détruite ou ne s'est jamais construite.

4. LA FOLIE DE LOL ?

Pour certaines critiques cette « folie » ne fait pas de doute. Julia Kristeva la nomme « dépression et mélancolie » et la juge dangereuse car susceptible de « contaminer » le lecteur. L'article sur Duras est intitulé « Rhétorique blanche de l'apocalypse ».

[Dans l'écriture de Duras] si recherche formelle il y a, elle est subordonnée à l'affrontement au silence de l'horreur en soi et dans le monde. Cette confrontation la conduit à une esthétique de la *maladresse*, d'une part, à une *littérature non cathartique*, d'autre part.

Julia Kristeva « Une rhétorique de l'apocalypse », in *Soleil noir, dépression et mélancolie*, Gallimard, Folio Essais, 1987, p. 233.

On comprend désormais qu'il ne faut pas donner les livres de Duras aux lecteurs et lectrices fragiles [...]. [Ils] nous font côtoyer la folie. Ils ne la montrent pas de loin [...]. Tout au contraire les textes apprivoisent « la maladie de la mort », ils font un avec elle, ils sont de plain-pied, sans distance et sans échappée.

Ibid., p. 235.

J. Kristeva souligne la tristesse « non dramatique, fanée, innommable » des femmes durassiennes ; l'abandon qui « structure ce qui reste d'histoire » :

On ne devrait sans doute pas prendre cette femme durassienne pour *toute* la femme. Cependant, quelques traits fréquents de la sexualité féminine y apparaissent. On est porté à supposer, chez cet être tout de tristesse, non pas un *refoulement*, mais un *épuisement des pulsions érotiques* [...], *une déliaison fondamentale.* Elle peut provoquer le ravissement, pas le plaisir. [...] Une certaine vérité de l'expérience féminine qui touche la jouissance de la douleur côtoie chez Duras la mythification du féminin inaccessible.

Ibid., p. 251-252.

Sont notés aussi tous les phénomènes de répétition et de dédoublement (par exemple entre les figures de Lol et de Tatiana). Mais cette interprétation très négative correspond, en fait, à une lecture très générale et superficielle des romans et ne prend pas en compte les structures de l'énonciation, qui font basculer le sens.

Raynalle Udris présente l'originalité de proposer une étude précise sur la question de la folie de Lol et une interprétation très positive, fondée sur l'opposition entre « folie » et « déraison », le deuxième terme désignant une mise en cause épistémologique et sociale à la fois.

La tentative de Lol pour l'établissement d'une relation triangulaire — tabou très fort dans une société basée sur la suprématie et l'exclusivité du couple — et pour une dynamique de triangulation enracinée dans les traits complémentaires de la perte de soi et de la non-préférentialité, devient la base d'un puissant renouveau du sens. L'effet de cela sur Jacques Hold devient de plus en plus sensible, tant au niveau fictionnel qu'au niveau narratif. « Lol devient transformante pour qui, par amour, fait l'effort de la connaître », écrit Alleins.

Raynalle Udris, *Welcome Unreason. A Study of « madness » in the novels of Marguerite Duras*, éd. Rodopi, Amsterdam, Atlanta, 1993, p. 75 (ma traduction). D.R.

Selon R. Udris, l'existence de Lol, si on ne cherche pas à lui appliquer des « étiquettes », même pas la plus « tentante », celle d'hystérique, postule « une nouvelle position du désir et un défi majeur aux attentes sociales ». Duras offre donc « la peinture d'une vision poétique sans compromis de l'impossible qui réside au cœur de l'existence humaine ».

L'impossible est conçu ici comme un chemin menant à toutes les possibilités, comme une source infinie de création et de sens, et si les figures féminines sont les collaboratrices les mieux adaptées de cet ordre nouveau c'est surtout parce que, comme Lol, Anne-Marie Stretter ou la femme du *Camion*, elles restent, en termes durassiens, la seule incarnation possible de la potentialité multiple de l'existence humaine. « Il pourrait y en avoir mille possibles, mille autres possibles de cette femme », déclare Duras. [...]

Marguerite Duras a toujours compris que « la politique de l'impossible est la meilleure voie pour découvrir la politique du possible qui ne peut être qu'une inconnue à plusieurs solutions » (Bataille).

Ibid., p. 236-237.

5. MOTIFS DIVERS

Sharon Willis :

Le chien mort, figure tout à fait inassimilable, cadavre répugnant qui crève la scène de la plage [...], interrompt la continuité sémantique, thématique et même logique du texte du *Ravissement*. Figure énigmatique de la mort et du dégoût, il signifie seulement une pure et stupide résistance au sens, en même temps qu'il attire la pulsion épistémologique, créatrice de sens [...] Dans sa résistance, son action de point de résistance à toute maîtrise, cette figure double aussi Lol V. Stein.

Sharon Willis, *Marguerite Duras : Writing on the Body*, University of Illinois Press, Urbana et Chicago, 1987, p. 90 (ma traduction). D.R.

À travers plusieurs passages, situés dans le contexte immédiat de celui du chien mort sur la plage (p. 184), Sharon Willis montre une association textuelle entre le chien mort et la « faim » de Lol : « Elle meurt de faim. » Le narrateur est fasciné par Lol assouvissant cette faim et le texte opère un autre rapprochement, entre « faim » et « fin » :

Elle mange, elle oublie. Au milieu de spéculations anxieuses sur la fin, dont le déni oblige à accepter une autre inconcevable fin sans fin, nous entendons « la fin sans fin ». [...]

La phrase se brise en formes diverses : « la fin sans faim », « la faim sans fin », « la faim sans faim ». De plus, la relation entre la faim et la fin, ou son impossibilité, rejoint aussi le problème de la mémoire. Manger, dans cette scène, c'est commencer le processus de l'oubli.

Ibid., p. 91.

Une autre figure textuelle (inverse) conforte ces « corrélations fragiles » : et S. Willis cite un passage (p. 174), où l'effort de mémoire de Lol est comparé à un « vomissement » :

La mémoire de Lol s'ouvre, surgit dans des mots qui ne signifient rien, des mots vomis ; les endroits indestructibles apparaissent comme des morceaux, des fragments demeurés intacts, c'est-à-dire non digérés. [...] Le souvenir non digéré est l'obsession centrale et répétée du texte. [...] Le travail du deuil étrange, incomplet, ne laisse rien à raconter, pas d'histoire à narrer.

Ibid., p. 92.

VI. AUTRES LECTURES

1. INTERPRÉTATIONS MYSTIQUES

La présence, récurrente, du vocabulaire du sacré, le caractère irréductible par le langage des expériences mises en scène, l'usage répété de l'antithèse et de l'oxymore entraînent des interprétations mystiques du *Ravissement* et, plus largement, de l'écriture durassienne.

Madeleine Alleins :

Qui est Lol dans le temps où nous la rencontrons ? Quelqu'un qui dit non à la subjectivité et à ses limites. Ce serait se tromper gravement sur elle que de la croire hantée par le souvenir d'une extase naturelle et mettant tout en œuvre pour goûter de nouveau la même extraordinaire émotion. [...] La nuit dans laquelle tente de plonger Lol est plus vaste que celle de l'inconscient, elle est du domaine de l'être. Chercheuse du sens caché derrière les données du sensible, il paraît plus juste de voir en elle une mystique sauvage. Il ne faut pas se laisser effrayer par le mot, *Le ravissement de Lol V.Stein* est écrit dans une perspective de transcendance.

Madeleine Alleins, *Marguerite Duras, médium du réel*, L'âge d'homme, Lausanne, 1984, p. 123.

Philippe Le Touzé, en proposant une interprétation mystique, se montre beaucoup moins catégorique et plus nuancé que Madeleine Alleins. Il ne prétend pas du tout « réduire » le sens du roman de Duras, « texte irréductible », écrit-il.

La danse suspend la durée. Toute la scène est célébrée comme une sortie du temps, un accès à l'éternité. Et par un déplacement insolite, la catastrophe traumatisante semble être non pas la transition amoureuse, mais la « fin », la désastreuse transition

Jean Bessière et Philippe Le Touzé, « *Le ravissement de Lol V. Stein* de Marguerite Duras : désir, transition et vide », in *Signes du roman, signes de la transition*, PUF, 1986, p. 205-221.

par laquelle Lol retombe dans le temps. [..] Le mot capital du titre, sujet même du roman : « ravissement », appose une sorte de sceau mystique à tout le livre, et l'état qu'il désigne se caractérise par ce que les grandes doctrines spirituelles nomment la *coincidentia oppositorum* : la « plus grande douleur » et « la plus grande joie confondues » [...].

Vient le moment de l'étreinte sexuelle. Jacques Hold, narrateur, relate que Lol passive donne des signes de délire, ne reconnaît pas son amant, confond sa propre identité avec celle de Tatiana Karl. Désincarnation, sortie du temps, perte d'identité, caractéristiques de la folie ? Symptômes troublants, certes. Mais n'est-elle pas troublante aussi, cette insistance mise sur l'universel, qui fait ressembler Lol à une « délivrée » du bouddhisme, une « éveillée » au grand tout, pour qui toute étreinte sexuelle particulière constituerait désormais une régression ? [...]

D'autre part, quand Marguerite déclare à Bernard Pivot avoir enfin trouvé une « écriture presque distraite » qui « courrait sur la crête des mots », ne peut-on rapprocher cette déconcentration de celle des anciens calligraphes chinois, dont l'écriture « rapide, fulgurante », s'obtient, selon Mi Fou, grand lettré du XIe siècle, en laissant « jouer le pinceau » « spontanément, la main et l'esprit restant vides » ? Le jaillissement créateur est conquis par une ascèse de la vacuité ; dans les tableaux des peintres chinois, on trouve, entre le haut et le bas, entre le ciel et la terre, ce vide central d'où naît le tableau lui-même, car selon Lao-Tseu, le Tao est « l'abîme » qui est « l'ancêtre de tous les êtres ».

[...] Ce qui, en Lol Valérie Stein, fascine et touche Jacques Hold et, par sa médiation, Duras elle-même, c'est que ce vide, cette infirmité [...] est précisément ce qui fait surgir d'eux la vie : l'élan d'amour de Jacques Hold, figure de l'élan créateur de Duras. On est loin de la pathologie : Lol, c'est la pulsation même de la pensée de M. Duras ; elle sort des limbes et y replonge. Emblème, enseigne du personnage, car non seulement produit d'une création, mais figure de sa propre création.

Danielle Bajomée :

Danielle Bajomée, « La nuit battue à mort », in *Duras, RSH*, n° 202, 1986, p. 18-22. Repris dans *Duras, ou la Douleur*, De Boeck, 1989.

Approcher passivement ou activement l'illimité ou l'illimitation. C'est là sans doute ce qui échoit aux personnages les plus emblématiques de l'œuvre [...]

Faut-il interpréter cette apparente apathie comme ce que Bataille désigne, à la suite de la théologie, par état théopathique (« de tels états qui peuvent être invoqués indépendamment de leurs formes chrétiennes, ont un aspect très différent, non seulement des états érotiques, mais d'états mystiques [...]. Il n'y a plus de désir dans l'état théopathique, l'être devient passif, il subit ce qui lui arrive en quelque sorte sans mouvement » (Georges Bataille, *L'érotisme*, UGE, 10/18, 1965, p. 272). Je ne sais. Ce que je lis, c'est que Lol atteint à l'égarement absolu. Où le sujet se brise. Où il approche sans doute cette continuité qui délivre de la séparation, du sentiment de séparation en laissant l'être accéder à l'existence impersonnelle, dans ce mourir-à-soi — que Bataille identifiait avec l'érotisme, le meurtre ou la violence — que Duras fait coïncider avec un au-delà ou un en-deçà de la douleur, avec ce qu'elle appelle « un anéantissement de velours de sa propre personne » (p. 50).

Comment parler de ce qui, chez Duras, me paraît faire signe du côté du langage mystique sans donner le sentiment qu'elle — ou ses personnages — serait mystique sans le savoir ? « Je ne connais pas », dirait Lol, et moi, avec elle. Je crois pourtant ne pas me tromper en prolongeant ou en aménageant ce qu'ont pu exprimer sur la question un Michel de Certeau ou un Ishagpour, quand Duras a elle-même manifesté son attachement à cette non-orthodoxie du penser-mystique : « je n'ai jamais été croyante, même enfant. J'ai toujours vu les croyants comme atteints d'une infirmité d'esprit. Plus grande, j'ai lu Spinoza, Pascal, Ruysbroeck. J'ai vu la foi des mystiques comme un désespoir du non-croire... » (*P.*, p. 239).

Je rappelle aussi, par souci de clarté, que le mysticisme, étymologiquement parlant, renvoie d'abord à une initiation et qu'il a pris, le temps venant, le sens d'état intérieur d'union de soi avec un absolu [...]. Cet « autre état » dans lequel [le mystique] s'abîme ou auquel il accède par l'ascèse ou la prière rejette la raison au profit d'un connaître différent.

2. LA SCÈNE DE L'ÉCRITURE

Christine Blot-Labarrère lit *Le ravissement* d'abord (mais pas exclusivement) comme une métaphore de l'écriture :

L'histoire de Lol peut être lue comme celle de l'écrivain quand l'écriture l'envahit et le ravit à lui-même. Ce qui ne signifie pas que l'histoire de Lol n'est pas aussi l'histoire d'un ravissement amoureux. Tout au contraire.

Christiane Blot-Labarrère, *Marguerite Duras*, Paris, Le Seuil, « Les contemporains », 1992, p. 141.

Lol-Eurydice est tirée vers le jour par un Jacques-Orphée qui, voulant la délivrer, la tue.

Ibid., p. 143.

À propos du triangle :

Il y a beaucoup d'indices que les triangles pourraient bien n'être pas ce qu'ils ont l'air d'être [...]

La structure triangulaire de cette scène (p. 47), telle que Lol la rejoue, est plus apparente que réelle. Lol n'est pas fermement positionnée comme spectatrice à mi-distance entre Michael Richardson et Anne-Marie Stretter, comme

Leslie Hill, Marguerite Duras, *Apocalyptic Desires*, *op. cit.*, p. 75. D.R.

l'implique l'exposé de Lacan et comme l'ont affirmé depuis d'autres critiques. Lol est placé à l'endroit précis où les premiers rayons de l'aurore, illuminant la scène avec une précision du genre de celle qu'on trouve seulement dans *Nosferatu* de Murnau, coupe une ligne imaginaire allant de Michael Richardson et Anne-Marie Stretter à Lol. La relation entre ces points n'est pas simple. L'aurore, appartenant au jour qui menace, fonctionne comme une figure de séparation ; mais le couple, qui traîne encore dans la nuit précédente, continue à dramatiser la possibilité d'une fusion amoureuse. En éclatant, l'aurore signifie une séparation soudaine et brutale, mais ce qu'elle révèle, c'est une scène dans laquelle la séparation est suspendue. Le temps est suspendu entre ce qui est déjà arrivé et ce qui n'a pas encore eu lieu. Entre le jour et la nuit, l'aurore et les deux amants, entre séparation et fusion, c'est Lol qui maintient l'équilibre, et son regard est moins un point de vue privilégié qu'un mouvement oscillant ; allant et venant du couple à l'aurore.

Le moment de bonheur de Lol ne tombe ni avant ni après le moment de sa séparation des deux amants, mais au point exact où la distinction entre séparation et fusion est elle-même inéluctablement effacée, quand elle-même est déjà détachée de son fiancé mais unie au spectacle des amants devant elle, les aimant encore apparemment, comme une mère très âgée. La scène est une scène de perte et de désir, mais, comme le montre Lol quand elle tente de la reproduire plus tard, avec l'aide de Jacques et de Tatiana, sa signification n'est pas fixe ; car Lol ne reproduit pas la scène passivement, comme si elle n'était rien d'autre qu'un symptôme pathologique et hystérique, elle la transforme en substituant à l'aurore comme elle le fait dans le champ de seigle — une autre sorte de demi-lumière, la demi-lumière du crépuscule qui, comme ailleurs dans Duras, promet un retour de l'obscurité mais aussi l'espoir d'une aurore différente.

Ce que répète Lol, c'est moins un triangle statique, avec son répertoire inchangé de participants masculins et féminins, qu'un scénario dynamique, oscillant, dans lequel il n'y a pas de positions fixes, mais une série de relations mobiles.

VII. INTERTEXTUALITÉ

Comme nous l'avons vu, le texte du *Ravissement* entretient des relations intertextuelles avec des mythes encore actifs dans le monde actuel et avec des contes, en particulier *La Belle au Bois Dormant*.

1. « LA BELLE AU BOIS DORMANT »

Une grande partie de la force du roman repose sur la structure de conte de fées sous-jacente à l'histoire moderne.

Dans le contexte du conte de fées, le bal de T. Beach est le baptême de la Belle et Anne-Marie Stretter la fée non invitée qui prive le bébé de ses heureux sorts (Michael Richardson). La convalescence de Lol à S. Tahla devient alors l'enfance de la princesse ; sa sortie vers la maison de Jean Bedford et le baiser de celui-ci, l'équivalent de la rencontre avec la vieille femme dans la tour et du doigt piqué ; les dix ans de mariage équivalent aux cent ans de sommeil [...]. Jacques Hold est, évidemment, le prince dont le baiser réveille la princesse.

Jennifer Waelti-Walters, « Sleeping Beauty : the Rapture of Lol .V. Stein », in *Fairy Tales and the Female Imagination*, Eden Press, Montréal, 1982, p. 58.

Tatiana pourrait être la dernière bonne fée qui pouvait modifier la malédiction et empêcher la mort de la princesse. (Son nom, Tatiana, rappelle Titania, Reine des Fées.)

Ibid., p. 61.

2. MYTHES

Avec le personnage d'Anne-Marie Stretter, connotant à la fois la séduction et la mort, c'est bien l'imagerie de la grande faucheuse qui est convoquée,

Mireille Calle-Grüber, « L'amour fou, femme fatale. Marguerite Duras : une récriture sublime des archétypes les mieux établis en littérature », in *Le Nouveau Roman en question*, I, « Nouveau Roman et archétypes », *Revue des lettres modernes*, Minard, avril 1992, p. 30.

squelette décharné [...], vêtement noir qui ne revêt pas, et jusqu'au « fourreau » qui appelle quelque arme, tranchante — épée, peut-être, à défaut de la faux. Telle l'épée entre les amants, Tristan et Iseut — autre fable. Anne-Marie Stretter donc, ou la Mort telle qu'en elle-même l'allégorie nous a appris à la figurer.

Ibid., p. 48.

[...] La narration du *Ravissement* de Lol V. Stein n'aura de cesse qu'elle ne parvienne à extraire de l'archétype la figure triangulaire de l'Amour. Afin de délaisser « la vieille algèbre des peines d'amour » (p. 19) et d'éviter que le roman ne se rabatte sur la thématique préfabriquée d'un vaudevillesque « ménage à trois », le récit a certes besoin de construire *une relation* hors psychologisation. [...] Il s'agit en effet, chez Duras, de *penser autrement* le rapport d'amour et le rapport de couple. Ceci : qu'il n'y a d'amour que Désir d'Amour ; que l'amour du couple est expérience du néant ; que la seule possibilité de prendre conscience de cet (son propre ?) anéantissement c'est de voir une autre à sa place (« remplacée par cette femme, *au souffle près* ») [p. 50], c'est-à-dire s'exclure-inclure (« cet anéantissement de velours de sa propre personne ») [p. 50].

Susan Cohen va plus loin, en montrant que la structure même des récits durassiens et de la lecture qu'ils imposent est analogue à celle des récits légendaires et mythologiques.

Les configurations narratives de Duras forment un cadre qui conduit à la mythologisation. L'ignorance narrative [...] se combine avec une attitude de fascination respectueuse pour les histoires racontées. Sans cesse, les « parleurs » racontent de nouveau ou réinventent des reconstructions multiples des histoires inaccessibles et absentes. Répétition, distance, caractère invérifiable caractérisent la matière textuelle des légendes, tandis que la révérence et/ou la fascination caractérisent leurs récits.

Susan Cohen, *Women and Discourse*, p. 179.

3. « NADJA »

À une question de Claude Cézan : « Le surréalisme a-t-il beaucoup compté pour vous ? », Marguerite Duras répondait, en 1963 : « Non, mais nous sommes tous passés par ce traumatisme » (« Marguerite Duras, le vertige et l'absurde », Les *Nouvelles littéraires*, 21 février 1963, p. 11).

Quelques passages extraits du récit d'André Breton montrent les ressemblances — un peu ténues — soulignées par quelques critiques, entre Lol et Nadja. (*L'amour fou* est aussi le titre de l'un des livres d'André Breton, texte essentiel du surréalisme, Gallimard, 1937, rééd. Folio.)

L'errance, le mensonge : Dès la première rencontre, Nadja erre et ment : « Elle devait reconnaître par la suite qu'elle allait sans but aucun » (Folio, p. 73). Elle répond à la question « Qui êtes-vous ? » : « Je suis l'âme errante » (*ibid.*, p. 82). « Qui est la vraie Nadja ? [...] la créature toujours inspirée et inspirante qui n'aimait qu'être dans la rue, pour elle seul champ d'expérience valable... » (*ibid.*, p. 133).

Les incertitudes du narrateur :

Je suis mécontent de moi. Il me semble que je l'observe trop, comment faire autrement ? Comment me voit-elle, me juge-t-elle ? Il est impardonnable que je continue à la voir si je ne l'aime pas. Est-ce que je ne l'aime pas ? Je suis, tout en étant près d'elle, plus près des choses qui sont près d'elles.

André Breton, *Nadja*, Gallimard, Folio, 1964, p. 104.

(À mettre en relation avec cette remarque de Jacques Hold : « Mon nom prononcé ne nomme pas », p. 113.)

Puis, soudain, se plaçant devant moi, m'arrêtant presque, avec cette manière extraordinaire de m'appeler, comme on appellerait quelqu'un, de salle en salle, dans un château vide : « André ? André... ? Tu écriras un roman sur moi. Je t'assure.

Ibid., p. 117.

Ne dis pas non. Prends garde : tout s'affaiblit, tout disparaît. De nous il faut que quelque chose reste... Mais cela ne fait rien : tu prendras un autre nom : quel nom, veux-tu que je te dise, c'est très important. »

La folie finale :

Quelque envie que j'en ai eue, quelque illusion peut-être aussi, je n'ai peut-être pas été à la hauteur de ce qu'elle me proposait. Mais que me proposait-elle ? N'importe. Seul l'amour au sens où je l'entends — mais alors le mystérieux, l'improbable, l'unique, le confondant et l'indubitable amour — tel enfin qu'il ne peut être qu'à toute épreuve, eût pu permettre ici l'accomplissement du miracle.

Ibid., p. 159-160.

On est venu, il y a quelques mois, m'apprendre que Nadja était folle. À la suite d'excentricités auxquelles elle s'était, paraît-il, livrée dans les couloirs de son hôtel, elle avait dû être internée à l'asile de Vaucluse.

4. « L'ANNÉE DERNIÈRE À MARIENBAD »

***L'année dernière à Marienbad*, dont le scénario est de Robbe-Grillet, est un film d'Alain Resnais (pour qui M. Duras avait écrit le scénario d'*Hiroshima mon amour*). Le détachement absent des personnages, l'incertitude généralisée de l'histoire, liée à la mémoire, les répétitions et les glissements des mots, des phrases et des situations, offrent des ressemblances avec le *Ravissement* mais sous une forme beaucoup plus intellectuelle et abstraite.**

« Je suis parti, confiait l'auteur à *L'Express*, de cette idée : une forme d'itinéraire qui pouvait être également une forme d'écriture, un labyrinthe, c'est-à-dire un chemin qui a toujours l'air guidé par des parois strictes, mais qui néanmoins à chaque ins-

Gaston Bounoure, *Alain Resnais*, Seghers, 1974, p. 71.

tant conduit à des impasses et oblige à revenir en arrière, à repasser plusieurs fois aux mêmes endroits, sur des parcours plus ou moins longs, à explorer une nouvelle direction et à retomber sur une nouvelle impossibilité... » Au travers de ces paysages intermédiaires, dans ce labyrinthe mental, seuls trois « inconnus » se déplacent. A, X et M hantent un monde comme empli d'une pensée mathémathique pure. Leurs itinéraires dessinent les figures du souvenir géométrisé. Ils tentent d'extraire — par une sorte d'« algèbre des actes » — du monde des choses et des nombres les racines de la mémoire.

5. AUTRES TEXTES

Michael Sheringham propose de nombreux rapprochements intertextuels :

La dimension de l'intrigue, des histoires, des anecdotes [dans le *Ravissement*] est essentiellement publique et implique un monde fait d'un étrange assortiment d'éléments stéréotypés : le cadre semble situé quelque part sur la côte est des États-Unis mais il y a des incohérences et elles ont pour effet de défamiliariser le contexte. Il y a une atmosphère à la Tennessee Williams dans les ingrédients de l'histoire et, en général, un parfum de cette Amérique impeccable des films des années cinquante — le cadre a vraiment la vraisemblance délibérée d'un décor de cinéma.

Michael Sheringham, « Knowledge and repetition in *Le ravissement de Lol V. Stein* », Londres, *Romance Studies*, n° 2, été 1983, p. 127 (ma traduction). D.R.

La logique narrative dans cette dimension dépend en grande partie d'une situation stéréotypée : quel sera le résultat du retour de Lol ? A-t-elle réellement surmonté son « ravissement » de T. Beach ? Va-t-elle s'effondrer et probablement devenir folle, comme Tatiana le craint et en un sens l'espère ? Les

Ibid., p. 128.

ordres de réalité impliqués ici sont psychologiques, sentimentaux et psychopathologiques, une mixture éminemment hitchcockienne que nous pouvons placer sous l'égide de Tatiana qui est au cœur de cette dimension parce qu'elle incarne tout au long du récit une perspective sur Lol qui fait d'elle la source d'énigmes très ordinaires et banales.

Mais tout change si l'on prend en compte la dimension de la narration :

Comme beaucoup de récits modernes à la première personne, le *Ravissement* insiste sur une fracture possible entre les ordres de la fiction et de la narration [...] Dans le *Ravissement*, à tous les niveaux se manifestent les signes d'un conflit, chez Jacques Hold, entre le sens normal de son être propre et les nouveaux ordres d'expérience auxquels il est confronté.

Ibid., p. 133.

M. Sheringham cite un « beau passage » (p. 166) tiré du récit du voyage en train vers T. Beach, dont il fait remarquer les intertextes (Baudelaire, Valéry, Breton).

L'un des *Fragments d'un discours amoureux*, de Roland Barthes (Le Seuil, 1977), s'intitule « Ravissement » : la « scène initiale » y est définie comme toujours « reconstituée », « déjà (encore toujours) un souvenir ».

VIII. BIBLIOGRAPHIE

I. ŒUVRES DE MARGUERITE DURAS

(Ne seront signalés ici que les textes explicitement cités ; voir les jaquettes des livres pour une bibliographie complète.)

Les impudents, Plon, 1943, Gallimard, coll. « Folio », 1992.
Un barrage contre le Pacifique, Gallimard, 1950.
Des journées entières dans les arbres, suivi de « Le boa », « Madame Dodin », « Les chantiers », récits, Gallimard, 1954.
Moderato cantabile, éd. de Minuit, 1958.
Hiroshima mon amour, scénario et dialogues, Gallimard, 1960.
L'après-midi de Monsieur Andesmas, Gallimard, 1962.
Le ravissement de Lol V. Stein, Gallimard, 1964.
Le vice-consul, Gallimard, coll. « L'imaginaire », 1965.
Détruire, dit-elle, éd. de Minuit, 1969.
L'amour, Gallimard, coll. « Folio », 1971.
Nathalie Granger, suivi de *La femme du Gange*, scénarios, Gallimard, 1973.
Les parleuses, entretien avec Xavière Gauthier, éd. de Minuit, 1974.
Le camion, suivi de *Entretiens avec Michelle Porte*, éd. de Minuit, 1977.
Les lieux de Marguerite Duras, en collaboration avec Michelle Porte, éd. de Minuit, 1977.
Les yeux verts, Cahiers du cinéma, 1980.
La vie matérielle, P.O.L., 1987.
Marguerite Duras : Œuvres cinématographiques, Édition vidéographique critique, ministère des Relations extérieures, Bureau d'animation culturelle, Paris, 1984 (coffret de cinq cassettes vidéo des films de Marguerite Duras, accompagné d'un livret contenant, en particulier, des entretiens avec Dominique Noguez, dont « La couleur des mots » [sur *India Song*]).

II. OUVRAGES CRITIQUES SUR L'ENSEMBLE DE L'ŒUVRE CONTENANT DES CHAPITRES OU DES PASSAGES SUR LE « RAVISSEMENT ».

Madeleine Alleins, *Marguerite Duras, médium du réel*, L'Âge d'homme, Lausanne, 1984.

Danielle Bajomée, *Duras, ou la Douleur,* De Boeck, Université de Bruxelles, 1989.

Christiane Blot-Labarrère, *Marguerite Duras*, Le Seuil, coll. « Les contemporains », 1992.

Madeleine Borgomano, *Duras, une lecture des fantasmes*, Cistre, coll. « Essais », Petit-Roeulx, Belgique, 1985.

— *India Song,* éd. L'Interdisciplinaire, Limonest, 1990.

Philippe Boyer, « L'instant fulgurant », in *L'écarté(e), Fiction théorique*, Seghers-Laffont, coll. « Change », 1973, p. 187-205.

Susan Cohen, *Women and Discourse in the Fiction of Marguerite Duras*, Macmillan, Londres, 1993.

Martha Noel Evans, *Masks of Tradition, Women and the Politics of Writing in Twentieth-Century France*, Cornell University Press, Ithaca et Londres, 1987, p. 123-156.

Yvonne Guers-Villate, *Continuité et discontinuité de l'œuvre durassienne*, éd. de l'Université de Bruxelles, 1985, p. 97, 115.

Leslie Hill, *Marguerite Duras, Apocalyptic Desires,* Routledge, Londres et New York, 1993, p. 64-84.

Alice Jardine, *Gynesis : Configurations of Women and Modernity*, Cornell University Press, New York, 1985, p. 172-177.

Julia Kristeva, « La maladie de la douleur : Duras », in *Soleil noir, dépression et mélancolie*, Gallimard, coll. « Folio Essais », 1987, p. 229-265.

Jacques Lacan, « Hommage fait à Marguerite Duras du *Ravissement de Lol V. Stein* », *Cahiers Renaud-Barrault*, n° 52, décembre 1965, p. 7-15 ; repris dans F. Barat et J. Farges, *Marguerite Duras*, Albatros, 1975, p. 131-137.

Marcelle Marini, *Territoires du féminin avec Marguerite Duras*, éd. de Minuit, 1977. (Le livre étudie plus spécialement *Le vice-consul*, mais aborde aussi le *Ravissement*, en particulier p. 34-48.)

Michèle Montrelay, « Sur *Le ravissement de Lol V. Stein* », in *L'ombre et le nom : sur la féminité*, éd. de Minuit, 1977, p. 7-23.

Jean Pierrot, « Le cycle de Lol V. Stein », in *Marguerite Duras*, José Corti, 1986, p. 201-268.

Janine Ricouart, « La voyeuse regardant dans le vide », in *Écriture féminine et violence*, Summa Publications, Inc., Birmingham, Alabama, 1991, p. 73-78.

Marie-Claire Ropars-Willeumier, *Écraniques. Le film du texte*, Lille, Presses universitaires de Lille, 1990.

Trista Selous, *The Other Woman. Feminism and Femininity in the Work of Marguerite Duras*, Yale University Press, New Haven et Londres, 1988.

Daniel Sibony, *La haine du désir*, Christian Bourgois éd., 1978, p. 81-141.

Susan Rubin Suleiman, *Subversive Intent : Gender, Politics, and the Avant-Garde*, Cambridge, Massachusetts, Harvard University Press, 1990, p. 88-118.

Micheline Tison-Braun, *Marguerite Duras*, éd. Rodopi, Amsterdam, 1985, p. 57-65.

Raynalle Udris, *Welcome Unreason. A Study of « madness » in the novels of Marguerite Duras*, éd. Rodopi, Amsterdam, Atlanta, 1993, p. 43-97.

Sharon Willis, *Marguerite Duras : Writing on the Body*, University of Illinois Press, Chicago et Urbana, 1987, p. 63-95.

III. ARTICLES

Jean Alter, « *Le ravissement de Lol V. Stein* », *The French Review*, 23-2, décembre 1964.

Verena Andermatt, « Rodomontages of *Le ravissement de Lol V. Stein* », *Modern French Fiction*, n° 57, Yale French Studies, 1979.

J. Baladier, « Ravissement et douleur chez Marguerite Duras ou les figurations de l'objet perdu », *Esquisses psychanalytiques*, nº 9, 1988.

Michelle Calle-Grüber, « L'amour fou, femme fatale. Marguerite Duras : une récriture sublime des archétypes les mieux établis en littérature », in *Le Nouveau Roman en question*, I, « Nouveau Roman et archétypes », textes réunis par Michel Allemand, *Revue des lettres modernes*, Minard, avril 1992.

Didier Coste, « S. Thala, capitale du possible », in *Écrire, dit-elle*, Université de Bruxelles, 1985.

Béatrice Didier, « Thèmes et structures de l'absence dans *Le ravissement de Lol V. Stein* », in *Écrire, dit-elle*, Université de Bruxelles, 1985.

Michèle Druon, « Mise en scène et catharsis de l'amour dans *Le ravissement de Lol V. Stein*, de Marguerite Duras », *The French Review*, vol. LVIII, février 1985.

M. Erman, « M. Duras : *Le ravissement de Lol V. Stein* », *L'École des lettres*, nº 12-13, 1984-1985.

Pierre Fedida, « La douleur l'oubli », in *Déraison désir*, revue *Change*, nº 12, septembre 1972, p. 141-146.

F. Larsson, « Écriture, mémoire, identité dans *Le ravissement de Lol V. Stein* », *Ariane*, Université de Coimbra, III, 1985.

Philippe Le Touzé, « *Le ravissement de Lol V. Stein* de Marguerite Duras : désir, transition et vide », in *Signes du roman, signes de la transition*, textes réunis par Jean Bessière, PUF, 1986.

Mary Lydon, « The forgetfulness of Memory : Jacques Lacan, Marguerite Duras, and the Text », *Comparative Literature*, 29-3, automne 1988.

Christine Rabant, « La Bête chanteuse », *L'Arc*, nº 58, 1974.

Michèle Ramond, « Le déficit, l'excès, l'oubli dans *Le ravissement de Lol V. Stein* », in *Le personnage en question*, Université de Toulouse-le Mirail, 1984, p. 141-151.

Ragnhild Evang Reinton, « *Le ravissement de Lol V. Stein* — un livre sur rien », in *Point de rencontre : le roman*, Conseil norvégien de la recherche scientifique, KULTs skriftserie n° 37, t. II, 1995, p. 341.

Michael Sheringham, « Knowledge and repetition in *Le ravissement de Lol V. Stein* », *Romance Studies*, n° 2, été 1983.

Susan Rubin Suleiman, « Nadja, Dora, Lol V. Stein : women, madness and narrative », in *Discourse in Psychoanalysis and Literature*, Shlomith Rimmon-Kenan, Methuen, Londres et New York, 1987, p. 124-151.

Anne Tomiche, « Repetition, memory and oblivion : Freud, Duras, and Gertrude Stein », *Revue de littérature comparée*, n° 3, 1991.

H. Veyssier, « *Le ravissement de Lol V. Stein* », in *Cahiers de recherche de Sciences des textes et documents*, Université Paris-VII, I, 1976.

Jennifer Waelti-Walters, « Sleeping Beauty : *The Rapture of Lol V. Stein* », in *Fairy Tales and the Female Imagination*, Eden Press, Montréal, Canada, 1982.

TABLE

ESSAI

DANS LA MÊME COLLECTION

Claude Allaigre, Nadine Ly, Jean-Marc Pelorson *L'Ingénieux Hidalgo Don Quichotte de la Manche* de Cervantès (126)
Pascale Auraix-Jonchière *Les Diaboliques* de Barbey d'Aurevilly (81)
Jean-Louis Backès *Crime et châtiment* de Fédor Dostoïevski (40)
Emmanuèle Baumgartner *Poésies* de François Villon (72)
Emmanuèle Baumgartner *Romans de la Table Ronde* de Chrétien de Troyes (111)
Annie Becq *Lettres persanes* de Montesquieu (77)
Patrick Berthier *Colomba* de Prosper Mérimée (115)
Philippe Berthier *Eugénie Grandet* d'Honoré de Balzac (14)
Philippe Berthier *Vie de Henry Brulard* de Stendhal (88)
Philippe Berthier *La Chartreuse de Parme* de Stendhal (49)
Dominique Bertrand *Les Caractères* de La Bruyère (103)
Jean-Pierre Bertrand *Paludes* d'André Gide (97)
Michel Bigot, Marie-France Savéan *La cantatrice chauve/La leçon* d'Eugène Ionesco (3)
Michel Bigot *Zazie dans le métro* de Raymond Queneau (34)
Michel Bigot *Pierrot mon ami* de Raymond Queneau (80)
André Bleikasten *Sanctuaire* de William Faulkner (27)
Christiane Blot-Labarrère *Dix heures et demie du soir en été* de Marguerite Duras (82)
Gilles Bonnet *Là-bas* de J.-K. de Huysmans (116)
Éric Bordas *Indiana* de George Sand (119)
Madeleine Borgomano *Le ravissement de Lol V. Stein* de Marguerite Duras (60)
Arlette Bouloumié *Vendredi ou les limbes du Pacifique* de Michel Tournier (4)
Daniel Bougnoux et Cécile Narjoux *Aurélien* d'Aragon (15)
Marc Buffat *Les mains sales* de Jean-Paul Sartre (10)
Claude Burgelin *Les mots* de Jean-Paul Sartre (35)
Mariane Bury *Une vie* de Guy de Maupassant (41)
Belinda Cannone *L'œuvre* d'Émile Zola (104)
Ludmila Charles-Wurtz *Les Contemplations* de Victor Hugo (96)
Pierre Chartier *Les Faux-Monnayeurs* d'André Gide (6)
Pierre Chartier *Candide* de Voltaire (39)
Dominique Combes *Poésies, Une saison en enfer, Illuminations*, d'Arthur Rimbaud (118)
Mireille Cornud-Peyron *Le voyageur sans bagage* et *Le bal des voleurs* de Jean Anouilh (31)
Nicolas Courtinat *Méditations poétiques et Nouvelles méditations poétiques* de Lamartine (117)
Marc Dambre *La symphonie pastorale* d'André Gide (11)
Claude Debon *Calligrammes* d'Apollinaire (121)

Michel Décaudin *Alcools* de Guillaume Apollinaire (23)
Jacques Deguy *La nausée* de Jean-Paul Sartre (28)
Véronique Denizot *Les Amours* de Ronsard (106)
Philippe Destruel *Les Filles du Feu* de Gérard de Nerval (95)
José-Luis Diaz *Illusions perdues* de Honoré de Balzac (99)
Béatrice Didier *Jacques le fataliste* de Denis Diderot (69)
Béatrice Didier *Corinne ou l'Italie* de Madame de Staël (83)
Béatrice Didier *Histoire de Gil Blas de Santillane* de Le Sage (109)
Carole Dornier *Manon Lescaut* de l'Abbé Prévost (66)
Pascal Durand *Poésies* de Stéphane Mallarmé (70)
Louis Forestier *Boule de suif* suivi de *La maison Tellier* de Guy de Maupassant (45)
Laurent Fourcaut *Le chant du monde* de Jean Giono (55)
Danièle Gasiglia-Laster *Paroles* de Jacques Prévert (29)
Jean-Charles Gateau *Capitale de la douleur* de Paul Eluard (33)
Jean-Charles Gateau *Le parti pris des choses* de Francis Ponge (63)
Gérard Gengembre *Germinal* de Zola (122)
Pierre Glaudes *La peau de chagrin* de Balzac (113)
Joëlle Gleize *Les fruits d'or* de Nathalie Sarraute (87)
Henri Godard *Voyage au bout de la nuit* de Céline (2)
Henri Godard *Mort à crédit* de Céline (50)
Monique Gosselin *Enfance* de Nathalie Sarraute (57)
Daniel Grojnowski *À rebours* de Huysmans (53)
Jeannine Guichardet *Le père Goriot* d'Honoré de Balzac (24)
Jean-Jacques Hamm *Le Rouge et le Noir* de Stendhal (20)
Philippe Hamon *La bête humaine* d'Émile Zola (38)
Pierre-Marie Héron *Journal du voleur* de Jean Genet (114)
Geneviève Hily-Mane *Le vieil homme et la mer* d'Ernest Hemingway (7)
Emmanuel Jacquart *Rhinocéros* d'Eugène Ionesco (44)
Caroline Jacot-Grappa *Les liaisons dangereuses* de Choderlos de Laclos (64)
Alain Juillard *Le passe-muraille* de Marcel Aymé (43)
Anne-Yvonne Julien *L'œuvre au noir* de Marguerite Yourcenar (26)
Patrick Labarthe *Petits poèmes en prose* de Charles Baudelaire (86)
Thierry Laget *Un amour de Swann* de Marcel Proust (1)
Thierry Laget *Du côté de chez Swann* de Marcel Proust (21)
Claude Launay *Les fleurs du mal* de Charles Baudelaire (48)
Éliane Lecarme-Tabone *La vie devant soi* de Romain Gary (Émile Ajar) (128)
Éliane Lecarme-Tabone *Mémoires d'une jeune fille rangée* de Simone de Beauvoir (85)
Jean-Pierre Leduc-Adine *L'Assommoir* d'Émile Zola (61)
Marie-Christine Lemardeley-Cunci *Des souris et des hommes* de John Steinbeck (16)
Marie-Christine Lemardeley-Cunci *Les raisins de la colère* de John Steinbeck (73)

Olivier Leplatre *Fables* de Jean de La Fontaine (76)
Claude Leroy *L'or* de Blaise Cendrars (13)
Henriette Levillain *Mémoires d'Hadrien* de Marguerite Yourcenar (17)
Henriette Levillain *La princesse de Clèves* de Madame de La Fayette (46)
Jacqueline Lévi-Valensi *La peste* d'Albert Camus (8)
Jacqueline Lévi-Valensi *La chute* d'Albert Camus (58)
Marie-Thérèse Ligot *Un barrage contre le Pacifique* de Marguerite Duras (18)
Marie-Thérèse Ligot *L'amour fou* d'André Breton (59)
Éric Lysoe *Histoires extraordinaires, grotesques et sérieuses* d'Edgar Allan Poe (78)
Joël Malrieu *Bel-Ami* de Guy de Maupassant (105)
Joël Malrieu *Le Horla* de Guy de Maupassant (51)
François Marotin *Mondo et autres histoires* de J.-M.G. Le Clézio (47)
Catherine Maubon *L'âge d'homme* de Michel Leiris (65)
Jean-Michel Maulpoix *Fureur et mystère* de René Char (52)
Alain Meyer *La Condition humaine* d'André Malraux (12)
Michel Meyer *Le Paysan de Paris* d'Aragon (93)
Michel Meyer *Manifestes du surréalisme* d'André Breton (108)
Jean-Pierre Morel *Le procès* de Kafka (71)
Pascaline Mourier-Casile *Nadja* d'André Breton (37)
Jean-Pierre Naugrette *Sa Majesté des mouches* de William Golding (25)
François Noudelmann *Huis clos* suivi de *Les mouches* de Jean-Paul Sartre (30)
Jean-François Perrin *Les confessions* de Jean-Jacques Rousseau (62)
Bernard Pingaud *L'Étranger* d'Albert Camus (22)
François Pitavy *Le bruit et la fureur* de William Faulkner (101)
Jonathan Pollock *Le Moine (de Lewis)* d'Antonin Artaud (102)
Jean-Yves Pouilloux *Les fleurs bleues* de Raymond Queneau (5)
Jean-Yves Pouilloux *Fictions* de Jorge Luis Borges (19)
Simone Proust *Quoi ? L'Éternité* de Marguerite Yourcenar (94)
Suzanne Ravis-Françon *Les voyageurs de l'impériale* d'Aragon (98)
Frédéric Regard *1984* de George Orwell (32)
Pierre-Louis Rey *Madame Bovary* de Gustave Flaubert (56)
Pierre-Louis Rey *L'éducation sentimentale* de Gustave Flaubert (123)
Pierre-Louis Rey *Quatre-vingt-treize* de Victor Hugo (107)
Jérôme Roger *Un barbare en Asie* et *Ecuador* de H. Michaux (124)
Myriam Roman *Le dernier jour d'un condamné* de Victor Hugo (90)
Anne Roche *W* de Georges Perec (67)
Colette Roubaud *Plume* de Henri Michaux (91)
Mireille Sacotte *Un roi sans divertissement* de Jean Giono (42)
Mireille Sacotte *Éloges* et *La Gloire des Rois* de Saint-John Perse (79)
Corinne Saminadayar-Perrin *L'enfant* de Jules Vallès (89)
Marie-France Savéan *La place* suivi d'*Une femme* d'Annie Ernaux (36)
Henri Scepi *Les complaintes* de Jules Laforgue (92)
Henri Scepi *Salammbô* de Flaubert (112)

Alain Sicard *Résidence sur la terre* de Pablo Neruda (110)
Michèle Szkilnik *Perceval ou Le Conte du Graal* de Chrétien de Troyes (74)
Marie-Louise Terray *Les chants de Maldoror* de Lautréamont (68)
G.H. Tucker *Les Regrets* de Joachim du Bellay (84)
Claude Thiébaut *La métamorphose et autres récits* de Franz Kafka (9)
Bruno Vercier et Alain Quella-Villéger *Aziyadé* suivi de *Fantôme d'Orient* de Pierre Loti (100)
Dominique Viart *Vies minuscules* de Pierre Michon (120)
Michel Viegnes *Sagesse – Amour – Bonheur* de Paul Verlaine (75)
Marie-Ange Voisin-Fougère *Contes cruels* de Villiers de L'Isle-Adam (54)
Jean-Michel Wittmann *Si le grain ne meurt* d'André Gide (125)

COLLECTION FOLIO

Dernières parutions

4062. Frédéric Beigbeder	*99 francs.*
4063. Balzac	*Les Chouans.*
4064. Bernardin de Saint Pierre	*Paul et Virginie.*
4065. Raphaël Confiant	*Nuée ardente.*
4066. Florence Delay	*Dit Nerval.*
4067. Jean Rolin	*La clôture.*
4068. Philippe Claudel	*Les petites mécaniques.*
4069. Eduardo Barrios	*L'enfant qui devint fou d'amour.*
4070. Neil Bissoondath	*Un baume pour le cœur.*
4071. Jonahan Coe	*Bienvenue au club.*
4072. Toni Davidson	*Cicatrices.*
4073. Philippe Delerm	*Le buveur de temps.*
4074. Masuji Ibuse	*Pluie noire.*
4075. Camille Laurens	*L'Amour, roman.*
4076. François Nourissier	*Prince des berlingots.*
4077. Jean d'Ormesson	*C'était bien.*
4078. Pascal Quignard	*Les Ombres errantes.*
4079. Isaac B. Singer	*De nouveau au tribunal de mon père.*
4080. Pierre Loti	*Matelot.*
4081. Edgar Allan Poe	*Histoires extraordinaires.*
4082. Lian Hearn	*Le clan des Otori, II : les Neiges de l'exil.*
4083. La Bible	*Psaumes.*
4084. La Bible	*Proverbes.*
4085. La Bible	*Évangiles.*
4086. La Bible	*Lettres de Paul.*
4087. Pierre Bergé	*Les jours s'en vont je demeure.*
4088. Benjamin Berton	*Sauvageons.*
4089. Clémence Boulouque	*Mort d'un silence.*
4090. Paule Constant	*Sucre et secret.*
4091. Nicolas Fargues	*One Man Show.*
4092. James Flint	*Habitus.*

4093. Gisèle Fournier	*Non-dits.*
4094. Iegor Gran	*O.N.G.!*
4095. J.M.G. Le Clézio	*Révolutions.*
4096. Andréï Makine	*La terre et le ciel de Jacques Dorme.*
4097. Collectif	*«Parce que c'était lui, parce-que c'était moi».*
4098. Anonyme	*Saga de Gísli Súrsson.*
4099. Truman Capote	*Monsieur Maléfique* et autres nouvelles.
4100. E.M. Cioran	*Ébauches de vertige.*
4101. Salvador Dali	*Les moustaches radar.*
4102. Chester Himes	*Le fantôme de Rufus Jones* et autres nouvelles.
4103. Pablo Neruda	*La solitude lumineuse.*
4104. Antoine de St-Exupéry	*Lettre à un otage.*
4105. Anton Tchekhov	*Une banale histoire.*
4106. Honoré de Balzac	*L'Auberge rouge.*
4107. George Sand	*Consuelo I.*
4108. George Sand	*Consuelo II.*
4109. André Malraux	*Lazare.*
4110 Cyrano de Bergerac	*L'autre monde.*
4111 Alessandro Baricco	*Sans sang.*
4112 Didier Daeninckx	*Raconteur d'histoires.*
4113 André Gide	*Le Ramier.*
4114. Richard Millet	*Le renard dans le nom.*
4115. Susan Minot	*Extase.*
4116. Nathalie Rheims	*Les fleurs du silence.*
4117. Manuel Rivas	*La langue des papillons.*
4118. Daniel Rondeau	*Istanbul.*
4119. Dominique Sigaud	*De chape et de plomb.*
4120. Philippe Sollers	*L'Étoile des amants.*
4121. Jacques Tournier	*À l'intérieur du chien.*
4122. Gabriel Sénac de Meilhan	*L'Émigré.*
4123. Honoré de Balzac	*Le Lys dans la vallée.*
4124. Lawrence Durrell	*Le Carnet noir.*
4125. Félicien Marceau	*La grande fille.*
4126. Chantal Pelletier	*La visite.*
4127. Boris Schreiber	*La douceur du sang.*
4128. Angelo Rinaldi	*Tout ce que je sais de Marie.*
4129. Pierre Assouline	*État limite.*

4130. Élisabeth Barillé — *Exaucez-nous.*
4131. Frédéric Beigbeder — *Windows on the World.*
4132. Philippe Delerm — *Un été pour mémoire.*
4133. Colette Fellous — *Avenue de France.*
4134. Christian Garcin — *Du bruit dans les arbres.*
4135. Fleur Jaeggy — *Les années bienheureuses du châtiment.*
4136. Chateaubriand — *Itinéraire de Paris à Jerusalem.*
4137. Pascal Quignard — *Sur le jadis. Dernier royaume, II.*
4138. Pascal Quignard — *Abîmes. Dernier Royaume, III.*
4139. Michel Schneider — *Morts imaginaires.*
4140. Zeruya Shalev — *Vie amoureuse.*
4141. Frédéric Vitoux — *La vie de Céline.*
4142. Fédor Dostoïevski — *Les Pauvres Gens.*
4143. Ray Bradbury — *Meurtres en douceur.*
4144. Carlos Castaneda — *Stopper-le-monde.*
4145. Confucius — *Entretiens.*
4146. Didier Daeninckx — *Ceinture rouge.*
4147. William Faulkner — *Le Caïd.*
4148. Gandhi — *La voie de la non-violence.*
4149. Guy de Maupassant — *Le Verrou et autres contes grivois.*
4150. D. A. F. de Sade — *La Philosophie dans le boudoir.*
4151. Italo Svevo — *L'assassinat de la Via Belpoggio.*
4152. Laurence Cossé — *Le 31 du mois d'août.*
4153. Benoît Duteurtre — *Service clientèle.*
4154. Christine Jordis — *Bali, Java, en rêvant.*
4155. Milan Kundera — *L'ignorance.*
4156. Jean-Marie Laclavetine — *Train de vies.*
4157. Paolo Lins — *La Cité de Dieu.*
4158. Ian McEwan — *Expiation.*
4159. Pierre Péju — *La vie courante.*
4160. Michael Turner — *Le Poème pornographe.*
4161. Mario Vargas Llosa — *Le Paradis — un peu plus loin.*
4162. Martin Amis — *Expérience.*
4163. Pierre-Autun Grenier — *Les radis bleus.*
4164. Isaac Babel — *Mes premiers honoraires.*
4165. Michel Braudeau — *Retour à Miranda.*
4166. Tracy Chevalier — *La Dame à la Licorne.*
4167. Marie Darrieussecq — *White.*
4168. Carlos Fuentes — *L'instinct d'Iñez.*

4169. Joanne Harris — *Voleurs de plage.*
4170. Régis Jauffret — *univers, univers.*
4171. Philippe Labro — *Un Américain peu tranquille.*
4172. Ludmila Oulitskaïa — *Les pauvres parents.*
4173. Daniel Pennac — *Le dictateur et le hamac.*
4174. Alice Steinbach — *Un matin je suis partie.*
4175. Jules Verne — *Vingt mille lieues sous les mers.*
4176. Jules Verne — *Aventures du capitaine Hatteras.*
4177. Emily Brontë — *Hurlevent.*
4178. Philippe Djian — *Frictions.*
4179. Éric Fottorino — *Rochelle.*
4180. Christian Giudicelli — *Fragments tunisiens.*
4181. Serge Joncour — *U.V.*
4182. Philippe Le Guillou — *Livres des guerriers d'or.*
4183. David McNeil — *Quelques pas dans les pas d'un ange.*
4184. Patrick Modiano — *Accident nocturne.*
4185. Amos Oz — *Seule la mer.*
4186. Jean-Noël Pancrazi — *Tous s'est passé si vite.*
4187. Danièle Sallenave — *La vie fantôme.*
4188. Danièle Sallenave — *D'amour.*
4189. Philippe Sollers — *Illuminations.*
4190. Henry James — *La Source sacrée.*
4191. Collectif — *«Mourir pour toi».*
4192. Hans Christian Andersen — *L'elfe de la rose et autres contes du jardin.*
4193. Épictète — *De la liberté* précédé de *De la profession de Cynique.*
4194. Ernest Hemingway — *Histoire naturelle des morts* et autres nouvelles.
4195. Panaït Istrati — *Mes départs.*
4196. H. P. Lovecraft — *La peur qui rôde et autres nouvelles.*
4197. Stendhal — *Féder ou Le Mari d'argent.*
4198. Junichirô Tanizaki — *Le meurtre d'O-Tsuya.*
4199. Léon Tolstoï — *Le réveillon du jeune tsar et autres contes.*
4200. Oscar Wilde — *La Ballade de la geôle de Reading.*

4201. Collectif — *Témoins de Sartre.*
4202. Balzac — *Le Chef-d'œuvre inconnu.*
4203. George Sand — *François le Champi.*
4204. Constant — *Adolphe. Le Cahier rouge. Cécile.*
4205. Flaubert — *Salammbô.*
4206. Rudyard Kipling — *Kim.*
4207. Flaubert — *L'Éducation sentimentale.*
4208. Olivier Barrot/Bernard Rapp — *Lettres anglaises.*
4209. Pierre Charras — *Dix-neuf secondes.*
4210. Raphaël Confiant — *La panse du chacal.*
4211 Erri De Luca — *Le contraire de un.*
4212. Philippe Delerm — *La sieste assassinée.*
4213. Angela Huth — *Amour et désolation.*
4214. Alexandre Jardin — *Les Coloriés.*
4215. Pierre Magnan — *Apprenti.*
4216. Arto Paasilinna — *Petits suicides entre amis.*
4217. Alix de Saint-André — *Ma Nanie,*
4218. Patrick Lapeyre — *L'homme-soeur.*
4219. Gérard de Nerval — *Les Filles du feu.*
4220. Anonyme — *La Chanson de Roland.*
4221. Maryse Condé — *Histoire de la femme cannibale.*
4222. Didier Daeninckx — *Main courante* et *Autres lieux.*
4223. Caroline Lamarche — *Carnets d'une soumise de province.*
4224. Alice McDermott — *L'arbre à sucettes.*
4225. Richard Millet — *Ma vie parmi les ombres.*
4226. Laure Murat — *Passage de l'Odéon.*
4227. Pierre Pelot — *C'est ainsi que les hommes vivent.*
4228. Nathalie Rheims — *L'ange de la dernière heure.*
4229. Gilles Rozier — *Un amour sans résistance.*
4230. Jean-Claude Rufin — *Globalia.*
4231. Dai Sijie — *Le complexe de Di.*
4232. Yasmina Traboulsi — *Les enfants de la Place.*
4233. Martin Winckler — *La Maladie de Sachs.*
4234. Cees Nooteboom — *Le matelot sans lèvres.*
4235. Alexandre Dumas — *Le Chevalier de Maison-Rouge*